THE GIFT OF RUIN

DANIELLE FERRARO

THE GIFT OF RUIN

THE GIFT OF HEARTS
BOOK ONE

DANIELLE FERRARO

VAM GROUP LLC

Library of Congress Cataloging-in-Publication data is available.

ISBN
979-8-9923038-1-0

For Celine—

Whose little hands broke my phone and the curse of the scroll, and allowed this story to find me.

CHAPTER 1

HARD AND COLD. Smooth and leathery. The skin of her dead grandmother's forehead felt right and wrong as she traced a small cross with her thumb. The priest had told them to do it. A tradition he said. Era knew nothing about it—Christianity, dead people or otherwise.

Then, compelled beyond reason, her hand moved down Grandma's face towards her neck. The silver medal gleamed against the crisp white of her pressed shirt. Era reached for it, felt the raised stars around the relief of a woman on the silver oval. When she cupped it, the necklace detached into her hand. Or maybe it hadn't been secured at all, but Era was too embarrassed to be caught fiddling around with the body. Instead, she palmed the item and pulled her hands together in a prayer pose that made her even more self-conscious. As she spun away from the casket and hurried down the aisle, her eyes caught her mother's gaze as she passed their pew. "Bathroom," Era mouthed.

The sign for the bathroom pointed downstairs—to the basement—unsettling and novel for a California girl. She descended into the small, empty room with two stalls and a sink. Quiet.

Muffled. She glanced at her reflection, her pale face contrasting sharply against the scratchy black wool dress before looking down at the object gleaming in her open hand.

Oh my gosh, I've robbed Grandma's grave.

She stared at the relic in her palm. The stars around the veiled woman in the long dress sparkled and a jolt of pain went up her arm. Her heart cramped, then pricked, then burst into agony, as each heartbeat pushed the delicate muscle onto spikes within her. The pain marched on with each breath, compounding until she sank to the floor, clutching her chest, stars breaking out in glittering points across her vision. The smell of lemon cleaner mixed with sweet almond soap shoved in and out of her nose as she took in tremendous breaths to manage the pain, as if the air could soothe it.

I won't make it out of this bathroom, she thought, her vision darkening. She gripped the sink, desperately trying to pull herself up, but the pain pressed harder, grinding through her chest. She had to make herself walk, to get help, even if she had to crawl.

Do twelve-year-olds die of heart attacks? She fought back the panic and her other hand slapped against the sink. The medal— still hanging on its delicate chain—clinked against the porcelain, but Era didn't hear it. All she saw was the image of the woman again. As she collapsed, slipping against the floor, the medal flipped over. Two hearts. One, burning, wrapped in thorns. The other, pierced by a sword.

A pulse of pain shot through her skull, like a harp string plucked at a million decibels, thrumming deep within, exploding in her ears.

Her body lay prone on the waxed linoleum. *I'm dying.* She had stolen a holy object—from a dead body. In a church. She'd brought down a curse.

But the pain? It retreated. Slowly. Tiny knives in her chest retracted from her heart into the boobytrap she had set off by robbing the tomb. Then gone.

Era groaned, pushing herself up, legs trembling beneath her. She stumbled to the mirror. Sweat slicked her forehead, her nose, dripping in response to the agony. Blood—two small trickles—ran from her earlobes, tracing down her neck.

She splashed cold water on her face. Should she tell her parents? Would they care? Would they even believe her if she couldn't prove she was physically hurt? She didn't want to risk their disappointment, their accusations that she was making it all about her.

Her feet scraped up the stairs, the old wood creaking underfoot. She gripped the medal tightly in her hand, wishing the dress had pockets, wishing for an escape.

Maybe it was a one-time thing. A blip. But what if it happens again? She shuddered at the thought. *If it happens again, I'll have to say something.*

She scanned the sanctuary from the back entrance. Grandma's casket stood closed, a shiny grey pod ready for the earth to take it. Everyone was gone except for a pair of yappers that lingered inside by the exit door. She'd missed most of the funeral Mass.

The air outside stung her face. The wind whipped around the church, and Era wished for her sweater though she should really have a jacket. It hadn't snowed in some time, but little pockets of dirty ice clung to the corners of buildings and walls. She hoped her mom grabbed it from the pew so she wouldn't have to bother them to wait while she went back inside to look for it.

Her eyes canvassed the parking lot. There, in the idling silver Ford Escape, sat her father, her mother standing outside with a perturbed posture, scanning for her. She spotted Era from afar, beckoned with an impatient wave, and ducked into the rental.

Era waved back and hurried, clutching her chest that held only the echo of an ache.

"Sorry Mama," she said, pulling the door shut behind her, relieved to see the sweater thrown onto the back seat. "I didn't feel good, but now I'm okay."

Her mother didn't look up. The silence in the car told her everything she needed to know.

Salt crunched under the rental's tires as her father sped off to make up for the minutes they'd waited for her. Her mom flicked through her phone, digging for photos of Grandma. There weren't many and she had to pour over old albums in Facebook and download what she could find.

"Who is doing the slideshow again?" her mother asked her father and like that, Era's mind exploded.

Screens playing little movies filled the small car. On one she watched her mother, younger, more vibrant, handing Grandma a bouquet of yellow tulips—their first meeting. On another, she saw her mother on the phone, sitting with Era as a toddler, telling a woman that the flight was simply too long for them to make with a small child.

As Era's eyes flicked from one image to the next, she could feel Grandma's smooth handshake as she grasped her mother's hand, smell something cooking off in the distance during that phone call.

Era's breath caught in her throat. She didn't want to see these images, these memories that weren't her own. Her hand flew over her eyes, but the images merely continued to play against the rainbow backdrop of her eyelids.

It's okay, I'm okay, just a little hallucination. Worst case it's early onset schizophrenia. They say it hits around puberty. Era's cool collected thoughts tried to talk her through the madness.

But then her father spoke. "My cousin Martha. She's playing the slideshow after the wake so you'd better hurry. You should have worked on this during the plane ride. You had hours."

The screens flashed on again, but this time they felt different, harder, more rational, more her father. Era dared to drop her hand, to peek into the slit of light. Her father looked back at her.

"What's wrong with you? You going to be sick? Because not in the rental—"

"No I—"

Then it began. The memories—her father's thoughts—pressed against her, suffocating.

Selfish.

Selfish, selfish, selfish.

Era could feel the weight of it. His disappointment. His irritation. His frustration with her. How these ideas of her could never change because they were tied to something deep in himself, anchored there to a foundation of selfishness, one with roots that wound and reached beneath what she could see.

There was the truth he'd buried beneath his actions. He didn't want a daughter. He wanted a son.

Everything made sense now. Why he pushed her so hard to play sports and the disappointment when she picked tennis over basketball two years ago. Why he never understood her. Why he hated the things she liked. Why he called her interests "useless girly crap."

A thousand chunks of plaster and cement rained down on her, ricocheting off her tender body as her sad little castle collapsed around her. She suspected she was a perpetual inconvenience to them, her parents. Now she saw it. His heart tore open and bore the black secret to her.

He doesn't love me.

Era sat up straighter, her mind a storm of realization. The memories blurred, exploded, crackling like fireworks in her head.

She took small sips of the air through her nose, desperately willing herself not to cry. But a tear slipped down her cheek regardless.

Mother, who leaned into the mirror fixing her eyebrows, noticed. "Oh, come on, Era. You barely knew Grandma. You only saw her what? Five or six times in your whole life?"

The words hit her like a blow to the gut. The air left her lungs. Her hand clenched around the medal, hidden tightly in her palm.

There was no escape.

Sparks of memory flared again, burning her like pops of hot oil from a pan. Her mother's voice, talking to her father in the park, clear in her mind. "I don't want children."

Her father's nonchalant response, "I'm fine either way. Whatever you want."

Another clip. The antibiotics. The pregnancy. The threats.

Her grandmother had threatened to cut them out of her will if her mother had an abortion. Said it was an unforgivable crime against God. She had been a religious woman.

She wanted to murder me.

Now she understood why they only visited Montreal once. Mom hated Grandma after that and Grandma never respected her again.

Era peeled back her fingers slightly and stared at the metal edge hidden in her hand and remembered the cool forehead she touched.

Thank you, she thought, *for fighting for my life. Wherever you are, Grandma. Thank you.*

CHAPTER 2

THE END BECKONED, and the sweet song of freedom sang to Era from the constricting confines of her high school routine. Three more weeks until her new beginning. No more pretending to fit into a family or a school that would never understand her. With graduation looming, every pointless class felt like an eternity. Senioritis prickled under her skin, tingling in her fingernails as visions of her future flickered before her like a distant flame.

She glanced at the clock, heart racing. Only an hour left to finish her comparative Supreme Court case history paper—the last hurdle before she could leap into freedom. She flung her racket down and tossed her towel into the hamper, casting one last glance at her drawer, where the crisp envelope sat like a portal to take her into the future she had long awaited. Her acceptance letter, the ticket to her dreams, burned with urgency in her mind.

Era had promised herself she'd tell Cole the moment it arrived, yet here she was, two weeks later and dying to break it to him in person. It was too important to tell him over the phone, so her acceptance letter had sat like an overripe banana, blackening with each day she had to wait. She turned her focus back to her laptop and busied herself with her work, trying to suppress the anticipation bubbling inside her. If she could just finish this paper, she could finally turn her attention to something much better, the packed weekend of pre-graduation festivities ahead.

Mr. Ent is the devil incarnate, she thought, rolling her eyes at the thought of her AP US History teacher. Mr. E was notorious for assigning papers after finals, forcing students to suffer through busywork at the end of the year. He had been her nemesis, cracking down on her for too many absences and never letting her slide on deadlines. She could just picture him: the scraggly beard, the high-waisted dad jeans, always looking to make an example of someone, usually her.

School was Era's domain. Her parents were too self-absorbed to care about her academic achievements, despite their demands for straight A's and all honors. They hadn't even bothered to check her report card since freshman year.

She hammered away at the keyboard, her focus disrupted by the image of Mr. Ent's (not his real name) scowling face. With each sentence she pounded out, a mixture of triumph and impending sadness tugged at her heart. "Ugh, let that man think he's reading his own thoughts," she muttered, as she made sure to throw in a phrase he pointedly used during the lecture that day and closed the laptop with a sense of finality.

The paper was a slam dunk, and her future lined up before her and bowed as she walked past. She knew she held a royal flush. Her Gift, plus beauty, intelligence, and youth. Given the right circumstances, she could be an unstoppable force. But up until now, she had been too afraid to think of what she really wanted her life to look like after high school because she had been so focused on the number one Rule—hide the Gift at all costs.

She gazed blankly out the window at the warm afternoon sun, thinking about all the dances she'd missed, and wondered if anyone would even clap when they called her name at graduation. She chastised herself, knew how cliché it was to reflect on the past, but she couldn't resist. Many classmates were equally nostalgic this time of year, staring at the twilight of their youth, but Era felt only the thrill of impending freedom.

She shook off the unexpected wave of sentimentality and reminded herself that high school had only ever been a place of confinement for her, as if she existed in a small aquarium when really she should have dominion over the big wide ocean. Era wanted to do grand things with the Gift, knew it capable of so much. But she recognized that wielding it necessitated certain governing principles—never talk about the Gift, never use it in a way that makes people suspicious. Small doses, right time, right place, right person.

The fishbowl of Emerald Prep was not the right place to use it, too many eyes that watched endlessly, that talked about everything. Nowhere to hide.

Era glanced at the picture of Cole's face pressed next to hers on the desk, her love, her life, carefully chosen and separated from school.

She never would have guessed that the world she had curated, piece by piece, was about to implode.

CHAPTER 3

ERA PICKED UP HER PHONE, her thumb hovering over Cole's name, her stomach fluttering. Even after nearly a year together, those damn butterflies never really went away. As the phone rang, her heart skipped, wondering—no, *dreading*—that he wouldn't pick up. By the fourth ring, the flutter shifted into a tight knot of anxiety.

"Hey Babe, sorry you caught me in the middle of a study group. What's up?" he said.

"Oh, sorry," she replied, biting her lip. She could never seem to catch him at a good time these days. "Should I call back later?"

"No, no, it's fine. I'm pretty busy later. You need something?"

Her stomach sank. They hadn't really talked lately, not properly. She missed him. She missed the sound of his voice like the air she breathed. But she didn't want to be needy. "Just... haven't heard your voice much. I miss you, that's all. But I get it, I have a lot going on too."

"Oh, yeah?" His voice was flat, distant. She didn't know if it was because of the study group or something else, but she could feel that space between them, an alien thing she'd never experienced with him before.

Era wanted to gush over all the festivities—the huge party that the Ridgewell heir was throwing that night, the beach party tomorrow at Clarissa's. She lived in one of those sick houses that looked directly onto the water with a little trolley that took your stuff down to the sand. But she took a beat. She knew he was dealing with some sort of crisis at home. She couldn't expect him to care about some trifling high school celebration.

"Party at a classmate's house tonight, party at the beach for the graduating seniors tomorrow at the Cove," she said, imparting the information without embellishing to keep from bothering him too much with the details.

Cole scoffed. Era could almost see his incredulous facial expressions "Should be interesting, you partying with kids your own age for once."

"Yeah," she said, trying to sound enthusiastic. "It's at this kid's house—he's the richest kid at Emerald Prep. His family owns Ridgewell Enterprises. Like stupid money." She couldn't help the pride creeping into her voice. The name alone could make a room go silent. "It'll be insane."

"Hmm... sounds like it could get out of hand." He paused, then added, "I hope you're not driving."

Era laughed. "Don't worry. We're walking. It's only a few blocks."

Cole's voice softened. "Okay, just be careful."

The warmth in his tone almost caught her off guard. She held the phone to her ear a moment longer, savoring the sound of his voice. "Of course," she murmured. "And, hey... everything okay with you? With your family?"

There was a long pause on the other end of the line. A soft rustling, like papers shuffling. "Not a good time," he said finally, the edge in his voice unmistakable.

Era nodded, even though he couldn't see her. She was used

to this—his walls, his reluctance to talk about things that made him uncomfortable. "I get it. We'll talk later... Sunday. I want to hear everything."

"Yeah, we'll talk then," Cole replied quickly. "Can't wait to see you. I'll pick you up at 6."

Era felt a pang of disappointment, but she masked it. She wanted to believe things were fine between them, despite the distance. But something was... off.

"Yeah, hang in there with your studying. Love you," she added, but could feel his attention already shifting elsewhere.

"You too." And he hung up. Era stared at her phone, taking small sips of air.

You too? she thought. He always said, "love you too." Not "you too." Of course, she was probably reading too much into it. Still, the nagging tugged at her stomach.

Era ran a hand through her hair, feeling the weight of the silence that hung between them. She glanced at the Cartier heart bracelet on her wrist, a reminder of their anniversary, of promises made and yet unfulfilled. She *wanted* him to be excited, to share in the news she'd been dying to tell him: the freedom she'd gained, the plans they'd make together. But this strange distance—this gap that had grown between them—was like a cold draft, creeping into their relationship.

The past month had required a painful length of time apart. He'd had to skip quite a few weekends together as papers became due and finals drew near. And she struggled with these clipped conversations even though she knew they stemmed from some sort of crisis going on in his family.

Whatever was going on sounded alarming. She loved Cole's family life, loved how consistent, how normal, even a bit boring they all were until about three weeks ago, when he mentioned that his parents had some blowout fight. She tried her best to be there for him which wasn't an easy thing to do over the phone. His cagey demeanor on the details when she brought it up carved a strange distance between them. He changed the subject and then cut the conversation short every time. And she missed him so much that she found it better to skirt the subject, than deal with the pang of rejection he dealt out when she brought it up.

She walked on unfamiliar territory. If only she could see him and let the Gift unravel his guarded thoughts.

She stared at their picture on her desk, his wide smile beaming at her and thought of the first moment they saw each other, twenty feet apart on the boardwalk as Era walked towards the sound of Catalina Dreams' opening set.

Era had felt his whole soul reach for her, pulling her towards himself. His determined eyes locked on hers and unlocked something deep within. She had responded with a surge of power from her Gift, reaching back out to him and in that instant, the entire world fell away. They were inseparable from then on and he became something for which she had always longed, a feeling of coming home. Her home sucked but he was her refuge, the place she never felt rejected, like an inconvenience.

Era frowned at her reflection. Her tennis visor had flattened a dent in her blowout. *Ugh, hair shower is it.*

Era set down her blow dryer and as if on cue, a FaceTime from Alex lit up her phone. She picked it up and walked into her room towards the closet.

"Era! Are you serious? You're still doing your hair? How on earth am I supposed to know what to wear to Christopher's tonight?"

"Babe, you're going to wear the green dress. You know how it sets off your eyes and flatters your…you know," Era said nonchalantly, rifling through her hangers.

Alex gasped audibly. "Seriously, you know I hate showing off my boobs."

"I know, I know, but you need to get over that. Not every

guy is looking for a size zero stick figure. Your curves are womanly! Own them."

"Ew. No. Womanly is the last thing I want. Can't I be cute and petite? I'd love to be more flat-chested like you," Alex said.

"Listen," Era said, forcing a lighter tone, "you're not going to see these people much longer. Why not go bombshell on them? Confidence is everything."

Alex cracked a smile, and rolled her eyes as she replied, "I'm sure you're right. I just wish I could do whatever it is that you do. I swear you tilt your head, flash one smile and then turn around and swish that booty, and every guy is yours."

Era made a gagging sound. "I've gotta finish getting ready. Remember, don't wear anything super high-heeled. We're walking there and back. Can you still meet me here at 9?" Her attention was already elsewhere.

"Yup, see you soon!" Alex would likely obsess over her outfit for the next twenty minutes before settling on the green dress.

Era finished curling her hair, perfecting her liner, contouring her face and picking out her favorite jewelry. She decided to live a little, stacking on Hermes bracelets, an anklet, and a Tiffany's ring, the one gifted by her father on her 16th birthday. She guilted him into it.

Finally, she slipped on a snug white halter dress and white sneakers—something she'd never do abroad but here at home, high heels were seen as trying too hard. Nope, never mind, she couldn't do it.

Era kicked off the sneakers and snatched a low block heel from her closet. The booty must be maintained. After snapping a quick selfie for Cole with the message,

See what you're missing with all this studying.

It was go time. She saw his reply a minute later.

You look hot. Be safe.

She felt a little better. Moments later, Alex, who didn't bother ringing the doorbell anymore, barreled into Era's room and froze. "Era, you need to STOP! You picked something from the other side of the closet!? Gasp!"

"Settle down. You know I've always tried to keep my school reputation drama free, but senior year is over. Nothing matters now. I'll let them see me the way I've looked everywhere else except school, with make-up and clothes that actually complement my body. This weekend is going to be perfect and I feel amazing. I'm done hiding."

Alex walked over to the curling iron, deciding to fix a few pieces that had fallen too straight. "I get it. It's kind of exciting actually. I mean, I know you've already got Cole and he's in college but you're still the only girl I've ever known who never cared about getting guys from her own school to like her, unless you do care..." Alex joked with a hint of seriousness.

Era smiled at her friend, the only girl who had ever got her. Alex let Era shine without feeling like she was left in the darkness. Her true heart allowed her to love Era just as she was. With no siblings, no cousins, and parents that tolerated rather than loved her, Alex was a balm over the wound of her rejection at home. Her unconditional acceptance filled Era with a warmth that kept her hope of being loved alive.

Era would give her anything, including all the admiration she received if she could. And she told herself that nothing mattered to her except for whatever happiness she could give Alex.

Era knew she could use her Gift to protect Alex, to teach her some of the wisdom she had gained from looking deeply into human nature, help her avoid some of the pitfalls of being a teenager. It wasn't an easy task to accomplish all this with subtlety, to keep the Gift hidden, the source of so much secret knowledge from her keen-eyed friend.

When she snapped out of her reflection, Alex was still going on, "Seriously though, you better watch out because no one is prepared. Leave some boys for the rest of us!"

"No one at school was ever worth compromising the Rule. Privacy over proximity," she answered.

"Separate and safe," Alex chirped back.

Almost no one, she thought, the face of one handsome class-mate flashing in her mind before she pushed his picture away. *Probably not worth it,* she reassured herself.

Era glanced over at her closet, frowning at the left half, all boring basics and conservative pieces in bland colors. The other side glimmered with silky dresses, gowns, and bits of tailored perfection. Four long years had passed since she'd made a conscious decision to painstakingly divide her life the way she divided her closet. Why couldn't Emerald Prep have a uniform like everywhere else?

Era fingered a muddy shapeless dress and reflected on the closing of a long chapter, one that began a lifetime ago, in 8th grade. She spent the first few years with the Gift figuring out how to use it, testing its limits, and staying mostly on the sidelines.

It had made her grow up quickly, and in some ways it had robbed her of her childhood, her innocence. It also became the source of a growing insecurity complex. Despite fighting against it with all her spirit, the scalding rejection from her ruthlessly critical and emotionally detached parents whittled an emptiness into her. Nothing was given without a price.

But by eighth grade, she got too free with its use, drunk on middle school popularity and the adoration of middle school boys.

To make matters worse, the Gift had an ill effect she hadn't been able to control. It was a spotlight stealer. People treated Era with greater preference, liked her little better, and made her the center of attention without realizing it. Eventually, any girl friend she made became resentful.

Finally, she gave up on girls. It was a lot more fun to be liked by boys than the exhaustion of catering to the insecurities of pseudo-friends who were always competing with her.

She had been naive. And for this reason she'd made her first enemy, an insecure girl who viciously slandered her, turning her life at school into a living nightmare.

It became an important lesson, to keep her Gift concealed in places where she didn't have control, only using it to its full potential when necessary and one on one. She begged her father to send her to private school where she could have a fresh start. There she formed a charter of absolute unbreakable rules beginning her first day at Emerald Prep.

1– No dating anyone at school.

2– Avoid anyone who liked her (well, with one exception). Deflect unwanted attention gently so as not to create resentment.

3– No talking about her personal life at school or with anyone in Emerald Beach.

This last rule could not be broken, ever, with anyone, except Alex. Most importantly, Alex swore to her to keep the Rule as well, and so, their journey began together.

The pact allowed Era to move on from the part of her that middle school destroyed. She vowed to protect and nurture her friendship. And driven by a guilt of depriving Alex of the typical high school experience, she began finding adventures for the two of them. But what started out as a mission to give Alex something better than high school parties and popularity morphed into a pursuit of elevated living. Era relished the thrill of using her Gift to its full potential, so long as it took place in a compartment of her life that she could keep at a distance.

The Rule appeared to justify itself. Following it caused Era to realize that her high school was one of seven in the immediate area. There was no point trying to be a big fish in a small pond. With Alex at her side, they partied their way through every club in the City and flew private to ski in the French Alps at Val d'Isere and dance at La Folie Douce. She had left a trail of broken hearts in nearly every spot they'd been to, enjoying a fair number of romances—with the flings ending when she finally met Cole.

Alex kept her secrets, and on Mondays when they settled back into the humdrum of classes and homework, the girls smiled to each other knowingly, carrying on as if the announcement of homecoming court was still the most important thing in the world.

Now with the final weeks of school approaching, a college acceptance letter tucked away in her drawer, and Cole's unwavering love for her in her heart, Era knew the time had come for the charade to end. Arm-in-arm, she and Alex set off down the block, hearing music faintly in the distance, as they made their way to the party of the year.

CHAPTER 4

AT THE END of the street stood Christopher Ridgewell's house, arguably the only quasi-friend Era had allowed herself to have at Emerald Prep. His prominent family held formidable power over the area, and enjoyed a level of wealth that impressed even the rich kids at school.

The Ridgewell estate sprawled across an entire cliff overlooking the glimmering bay that reached into the ocean nearby. A thick screen of trees wrapped around the property like a fortress, giving it a sense of seclusion and exclusivity that reflected the wealth and power of its owners. The fortifications hinted at the importance of maintaining privacy from prying eyes though the intricate gates remained uncharacteristically ajar allowing a slow stream of people to pass through.

Beyond the gate, the sheer size of the massive building made Era pause mid-step to admire all 20,000 square feet and turned her head to take in the outbuildings for maids, groundskeepers, and guests. At one side, the sports courts added a touch of athleticism, while at the other, the stables spoke to the aristocratic lifestyle of the inhabitants. And at the very edge of the cliff, a sparkling pool caught the last of the sunlight, offering a stunning view of the calm bay and the private yacht bobbing lazily in its own slip below.

Alex let out a low whistle. "Pheeeeeeeeew. How in the world did we let this one get past us? He has been sitting under our nose this whole time?"

Era smirked at the comment. She'd seen the estate from afar a thousand times on her run around the bay, but it was a different experience walking the grounds. She'd even peeked at the Zillow which someone had carefully scraped of information and pictures, a telling sign of real money.

"This house is at the end of your street? You have a really nice house, don't get me wrong, but how did we never get invited over to THIS?"

"Looks like we weren't the only ones keeping secrets," Era replied. "I'm sure he didn't want to be judged for his family's wealth. Now that school is over, he probably doesn't care if people see his lifestyle. Maybe I underestimated Christopher. We might have more in common than I thought." Era turned toward her friend with a crafty knowing look, "But don't pretend he 'got past you' when you've had your eye on him since sophomore year."

"Fine, busted. You got me ok? I know the rules, but I couldn't help it with Christopher. He helped me in chemistry, the worst subject ever invented, and besides that, he's really really hot— Oh my gosh, is that a valet? I can't wait to see inside. Let's go!" Alex squealed as she slipped into a frenzy and yanked Era's arm towards the waiting scene.

The house's transformed interior diminished the intimidation of the exterior. Stylish and elegant but cleared of some furnishings to make space for the raucous guests, the party's attendance didn't disappoint. Faces known and unknown to them of varying ages spread out into every corner, flowing in and out towards the beating heart of the event, a dance party outside.

This was no ordinary high school party. Between the famous DJ spinning in a custom built stage on the deck, the hand-passed appetizers, and the massive photo-op flower walls, daddy's money had clearly met mommy's taste though neither of them seemed to be present.

Three bartenders manned a bar with at least ten seats and buckets of ice topped with chilled beers and hard seltzers dotted the exterior. Cabanas with flowing fabric surrounded the pool, tempering the rager with islands of private sanctuary. The night would rival the sponsored pool parties that took place in the desert during festival season and were likely an inspiration to some of the details here.

And yet in the midst of the excitement, the throng of party-goers seemed to grind to a halt when Era and Alex walked through the door. Alex's full chest burst atop the mint dress that simultaneously snatched in her waist. Era stepped through the doorway, her shapely tanned legs stretching across the foyer. Long blonde curls cascaded around the graceful symmetry of her face and down her backless white halter dress. Two rooms away, Christopher appeared anchored to the fireplace before making his way through the crowd to personally meet his guests.

She and Christopher were just friends, flirty friends but still just friends. She couldn't help preferring his company, sitting in front or behind him in classes so they could pass notes. He had a quick wit and a brilliant perceptive mind. He challenged her and even when they went toe to toe for the highest number of medals in Academic Decathlon, she enjoyed the rivalry as much as the awards. Era trumped him with a perfect score in Essay, and a first place in Interview and Speech but he took home firsts in Math, Science, and Economics.

And when Era showed up jet-lagged on Mondays from too much time galavanting around, Christopher could always tell. Without being asked, he never hesitated to slide his homework over for her to copy with a dimpled smile. She had never used her Gift on him and yet he always seemed to track her with his eyes, to remember her plans, and to ask pointed questions about her. Their playful banter had died out a bit last year when she mentioned her new boyfriend Cole, but never extinguished entirely. Era hadn't noticed the way he faded out of her attention. Everyone had similarly gone out of focus the moment she met Cole.

Now a tiny bit glassy eyed and red cheeked, Christopher greeted the two of them with a warm embrace, swept up like the rest of them in the end-of-school emotions that ran high. As he reached for her, his hand rested on her back and stayed there a beat too long. When he pulled away, his fingertips managed to trail casually down her exposed spine and over the silky fabric covering her hips, sending a jolt through her. She checked the corner of her eye to see if Alex had the angle to observe the gesture, but thankfully her body had been turned away just enough to conceal it. Thank goodness. Era certainly didn't want to depress the mood of the best party of the year by squashing her best friend's crush-hopes upon entry.

"Look at you guys! How could you wait until we've practically graduated to break my heart like this? And Era" –Christopher paused, his eyes boring into her and sucking up every detail– "you've clearly been playing us. Somehow you've grown all the way up since fifth period," he said with the most devious grin across his face. His impeccable manners to compliment the both of them were not lost on Era, eliciting a small smile from Alex.

She returned his compliment with a touch of condescension. "Thanks Christopher. You look pretty good yourself."

She cocked an eyebrow at him. The blazer *was* doing great things for his broad shoulders. She'd never seen him dressed up since they'd never hung out outside of school. Suddenly, she looked at him with fresh perspective.

His green eyes gleamed, framed by the golden brown hair swept dashingly into a side part. This crisp and clean look struck her. *Watch out girl,* she thought. If Alex liked his usual youthful casualness in sweats and designer sneakers she might faint over the new and improved grown-man look.

"Appreciate you throwing the invite our way. Clearly, I wasn't the only one holding back," Era said, waving her hand over their ostentatious surroundings.

Just then a woman approached Christopher to direct his attention to something related to the party. She was older and appeared to be part of the staff so he gave their arms a squeeze and headed off with her.

The girls made a beeline for the bar where a familiar face shook a round of Washington Apple shots. Standing head and shoulders above the average man at the party, a handsome face in a pressed white shirt and black dress pants lost his concentration and smiled at the approaching duo.

"Jesse, what a surprise to see you here! Aren't you a little far from the City for a one night gig? Only the best for the Ridgewells I see," Era said, honey dripping from her sweet voice. Era knew this bartender from the Social Club in the City. He always made polite conversation with her and didn't mind the girls dropping his name to get into the back room where private parties often meant access to every kind of A-lister.

A minor aspect of her Gift, she never forgot a person's name. She knew how to subtly flatter the vain or draw out the shy with a few words. With a quick read of people's insecurities or suspicions, she could put the wary at ease and leave them glowing in her warmth. She spoke without insecurity, unfazed in this case by the fact that Jesse had seven years on her at twenty-five and possessed the kind of undeniable appeal anyone between the ages of 15 and 40 would recognize.

Jesse's face beamed at the recognition as he stood clacking the ice inside the frosty glasses. "It was worth the drive. Trust me. What'll you have, sweetheart?" he asked with bedroom eyes as he tilted the shaker, sending the liquid cascading into a row of shot glasses with precision.

Era's Gift kissed the information around him. She felt the stress hidden behind his glowing smile—money trouble, and the gratitude for the gig at three hundred dollars an hour plus tips. Wow. A little dollar sign spun off him and melted into a shot glass he lined up on the bar.

When he looked up, she saw his gorgeous smile shift slightly, the incisors lengthening and understood that if he saw her again in a few months, he'd ask for her number. Era didn't register the least bit of surprise. She knew from seeing into the hearts of men that they didn't give a damn about age. They felt only primal attraction and the laws labeling some pretty girls as "minors" only dulled the desire. She noted the aversion to the taboo of going for a high school girl and saw his will yield to better judgment, that he should wait until she graduated high school.

"Mezcal margarita—Tajin, no salt on the rim, please. I'm feeling a little spicy tonight," Era said with a wink before spinning around to scan the room again. She left dealing with Jesse for another time.

The inside crowd stood shoulder to shoulder, and the air thickened as the AC struggled to keep up with the heat of so many bodies with the doors propped open. She decided they should head outside.

Twenty kids lined up on either side of what looked to be a very nice table on the outdoor patio poised for a rowdy game. The tang of beer filled Era's nose and she got a jolt when a girl screamed into her ear, as the anchoring cup on her side flipped and stuck upside down on the surface. As elegant as the party wanted to be, it couldn't get past the stereotype of drinking games and red keg cups. Well, it was a high school party after all. A few classmates waved them down to join the game of flip cup, but Era held up her cocktails and shook her head, continuing along.

Past the outdoor patio, the night air filled with electricity. A massive crowd had formed in front of the DJ stage and Era absorbed the heightened energy as the beat prepared to drop, foam light sticks waving in the air. As the bass hit her chest, she tasted the first lick of spicy Tajín, the tang of lime, and the smokey seduction of mezcal slide down her throat. Closing her eyes for a moment, she drank in the energy of the night, the feeling of elation pulsing off the bodies around her. The Gift could be good in a crowd.

Era and Alex walked hand in hand, faces tipped up to the starlit sky. By the time the girls pushed past the outer edges of the crush, the song cut off. The mood boomeranged as the DJ transitioned to a very popular hip hop track, triggering a collective scream as everyone went absolutely crazy. Bass enveloped the crowd and when everyone joined together on the lyrics, the speakers went silent, leaving the assembly to hear only the unified shout of their own youthful voices filling the night air.

The euphoria of electronic music hit on one level, but the energetic groove of this song brought out something else entirely. Era's body swayed and rocked with the rhythm in perfect synchronization. Her Gift allowed her to connect with music in a deeper way and her body moved with a fluidity that made the crowd around her step back and admire her. She knew her dancing often attracted too much attention, but after shedding the guarded, reserved persona she maintained to protect herself, tonight she allowed the full brilliance of her true self to shine for all to see.

Two young men brave enough to step towards Era and Alex in the midst of a small circle shook her out of her trance. She didn't mind a brief, playful dance with them, but anything that lasted beyond that moment could easily leave them stuck with random guys who believed they had a claim on the girls for the rest of the night. It'd happened more times than she could count, and Era knew that most guys didn't care that she had a boyfriend, especially if he wasn't around.

Era grabbed Alex's hand, pulling her through the crowd so that they could cool off at one of the pool cabanas near the bar. She thought they had successfully lost the two guys when suddenly she felt a hand on her elbow.

"Oh hi," she clipped robotically at the dark-haired guy. He appeared to be about twenty two with a cocky expression across his thin lips. His tall frame filled out a navy blazer and crisp white pants in a way that said, "I will not have a problem pulling a girl tonight."

"We're going to take a minute to cool down. Also, I have a boyfriend so you might consider improving your chances by trying elsewhere." Though spoken in her most disarming tone, her words were clear: he would not find success with her even if he tried.

"Is that so?" the now unwelcome stranger mocked. "I'm Simon and I'm not as concerned about my chances as you seem to be," he said, brushing his hand from her elbow up her arm. The persistence emanated from his words and something hidden and foul burned her nose, almost an odor, like getting a whiff of spoiled garbage after passing a row of dumpsters in an alleyway behind a seafood restaurant.

Era held her breath reflexively, her eyes scanning the crowd but not finding anyone she knew well. She needed an exit, didn't want the knowledge of a depraved heart. If she could just escape his voice, if she didn't hear it, she wouldn't see any more.

It wasn't all that rare to come across someone—like him. Dark hearts like his walked invisibly through the world, laid completely bare to her. She hated it. Sometimes the things she saw ruined her for days. Mostly she clung to a trick she'd invented. She pretended she was a surgeon, that they were merely diseased sick individuals. In this way, she diagnosed and dismissed the evil ones with a clinical detachment that kept her from dwelling too much on philosophical realities—like the absolute horrendous disgusting fallenness of man.

Thankfully, her life raft floated over from behind, the warm earthy scent of sandalwood hitting her nose with a calming familiarity. Era reached for Christopher's leg as he interrupted the unwanted exchange, allowing the desperation for his help flicker in her eyes.

Without missing a beat, Christopher butted in with grace, "Hey, Simon. You enjoying the party? It's great isn't it?" Era's eyes went wide and she had to turn her head to hide a smile at hearing Christopher answer himself condescendingly without giving the guy a chance to reply.

He might have been an arrogant know-it-all sometimes, but rude, never. "My girl Era and I were just going to get caught up. You wouldn't mind grabbing us a drink from the bar would you?" he asked with more insistence than politeness. He sounded as if he had told a junior associate at his company to make coffee for the meeting—not exactly a request.

Era swallowed the impolite giggle that nearly burst out of her. It didn't escape her that he said "my girl Era," and not "my friend Era" but she chalked it up to him playing the knight and nothing more.

"No problem—Era," he said, repeating her name, savoring the little slip. "See you later."

"You know him?" she asked, relaxing a little with each step the intruder took away from her while stirring the melted ice in the bottom of her drink.

Christopher swiped the half empty contents, replacing it with a fresh replica in one smooth motion. "He works in my dad's office."

"How did you...?" Era stammered looking down at a mezcal margarita with red flecks of Tajín lining the rim.

"Oh, that's compliments of your boy Jesse. Heard you guys

know each other," Christopher said with fake enthusiasm, "from the Social Club!" Dropping the act, he lowered his voice and leaned in more seriously making her heart speed up. "Now I happen to know that almost nobody gets into that club—unless they're a member of course *or* they're taken in by someone really important." He leaned back and eyed her suspiciously before continuing. "I also know they're very strict with ID and no matter who you know, you're not getting in there underage."

Era found herself ambushed by the interrogation. Christopher took a beat to study Era's face and see if she would interrupt him to incriminate herself. When she showed no sign of cracking he continued, "So I'm left to deduce that you are absolutely nothing like the girl that sits across from me in Calculus with those phony non-prescription glasses and an endless list of excuses as to why you don't have a social life outside of school."

Era snorted indignantly. "Those are blue light glasses, you ass!" But in truth she couldn't help herself from laughing at his astuteness, how he drew a perfect set of conclusions about her with only a few new pieces of information. *Congrats Sherlock,* she thought, eyeing him with a mix of appreciation and delight.

Glancing over her shoulder, she saw Alex happily chatting with a friend from school over at the bar which she noted before continuing, "Listen, you got me. Alex and I don't have much time for social events with people from *this* school because we have plenty of friends *outside* of school. It's as simple as that, and it's cleaner for us, much cleaner." She sipped her tangy margarita and hoped he would leave it at that. But he leaned in even closer, as if he'd only just begun with her. Who knew one outfit would burst her entire facade?

"What sort of people do you hang out with? What's the last event you went to with these 'friends'?" he asked, throwing up cheesy bunny ears with his fingers.

Normally Era would have sidestepped this question and redirected the conversation elsewhere, but the feeling of genuine interest she got from him chipped at her wall of general secrecy. And if anyone could handle hearing about some of the whirlwind of her double life outside of school, Christopher could, with his estate and yacht and who knows what else.

Shrugging away her apprehension she began, "We were at the Four Seasons over Spring Break... in the... ah... Maldives... with a rather large group of people."

"Huh, so let me guess, the 'budget concerns' that made you miss out on Senior trip were linked to splurging on cocktails in the Indian Ocean?" he inferred as he chewed on the newly imparted information, looking back in his memory to discover more of her secrets. "Jeez Era who are you? And I bet you're living your weekend life looking like *this* everyday," his hand mimicking the shape of an hourglass over her figure.

"Oh please, don't act like you sit at home with your home-work stalking your crushes on Insta. I know for a fact that you've hooked up with plenty of girls, go on lavish vacations with your family, and attend all the big galas. I saw your picture in Emerald Magazine, three times! You could have any girl you want in the whole school, including this smokeshow–" she said, flipping her hand towards Alex at the bar.

"Don't do that. Don't pretend you don't know that I've liked you since freshman year. You know everything." His eyes burned into hers and his pupils blew out wide, making her shiver.

"I don't know how you do it, but I know you do... well... something. I've watched you. How you manage to control every situation with astounding precision. It's subtle, but you get exactly what you want from everyone, every time.

"I also know that you're not a sociopath, I can tell you have concern for others. I saw you shield that dorky kid in our English class that wouldn't stop going on about his anime shows. You somehow fixed him, made him more likable and convinced the rest of the class that Korean cartoons were the new trend.

"I see how guys hit on you constantly and you somehow always find a way to turn them down without hurting their ego. And even now you're trying to spare Alex's feelings, holding her up to me as an option, even though we both know I never meant to lead her on by helping her in chemistry."

Then his tone dropped, becoming gruff and Era felt her stomach clench. "And I'm sure that you felt something for me too, at least at some point, but you still decided to go for that college guy that could never match you like I do."

The last line hit her like a punch to the gut and she aspirated on a gulp of liquor, burning her trachea. Her watering eyes locked with his as she coughed, a deer in the headlights.

Welcome to uncharted territory.

Someone had finally come close to understanding her mind. She felt completely naked before him, as if his words had shredded her clothes to pieces and there she stood, in a cliché nightmare before a crowd of people staring at her. She had grown so used to having the upper hand in every conversation that this shift in power truly caught her off guard. Not only had he known that she kept a secret, but he had been a keen silent witness as she exerted her power over others. She thought she had been so careful in how and when she used the Gift on others, that she'd covered her tracks. Panic welled in her throat and her tongue felt thick.

Being called out on her secret affection for him remained by far the worst of it. Era believed she had kept that little indulgence tightly guarded but he had seen through her forced boundaries. How had she not seen this coming? The Gift left little room for people to surprise her.

Christopher may not possess anything like the Gift but he had knowledge and understanding where most did not. She felt a sudden dread for which she had no explanation. His eyes demanded a truth from her and in that moment, she had no reason to hold back. A spontaneous compulsion to reward his curiosity with the whole truth took hold of her.

Unconsciously, she leaned into him, her face close enough to warm his face with her breath, ready to reveal more of herself to him than she had to anyone in a very long time.

"I was bullied in junior high by this terrible group of girls exactly because of what you described. In fact, this one girl pretty much ruined my life," she began to explain and paused to sip her drink again.

"Go on." His eyes looked deeply into hers, pulling the truth into their depths.

"I dated her crush, this sweet guy who also happened to be the most desirable at our school. When he had to move away unexpectedly, the girl spread terrible rumors that I had done things with him that I never did. Everyone treated me differently after that, especially the boys, who harassed me with sexual comments every day. I think I cried without missing a day until the end of the year. After that, I made a personal rule to keep my private and love life completely separate from my school life.

"You've always felt... ah... special to me but I couldn't pay that price again, especially not when I knew how many girls already liked you," Era finished with a huff, a strange relaxation sweeping over her with the admission of truth.

Christopher stared back at her in disbelief. "So *that's* what you meant when you said it was cleaner this way! You and I could have been happy together since freshman year. I could have made you happy, I know it. You threw away four years of happiness. For what? A stupid rule? To keep your reputation unsullied? How could you do it?"

"Woah, Christopher. I think you may have gotten the wrong idea. I don't know how you just pole-vaulted to that conclusion, but let me remind you that I have a boyfriend. I've been with Cole for a year. I love him. There was never any *us*."

"I remember your boyfriend. I saw him the one time you brought him to a football game in the fall. He didn't look too happy to be there, a bit old for you too," he spat with some venom. "Anyways, you wouldn't even be with him if you had given me a chance."

"Alright, I think we're done here. I'm not going to have you rewriting history in an attempt to make the past something it was not. The rule was my choice. It protected me–"

"I could have protected you too."

"No, you could have ruined me," she said standing up, grabbing her phone. Era bit her lip and frowned at not finding her friend still at the bar. She knew that her response, though true, could give him the wrong idea. She didn't mean it like that, or thought she didn't. She never imagined the night turning out this way. The press of the crowd suddenly felt suffocating rather than exhilarating and she wanted to get out of there.

She pushed past a couple making out and wove through bodies until she was on the far side of the pool. The guest house, a perfect hideout, sat quietly off to the side, far enough away from the music and booze that few ended up so far out.

She walked into a perfectly staged living room, one that looked bigger than the average apartment and threw herself down on the thick couch cushions. Pulling out her phone, she found the one name she wanted to see, Cole.

His phone rang and went to voicemail. *That's so strange,* she thought to herself. *Why wouldn't he pick up his phone if he's just studying in his room?* She really needed to hear his voice. Her body trembled after being sideswiped by the most outlandish conversation of her life. The drop in the pit of her stomach happened a second time since arriving and it did not make any more sense to her than before.

Without warning, the door to the guest house swung open

and Simon swaggered into the room. He tried to look casual about it, but Era instantly detected his direct intention to find her alone.

She greeted him casually, "Hi again," remaining on the couch and looking at her phone so as not to give away how defensive she felt in his presence. "Is my friend still at the bar?" seemingly inviting him to leave the guest house with her.

"I'm overdue for another drink," she finished, standing up from the sectional.

"Why don't we have one in here?" he asked with a kind of weaponized oblivion to her meaning, moving towards the small bar in the kitchen to make them a drink.

The Gift flared angrily. Small licks of fire trailed behind his jacket as he moved towards the decanter on the bar. And then she saw the memory—the liquid he poured into another girl's shot glass on Halloween last year. His playful demeanor as he carried the stumbling and slumped pirate girl to his car, had his way and then dropped her back off on the front lawn. Era's mind revolted at the image but plastered a practiced smile on her face and said, "Hmm why not?" Then she held her phone in her lap while she texted a very capitalized message to Alex to get to the pool's guest house *NOW* followed by a creeper emoji.

He poured a shot from the decanter into two glass tumblers then opened the mini fridge to grab a small ice cube tray and can of ginger ale. Her warning bells were sirens in her ears now. She saw the fire coming off him turn to green and understood— poison. He had taken a pill from his pocket when he bent down to open the mini fridge and planned to make her his next victim. Even while watching his every movement, she never caught the moment the pill slipped into her drink before he stirred it—that's how smooth this preppy-looking finance bro operated.

She would have to get past him to get out the door. A tight squeeze.

He approached her with the drinks, his wide frame filling the space between the couch and the credenza in a way that left her little room to navigate. If she retreated, she would give herself away. She decided she would approach him as if to take the drink and bump him hard enough to spill them, then try to make a break for it past him during the confusion.

She grinned at him, extending her hand as she reached for the drink, letting her purse slip down at the last moment. The baguette handbag swung off her shoulder, hitting the drink with perfect aim.

Era let out a fake "Ooh" of surprise and spun her body like a football receiver, pretending to trip as she caught the purse. She had nearly completed the maneuver except that Simon dropped the glass without a thought and his empty hand shot out to wrap around her arm.

"Careful!" he said, tightening his grip as if he was steadying her instead of stopping her escape when Alex came busting loudly through the door.

"ERA! You ho! How could you leave me out at the bar for nearly half an hour and then ditch me to come in here to call your BOYFRIEND? He's out front waiting for us. Let's go!"

Simon's face turned towards Alex's in surprise and then twisted momentarily into anger as she grabbed Era's other arm and yanked his prize out the door.

CHAPTER 5

ALEX'S wide white eyes shone even in the dark but they moved quickly away from the guest house before speaking. They headed straight for the crowded main house and up the stairs into the Master bathroom.

"What was that all about?" Alex questioned without hiding her alarm. "I saw him grabbing your arm. There were indents on your skin. What happened?"

"Alex, have I ever told you that I love you?"

"I love you too. You know that."

"He followed me to the pool house. That's what happened. I had one of my gut instincts the second he walked through the door and you *know* I'm never wrong about those. He insisted on making us drinks. And drugged mine," Era said, tears starting to sting her eyes.

"Shit—that's terrifying. Thank God you texted me. Let's get out of here."

Despite the fact that Era had been the target of a serial rapist, she couldn't help feeling guilty. "Hey, I'm so sorry. I know you were having a really good time and finally hanging out with our classmates–"

"Ahem," a sound came from the Master closet.

"Are you kidding me?" Alex's voice rang out, rising in irritation. "Who's in there? 20,000 square feet and we can't get an ounce of privacy!"

From the closet, Christopher stepped out, buttoning a new shirt, a scowl on his face. "Are you fricking kidding me? Era, are you alright? I'm going to have security kick that guy's ass right now." Christopher grabbed his phone and sent off a quick text to his staff.

He walked over to Era and wrapped his arms around her. For the first time, they embraced, and the feeling turned out to be surprisingly soothing and safe. His arms felt strong, and with his tall frame, her head rested just above the center of his broad chest. His solid body eased her sense of vulnerability.

"Hey, really," his voice softened as he looked down at her. "Are you okay?" he repeated. As he paused, his face tilted down towards her, illuminated by the bathroom lights that highlighted every detail, Era couldn't help but stare at the shape of his mouth. His lips were full and perfectly sculpted, with a natural curve that hinted at both strength and sensuality. His positively arched eyebrows squinched down in concern while his turquoise eyes bored into her as she grasped for a response.

Instead of forming words, her brain glitched, taking in the dramatic dark lashes that dragged her attention back to his eyes, contrasting with the golden streaks in his sandy brown hair that swept up and off his smooth forehead. The awkwardness of their previous conversation vanished into thin air replaced by a riptide that pulled her out to him.

"Um." Now Alex had the duty to break up the party, her presence forgotten amid the intense unspoken exchange.

"I'm fine," Era muttered, finding her voice at last and stepping out of Christopher's arms. "I didn't see him put the pill in the drink even though I know he did. Let's just forget about it. We're about to head out." She paused, looking at his shirt quizzically. "Why are you even up here anyway? Not feeling the outfit?" Era asked, trying to change the subject.

"A drunk girl spilled gin on me downstairs which I hate, nasty stuff, smells like medicine. I came up to change and over-heard someone's *very* echoey conversation taking place in a *marble* bathroom. Who picks the Master bath for a private moment at a party? You girls are too funny. 20,000 square feet...." he trailed off, chuckling to himself.

Alex turned beet red and spun around to hide her embarrassment. She crossed the floor of the bedroom so quickly that Christopher and Era had to bolt to catch up.

"I'll take you guys home," Christopher offered. "It's the least I can do."

"It's fine, I live down the street and you've been drinking. Plus, you're not going to leave your whole party to take me home. We can walk."

"I know where you live. I've been driving past your house every day since you moved in there the summer after 8th grade. And some predator tried to drug you, what? Five minutes ago? Do you really think I'm going to let you walk off into the night by yourself?" Christopher asked, his hand reaching for her, then dropping to his side. He turned to Alex with authority and continued, "If you're not staying at Era's house, I'll have one of the valet's drive you home."

"Thanks Christopher." Era noticed with some annoyance that Alex looked down at her feet when she replied. She struggled to deal with guys she liked acting thoughtfully towards her, something Era made a point mentally to work on with her.

"Get my girl home safe, ok?" she said as the valet shut the door of Christopher's dad's Bentley.

Era's hand reached out, her thumb stroking his forearm below the rolled up cuff of his sleeve. "That was sweet, but seriously, I can walk home. It's not far and as much as I know you could snap your fingers and pull a Ferrari out of thin air, I need to walk. I need to think," she explained.

"Fine. No problem."

"Thanks I knew you'd understand," Era said, relieved.

"I'll walk you home."

"Ah you're so stubborn. Let's just go so you can get back before you have any more staff emergencies," she said, stomping off into the driveway.

They walked into the dark and quiet street without saying anything further. The night had turned cool. Dew hung in the air like a wet blanket around them, the hushed fog broken only by the muted patter of Era's heels on the cement.

What a weird night. She tried to forget the smell of rotting garbage, the vision of green poison. Era usually found a way to dodge the worst kind of people. In fact, rapists were a dime a dozen among the men hitting on her in the club. Only a few months ago, she'd sat crammed next to a seasoned murderer in a middle seat on the longest flight of her life from Heathrow to JFK.

She wondered how shocked people would be to know without a doubt how many murderers she'd crossed paths with in her short lifetime. Yep, if she had to choose between being found alone in the woods by a random man or a bear, she'd pick the bear, everytime. Because not only had she discovered that a good hunk of the male population were outright depraved, but more chilling was the knowledge that an even greater proportion of them were opportunists.

Based on her experience, out of ten men, two would be truly frightening, five would take their chances to get away with being a creep, and three would be decent. For that reason, Era did her best to avoid unnecessary conversations with strangers. She didn't want to read any more hearts than necessary and gathered people with good intentions around her for her own safety as much as for her benefit.

Her mind began to wander, seeing a carousel of faces—
Christopher, Cole, Jesse, Simon, Christopher. She looked over
and to her surprise saw Christopher's face in the soft moonlight. She had forgotten his presence, he walked so silently by
her side.

"I'm sorry for what I said about your boyfriend, earlier. I'm
sure you have good reason to be with him, ehm, love him," he
said, choking on his own correction. "I don't regret telling you
how I feel though. I knew you didn't want to hear it, but I had to
say it anyway, especially if I don't get another chance. I feel like
it's been weighing on me for a long time." Christopher paused
then continued, "So where did you end up picking for school
next year?"

"Actually, I was holding out for Cal University and finally
got off the waitlist. I'll be going there in the fall, with Cole," she
answered sharply, more sharply than she had intended.

His face perked up with excitement, "Really? Me too. I
thought for sure you'd end up on the other side of the country.
Looks like you won't be able to get rid of me just yet," he said
and smirked, pushing her gently with his shoulder.

The Gift pulsated. Even in the dark, looking straight ahead,
she felt hope and happiness and yes, something else—patience,
beating towards her. Era didn't feel ready to sort through it all,
but despite the pang of guilt, she couldn't help but harbor a
smug satisfaction to have Christopher coming with her to Cal.
Surely, it would be good to have a familiar face in a class, and
maybe—if she put up the right boundaries—they could still be
friends.

Cole had never been jealous at all so she didn't see why the
two of them couldn't get along if they had to. Era knew
corralling Christopher into the friend zone might be selfish, but
no other option came to mind on how they could still talk after
tonight's confession. There might not be any room left in her
heart for anyone but Cole, but that didn't negate the fact that

Christopher had shown her something beautiful about himself tonight. They understood each other and letting that go didn't feel right either.

"Stop being dramatic. I don't want to get rid of you. You're the only person other than Alex I actually enjoyed spending time with at school. And yeah you caught me off guard with some of what you said, which was super weird because that never happens—um nevermind. Anyway, I do agree that part of me feels like I missed out on something with you... even if it's only *the friendship* that we could have had if I hadn't been such a stickler for 'the Rule,'" she whispered as her house came into view. Era felt the Gift radiate his anger when she said the word friendship but it dissipated as she stepped towards him.

"Thank you for getting me home safely," she said as she pivoted towards him on her toes with her arms outstretched. He swept her into another tight hug and answered back into her hair.

"You're welcome...friend. Whatever it is that you need. I'm here. The rule is dead, you're free. Keep yourself safe for me, okay? And call me if you need a ride to the beach tomorrow. I'll be heading out around noon. You're on the way you know," he teased.

Era went upstairs to her room. She checked the time on her phone, only 10:30, easily the earliest she'd ever gotten home from a party. Somehow she felt utterly exhausted. She rubbed the aching orbital of her eyes and kicked off the heels that left her sore feet humming from hiking through the whole neighborhood.

Using the Gift drained her, not in itself, but the constant barrage of other people's emotions and memories did take a toll on her after a while. She closed her eyes in relief to be alone in the noiseless room then winced at the brightness of her phone. She almost forgot to send off a last text to Cole.

Came home early from the party. Not as fun as I hoped. Heading to bed exhausted. Good night my love. Call me in the morning.

She decided to leave out the date rape drug, the love confession and the long walk home with another boy. For some reason she didn't even ask him to call her or word the message so he'd respond. Part of her knew she wouldn't be hearing from him tonight. She brushed off the uneasy feeling. Cole had never given her any reason to worry about him. She trusted him like she trusted the sun to rise in the morning.

CHAPTER 6

THE NEXT MORNING gave Era the perspective that she needed. Her future happiness with Cole and the promise of inseparable bliss together in college dissolved any remaining worry about Christopher, her classmates, or her reputation. It all appeared so trivial and nearly in her rear view mirror.

She jumped up with incredible vigor, feeling like a lion poised to pounce on her day like so much helpless prey. She grabbed her Airpods, phone and a water and was out the door, jogging down the street for her usual ten mile loop around the bay. 8 a.m. was early enough to beat the sticky air while the sun hid behind the last hour or two of morning cloud cover. She decided on a whim to alter her route slightly, heading all the way down her block to get a peek at the aftermath of Christopher's party before ducking down the trail that started at the edge of his property. From there she could make her way down the winding dirt trail to the marshy water below.

The estate looked as it normally would, deceptively unassuming from the street, behind the rows of trees with the large gate closed tightly against wandering eyes. The only evidence that the spot held the largest party of the year was an errant

cigarette butt on the ground and a few beer cans she saw
stashed in the bushes across the street.

It wasn't until she was on the dirt path that she glanced over
her shoulder and spotted the gleam of sunlight off Christopher's
sandy hair as he sat on one of the high balconies, drinking
coffee in a lavender polo and gray pants, dark sunglasses on his
face. For a moment, she thought he hadn't seen her, until he
tilted his head and waved in her direction. She gave a weak
wave and sped quickly around the corner so the brush could
conceal her from view.

His ego was already big enough. The last thing she needed
was for him to think she was snooping around his house. A
minute later she looked at her watch and saw his message.

> Good morning early bird. I'd join you but I have
> a raging headache. What time am I picking you
> up for the beach?

That cheeky bastard, she thought, *I never agreed to ride with him.*
However, on second thought, she remembered the parking situation at Clarissa's house, a private cove with only four parking
spaces and at least fifty kids from their class coming. She imagined herself having to park at the top of the gated community
and walk down the steep hill and then the stairs with her stuff,
arriving at the beach drenched in sweat. *Ew, no thanks,* she
thought and dictated a message back to him from her watch.

> 12. We'll have to pick up Alex on the way.

Of course. It wouldn't be appropriate for us to ride together unchaperoned now would it?

She knew he was toeing a fine line with their newfound friendship and her relationship. Turning into the driveway, she wiped the sweat from her nose. She'd pushed herself hard on interval sprints over the last three miles. Thankfully, her grocery order sat waiting for her at the front door. She had decided not to be a mooch and actually bring some of her own spread down to the beach. Plus, with Era's mom and dad out of town wine tasting for the weekend, she would be cooking her own meals.

After putting everything away, she mixed up an extra large pitcher of rosemary jalapeño daiquiris and put it in the largest thermos to chill. Then she chopped her sushi grade fish and marinated the Ahi. She finished off her beach picnic basket with appetizer plates, sparkling mineral water, and a veggie with pesto dipping bento box. *Ah, perfect!* she thought. So what if the menu was slightly borrowed from the chartered yacht she and Alex had taken off of Croatia last summer? She showered and dressed, reminiscing fondly on that terrific spread and then FaceTimed Raquel, her dearest friend in London.

"Hi, love! I know you're probably getting ready for dinner there but I was thinking about you—my don't you look lovely!" she chirped, interrupting herself. "Where are you headed? Is that Givenchy?"

"Ah yes, darling it's the summer line. It wasn't exactly ready to wear, but I had to have it after the show. George is picking me up in about 20 minutes. What are you up to?" Raquel asked.

"Just getting ready to head out to the beach… with some classmates. This girl is having something of an end of the year get together. It's kind of a coming out party for me since no one has seen me in anything other than my boring t-shirts and jeans. I thought I'd get your opinion on my outfit. Too much?" Era asked, spinning around.

She wore the same outfit that she had worn in St. Bart's last Christmas, a white two piece with a gold ring in the center and a chain that connected to the bottoms. It fit like a tailored dream, the thick stretchy fabric snapping over her curves without a wrinkle. It also didn't leave much to the imagination, especially in the back.

On her wrists were stacks of designer gold bracelets, gold hoops in her ears and two dainty gold necklaces. Her shoes were tall flatforms that flattered her without being too impractical for the walk down to the sand. Long blond curls fell down her back with two braids twisting strands from her temples away from her face. Her legs were oiled with gold bronzing powder dusted down her shins, toned abs, bust and collarbones. Her poised graceful figure looked as if she had stepped off the pages of a swimsuit shoot and knew it. She didn't really need Raquel to approve her outfit but she knew that she loved to be consulted in all manners of fashion.

Raquel squeaked happily, "Era, you look positively scrumptious! You know you always kill it in swimwear, but did I hear you right? I thought you didn't hang out with 'school kids.' One tip, darling, swap the hoops for the diamond studs. Plenty of gold already going on, and go big or go home, right?" she stated matter of factly.

"Three carats at the beach? I hope I don't get hit by any big waves. You're right though. A little much for the beach and I bet anyone who sees them will think they're fake anyway," she replied with a sly smile. "I miss you and George so much. Where are we going this summer? I'll be losing my mind with boredom by the time finals are over."

"Not sure yet babes but I'll let you know. George might be able to get us a week or two at his villa in Como, wouldn't that be lovely?" Raquel finished. "Oop okay he's here, gotta run. Bye love."

Era met Raquel Freshman year when her family took a ski holiday to Aspen. Era's father imagined he was a quasi-pro skier when really he ended up sitting most of the day in the lodge bar drinking steins of beer and reminiscing about his double black diamond days. Alone most of the time, Era ended up riding the gondola with a sweet British socialite and her mildly attractive though round-faced brother.

It only took Era one compliment about the puppy on her lock screen and recognition of the rare trendy bracelet she wore to get invited to ski the rest of the day with them. The afternoon together turned into nearly five days of joint holidaying.

Raquel's brother developed quite the crush and it wasn't long before Era and her trusted travel companion Alex became the American extension of a British crew of jetset kids, joining them on trips all over.

Back at home, Era had no trouble linking into a circle of party friends in the City where they could play anonymously closer to home. The adventures snowballed. By junior year, they needed to order extra pages for their passports. They rarely stayed in the sleepy beach town for breaks until senior year when Cole came into the picture.

After swapping the earrings, she tried Cole for the second time that morning. He picked up on the third ring, his voice raspy and parched. "Hello, sleeping beauty," she said sunnily, "I've only been trying to get a hold of you all morning and it's what, 11:30? How are you sleeping in so late? I thought you went to bed early last night since I never heard back from you."

"Sorry babe. I actually did get most of my papers done although I ended up heading down to the coffee house and running into some buddies. Hung out there for a lot longer than I meant to. How did last night go?" he asked, clearly wanting to move the spotlight off himself.

"Well, the party started out great. Alex and I were dancing and Christopher's DJ was incredible. Unfortunately, there was a guy who was following me around and I didn't feel like dealing with it so I came home early," she explained. It was a highly condensed version of the night's happenings but she didn't think it necessary to upset him with every last detail. "Any chance you might make it to the beach today? I'm bringing cocktails and my famous poke!"

He stammered in reply, "Uh, not today babe. I wish. Accounting study group this afternoon and I really need to stay on campus until I finish all my work or I'll never get it done. I'll see you tomorrow for our date though."

Even though Era loved responsible Cole, she wasn't used to him saying no to her. This was the third weekend in a row that they hadn't spent completely inseparable and she did not enjoy the change. She took a breath and reminded herself that the semester was almost over and that they'd have all summer together, possibly even in Como. The thought brightened the flicker of her dark mood.

"Sure. Kill it at your group sesh. Love you." She tried to sound positive despite the disappointment she felt.

"You too. Bye," he said and hung up.

You too? Again? she thought. *No need to panic. He's probably still just waking up. Right?*

Her phone lit up again with a text from Christopher announcing his arrival outside. *Dammit, ten minutes early?* Her stomach flipped over again, butterflies. *Why do I feel so weird around him?* she thought. *And who shows up EARLY to a girl's house? Doesn't he know that's a cardinal sin?*

Flustered, she snatched a white cover up from her closet and rushed downstairs to assemble the basket. Crap, she hadn't even packed her beach bag yet, and gosh knows she still needed her towel, sunscreen, lip balm and about ten other items.

She ran to the front door, motioning to Christopher to come

inside. Better to make some small talk with him rather than hurry frantically around the house. Era hated making people wait. Feeling like an inconvenience gave her a sick feeling. Thanks mom and dad.

He strolled through the door casually, and Era's frantic mood shattered with a tiny gasp. He wore sea foam green trunks that cut off inches above the knee, showing off a thick cut in his muscular thighs she'd never seen. But even more scandalous was the loose white tank with some sort of throwback 80s squiggle on the front and giant armholes that exposed an obscene amount of tan skin, rippled with muscle across his broad shoulders and chest. His sandy golden hair framed his clear features in an effortless way that made him look like a California dream.

Era froze in the hallway, forgetting her task list entirely, peering intently at the sight of his lat muscles peeking out from under the loose tank. *Woah, this body. He doesn't even play a sport?* she thought before remembering how irritated she was at him for being early.

His eyes checked hers, and he gave her a half wink.

"Christopher, you're killing me! Never arrive early to pick up a girl! Have you no manners?" she said, storming off and speaking to him over her shoulder. "I still need to grab my stuff. Come sit in the kitchen while I finish up." She took a breath, remembering her own manners and asked, "Can I get you a water or a coffee or something?"

"I'm good. Take your time. I already had plenty of coffee this morning. You know, on my balcony where you saw me during your run," he answered devilishly. Ignoring the obvious flirt attempt, Era deftly assembled the drinks and food into her picnic backpack and started gathering items for her beach bag from the hall cabinet.

"Dammit," she muttered when she grabbed the sunscreen. She always liked to apply her sunscreen before going to the beach. Era spent a good amount of time in the sun and worried about looking like a raisin one day so she took very good care of her skin.

"What's the matter?" she heard Christopher call from the kitchen.

"Nothing, I just haven't put my sunscreen on yet and I know you want to get going," she answered.

"Why can't you put it on at the beach like everyone else?" he asked, clearly confused.

"Look, with all the time I spend playing tennis and in the sun, I always put it on before. I'm not going to end up looking like a crocodile bag. Give me a second and I'll be right back," she called over her shoulder as she walked towards the back patio doors, annoyed at hearing him chuckle behind her.

Era set down the spray and had whipped off her dress when she heard the bottle being shaken behind her.

"I got you," Christopher said as he stepped behind her and sprayed the cool aerosol down her back. The sensation sent a wave of ice and electricity jolting through her. He sprayed every curve of her bare skin including the sides around her bikini bottoms until goosebumps were visible over her entire body. With the cold torture finished, she felt the chill replaced by his warm hands as he massaged her shoulders, rubbing up into her hair. There was nothing awkward about his touch and she had to hold herself rigid to keep from giving away how good it felt.

When his hands had finished her lower back, his touch began to trail further down which is when she spun around quickly with a, "Thank you." She finished the job herself, then rubbed the clear liquid into her chest and stomach before bending all the way down to get her legs.

As she did so, she could feel Christopher's eyes on her exposed body and rebuked her own sensitivity. Her entire class would soon see her in just as much. She threw the dress back over her head and began walking towards the patio door when his deep voice rang out from behind, "Um, excuse me, but if we're going to be friends, then you certainly wouldn't want *me* getting skin cancer would you? I could use some help."

The fake cluelessness in his voice was cute but irritating. Still feeling a little embarrassed by his earlier appraisal of her body, she turned to find him tugging his tank top off with one hand and pivoting so that his broad back was facing her.

Holy smokes, what a body this boy had! He'd hid his frame as well as she'd hid her own. She couldn't help but notice his well-defined muscles or the athletic curve of lats and traps which were her favorite part of the male form. Surely, it wasn't her fault that she was programmed to appreciate beauty and his form was nothing if not beautiful.

Era's teeth gleamed as she gave him a punishing icy blast with the spray, hitting him in the more sensitive spots with a little bit extra. That would teach this brazen flirt. Next, she began roughly rubbing his skin until without realizing it, she had slowed down and was tracing her hands over the cuts of his muscles, up the back of his neck, and around the sides of his abs.

The Gift showed every breath he took even though he faced away from her. She could see the hot tendrils like smoke curling towards her. Embers of desire smoldered on the ground around them before she could stop it.

As the smoke touched her face, she became aware that she had her hands in places that he could easily reach himself. "That should do it," she sputtered with some embarrassment and stepped away.

Era almost never felt embarrassed but in that moment her mind flashed to a scenario in which Cole suddenly stood in the doorway, seeing the two of them together and she felt shockingly guilty. Pushing the thought from her head, she once again began walking to the kitchen to collect her things. It wasn't until they were in front of Alex's house that she had fully pulled herself together.

True to his gentlemanly manners, Christopher got out to ring the doorbell and help carry Alex's beach chair. She gave him a brief hug and sauntered towards the truck with a crooked smile on her face.

Once everyone was settled in the cab, she raised an accusatory eyebrow at Era. "Christopher, I see you've sampled some of Era's signature sunscreen. Isn't it so refreshingly minty?" she asked without disguising her fiendish tone.

Christopher gave a cute smile and nod in agreement, not wanting to draw more attention to the subject, but Era knew she would be questioned further on the matter.

Once at the beach, there were, of course, no spots left so Christopher dropped them at the top of the stairs and drove up to find parking. Without wasting a moment, Alex was grilling her about the distinctive sunscreen smell on Christopher she detected during their hug. "Babe, listen, you know me. I'm no snitch, but it's one thing to have the hottest guy from our school who, yes, happens to be your neighbor, pick you up at your house to take you to the beach, but it's another thing to be rubbing sunscreen all over each other before you get there! What did you guys do? Whip off each other's clothes in the kitchen? What would Cole say if he knew?" she finished dramatically, shaking her head.

"It's not like it was planned! He showed up early and offered to get my back when I was finishing getting ready. I couldn't exactly refuse when he asked me to reciprocate," Era defended.

Alex coughed out, "Woah, wait a second, you let him touch you? That does sound pretty bad. Let's just move on but better be careful with that boy. It wouldn't be worth pissing off Cole just because you want to play around with your neighbor."

Now even more humiliated and defensive, Era couldn't stop herself from justifying her actions. "It's not like that at all. He and I have always gotten along really well though I never gave him a chance to get to know me because you know...the Rule. Last night, he found out I knew Jesse and started piecing it together. He was grilling me and wore me down so I maaaaay have explained it to him."

Era paused, checking Alex's emotions to see if she was buying it and if she was pissed that Era had divulged their most highly guarded secret to her own crush before continuing, "And don't worry, he knows about Cole. He even remembers seeing him at that one football game I took him to in the fall."

Sending a shock of exuberance rather than judgment at Era, Alex broke in, "Woah you told him about the Rule!? Wow, you are really busting out of your shell. I'm glad that you did. The old cliques are already dissolving and no one cares about the drama at this point. Let's just enjoy the end of high school. We've got nothing to lose at this point anyway," Alex said, surprising Era with the display of perspective and maturity.

Era agreed with her whole heart. But though she felt herself to be omniscient, and all-knowing, she had neither wisdom nor life experience. What did she have to lose? Only everything.

CHAPTER 7

BY THE TIME the girls reached the bottom of the stairs and laid eyes on one of the state's most stunning beaches, their conversation dissolved into the warm, salty air, as if it, too, had been swept away. The tawny sand folded into jagged red cliffs that seemed to guard the cove like ancient sentinels. Rocks and tide pools clung to the cliffs, where waves broke with a force that sucked the foam back into the sea, only to crash again in a relentless rhythm. The pewter ocean shimmered under the sun, turning a vivid aquamarine as it rose up against the steep shelf of sand in violent shore break.

Above, the sky was an endless, serene blue, and the sun radiated warmth without the usual heaviness of heat. A soft briny breeze lifted Era's hair off the back of her damp neck, and for a brief moment, her heart was enraptured by the beauty of the scene, an intoxicating sense of magic in the air. Yet, beneath the picturesque calm, there was something else—an almost imperceptible shift in the atmosphere, a subtle heaviness that whispered of things just beyond reach. She had been to many beaches across the world, but this one—this one always had something the others lacked. A promise. But a promise of what? It was too elusive to grasp, and yet Era couldn't shake the sense that something was stirring beneath the surface, waiting.

Just beyond the stairs, towels and beach chairs lay strewn haphazardly into loose circles. A frisbee sailed casually through the air near the surf while another group stumbled in the soft sand playing touch football.

Clarissa's house sat on the cliff directly above the beach, affording her a private strip of sand in which to station speakers and a table of drinks. Someone must have made arrangements because usually you couldn't drink alcohol openly on the beach. Not so today.

As they walked closer to the most crowded section, she saw that a group of guys from the soccer team stood around a hose coming out of the sand, filling up red cups. Ha! They had a keg buried in the sand! That had been explicitly banned a while back but apparently, no one was worried about tickets here.

A motley crew of kids waved to Alex and Era to join them— a few girls from tennis and cheerleading mixed with super ambitious kids from the Advanced Placement track and a couple of football players. Alex was right, the cliques had all but evaporated.

They squeezed into a circle of kids with towels laid out to face each other. But the lighthearted atmosphere of laughter and conversation ended as Alex peeled off her dress. Somewhere a ways off, a soft whistle rang out. The seniors met Alex's perfect chest for the first time. She had really gone for it with a full push-up. Era noticed the elbow a guy on the soccer team threw into the side of his teammate with satisfaction before whipping off her dress. Her body glistened in the blinding white and gold, standing out among the more demure florals and classic cuts of her classmates. Several seconds of blaring silence passed before the conversation picked back up.

One small secret that Era had kept well hidden in thick mom jeans and skirted tennis shorts was her incredible backside. It was unmistakable that she was fit from years of tennis but this particular asset was a gift of genetics as well. The girls looked like supermodels off a yacht rather than embarrassed teenagers, stripping out of jeans for their first time in front of classmates.

Christopher arrived and without hesitation, squeezed into the circle, forcing a guy on Era's right to move over. He overlaid his towel with hers, the California code signaling their apparent togetherness. Turning towards Alex with a subtle cough to mask her disbelief, she allowed him to take the liberty, much to the chagrin of several male onlookers.

The day proceeded without much fanfare. Conversation between kids remained more polite, more open, and friendlier than usual. The topics revolved mostly around people's college and summer plans. Era passed around her thermos of daiquiris down the appreciative circle wishing all of high school could have been like this, no ladder to climb, no rigid friend groups to protect. Every thirty minutes or so a few people would wobble down to the water in shifts to swim and cool off (and probably pee) and then flop back down to bake in the hot sun.

Thoroughly buzzed and content, Era rolled over on her side to face Christopher who read quietly under the brim of his hat. She noticed the title, *Discrimination and Disparities*, a Thomas Sowell book that she had on her reading list, a bit heavy for a beach read.

She had no qualms interrupting his study. "Sowell is the man. I saw something about him on my feed and ended up reading a few of his books. I bet you'd like my favorite quote. He said, 'I have never understood why it is greed to want to keep the money you have earned but not greed to want to take someone else's money.'"

"Ha," he said, his eyes sparkling at her, "That's a good one considering how people think my family should give away half their fortune. My adviser recommended I read *Basic Economics* and despite the dauntingly boring name, it was incredible so I got interested in a few of his other books."

"Adviser huh? Aren't you a little young to be groomed for a corporate takeover?" she asked with a little snark, even as her earnest interest caused her to lean into him just a little closer.

"I've been doing my own succession planning since the fourth grade. Alexander the Great was a general with his own army by 18. There's no need to screw around finding myself. If I figure things out early and apply myself, I can be ready to run my own business unit within a few years. So you have to admit it makes sense for me to be reading Sowell, but a little strange to hear you're into him."

Era felt an odd twinge, he hit on something that she had wondered about herself. She'd been drawn to the books because after reading the hearts of the rich, middle class, and poor, people appeared to be unfulfilled everywhere. What could make a person happy, what could solve a real world problem?

"He looks at things differently. He doesn't think that if you throw money at a problem, you can improve it. Part of me used to think about going into politics because I have this desire to fix things, to fix people. I'm still figuring out how exactly I can best do that without being misguided and making things worse," she said, studying the way his eyes narrowed as she spoke. He listened so intently working out her secrets a little at a time.

Her head was fuzzy, the sweet spiked strawberry elixir hitting her, ill-timed with the serious turn of the conversation. The feeling intensified her admiration of his intellect and now his razor-focused ambition.

She touched his arm. The Gift shocked her like a correction from an electrified dog collar. His head snapped over to look at her and down to the simple gesture, simultaneously rolling towards her. Their faces hovered above the sand, only a foot apart, his cerulean eyes gazing quizzically into hers. No, she had definitely never reached out to him like that before and he noticed. How was this guy so perceptive?

They spent the next hour that way, talking softly while the beach party ramped up around them. He told her all the things she could never bring herself to ask him, for fear of becoming too intimate.

His grandpa had built their family's business in the 50s, buying up large swaths of wilderness and agricultural land across the country and developing it. Whole cities were practically owned by the Ridgewells. Master-planned communities, sprawling retail complexes, high rise commercial office buildings in major cities from coast to coast combined to make them one of the most powerful landlords in the country.

He was planning on getting his MBA from Cal University and working for his family's company, taking the baton from his dad one day. However, he made it clear he didn't expect it to be handed to him. He wanted to make sure he could lead the company better than any hired help.

His mom and dad sounded like hard-working people and caring parents. They took an interest in his life, supported his goals, and apparently even enjoyed each other's company. His mom in particular must be a force of nature. She oversaw the hospitality arm of their holdings, including a massive five star resort north of the City, was a fabulous cook, and still made time to play backgammon with her son. From the sound of it, she took Christopher and his friends for all their money if they tried their luck.

Christopher's dad came off as the typical CEO type, hard-working, direct, but he also loved to ski and scuba dive with his son so they had shared more than a few adventures.

The vision that began forming in Era's mind of this handsome boy surrounded by his happy family, swimming with dolphins off their boat, and sitting before his mother's home-made feast at Thanksgiving was an appealing picture. He morphed from the cute and witty albeit shallow classmate she had created in her mind into an unaffected well-mannered man with a bright future before him. As the shift took place, she began to feel the heat of the sun mix with the radiating warmth of the Gift and her guard slipped down with the sun in the sky.

Before she knew it, she was allowing the Gift to form deeply introspective questions to his stories, prodding him with tantalizing interest so that he couldn't help but be completely drawn out.

When the conversation naturally came to a close and Christopher realized he had been talking about himself for quite some time, Era shut her eyes and breathed in. When she opened them, the Gift breathed out of her, reaching directly into his chest, the words flowing through rather than from her. She repeated back a summary of him, filled in his truest intentions, his fears, his most secret desires. It was likely the way the Gift was meant to be used, not to mine the heart of a soul for selfish proposes, but to allow the Gift to open the eyes of the person to themselves.

"I understand everything Christopher. You're deeply afraid of disappointing your grandfather's legacy. You question whether or not you'll ever be as great a man as your father or grandfather before him, though you're willing to outwork anyone in order to be.

"Your parents are invested in your success and love you wholeheartedly, but they're not home all that much and you're often alone in a big house. The flings you've had with girls from school were more about you craving companionship than wanting to hookup which is why they never became anything more serious. And you have a hard time trusting anyone outside of the family because you're worried that you'll let someone in, only to discover that they're using you to get a job, a favor, or access to your family's wealth.

"You actually enjoy what the money can do, but wish you could maintain your anonymity which is why you drive a tricked out truck instead of a sports car... as if you're fooling anyone with that aftermarket spectacle. It was what? $100k?" she teased, lightening the mood for a quick second before launching back into him.

"You're polite but you also know that you're smarter than most everyone around you so you think you're usually right in a difference of opinion. And while your fears are certainly valid, what you should be worried about is the part of you that will do almost anything to get exactly what you want. It'll cause you pain and great destruction in the end," she prophesied without a thought as to how he would react.

Era had not allowed the Gift to speak in this way, not even with Cole. The air crackled around her with power as she observed the emotions sliding across Christopher's face—stupor then disbelief and finally a sort of joy. Her mistake was now etched into his heart. No man could be known so totally by Era through her Gift without a feeling of being united to her.

His mind and his heart were illuminated with perfect clarity and he stared in wonder at her beautiful face, transfixed by features which were now transformed by the Gift. He perceived the excellence of her soul, her intellect, her wisdom wrapped into a single form which was further entangled with the carnal desire of his body for her physical beauty. Possessing her became the singular desire of his heart and as Era had ascertained, he would stop at nothing to have her.

Still buzzed from the daiquiris but realizing the gravity of her error, Era jumped up, walking down to the water to clear her head and cool off. She pulled Alex along with her on the way, interrupting her conversation with a few intoxicated soccer players. They wouldn't mind.

Before throwing down her phone so they could jump into
the waves, Alex showed off a picture she had posted to her
profile. Four guys from the soccer team were holding her up
horizontally, an innocent pic for the most part which she had
taken to prove to her extended family that she did normal
things like a normal high schooler. Neither of them ever posted
extravagant showy pictures from their vacations or with
conspicuous friends as it had become a necessary extension of
"the Rule."

The picture contained one alarming misstep. In the background behind Alex, Era and Christopher lay inches from each
other on their towels, her backside highly exposed and Christopher's hand appearing to touch her. It was a trick of the
perspective of the photo of course, but damn if it didn't look
incriminating.

A sharp weight pressed against Era's throat, making it hard
to swallow. Below the caption, the first comment was Cole's.

"*Hope you girls are having fun,*" it read, clearly referencing
both of them. So he had noticed. The twist of acid in her
stomach was real then. She felt guilty until proven guilty.

Diving headfirst into the jarringly cold water didn't cool the
self-reproach. The girls swam out past the break to tread water
where she knew they couldn't easily be seen or heard. "First of
all, how could you not notice the background of your post?
Haven't I taught you anything? Christopher looks like he's practically laying on top of me and my whole ass is showing!" Era
berated.

"What? Are you serious? Oh crap, I had no idea. I swear I'm
buzzed and I threw it up so fast after we took the picture that I
must have missed it," she said, defending herself in earnest.

"Well, Cole sure didn't. First comment." Era had wanted to
talk about what happened but was too freaked out to find the
words. "I know it was an accident. Leave it up since it's too

suspicious to take down now. I've got another problem on my hands anyway," Era continued miserably while treading water.

"Girl, what trouble have you got yourself into now? Let me guess, Christopher's in love with you," Alex guessed flippantly.

"This is serious. I really messed up. We were just talking and suddenly he's telling me his whole life story and we're discussing his deepest insecurities and life's goals and... ugh, I couldn't stop myself," she groaned.

"I get it," said Alex softly. "I've seen you in action, I know what happens when you get into those deep conversations with people. It's like you hypnotize them and they fall for you. It's what you do. It's why we go everywhere, get in everywhere, know so many incredible people. Just be careful. Christopher isn't some random friend of a friend or a guy on vacation. He's your actual friend, your neighbor! And not intentionally, but after that picture, Cole is going to be wondering about him. I'd steer clear until you can assure Cole that nothing is going on," she finished, with a dose of her usual pragmatism.

Era pouted sheepishly, "Are you mad? I know you kind of like him."

"Are you kidding me? Didn't you see the hot Argentine the soccer guys brought with them?" she asked. "I'll be just fine."

Era perceived the mix of guilt, hurt, and concern pouring off Alex. She knew Alex was being gracious about her crush on Christopher. She really had meant to do her best to push them together, it just hadn't been in the cards.

Era felt an unexpected fury come over her. How could she let this happen? With her anniversary approaching, she stood ready to celebrate with the love of her life and to start planning their new chapter together. How could she let this background character get in the way?

Sure, he made an incredible catch for someone, but she had already met her soulmate. The Gift had confirmed their love on many occasions, highlighting the elegance of their perfect match. No one could be worth jeopardizing that, nothing.

She would take Alex's good counsel and stay the hell away from Christopher. He had lured her in, disarming her with the openness and genuineness of his feelings for her. She told herself that he had appealed to her vanity, not her heart. But the truth itched. Though her vanity had opened the door, something much deeper responded to him, something that she couldn't possibly admit

Why couldn't he simply like Alex? She possessed beauty, intelligence, and virtue, yet remained perpetually outshined by her best friend. Era couldn't bear to know that sometimes Alex believed this happened due to some inadequacy in herself. If only Era could explain to her that the Gift pulled people to her. She loved that she could give Alex so many experiences but she couldn't help feeling guilty about stealing a spotlight that would normally shine on her friend more brightly if she were with any other regular girl.

The two walked back up the steep wet sand bank dripping wet with slicked back hair, more Bond girls than high school seniors. She noticed the eyes of several girls in their class turn away as if they hadn't been jealously scrutinizing Era and Alex's bodies. Grabbing their stuff, they headed over to Clarissa's private shower to rinse off when Christopher came charging in playfully, stealing the water from Era as he shoved her off the stream. She pushed back when he caught a handful of the chain on her bathing suit, giving it a yank. Era's eyes snapped open wide in surprise while she smacked his hand away, her mouth gaping.

"You guys ready to head back already?" he asked naively, all the while glancing with too much familiarity at Era's assets.

"I think we've had enough sun and I'm ready for some real dinner," Era said.

"Also, she's a terrible day drinker," Alex scoffed.

"Is that so? Ready for bed then are we?" Christopher chided.
"Works for me. I think I got maybe four hours of sleep last night so I don't have much gas left in the tank anyway." He deferred to them readily. "I'll head up to grab my truck. Meet me at the top."

He grabbed both of their beach chairs and charged towards the stairs, taking them two at a time. Era caught Alex smiling after him, and knew the thoughtful gesture had won more points with her, with both of them.

CHAPTER 8

ERA BASKED in the euphoria of gliding home on a glorious California afternoon as a passenger princess. The highway ran parallel to the beach. A view of the gorgeous ocean stretched out beside the winding road while the wind lashed her hair so fiercely, she had to hold it off to one side.

The sun changed to an orange hue, expanding as it sank towards the horizon. Glancing over at Christopher and back at Alex, Era floated in an inexplicable peace. The three of them were easy together, like they had all been best friends for years.

Era thought back on Christopher's comment the night before, specifically about the time she had wasted following "the Rule." Spending time like this, with friends in her own home-town, certainly would have saved her ages in the airport and a lot of jet lag. His words rang with a hint of truth, even if he had been talking about missing out on more than friendship.

Nostalgia overpowered her as she interrupted the serene moment. "Hey guys, what if you both stayed for dinner at my house? I bought all the groceries this morning and anyways, I owe you," she said looking over at Christopher, "for driving us and for other things," she finished not wanting to explicitly mention why he walked her home after the close call the night before.

"Oooh somebody wants to play with fire. Okay, count me in!" Alex said, the corners of her mouth curving in a diabolical grin.

Christopher choked on his LaCroix and stammered out an acceptance of the invitation.

Era looked back over her shoulder, throwing daggers as hard as she could at her turncoat friend. Pissed that her good advice had been thrown completely out the window, she invariably prepared to bust out the popcorn and watch the drama unfold. Even Era recognized that this could be either entirely harmless or a terrible idea.

A few minutes later, they were slowing in front of Christopher's house when a literal "Jeeves" came walking out. The man didn't even attempt to make eye contact, and without a word, dropped a weekender bag into the bed of the truck and turned back towards the house. Christopher gave a wave of thanks before continuing down the street to Era's house.

"What was THAT!?" the two of them asked in unison, giggles filling the truck. "Did your butler literally pack you an overnight bag while we were driving? Is that who you were texting at the light?" Alex laughed hysterically. "Does he know which underwear are your favorite too?" she teased.

"Alex, stop! That was pretty funny but come on. I'm sure he doesn't want to wear his sweaty 80s tank for the rest of the day. Give him a break," Era said, feeling bad for making fun of him.

Back at the house, Era put Christopher in the downstairs guest suite to shower and Alex headed up to Era's room. She took her parent's bathroom to freshen up. It dawned on her that she should probably call Cole but time ticked away to get cleaned up and an entire dinner made, so she texted instead.

Hey babe. Home from the beach and making
dinner. Alex is over. Call you later.

"Stick to the trees, not the forest," she thought as she edited. And
though she never left out details with Cole, she didn't want to
make him needlessly jealous by mentioning Christopher. Her
phone immediately lit up.

Call me after.

Short and concise and weird. Uhoh. But she would deal with
that later. Era dashed into the shower and headed downstairs,
borrowing a spaghetti strap satin slip dress from her mom's
closet to save time. Downstairs, she tied on her favorite apron
and began tossing ingredients for the lamb's marinade into the
Cuisinart, plunking the heavy chops on the counter to come to
room temperature.

Era had another talent, one that ingratiated her with friends
as they traveled together—her cooking ability. She cooked well,
and coupled with a host of hospitality-related talents, she
invariably made people feel loved. She would arrange flowers
for their vacation homes, set gorgeous tables when she cooked,
bring thoughtful gifts when she visited, write beautiful thank
you notes when she returned, and even made highly personal-
ized curated welcome baskets for their group trips.

And really, who didn't love to eat? Even the wealthiest set of
jetset partiers were not used to their friends waking up after a
night in the club to squeeze fresh orange juice and set out hot
waffles dusted with berries and sugar. No one minded booking

an extra ticket with their miles or splurging on a coordinating dress for Era during a shopping spree when she made them feel so valued.

The stunning rack of lamb sat prepped to be popped into the oven, pressed with mint, rosemary, thyme, and garlic when Alex and Christopher simultaneously appeared in the kitchen. "Oh my gosh, smells amazing," Christopher said, breathing in the scent of fresh chopped herbs from her garden.

"I'll get the wine," Alex said with a smirk. "Let's do the Cab from Cakebread. Blackberry, cigar, and umami, perfect to go with your lamb. It's your favorite, right?" Alex asked with a slice of sarcasm paired with cheerfulness.

"Umm, YES!" Era said, closing her eyes for a second. She absolutely loved that one. "Mom and Dad will need some room in the wine fridge when they get back from their trip anyway."

When she opened her eyes she saw Christopher enjoying her private moment with a suppressed smile. She wondered how long it would be before he nonchalantly ordered a Cakebread cab for her and stifled a laugh, turning towards the oven to hide her face.

Alex corked the bottle and poured each of them a "house pour," as the girls called it. No sense in leaving any in the bottle. She had chosen violence and settled in to watch the evening burn as she threw gasoline on the fire.

"To new friends," Alex toasted, holding the dark red liquid up to the light. "That we had enjoyed each other's company sooner but to making many more memories together." Their glasses kissed with a satisfying clink and the three felt a solidification of something new.

Era took a long sip of the big minerally wine, anticipating the blissful relaxation a full glass of this would bring. However, she set the glass down and turned her attention back to the task of not only putting dinner on the table but hosting an impromptu party for the three of them.

Having to think quickly, she plagiarized one of her favorite menu items since she had all the ingredients for lamb atop a sweet potato mash finished with cilantro, sage and star anise. She would serve a curried squash soup defrosted from the freezer as a starter, alongside a frisée salad with apple, pecan, and blue cheese. Thankfully, she also had an extra apple crumble in the freezer that could go right into the oven and be bubbling hot by the time they finished dinner in about an hour.

Christopher watched captivated as she moved sprightly through the kitchen, juggling the tasks of five separate dishes at once. Era ducked out the patio doors with a pair of clippers, returning moments later with a handful of hydrangeas that she arranged on the table with practiced ease.

Alex moved through the house with familiarity, setting an elegant table with cutlery, plates and glasses placed with care. She even added sliver dumbbell-shaped knife rests to protect the tablecloth from the hefty steak knives. This pair had done their fair share of fine dining and damn if he wasn't impressed. With little left to contribute, Christopher filled up the water glasses and set them out on the table.

The dinner turned out fantastic, better than the ones that his parents spent thousands on only because of a Michelin star rating. Era's courses came out plated to perfection and they settled around the table, laughing, teasing, and speaking easily about their charmed experiences. Nobody had to edit, or minimize the details of the places they'd been. For the first time, Christopher and his peers stood on equal ground, and he enjoyed knowing no one judged him, regardless of how open he chose to be.

The crumble came piping hot out of the oven and they shared it with three spoons, fighting over the last bites until only a few burnt edges of sugar remained. With the bottle empty, Alex resumed her duties as cupbearer. "You guys ready for a digestif?"

Era groaned softly, "I don't know, I'm so full."

"Oh, but I thought we should bring something with us to the jacuzzi. It's already heated."

"You sneaky little fox! When did you turn it on? During dinner? I thought you were texting your mom!" Era accused a little too loudly. "You're so bad. You know I'm a sucker for a hot tub even though we all already took showers," she grumbled before surrendering, "Let's just do it."

Alex and Era giggled their way upstairs once again to change. They opted for simpler bikinis from Era's overstuffed bathing suit drawer. Alex teased her mercilessly now, lamenting her third-wheel status and threatening to Snap the guy from Argentina to join them.

As they headed downstairs, Era had to pretend not to hear Christopher suck in his breath as he took in the sight of her body, thinly veiled in the flesh-colored bikini. She hadn't even thought about how the skin-colored fabric might give the impression that they were skinny dipping rather than having a friendly soak. Alex had poured them shots from the bar and they looked each other in the eyes before throwing back the burning intoxicant.

As she passed by him, he spoke in a low hushed voice to her, "I thought that your apron over that satin dress was the sexiest thing I'd ever seen, but THIS," he reached out and touched the tie at her back lightly, as she walked briskly out the doors to the pool.

The tension and the alcohol began to fracture her wall of boundaries. She had been strong all day, constantly reminding herself of Cole, of their future, of their past. Yet when she turned to look behind her, she saw Christopher standing backlit by the pool's lights, his hunter green eyes catching the reflection and becoming even more brilliant. The shadows were enhancing the chiseled lines of his body, strong jawline, and his high cheekbones and she lost her composure.

She reached for his hand and pulled him the rest of the way into the water, muttering softly how he had no business being so hot. An innocent gesture, although to Christopher it confirmed what he already suspected: Era might not be as settled as she thought with this boyfriend of hers.

In the hot tub, they ended up with a few minutes alone as Alex dilly dallied inside making them a round of drinks—not that Era needed anymore. She noticed again the drifting detachment in her head and felt dangerously sexy in front of Christopher's appreciative gaze. He didn't bring up the character revelation, instead launching into a barrage of questions about "the Rule" which he appeared to be more than a little obsessed with. He didn't really care that much about "the Rule" per se, his concern centered on what happened to cause her to impose such a thing upon herself.

She found herself elaborating on the story she had summarized the night before. Era explained that she had been popular, giving herself free rein of the "Gift," though she described it to him as charisma since he already perceived she relied on some type of genius level social intelligence to get her way.

"I was on a high of all these kids liking me and wanting to be my friend. I got the idea in my head that I should use my popularity to run for President. I knew Brittany wanted to run but I didn't care. I thought I could beat her. Big mistake. I swept the election but I made a dangerous enemy. I was stupid, thought, 'you can't win em all!'

"Anyways, there was this boy, Beau. Pretty much universally accepted that he was the hottest boy in school. EVERY girl had a crush on him—"

"Did you have a crush on him?" Christopher asked.

"You know, I didn't at first even though I thought he was cute like everyone else did. I felt kind of sorry for him. He was clearly painfully shy and had no idea what to do with all the attention. Brittany hit on him all the time and I could tell he hated it though he always tried to be nice about it. So anyways, one day he and I got put together in Bio to dissect a frog and it was such a gross activity, it ended up being a good icebreaker. He turned out to be super sweet and about a week later he asked me to be his girlfriend."

Christopher chuckled, "Woah Beau, moving fast!"

"Not exactly. Boyfriend/girlfriend for us was basically us talking on the phone after school, holding hands walking between classes, and an occasional PG peck on the lips. We weren't ever really alone."

"All normal awkward junior high stuff so far," Christopher cut in.

"Yes, exactly. Be patient, I'm almost there. So Brittany took it very personal that Beau ignored her completely and went for me. It was obvious this girl lived and died by her need for attention and power. You should have seen what she wore, borderline dress code violation booty shorts every day. And the way she bossed around her circle of cronies who did her bidding like mindless zombies..."

"Everything might have turned out fine, except one day Beau broke the news that his dad's company got relocated to Texas. He moved within a week. And once he was out of the picture, that evil wench Brittany spread nasty rumors that Beau and I had gone to third base. We never even made out!

"It felt like no one even wanted to believe my side of the story, that girl's jealousy spread through the school like a cancer. Girls were whispering about me and the guys were even worse. I tried to ignore the inappropriate propositions and disgusting compliments. I'd barely make it through the day and then end up crying every day after school, until I didn't even want to go anymore. I was so angry with myself for ever allowing them to even have the opportunity to gossip about me. I saw how it could have all been avoided if I hadn't dated Beau knowing everybody liked him."

Christopher listened with rapt attention to her story, anger beating around him. He never interrupted, letting her finish with a sigh. "You can't possibly blame yourself for what happened. Kids can be terrible. My only question is, how did Alex make it into the inner circle if you vowed to keep such a strict separation between school and everything else? She does go to our school."

"Alex and I met at a youth group we were both forced to go to by our parents, the summer after 8th grade," Era answered. "I was still struggling through what happened and she was the first person that ever understood me and didn't try to compete with me. She had this big soft heart and once I got to know her, she felt like the sister I always wanted but never got. In fact, I never even had a close girlfriend before her. Every single friend I've ever had ended up turning on me either from jealousy or insecurity. She appreciated me for me from the start.

"So I decided to trust her with my story and what I thought my plan was going to be for high school. I didn't expect it, but she decided to join me. Alex got her boobs early and had experienced bullying at her school too. I don't know what I would have done without her. She really saved me, gave me a new purpose. I knew she would be giving up a lot to follow 'the Rule' and I wanted to make it worth her while, so I started making friends and finding adventures for us. It became us against the world. Neither of us knew how far it would go."

After digesting the rest of Era's explanation, Christopher continued, "I can't say I don't agree with your 'Rule.' Given your situation, it's pretty smart. I doubt any of the girls in our school weren't touched by rumors or bullies at some point. There's always a lot of drama going on. That girl Jessica got thrown in the pool by three of her own former friends last week!"

Era giggled. She'd heard about that, but didn't feel so bad for the girl. She was petty and mean.

"You have the perspective to realize that high school is a

very artificial environment. I obviously get keeping your private life private given that I never brought anyone over to my house for nearly the same reason. I keep my family's business confidential too," Christopher said, looking out in the dark sky before turning back and catching her eyes with ferocity. "It's just too bad that you didn't let *me* in on your secret," he continued, his voice dropping low, closing the distance between them. "Because I can be *very* good at keeping a secret," he finished, his green eyes unlocking the Gift's power.

Era saw herself through them. She saw little clips, years worth of clips. She watched him watching her around campus with Alex, the line up the back of her sensuous neck exposed by a high ponytail that drove him crazy as he sat in the desk behind her, felt his delight at the witty sparring they'd done in class.

She didn't see his memories like little movies playing, her mind took her all the way inside. Maybe because he wanted her to see. And there she was again, standing in the passageway between the math and science buildings with Alex and Clarissa, dressed in a slouchy oatmeal sweater pulled over an oversized knit dress. Yuck.

Christopher walked over with two friends and as Alex and Christopher chatted, his friend called out, "It's my man's birthday! We're partying tonight!"

Alex, well-mannered as always, wished him a Happy Birthday and gave him a hug. Clarissa did likewise. Then it came to Era. She didn't hug. Even if everyone else hugged twenty times a day, the standard California greeting, she always politely declined.

Then there was the moment that Era stepped towards him, and Christopher's heart sang. She remembered that moment, the solid feel of him, like a tree filled with honey. But through his eyes, she felt the burn of admiration as he wrapped his arms around her form, and felt, for the first time, the beautiful lines of her body. His mind constructed her, hidden beneath the layers.

He never spoke that time, merely accepted the gesture, and so her Gift never hummed to life exposing the raw desire simmering beneath his stoic face. She had no idea that little moment had been his most treasured birthday Gift that year.

She'd never experienced anyone's deeply invested interest in her, their devotion to each detail of her life. His unfettered appreciation and admiration. Cole loved her but he didn't notice her details, not like this. She was floored with flattery. Even the satisfaction he felt in passing her his homework to copy on occasion, to feel himself able to take care of her. How much more he wanted to do. She could live inside his mind forever.

But then he took her to his memory of seeing her for the first time with Cole, knowing she was out of reach. The rejection squeezed her chest. Indeed, she had rejected him often—with her vague responses to personal questions, refusal to join even group activities with him. She touched the black wall of rejection herself, low enough for him to see her on the other side, tall enough to keep him from crossing over.

Beneath the water and concealed by the jets, his hands found hers and she intertwined her fingers with his, unconsciously pulling him closer while tilting her head back.

In the moment of tipsy temptation, Era thanked the gods for the sound of the patio doors opening to interrupt their moment. Alex would be coming back with their drinks. But when she didn't hear her voice, Era felt a twinge of wrongness and looked up to see Cole's dark shape standing menacingly over her. Shock, horror and icy cold dread spread down to her toes despite the scalding water.

CHAPTER 9

"Why haven't you been answering my texts? I thought something was wrong. You've never ignored my messages when you're home!" Cole barked and then continued in a rage without waiting for an answer. "I guess you're *not* home alone are you? So dinner with Alex or a co-ed sleepover? Which is it?" he demanded, seething with jealousy.

O lord, Christopher's weekender bag! Era immediately jumped out of the hot tub, grabbing a towel from the chair to cover her nude-colored suit.

"I'm so sorry. I didn't have my phone. I was running around making dinner and Alex turned on the heater–"

"What are *you* doing here?" Alex interrupted cheerfully, disarming the explosiveness of the moment, carrying a tray of glasses. "If you're joining us, you can take mine. I'd be happy to make another."

Christopher took the interruption as his chance to get out of dodge. "He can have mine. I should get going… still recovering from my party. Thanks again for the dinner," he said, glancing at Era.

Era gave a weak nod in reply. "Do you mind seeing him out?" she asked, motioning to Alex.

Alex closed the glass patio doors to let the lovers quarrel in private and bent down to help gather his clothes. "I wouldn't want to be in her shoes right now." She puffed out a long breath. "Shit, this is all my fault. I posted a picture at the beach earlier today and the two of you were getting cozy in the background. Honestly, I didn't even notice until it was too late. Cole got the first comment."

"No wonder he showed up, must have guessed something was up. I definitely didn't mean to get her in trouble and I doubt she'll want to be friends with me after this. You should probably do something to make it right since this is partly your fault after all," he drawled strangely.

Suddenly, he pulled Alex up on her toes in a very tight hug, whispering into her ear, "You ok taking one for the team?"

Breathless from being caught all the way off guard, Alex whispered back, "You're going to have to do better than that if you're trying to do what I think."

Just like that Christopher turned his head towards her, landing a soft slow kiss across her full lips. Neither of them looked over but from the sudden stillness outside, it was obvious that Era and Cole witnessed the encounter.

Christopher pulled away, slick as a salesman. "Hope that helps."

"You'll know soon enough," she said, matching his evil grin, her heart thumping in her chest.

Outside Era and Cole were going back and forth. As soon as the door clicked shut, he launched into her. "Why is there a random guy over here with an overnight bag!?"

Holding her hands up to ask him to lower his voice, she did her best to explain as honestly as she could. "I know how it looks, but Christopher and I have had classes together since freshman year. He's actually a really nice guy–"

"Do you think that makes me feel better? So now you're telling me you're here with a longtime secret friend you have failed to mention in the past year we've been together?" he said, the anger escalating in his voice.

"Let me finish... please. All of these end of the year activities with my class have made me question what I missed out on by following the Rule. Most of my friendships are on the other side of the world, with an eight hour time difference, while I passed over good people on my own street—"

"You've got to be kidding me. That guy is your neighbor too? Is he the rich kid that threw the big party last night? The Ridgewell Enterprise heir?"

She stood crossing her arms across her body, "Stop it! You're not hearing me. I'm trying to tell you that I might have made a mistake isolating myself here and I am finally reaching out for a normal life, one where I don't have to hide my true self for fear of people making my life hell. High school is over in a week and no one is even going to remember me going to school with them. Maybe I don't want to feel like I never existed," she shouted.

He sucked his teeth, wanting to fight back, jealousy blinding him despite her excellent excuse. All the sudden, he remembered that soon enough she would have one less person to support her, and guilt coursed through him mixed with dejection.

Era caught the emotion immediately and felt her emotional escalation grind to a stop. She wanted to get to the bottom of this out of place feeling even though she knew she'd have to wait until his grudge subsided. After all, he had just dropped by unannounced to find his girlfriend buzzed and alone in a hot tub with an attractive rival.

By some miracle of perfect timing, an unmistakable movement on the other side of the doors pulled their focus, breaking the tension. The light between the two bodies disappeared as Christopher leaned in to kiss Alex.

Cole's jaw relaxed. "Huh," he huffed with surprise and a hint of relief.

Era's eyes grew wide at the scene. *What in the actual f–* she thought until she noticed Christopher's hand—the one facing away from them—hung casually at his side, rather than on his friend's waist. Then it clicked. It was all for her. *My girl...* she thought, suppressing a proud smile.

"So" —she turned back to Cole— "are we going to stand out here all night or do you think we could finish this on the couch? I would love to fight with you in something more cozy and I'm dripping wet."

Crisis averted, she headed upstairs to change into her favorite pajamas, a worn off-the-shoulder shirt and a pair of boyshort underwear. Alex danced nervously around in Era's room, raiding her drawers.

With the door tightly shut, Era whispered, "So how was it?"

"What? Saving your ass? You owe me so big for this one. But seriously, it was still pretty hot," she giggled, throwing a pair of underwear at Era's face.

"I knew it!" Era laughed back, shouting at a whisper.

"Did it work?"

"I think so. He suggested watching a movie so that means he's cooling off."

"Do you mind if I skip the movie and go to bed? I don't think I can take one of Cole's alien action movies right now. No offense," Alex said, a yawn breaking over her face.

"Yeah right. You just want to lay here and play back that kiss in your head a few times don't you?"

"You stop it! You know that you could get a taste of those luscious lips any day of the week–"

"SHHHH," she hushed, throwing her finger up to her lips. They did not need any more trouble.

CHAPTER 10

DOWNSTAIRS, Cole sat quietly, consumed with his thoughts. The hot tub incident dwindled in importance as he contemplated the weekend ahead and the weeks past. He hadn't seen Era in person in three weeks and it was not by accident. His life had exploded and his thoughts were still shredded by the shrapnel. Nor did he want Era's prying mind coming after him for explanations that he didn't have. He closed his eyes, feeling the familiar fury and hopelessness burning hotly in his chest before pushing the feelings down so deep that for a while, they were not even there. He shouldn't be there and he knew it.

When she appeared in the doorway, the breath left his body. There she stood, the love of life, exquisite even dressed in what could only be described as a raggedy pajama top, yet she oozed a sultriness that only Era possessed. Her long legs stretched out beneath the hem of the shirt, her hair pouring over an exposed shoulder, her chest barely visible behind the threadbare fabric.

So many nights apart had left him ravenous for her. He needed her more than he'd ever needed anyone as his life quietly fell apart over the past three weeks. He had avoided her so carefully, but now that he saw her staring at him with those sneaky cat-like eyes, his resolve to resist her dissipated with the steam from her still damp hair. And like stepping out of the total darkness of an endless night, Era blinded his eyes with a light that shined only for him.

Era's mood had been lightened by the quick exchange with Alex. Unsure exactly what temper she'd find Cole in, she froze mid-step through the doorway. His face glowed with an internal brilliance, dazzling her, and setting her heart on fire. She didn't realize at the time that his light was no different than the way the moon shines with stolen radiance from the sun. In that instant, Christopher faded from her memory, already a ghost of summer's past. It was Cole and only Cole that pulled her to himself, like planets and moons that danced around each other for all time.

The need for words finished, Cole pulled her into his lap. They were kissing, a deep slow kiss of yearning to satisfy the too-long separation. When she stopped to catch her breath, Cole's face continued to shine, his deep-set almond-shaped hazel eyes molten. He could have been an angel then, his features had become transfigured with pure beauty. Her heart burst with love and and then her pulse raced at the realization of how close she had come to ruining their relationship only an hour earlier.

She wanted him then, more than she ever had, to supplant any lingering confusion she had, if only momentarily, felt. Era knew that making love to him would smelt them to liquid and harden the bond back together, restoring any cracks caused by her carelessness.

Memories of him opening every door she ever walked through with him at her side, their trips to his family's cabin during the winter, the way he had patiently taught her to hit the ball straight at the driving range flooded her mind. She loved him for the way he cherished every part of her.

She had always yearned to feel irreplaceable, needed. If she could only grasp it, hold onto it. She had found him worthy of her love too. He had a generous open heart. And time after time he proved himself to be thoughtful, passionate, selfless. She could hardly contain her gratitude for him while thinking of his virtues—goodness which she embraced as belonging to her.

Cole sensed her need for him yet his touch moved across her skin unhurried. He savored her the way one might enjoy their last meal, taking no part of her for granted. Every slow and deliberate movement brought her further under his power.

By the time he finished fully appreciating every last detail of her, Era called to him, a call that was more than his name. She called out from a place deep inside her most vulnerable heart to all of him, to make them whole. They came together like two waves cresting, to become one rolling unstoppable power. And in the moment when lights flashed behind her eyes, bolts fired through her legs and fingertips, and she and Cole cried out in unified ecstasy, their singular form lifted an inch into the air for the briefest of moments.

Era saw her own essence then, reach out and fuse with Cole's. She understood how every human could experience the Gift in a small way. Men had long used the word "to know" to describe sex. Human intimacy allowed people to touch more than the bodies of one another, they shared also in the spiritual reality of their partner's soul. Thus, souls consummating a physical relationship resulted in an irrevocable spiritual union. And this intimate knowledge mimicked the knowledge Era received from her Gift.

The sight of their physical souls together with this new understanding left her in a state of wonder. She had never connected her Gift to a natural power as old and universal as the human race itself. The Gift gave her great knowledge of others while leaving her with great mystery as to its own origin. The thought sent a final shiver through her.

With their incredible moment passed, Cole wasn't entirely

sure if something strange had happened or if his mind had simply fabricated the sensation of floating. He took a last look at Era's peaceful face before closing his eyes to bask in the remnants of reprieve from his tortured thoughts.

Cole's moment of peace slipped away as the memory of his parents' fight bombarded him, his mind replaying the image of his mother's perfectly manicured fingernails violently throwing his father's phone across the room. The truth slammed into him like the glass of that phone cracking against the fireplace. Nothing had changed. He knew he had used Era for temporary relief from his internal agony. It had never been his intention in coming here, to sleep with Era. His mistake lay in thinking that he could trust the promise he had made to himself to resist her; he underestimated how strong the pull on him would be the closer they got.

He felt her stir beside him and knew she had already started sensing that something troubled him. This time Era's alarm bells sounded when she saw the shimmer of guilt around Cole considering what they had just done.

"What's the matter? How could you be feeling this way after such a perfect moment?" she interrogated with force. "I see the guilt coming off of you."

"You *see* the guilt?" he repeated incredulously. "What's that supposed to mean?"

Era halted knowing she had slipped up for the first time—ever. She had always been so careful to avoid letting anyone know that the Gift let her *see* (or sometimes hear) anything explicitly, accidentally or otherwise.

"I *know* you," she said, Pushing with her Gift, skirting the question. "You can't hide anything from me. Tell me what is going on, please," she begged, tears springing up in her eyes.

The only defense he had against her indomitable powers of perception were to get out of there as fast as he could. "I have to go. I need to be up early tomorrow morning and it's late."

Lies, lies—the Gift strobed little points of light at her.

"Leave? You can't leave! Why won't you talk to me?" she asked, her voice breaking and her heart hammering in her chest. Just like that, he dressed and headed towards the door, his face slack. "I'm sorry," he said without turning to look at her and retreated through the door.

Era sat there motionless for a full minute after hearing the door click, as stunned as if he'd slapped her. Tears rolled down her face and a mixture of emotions swirled around in her head driven by the roller coaster of the day's memories. Utterly frustrated and unbearably sad, Era trudged up the stairs and squeezed alongside Alex's warm back. She heard her soft regular breathing as she cried noiselessly into her hair.

CHAPTER 11

THE MORNING SUN streamed through the window hatefully. Era awoke parched and with a beating headache. Alex, the angel of morning, had left two Advil and a glass of ice water next to her pillow. A few minutes later, Alex returned with yet another blessed gift, a huge mug of coffee doused with cream and tucked in next to her in the cozy armchair with her own cup. "Not a great night for you was it?"

Era frowned miserably, "How much did you hear?"

"Well, I heard you kiss and make up. Then I heard you fighting followed by him leaving. Whatever happened, I'm sure you guys will work it out."

The prediction rang hollow in Era's ears but she needed to hear it anyway. "I hope so. Something is going on with him and he won't talk to me about it. I can tell he's been hiding it from me too. We don't keep secrets from each other and I don't know how to handle it."

They made a simple breakfast. Era's stomach roiled uncomfortably from mixing so many different alcohols the day before so she decided to skip her morning run and mope around the house instead. Alex would have stayed to keep her company except that she had to drive three hours away to her cousin's sweet sixteen party in the Valley.

After a few hours of useless brooding, she decided that she'd had enough. Cole may have hurt her deeply last night but that didn't negate their entire year together. He was still the love of her life and whatever was going on, he needed her. She needed to suck it up, get over the bruised ego, and focus on the challenge at hand. No matter the cause, Era believed that the Gift would help her understand what he needed and she would find a way to give it to him. She could fix it, fix him if necessary. She could hold them together through sheer willpower. What good was the Gift if it couldn't do this?

Her firm resolve blossomed into triumphant confidence and with that she sprang to life and began ripping through the hangers in her closet until she found the perfect one year anniversary outfit. This was no time to play coy. She went with a red satin dress that draped across her chest and hugged tight through her waist and butt, strappy heels and big sexy waves.

When Cole pulled up in his white Tesla, she jumped in happily, flashing him a gorgeous smile. "Hi, handsome. Happy Anniversary." She laid a sweet kiss on his lips, as if to say, that he had her free forgiveness and immediately felt him melt a little. They drove with his music playing, the sun shining over a picture perfect evening.

CHAPTER 12

COLE HAD RESERVED a table on the rooftop of a boutique hotel that perched over the water. It had the best sunset views in the area and fire pits that turned on after sunset to boost the romantic vibe. The rooftop belonged to them.

A young chatty hostess sat them and an overly enthusiastic server greeted them. Cole brushed off the guy's attempt to make recommendations and put in a curt order of their usual drinks and appetizers—he didn't want any nosy servers poking around their table for a while.

Finally, he took Era's hand across the table. "I want you to have this," he said and slid a box over to her.

She picked up the navy blue box, feeling the velvety finish and snapped it open dramatically. Inside, lay a stunning gold watch with a small diamond set into its crown. She pulled it out, feeling its weight in her hand and noticed an inscription on the back of the face. She held her breath as she brought it closer to her eyes and read the passage taken from Era's favorite book, Jane Austen's *Persuasion*.

I have loved none but you, it gleamed in letters etched into the flawless surface

Nearly choking on her happiness, she gushed her thanks while she struggled to open the clasp and put it on her wrist. In the moment of surprise, she didn't notice his mood change. When she looked up, storm clouds gathered around them in spite of the bright sun sinking towards the horizon.

He cleared his throat and stammered, "Era, there's ah— something I need to talk to you about—"

Oh no. Here we go. Showtime, she thought, interrupting him before he could get any more out.

"Yes, me too. Is it ok if I go first?" Era had anticipated this part of their reconciliation while getting ready. She knew he planned on breaking bad news of some sort, but she thought if only she could tell him her good news, it would outweigh whatever bad thing hung over him. She would give them something to rejoice over together, to look forward to.

He acquiesced with a nod. "Ok."

"I got off the waitlist for Cal. We'll be there together in the fall!" she squealed, hands clutched over her heart, the watch jangling along with her best bracelets. "I know we won't have any classes together since you finished all your general ed credits this year—still, we can study together and hang out on campus—" Era rambled on about the plans she had made for them, lost in her future fantasy without realizing Cole's face had grown very still.

"I thought I should live on campus the first year, so I can make friends and then sophomore year we could live together off campus when you're in your senior year. It's just like we always talked about and it's finally happening!" Era took a beat, waiting for his face to light up, to return her enthusiasm. Instead his eyes deadened and a hand came up to pull at the collar of his shirt. Era didn't need the Gift to tell her that the news wasn't eliciting the reaction it should have from a person who loved her, who wanted to be with her.

Then the Gift pummeled her with the prick of a thousand

points of ice. The chill crackled down her back and made her fingers go stiff as if she had taken off her gloves in a snowstorm.

"My parents are getting a divorce," he said, the darkness not leaving his eyes. "They told me out of nowhere—three weeks ago. My dad cheated on my mom. He's already moved out. I don't even know where he lives now."

Era reached for his hand. When she touched it, he didn't even seem to notice. "I'm so sorry. I didn't know."

Cole cleared the rasp from his throat and continued, "The worst part is that my parents are now fighting for custody over my little sister. I think my dad only wants her because he doesn't want to pay child support to my mom. They're both calling me, trying to convince me to be on their side. My dad even stooped so low as to throw money at me to get me to support his custody claim.

"It's disgusting. It feels like everything I've ever known in my life wasn't real somehow. My parents' relationship wasn't real; our family wasn't real. I've been doing my best to hold it together at school even though I'm angry... I'm so angry... all the time."

Era hadn't prepared for a scenario this serious. Cole's life was falling apart at the seams and she had no idea. He was in pain, so much pain. She could feel it coursing out of him and she wished she could take it from him. Her plan to overwhelm his bad news with her good news appeared painfully childish. No announcement could unbreak his family or stitch up the wound that gaped in his chest. And somewhere, a buried part of her grieved for herself at the news, at the perfect family, that perfect future, she could no longer escape to.

"That's why I couldn't see you since I found out. I didn't want to take my anger out on you and I couldn't face the truth of what was happening. I can never give you a happy family to be a part of now. Being with me means being forever tied to a thousand broken holidays." He made a wretched sound and continued, "The worst part is, this isn't something that is going away anytime soon. If anything, it's going to get worse."

He paused for only about five seconds then, seconds that could have been five eternities and spoke the words that brought down her entire world. "I think—I need to take a break from us while I sort this out."

The chill turned to a humid tropical storm. The heat of his frustrated helplessness steamed off him. Sparks punctuated the fury in his voice as he described the situation, likely when he thought of some particularly painful detail. And the rain of depression splashed her, dampening all happiness in its path.

The visceral experience of all his terrible emotions paled in comparison with the vision that came into focus before her, an impregnable shelter built around his heart to weather the storm. The squat structure fortified itself with a rusty metal door, and inside, she saw his beating heart, huddled in terror, seeking sanctuary from the hurricane battering the entrance.

Then a pang of understanding stabbed at her own heart as the Gift showed her that no amount of persuasion would convince him to open the door. Free will had the upper hand in this instance, and his spoke with sickening finality. She probed with the Gift but found no unease, no hesitation, no indecision in which to exploit.

Era froze like a movie character that had been shot, touching the fatal chest wound but not yet feeling the pain. She had been listening, drawing in his emotions to her, letting the Gift paint the full picture of his words. And so there it was. No matter what she did, he was breaking up with her.

The tide pulled back in her mind, a tsunami forming, sucking the water away from the beach. Then the anger began to surge forward in a solid wave, crushing everything in its path. She knew she would end up regretting every word tomorrow but for now she hated that she had let him become the center of her world.

After spending five years wondering if anyone could ever love her—seeing the void of love at home with a clarity that only the double-edged sword of the Gift could cut—she thought she had finally found someone to heal the wreckage in her heart. His weak words swirled in her mind. "I think" he had said, even though he *knew*. *Where is all his honesty now?* she thought.

The phrase "take a break" hit her with the most painful betrayal, one that tapped into her deepest fear. Her parents had been "taking breaks" from her for her entire life—endless vacations without her, hobbies, commitments. They crowded their lives with so much busyness that there was only a sliver left that required them to be parents.

He was wish-cycling her, throwing her in the recycling bin like so much plastic trash that would end up piled in a faraway landfill. So much for being supportive, she steadied her shaking voice, ready to crash over him with frightening force.

"Let me get this straight. You go through some adult shit and are too much of a coward to talk to me about it. Instead, you make up a bunch of lame excuses about study groups to avoid me and then show up at my house unannounced because you're jealous I'm with someone other than you. You berate me for not answering your calls when you're the one who hasn't been returning my texts or answering my calls. Then you f—k me to make yourself feel better and run off when I call you out for being guilty about it. Because you *knew* last night that you were going to dump me. You *used* me! I thought I could trust you with anything but you used me!"

She paused to get her voice under control once more, not wanting an ounce of hurt or weakness to creep in.

"Then you let me get all dressed up and take me to the place of our most happy memories together, on our *anniversary*, and you *dump* me? And what is this?" —she nearly screamed, throwing the watch back at him— "a door prize?"

It was clear how resolute Cole was in seeing this break up through. Rather than respond to her tirade, he simply took out his wallet, threw down a hundred dollar bill, picked up the watch and stood, heading towards the exit. He looked at her with those empty eyes once more before uttering his final words of the evening. "You should probably call an Uber."

That heartless bastard, she thought as she glowered at him from above, watching as he moved without emotion towards his car a block away.

CHAPTER 13

THE RIDE HOME passed in a blur. Had she been in an Uber? She couldn't remember. She knew that when she arrived home, her Dad's Mercedes sat parked in the driveway. She couldn't stomach forcing pleasant conversation about something only he cared about. No, she couldn't pretend to care right now and she didn't want to try. And if she saw any of his unpleasant thoughts about her, she'd scream.

Era did the only thing she could think of, she rushed upstairs to change into her running set and scram before anyone had a chance to exasperate her with chatter about wine country. Thankfully, she remembered to grab her night running reflectors and flashlight and even her sunglasses despite the fact that evening loomed. Walking down her street, she was grateful for the huge glasses covering her face so she could cry with some dignity.

Her brain worked overtime reconstructing the meaning of the missed calls, the weird tones, the clipped conversations. The Gift had a major blindspot, it didn't work through technology like texts or phone calls. She had missed all the signs with Cole because she hadn't physically seen him. She knew she relied too heavily on the Gift and blamed herself for being so quick to minimize the warning signs. Part of her knew that *he knew* he could keep his secret longer if they didn't see each other which is why he stayed away so thoroughly.

Coward.

She walked like that for a while, replaying the image of him striding away from the hotel, improving the memory with all the hurtful things she should have said. But as she turned onto the dirt path to the bay, the fabricated scenario dissipated. A mirage. A distraction to cope with the pain. She realized she was alone. Cole was lost to her.

Era took one last step and collapsed, sobbing into a large rock. What had he done to her? He must have surgically removed large parts of her lungs because they were too small to fill with enough air to keep her conscious. She clung to her phone. Should she dial 911? The dark had enclosed her in the tree canopy and somehow her legs were lead, too heavy for her to move them on her own.

Alex, my Alex, she thought momentarily before remembering that a hundred miles separated them. *Cole...* the thought scalded her. He should be the person she could depend on now, rather than the one causing this exquisite misery.

At long last, she gathered her wits enough to look at her recent call logs and saw Christopher's name. Tapping his name brought a ring and then an answer.

"Hellooo?" he answered, with a flirty lilt, misconstruing the nature of the call.

"Christopher... please... I need—" Era sputtered. "I'm on the running path. Can you come?" She choked on the question and hung up as another wave of sobs engulfed her.

Two minutes later, he spotted her lying sprawled over a sandstone boulder, the sunken sun turning the sky to a dim amethyst. His eyes scanned the path in alarm as he jogged over.

When he reached her, he stared intently into her eyes. "Are

you hurt?" he asked, confused when she barely acknowledged him with more than a grunt. His fingers passed over her body, checking for signs of injury, not knowing what he'd find.

Finding no sign of anything physically wrong, he pressed his fingertips on her back and asked again, "Are you alright? Can you walk?"

When she sobbed instead of answering, he scooped her up in his arms as if she weighed no more than an injured animal and carried her back down the path towards his house. Through the few incoherent words she got out while her cheek rested in the crook of his neck, he determined that she didn't have any physical injury so he brought her to the pool house. His parents were home tonight of all nights and he wanted to sort things out before getting anyone else involved.

Setting her down on the all too familiar couch, he wrapped her in a blanket and went to the kitchen to grab her a glass of water. Her jaw shook and he panicked for a brief moment thinking she was going into shock. The entire scene terrified him. If only he could calm her down enough to tell him what on earth happened?

After several excruciating minutes of silence, Era regained herself enough to find her voice.

"Last night, he... he... fu—ed me, and then he dumped me," she hiccuped. "On our anniversary dinner."

As a man, Christopher couldn't help his knee-jerk thought, *Woah, they had sex right after I left. That sucks.* But rather than dwell on his own crushed ego, he refocused on Era, the girl he cared about more than anyone, who had called out to him in her hour of need. Why should he be shocked that she had hooked up with her own boyfriend of a year after all?

Maybe Alex hadn't told her that the kiss had been a ruse to get Era out of trouble. He knew it was delusional to think that their brief moment in the hot tub negated an entire relationship.

Snapping back to the situation at hand, he saw again her total devastation. Comforting her over a breakup felt strange, especially considering he'd only crossed over from acquaintanceship to intimate friendship two days ago. Well, that and the fact that she knew he had feelings for her. Yet there they were.

He took her into his arms, letting her head rest against his chest, and shushed her, his hands stroking her hair gently. There were no words that he could say to take away her pain so he gave her the comfort of his body and the time to vent her suffering.

When she finally quieted down, he scooped her up once more—she didn't protest—and carried her into the small bedroom. He pulled off her shoes and stripped off her socks before tucking her under the down blanket and setting the glass of water on the bedside table.

Unsure what to do next, he rubbed the back of his neck. "There are clean towels, toothbrushes, toiletries, whatever you need in the bathroom. Snacks are stocked in the fridge. Help yourself to whatever. There aren't any extra clothes in here but here" —he pulled off his shirt and set it on the bed next to her— "you can wear this if you want."

As if in a dream she replied, "So tired," her voice thick and far-off. In her daze, she stripped off her own shirt in front of him, swapping it for his, clearly out of it.

He took that as his cue to exit and left her there to sleep off the remainder of what had probably been one of the worst days of her life.

As Era drifted into a fitful sleep, the last thing she remembered involved the confusing scent of a boy. It was the wrong boy, yet the familiarity brought her comfort all the same.

CHAPTER 14

LATE MORNING LIGHT streamed through the thick curtains, falling across the beige Bedouin rug of the well-appointed guest house bedroom. Era awoke with a start, perplexed at her environment. Looking down at the unfamiliar shirt on her body, her hand immediately shot down to her waist. Ok, her underwear were intact and no one else seemed to be around.

It felt like the morning after she and Alex partied way too hard in Tenerife and woke up in a similar state in someone's hotel room. Thankfully, nothing had happened that time either. In an instant, the scenes from last night snapped into place. A flash of a nightmare rushed at her, but no, not a nightmare. In another second, the fog in her brain cleared and she remembered, her life was the nightmare.

She whimpered and rolled to reach for her phone on the nightstand. The screen flashed at her, 11:30 a.m. along with multiple notification bubbles—Alex, Christopher, her dad. Alex wondered why she hadn't showed up to school again. Her dad didn't hide his irritation that she hadn't talked to anyone when she came in yesterday or told them where she would be staying the night. And Christopher had let her know that the chef dropped breakfast off in the pool house kitchen.

Peeling herself out of bed, she headed to the kitchen to see a tray with covered silver dishes straight out of hotel room service, an insulated pitcher, and a glass of juice. How thoughtful. Beneath the silver domes, she found a scrumptious breakfast that sadly had gone cold though the pitcher contained coffee that remained drinkably warm. She took one bite of yogurt parfait and a slice of bacon from the egg plate and went back to bed. Not that she had any appetite whatsoever, she only knew that she hadn't eaten any dinner last night and should have something in her stomach.

For the next few hours, she lay wrapped in the down comforter, torturing herself with pictures and videos of her and Cole together on her phone. When the agony became unbearable and sleep pulled her down once more, she forced herself to check the time and saw that the early afternoon had slipped by. Christopher would be getting home soon and so she begrudgingly motivated herself to leave the fortress of blankets, the wall of pillows.

The walk of shame stretched out before her aching limbs. The sunglasses did little to protect her from either the hot sun that tortured her eyes or the feeling that everyone who passed by could see her mental dishevelment. She gripped Christopher's t-shirt, a wave of guilt sweeping over her. Sure it could pass as a walking outfit if she tied it up, but she couldn't help thinking it felt like a scarlet letter across her chest. Even if Cole never saw it because he didn't love her anymore. As her house came into view, she let out a whimper. The garage stood open and her dad's freshly-washed black Mercedes gleamed inside.

Era's fist slammed angrily into her leg knowing she'd have to talk to him. "Ugh, can't I get a break?" she muttered aloud.

As expected inside, her dad swiveled in his office chair, engrossed in a work call on speakerphone that grated on her ears. She didn't attempt to sneak up the stairs a second time and turned towards the open doorway, bracing for impact. "Hey, I'm gonna have to call you back," he said as she walked through the door and slumped down into the lounge chaise in the corner.

"Glad you made it home," he said before launching into his tirade. "Your mom and I give you an incredible amount of freedom. We treat you like an adult and don't meddle too often. I let you travel with Raquel's family wherever you want. So I'd like you to remember that your participation in *this* family is not optional."

Too bad you think loving your daughter is optional.

"Your mom and I deserve the decency of being acknowledged when we're in the house together. How do you come home and not even say hello? Then you just leave for the whole night? With your car still here? And ignore my messages?"

She tried to break in but he lifted his hand to silence her, "And I know you have the attendance texts set to go to your phone but I got an email saying you had missed a whole day of classes without calling in an absence. You better watch it or they're not going to let you walk at graduation."

The violent surge of rejection returned in her mind, threatening to sweep her sanity away. She wished for the thousandth time that with her parents, she could turn it off. She was sick of listening to him tell her that whatever she struggled with should be easy, that life only got harder. He never invested himself in her education, yet he expected her to get As in everything, no excuses.

Even before the Gift whirred to life that day in the car, she had always sensed her parent's indifference to her. She observed other parents with their children, noticed the praise, the little tokens of affection that her own parents starved her of. She tried to tell herself that she didn't need their love, not even their approval to be happy. It still hurt.

She was tired of bitter medicine the Gift doled out, spoon by spoon at home. Though the silver lining was that it gave her a thick skin and an iron stomach.

The plaster face she learned to wear during the years of silently decoding his words began to crack. On any other day she would ignore the jab that came from knowing he loathed graduations and would be entirely peeved to sit through hers, listening to some other kid giving the valedictorian speech instead of her. In his mind, if she couldn't even be the best among 300 kids, the likelihood that she'd be anyone of significance was now zero.

She smothered the embers of her anger. Era knew that she was in a dark place and if she was going to get the space she needed to grieve she would have to tell her dad some of the bitter truth.

"Cole broke up with me yesterday. And no, I'm not alright." Era watched with satisfaction as her father's face went slack, the conversation veering into territory he was not expecting.

She didn't wait for the consoling words that wouldn't come before continuing matter-of-factly, "I had a panic attack on the Bay Trail and had to call a friend to carry me home. That's where I slept last night, at his guest house." The brutal honesty of the truth in her ears felt like ripping the bandage from a fresh wound and watching the unhealed skin begin to gush blood once again.

Her father cocked an eyebrow. "*His* house?"

"Yeah, a friend from school, the Ridgewell family's son. Last house on the street."

"The Ridgewells? Didn't know you were friends with their son. Good connection to have."

Era ruffled in irritation. Future connections with the Ridgewells were the least important part of this conversation. "Anyways… I'll handle things with the school, *you* don't have to worry about it," she said, unable to control the slight slip of sarcasm knowing damn well that all he wanted in life was to not have to worry about her.

He nodded in agreement while she continued, "I took a mental health day. I'll go tomorrow. Also, I'd appreciate it if you told Mom for me. I don't want to talk about it again for a while."

She watched the emotions roll off her dad in waves and colors—irritation, alarm, intrigue, and finally his last emotion swept over Era with a cool wind—relief. He was perfectly happy to not talk about it and unbothered about her broken heart. He also didn't want to deal with the school. He simply wanted her to handle her own business and be cordial in the house. Lovely.

"Yeah ok. Oh, I've been meaning to ask you—" he had no problem switching gears knowing that she would look elsewhere for sympathy, "have you made a decision about school for the fall? You can't wait forever on CalU. You might never get off the WaitList and going to school back East wouldn't be so bad."

Era glared with ice in her eyes. She had kept the news from her parents, wanting to break it to Cole first so that her joy wouldn't be spoiled by the tinge of disappointment that peppered her accomplishments at home. She knew her Dad wished she had better prospects.

"Yeah I have. Thankfully, I won't have to freeze my butt off in Michigan or sweat through the summers in North Carolina. I'm going to CalU." The bittersweet declaration rang hollow knowing that she'd arrive there as a jilted Ex instead of as part of a power couple the way she imagined.

"It's not the Ivies but it's a good school," he remarked.

She braced for the impact of soiled thoughts, doing her best not to react to the string of illuminations. She saw his relief at not having to be embarrassed about Era's future plans when talking to the other parents at graduation. She saw how he wished she hadn't gotten off the WaitList. She saw that he wished she'd go to one of the less expensive schools since he didn't think it mattered which school she picked after getting rejected from the Ivies. She saw how he wished she would pick something long distance.

Anybody else who only had to hear the words people spoke would have felt a little offended to have their accomplishment minimized by the condescending congratulations. Era had to stare the ugly truth in the face. And smile. He wrote the checks after all.

One day I'll be so rich, he'll be sorry, she thought and offered him a half-hearted smile. With that unpleasant exchange concluded, she fled up the stairs to her room, and sighed at the satisfying click of the lock on her door. Alone, with only her thoughts to trouble her, she pulled the curtains closed and blocked out the chaotic buzzing in her head, stinging her now and then as she thrashed under her covers.

When she awoke the next day, she registered with surprise the sun falling long through the slit in the curtains. 2 p.m. was by far the latest she'd ever slept in in her life. She had no clear thoughts except that she didn't want her parents asking questions about her confinement. Driven by the desire to avoid both sympathy and apathy to her plight, she shoved aside the covers and walked stiffly to turn on the shower, forcing herself to think through what she'd pack for a night at Alex's house and nothing else.

Alex's house, normally a welcome refuge, offered no lasting comfort. The daunting task of retelling the story remained and no surprise, Alex was justifiably pissed when she heard it. Era juggled a strange mix of feeling simultaneously furious with Cole but not wanting her friend to judge his horrible actions. For some reason, the indignation should be hers alone.

"You should have called me. You know I would have left that party in a second to come get you," Alex said, alarmed as Era described the rescue from Dreadstone as they coined it.

"I wanted to. You know I wanted you more than anyone, but

I was seriously considering calling an ambulance. I couldn't even walk. So I called the only person near enough to help," she explained.

It took all the energy Era had to retell the story. Funnily enough, hearing it didn't cause the pain she expected. She heard her own voice as if she listened to someone else recount a traumatic story, one that had nothing to do with her. The exhaustion overcame her again, and she barely said goodnight before being dragged back into the abyss of achingly real dreams that only the Gift could create.

Era spent two days and nights in Alex's room. Once when she woke up from an eerily long nap that spanned most of the middle of the day, she texted Cole.

I miss you.

Era blinked and fell asleep once more, then awoke with a jerk, remembering the message. She grabbed for her phone reflexively. Next to her text, a little check marked the message above the dreaded word "Seen," but nothing followed.

She swallowed the knot in her throat and felt the darkness sucking her back in. Some part of her was aware that she had promised herself to go back to school today, but the concern floated away as the drowsiness carried her under. Upon awakening yet again with the light creeping towards late afternoon, Era realized she should probably head home to get some clean underwear and eat an actual meal.

She snuck home like a thief, checking the cameras beforehand to make sure the house was empty before pulling into the driveway. After packing a few extra outfits and an actual toiletry bag, she hustled down the stairs and back into her car.

She reversed out of the driveway and crept slowly down the street realizing she had no idea where to go.

When a vehicle slowed a foot from her bumper, she moved towards the curb and threw up an exasperated flip of her hand. Rather than passing, the car stopped alongside her and rolled down a tinted window. Miffed by the unwanted intrusion, Era prepared to shout down a potential cat-caller when she heard her name.

Too cool in a shiny blue Porsche Cayenne, a handsome guy in dark sunglasses called out, "Era! Hey there stranger. I wondered when I'd see you again. Where you heading?"

"Christopher!" she called back in surprise, breaking through her stupor. "Well, I'm trying to figure out where to go for dinner. I'm starving."

Without missing a beat, he said, "Come over to my place. My parents are out of town, but I've got the chef." He didn't even wait for a response before speeding the rest of the way down the street.

This guy has some serious overconfidence issues, she thought while falling in behind him. She had to admit, the invitation made for a convenient answer to her current predicament. Before she knew it, her car rolled through the gate towards the impressive home Christopher had all to himself.

CHAPTER 15

UNUSED TO THE newfound awkwardness around Christopher, Era directed her attention towards the chef, a good-looking guy in his early thirties who moved confidently through the kitchen. She made sure to thank him for the incredible breakfast he had brought her during her stay in the pool house, assuring him that on a typical day, there would have been only crumbs left on the tray.

She jumped up into a bar stool at the island to watch as he pulled homemade fettuccine through a hand-cranked pasta maker. His hands gingerly guided the delicate noodles through the machine until he paused to cut them, draping the long strands over his arm. Era couldn't help but Snap a quick photo to Alex of the extravagance.

A few minutes later, Christopher appeared, freshly showered in an Essentials hoodie and high-top Nike Dunks. She gave him a little whistle and a glance that let him know she loved the look. He blushed under the scrutiny before sidling up next to her at the bar. Not wanting to get too personal with his chef standing only a few feet away, he launched into a discreet line of questioning. "Missed you at school today. You hanging in there?"

Era shifted in her seat before answering, "Barely. I've been staying with Alex for the past few nights. I had to tell my dad *something* when I got home but I don't want to talk about it with either of them. I'm avoiding them."

"I know what you need," he said, warming her with his genuine concern. Turning to the chef, he asked, "What's on the menu tonight?" and upon hearing the dish he got up and returned with a bottle of wine. "I think this would pair nicely, don't you agree?"

Unsure if the question had been directed to her or the chef, she squinted down at the label–Cakebread Cabernet Sauvignon, 2012, a good year. She freaking knew he'd bust this move on her; however, she hadn't expected it to happen so soon, five days to be exact.

A snarky comment perched on her lips when he leaned in, his breathy whisper tickling her ear, "I thought you could use a little cheering up." When he pulled back and looked into her eyes, the Gift melted her as she perceived his heart hurting on her behalf.

"A wonderful pairing," she answered, unsure if she meant the wine with the mood or the two of them.

He poured their glasses with more refinement than belonged to an eighteen year old senior, grasped the stem of the wide glass and tucked his nose into it before handing it over.

"No wet cardboard?" she asked, impressed that he knew to check for a skunked smell before giving it to her. She sucked in the calming scent of graphite and mulberries, fully aware that the only part of this wine she could truly savor was the numbing relief it would bring to the crushing ache in her chest.

Christopher continued to spoil her during dinner, opening a second bottle, a 2004 Maybach Cab that blew the Cakebread out of the water. "I still think it's unusual that a guy 'your age' drinks wine," she said, shoveling another mouthful of carbs drenched in the heavy white sauce into her mouth.

"My age?" he chuckled. "You know we're the same age right? My parents started pouring me a glass occasionally when we had dinner at 15. They didn't want me learning how to drink at a party. It sounds very European, but really I think they did it so I was less likely to screw up and end up in a tabloid. Oh hey—" he said, reaching for her face and wiping a dob of sauce that had flicked up from the long noodles onto the tip of her nose. His palm cupped her cheek for the briefest of seconds. Era laughed but her cheek tingled ever so slightly from the warmth of his touch. Christopher proceeded to scrape his bowl clean then leaned over to mop up the last of her noodles.

"Jeeze, trash compactor!" she teased as he slurped the pasta down. But she liked it, she enjoyed the feeling of friendship so close he didn't mind sharing her germs. He'd probably lick her fork if she let him. The bottles empty, Era forgot the misery of the past few days, content to breathe in an existence without unspeakable agony.

Dopamine and serotonin tingled through her, filling Era with unanticipated bravado. A sudden compulsion made her want to tour Christopher's room, as if seeing his private sanctuary might decode some of his mystery. He shook his head and snickered, trailing her as she bounced up the stairs without permission, opening up several doors before seeing the prize at hand.

Christopher's room rivaled the size of a master bedroom in Texas. It had enough space to contain a California King, a fireplace with a sitting area, and a desk, without being at all crowded. His style exuded masculinity and simplicity, yet retained a refined elegance that reminded her of a CB2 showroom. The room's most striking feature, a massive wall of windows framed by floor-to-ceiling curtains, offered an unobstructed view of the water, reflecting the twinkling lights of tall buildings across the Bay.

Kicking off her shoes, she swan-dived into his bed, messing up the pillows and cocooning herself under the comfort of a fluffy white duvet. His bed, much like the man himself, made for an irresistible invitation—strong yet soft, a sanctuary to envelope her. And even though this house was less than a mile from home, it felt a world apart. She wanted to sink into it and never leave.

He stood there laughing at her rolling around like a hamster before heading into the bathroom to brush his teeth and change. The night grew late, and Christopher's prudence kicked in, reminding him that an early morning awaited them both.

"Tap tap tap," came an unexpected noise. Era froze, still concealed by the fluffy covers and listened, realizing someone had knocked. Christopher strode over and opened the door, taking Era's leather duffle, the phone she left downstairs, and an extra charger from "Jeeves" the butler (she still hadn't heard his name spoken).

Era cowered under the blanket, astonished and mortified in turn. Who even saw the bag in her passenger seat and assumed she wanted it to stay the night again? Jeeves must have found her keys and dug around in her Jeep to get it. *These guys sure take some liberties,* she thought.

It struck her as odd, but tonight she didn't care. She shoved away the embarrassment she felt, sauntered over to the chair where Christopher dropped it, unzipped it to grab her toiletry kit, and joined him at the sink to brush her teeth. Except even Era, usually cool as a cucumber, couldn't shake the feeling of closeness in brushing her teeth in the en-suite bathroom of her new friend. *Why does this feel like second base or something?* she thought and spit into the sink, splashing the blue streak away before he saw it.

Rather than succumb to any awkwardness, Era embraced

the familiarity. Without a second thought, she strolled into Christopher's closet, shutting the door behind her before pillaging his drawers for a t-shirt and boxer briefs. "You better not be snooping around in there!" she heard him call through the door. When she emerged, she knew she was going straight to hell in a handbasket.

He eyed her in his t-shirt and white boxer briefs, his face still, his Adam's apple bobbing with a gulp. All guys love to see girls in their clothes; it stemmed from some primal possessive caveman thing. Before he had a chance to say anything, she dive-bombed back into his bed.

Christopher took a few cautious steps towards her. "It's clear how much you like my room. You're welcome to stay in here tonight if you like. I'll sleep in the guest room next door."

"Ok—but don't go yet. I'm not ready for bed."

"No? You wanna build a fort then?" he asked with a touch of humor, still trying to decide in which direction they were heading.

She laughed as he sat with perfect posture, hands on his knees on the outer three inches of the mattress. She knew he felt like an intruder sitting on his own bed now that he had relinquished it to her use. "Stop it, that's so awkward. Just get under here," Era said, motioning with the covers.

Christopher cast her a wary glance before slipping under the plush comforter, carrying with him a swirl of emotions. Despite the haze of alcohol, Era's Gift revealed the undercurrent of hesitation that charged the sheets. He was reluctant to let himself get too close to her, especially with her reckless emotional turmoil on full display. He doubted the sincerity of anything she said or did after downing an entire bottle of wine. And he hid it like a pro, but he felt an awkwardness about having her in his bedroom at all.

The Gift seemed to confirm something intriguing—no other

girl had crossed the threshold into his private space before. How very interesting.

Despite his mountain of hesitation, the Gift displayed his desire before her. She saw how he longed to pull her close and she ached for the soothing comfort of his body once more. Days of crying, of sleeping and sleeping left her with nothing to give, and a blind need to take, even if what she needed was the clothes-on, unrequited desire he offered. She knew she could take exactly what she wanted from him, and not an inch more, that he would let her draw him out and not push beyond any boundary she set.

As naturally as green branches reaching towards the sunlight, she pulled him over to her, his head landing on her pillow where she could relish the feeling of having his face so close to her own. His eyes opened up like green pools before her and she drank in their sweet vulnerability. She gazed at his perfect mouth, his full lips barely parted, trembling slightly before she pressed a soft kiss to them. The moment carried a fleeting spark, like licking a nine volt battery—briefly electric, then nothing but cold stillness.

Unsure what she had expected, she definitely didn't expect him to completely freeze. His breath paused and he remained motionless. As she pulled back and opened her eyes, she searched his face, immediately recognizing the conflict in his gaze—an unmistakable battle between hesitation and desire. Perplexed beyond words, she sat up to put some distance between their too close faces and threw back the covers.

Time to head to the guest room.

Imperfect circumstances or not, he couldn't let her slip through his fingers. As one foot touched the floor, Christopher grabbed her wrist. "Wait," he said, pulling her back into bed with him and lit up her lips, this time like a downed electrical wire. Reluctance, release, triumph, desire—a sea of emotions swirled around them, locking them together in currents of power. Their tongues merged and his hand ran up the length of her neck causing Era to moan directly into his mouth.

After four years of locking him behind a wall of friendship, the kiss torched her brain like lighting hitting a patch of over-grown parched brush after a dry California summer. Era ignited in his arms. And while his yearning burned her with fire, his need to protect her, even from himself, spread an aloe over her charred heart.

As they kissed, Era visited Christopher's luscious memories again, memories of the longing he felt for her every day since the moment she sat in front of him at freshman orientation. She relished the feeling of a thousand vicarious bolts striking him as his mouth finally touched the soft fullness of her pink lips and his fingers caressed the creamy skin of her neck. Her experience of him wrapped around them in 4D. She felt her pleasure and absorbed his too. The Gift could be good in a kiss.

As the kiss began to fracture her, to make her forget the pain of rejection, a jumble of little thoughts bombarded her, pulling her out of the moment. Accusations like, *How could you move on so fast after Cole?* And, *How could you use him as a rebound when you know he really likes you?* danced around her head.

She batted the thoughts away. She needed this. The way he wanted every part of her soothed an ache in her soul. And when she paused to look into his eyes, whatever they were before, crumbled like a child's sandcastle built too close to the tide.

Christopher often wondered how Era acted around her boyfriend after the fateful day she crushed him with the news. He had tried so hard to get her to hang out with him, casually or otherwise, though she never budged on rejecting every invita-tion save those that took place on campus, during school hours. Then without warning, his opportunity vanished.

Era was witty, funny, confident; however, she was also reserved even if he sensed that the disposition seemed forced. Now he kissed her, following the confident movements of her body against his. Era pulled back from the kisses and stared into his face, building a bridge of intimacy with her eyes. And he knew. He knew that sleeping with Era would be unlike anything else. How he wanted her! His body pulsed with wanting her while his head screamed at him to take it slow.

Era tucked her head into the crook of his neck, finding an especially soft spot to kiss there and to hide her face as she experienced his hesitation return when things heated up. Era couldn't hear exact thoughts—that's not how the Gift worked— but she could surmise his mantra, *You can't. You can't. You can't.* A devilish part of her enjoyed the internal struggle.

"Mmm," she moaned in encouragement. *You can, you can, you can,* she thought as his warm hands pushed under the back of her shirt and grasped her shoulders then stroked down over her round bum, snuggly tucked into his rolled-up boxer briefs.

She watched as the tug of war between pleasure and fear consumed him. He was afraid to be pushed away if he took too much.

She broke their kiss then, and looking dreamily into his eyes, said the words that unraveled him, "I won't hold it against you... later."

She knew he wondered how she knew. He wondered why it felt as if they were having a conversation instead of a single person breaking the silence. He held back a moment longer because as much as he wanted to believe her, he didn't think that she could be trusted with her promises right now.

The image of her lying broken on the rock flashed in his mind for the thousandth time. Era winced. His good sense delivered the crushing blow to his passion and he pulled his arms back against his sides. She didn't know how he managed it.

"I would hold it against myself," he said, gently combing the hair behind her ears with his fingertips. "I told you that I would be whatever you need me to be, and I think you need a friend more than you need an opportunist."

In that moment, a piece of the seemingly indestructible bond tethering Era to Cole snapped, crumbling into the abyss. What she needed more than anything was someone who prioritized her well-being over their own desires. That had been the missing element with Cole. He never had the chance to prove himself, and when the moment finally came, he failed to rise to the occasion.

With Christopher, she felt the way a person stumbling through a dark and airless cave would feel to suddenly catch a cool breeze and hope for an escape nearby. She breathed easy for a second before the traitorous thought came to her. *He'll only want you until it's inconvenient for him.*

He pulled her into his arms once more, the familiar tears dampening his shirt before her muffled crying turned to soft snores. She did need him, and no matter what, he would make sure that he gave her everything she needed.

CHAPTER 16

7 A.M. —Christopher's phone alarm went off, jarring Era awake and hoisting her from the depths of a tumultuous dream. The vapors of the memory floated around her.

She had been driving away from CalU on the first day of school. When she got to the dorms, someone had already moved into her room. The RA said her acceptance letter must have been a mistake. She drove away, humiliated and confused, with no home or family, no friends, no boyfriend, to go to. She called her dad, Alex, Christopher—but each attempt left her more distraught. The first two numbers were no longer in service, and on the third try, a stranger answered. *Damn, I'm dark,* she thought, as the vision slipped away.

As she reached over to annihilate the obnoxious intrusion, Christopher turned to her and announced simply, "You can shower first or second, but you're not skipping any more school. I'm driving and we leave in 45 minutes." His smile beamed brighter than the sun streaming through the wide windows and her heart felt a glimmer of his warmth, dispersing the memory of the nightmare.

She hadn't thought to pack school clothes and instead

slipped on a pair of basic Lululemon leggings and a cropped top that could barely pass the dress code without exposing her midriff—if she kept her arms down. Era knew she'd get some glances at school by showing off her figure after taking such pains to conceal it.

Downstairs, Chef finished plating a zesty asparagus and goat cheese omelet with from-scratch biscuits and homemade cherry jam. They ate quickly, finishing every last bite while Era teased Christopher about his perfectly organized undie drawer. He fired back, betting her ten dollars she'd get at least five comments on her leggings at school.

Era didn't even mind if anyone saw her holding onto his arm as they walked through the parking lot toward campus. They were friends and touching him comforted her, made her forget something that nagged at the back of her mind.

The realization finally smacked her, an icy wave crashing over her. "Oh NO, with everything going on, I never covered for my absence. What day is it again?" she asked, panic rising in her voice.

"It's Thursday. And it's the end of the year. They'll know seniors took finals last week. I'm sure you'll be able to sweet-talk them," he said, giving her arm a squeeze of reassurance.

Era bit her lip nervously and pulled her arm from his, "I hope so." As she let go of his steady frame, anxiety pummeled her. She had dealt with the administration on many occasions and after missing two full weeks of school to go to the Maldives with Raquel's crew, they basically hated her. She prepared to turn her Gift to maximum velocity and sort this out.

The moment she stepped through the doors and saw Ms. Lee in her matching grey tweed blazer and pencil skirt, she knew she was cooked. Maybe she could have worked Ms. Lackabee, the younger one, to overlook the daily call or email policy, but Ms. Lee was no nonsense and a stickler for the rules. Era looked around desperately for another option, but the office was eerily quiet this morning.

She launched into the excuse she prepared on the walk over, a mental health crisis and a private family matter. Ms. Lee listened with a blank expression, not even blinking as Era spoke. "I'm very sorry to hear about your situation," Ms. Lee began as Era finished her veiled sob story, "But you know school policy. Absences of three or more days require a doctor's note in order to be excused by this office."

A doctor's note, no problem, I'll call that homeopathic doctor we met in the Hills, she thought, before Ms. Lee interrupted her plan with a curveball.

"Since your issue stems from a mental health issue, you're going to need to provide a note from a Psychologist, on official letterhead.

"Wait, what?" she asked, baffled. "Is this a new policy I'm not aware of?"

"I'm afraid so. Students with more than 20 missed days per semester require a Psychologist note, if the subsequent days stem from mental health concerns. We want to make sure students are getting the help they need," she said with a conde-scending frown.

Era felt the ground sway under her as she scrolled through her mental contacts. She knew many people—lawyers, teachers, politicians, hedge fund managers, restaurateurs, CEOs, software nerds, influencers, and even several doctors for crying out loud! None were psychologists or psychiatrists no matter how far back she looked in her acquaintance circle. Panic bit at the edges of her mind.

Before she could stammer out a response, Ms. Lee clicked away on her laptop and hit her with an aftershock. "Era, there's a note in your file I must inform you about. Your history teacher says you had a major paper due on Monday, worth a third of your grade. He told the Vice Principal that he will refuse to accept the paper unless your absence is properly excused."

Era swallowed the acid rising in her esophagus. *I am going to fire his petty ass back to Middle-Earth,* she thought, sparks flashing behind her closed eyelids. As her already desperate situation now teetered on the edge of disaster, Era took the ultimate risk. She dug from the bottom of herself, tearing the Gift from its roots and threw it around the woman like a lasso, Pulling her heart close to examine every last crevice.

Era began to pry for any angle with the woman—pity, bargaining, promises, tears until she saw that the woman stood solid as a mountain before her. Until, *Ha!* She saw it. A little path lay carved into the side of what appeared to be an insurmountable cliff face before her, one that would get Ms. Lee to excuse the absence.

At the precipice of the path, an exotic black orchid bloomed and pulsed with her heart to remind the woman of its presence every second. The Gift's illumination brought the meaning to her like a wrapped present.

This particular administrative assistant had breast cancer. She felt completely out of control of her life, and clung to the rules in her profession as a way to make sense of a senseless disease in which she had no control. Era saw that the only way to break through to her would be to mention her cancer directly and call her out on the illusion of power in this temporary world.

But she couldn't bring herself to do it, to use the Gift with such abandon for its concealment. She also saw that by doing so, she would shatter this woman.

Era turned away without responding, nausea rising from her gut, and threw open the door, sucking in the fresh air. Her heart sank, she knew, utterly, that Mr. Ent would give her a zero on the paper, dropping her grade to a D.

Era watched her body walk from class to class from a thousand feet in the air. Only the self-satisfied look on Mr. Ent's face as she took her seat drew her down from the clouds. She fought back a snarl as his lips curled into a thin, self-congratulatory smile, barely hiding the gleam of superiority in his eyes. So he had gotten the email notification that her absence remained unexcused. Unable to be anchored even by the anger, she drifted off again, leaving her corporeal form, an empty shell to carry out the duties of the day while her mind spun the wheel of her imminent doom.

The distant chime of the fourth-period bell barely registered in her mind. It felt as if a boulder had just crashed onto her—the weight of a single D threatening to torpedo her GPA and revoke her admission to Cal University. She stared into the shattered mirror of her future, bewildered that one bitter man could so irrevocably alter the course of her life.

Then the fifth period bell rang. She still sat at her desk, now in the wrong class. Before she could get up, another realization sideswiped her like a truck—if she lost her spot at Cal, she'd never go to school with Cole. Her dream, her only desire, crushed in a single, brutal day. Still grappling with that gut-wrenching eventuality, it felt like the truck backed over her again when she remembered Alex. She'd leave Era behind, too. Everything she cared about, dust.

Alex had only ever bought into the dream to go to Cal because Era painted a vivid picture of them taking over campus, together. She pictured her friend's crushed expression, heard the veiled anger and disappointment in her voice when she broke the news. Then the soft whisper of a thought, an unbearable vision of Alex at school, finding a new best friend, passing the days with someone else. Era's stomach clenched.

See how easily you are replaced? Her vicious thoughts taunted her. It was too much. Cole, Alex, even Christopher. They were all little boats charting their own courses away from her, moving steadily into the distant future while she weathered the terrible storm alone. She pushed the thought away.

When the bell rang again, announcing the start of fifth period, Era understood that this had all happened because she had put all her trust in the Gift and all her hope in a single man. She had destroyed herself. She had taught herself that she could rely on the Gift and do what she wanted without consequences.

Era looked into her own heart and saw a pathetic, naive and selfish teenager. She might have been transported back to 8th grade, knowing that a single choice had ruined her life. Era seethed with self-loathing as she reflected on the past few days. How could she have cared more about losing Cole than her own future? A second chunk of her bondage to Cole splintered away, disintegrating into oblivion. Burning shame at her actions filled her, and a hatred of the one her heart still loved tore at her without mercy.

She resisted the instinctive allure to text her mom to get picked up from school. Despite wanting to be anywhere but school, she couldn't stomach a "talk" right now. She already knew how that conversation would go.

Era's parents stood on the weak principle that doing nothing on her behalf was best, believing it to be to her benefit to have to clean up her own messes. They wouldn't flinch to watch her suffer the academic ramifications of her choices.

Through a sheer act of will, Era forced herself to walk to Calculus, arriving ten minutes late. No assignments and no lecture meant she had no shield from Christopher. "What happened?" he asked.

"It's over, that's what happened."

"What's over?"

She put a hand to the side of her head as if she could block out the screaming whine and blaring lights. "My life, everything."

"What are you talking about? Tell me what happened," he asked again, more insistent.

"I couldn't get the absences excused. Mr. E is giving me a zero on the final paper which means I'll get a D in the class. They're going to revoke my admission to Cal in the fall and you and Alex and Cole" —her voice sputtered momentarily before she regained her disassociated composure— "will be there while I'll be condemned to at least a year in community college with the academic refuse of the system. I already passed on my other options when I got off the waitlist. Another year surviving my insufferable family."

Shock and then anger passed through Christopher as he heard her simple answer turn into a nightmarish domino effect of destruction. "How can he ruin an entire student's academic future over one paper? And you even wrote the paper! I'm going to talk to him. I bet if I offer to have my dad's company donate an entire rare book collection or sponsor a trip to DC or something for next year's class, he'll rethink zeroing that paper." She saw the wheels turning as he worked through scenarios of how money could solve the problem.

"It won't work. Not with Mr. E. He thinks he's at Custer's Last Stand. I've seen it," she replied, looking out the window.

"You've *seen* it?" he asked curiously, and she saw in his face that he thought it a weird turn of phrase.

Whoops, she thought. She'd been slipping up a lot lately.

Yet, he didn't doubt it. He saw the way Mr. E wanted to make an example out of her, for doing lord knows what, acing his tests? It was all absurd. "I think we have to try. I want you at Cal with me in the fall."

His words scraped her bruised heart. *Well, at least somebody does...* she thought.

"No, I don't want to give him the satisfaction. He won't budge. Save your dad's money for some other pathetic loser who lets a breakup completely destroy her life's work."

He hugged her again, not noticing the intrigued onlookers. But she didn't cry this time. In fact, she felt nothing at all.

CHAPTER 17

AT HOME, Era didn't speak of her personal tragedy. Anyway, it would be a long while before CalU received the updated transcript and then canceled her life. She skipped Senior Night at the theme park and spent three whole days with her phone turned off, not even bothering to plug it in. She didn't care, she didn't shower, and she ate alarmingly little.

Finally, graduation day arrived. Now with the displeasure of having to shower, dress, and make polite conversation with her classmates and family, she wished they had kicked her out of school so she could avoid the burdensome event.

In true juxtaposition to her own mood, she found her classmates in a veritable frenzy of affection for one another at the ceremony. She did her best to block out their chatter about college plans, each mention twisting the knife a little deeper. Once, she even found herself scanning the stands, half-expecting to see Cole sitting beside her parents. When he wasn't there, she quickly took custody of her traitorous eyes, refusing to let them return and face the disappointment again. Christopher glanced her way several times, trying to catch her attention, but she kept her face resolutely turned away.

Most of the day passed in a blur, even the moment when her name echoed through the speakers, and her body carried her across the stage to accept the diploma and shake a chapped, wrinkled hand. What should have felt like a joyous occasion now carried only bitterness and regret. She yearned for the comforting darkness of her room, for the escape hatch her bed offered from the harshness of this painful reality.

The next morning she woke up to a message from Alex.

> Why did you ghost everyone yesterday? Got your yearbook. Dropping it off at 10.

Era checked the time, 10:02, and heard the doorknob turn.

Alex entered cautiously as if unsure what she'd find on the other side. She set the yearbook down on the dresser and then threw open the curtains. "You peaced out of graduation before we even got a picture together. I was pretty bummed about it. I know that your breakup must be really hard but I don't understand why you're isolating yourself like this," she said, pulling up the chair to her bed for a second time this week. Alex had given her space when she stayed over. Now the time had come for a heart-to-heart.

Era laid out the whole truth for her then, how she had screwed up her grades and the subsequent consequence, that she wouldn't be joining Alex at school. Era felt Alex deflate and ice over, her mind working through the heavy confession. Era watched her oscillate between pity for her friend and resentment at the shared future that had been torched by a selfish choice.

She took a long breath, sorting out her feelings before replying, "I can see now why you didn't tell me right away. I'm sure you were worried about my reaction, and I *am* angry at you, but I know that this is much worse for you than me."

Relief flooded Era.

"It doesn't matter where we go to school, I will always love you as my best friend. And I plan to see you through worse in life than a college rejection letter."

Era jumped from her covers into Alex's arms, holding back tears. She would allow no self-pity right now, not when her friend had shown heroic fortitude. And like that, the hateful vision of Alex with her new best friend dissolved and she let herself look into a future of at least the summer.

"I'm so sorry. I should have leaned on you, it's just not something I've ever done or even know how to do. I haven't figured out what my backup plan is, but at least we can look forward to Lake Como with Raquel. We could even backpack like we always talked about starting in Italy. Now that we're both single, we'll probably get invited to go everywhere—"

"Oh... ah Raquel. I haven't gotten the chance to tell you since it just happened this past week, but Raquel hooked me up with an Au Pair job this summer. The family is a friend of her father's. And rich rich. They're summering in southern Spain and Greece, and need a nanny to look after their twins.

"They're paying for all my expenses and enough of a salary to cover my tuition for next year. Plus, you know I love kids and this will look good on my resume some day if I go into education. It's kind of a dream gig," Alex finished excitedly though clearly nervous to break the news at such a time.

Era fell back, crushed, but how could she show it? She really needed her friend and now she would be spending the entire summer alone. The irony didn't escape her—her only true friend, leaving, all because Era had expanded their circle with so many connections.

She barely resisted the urge to head straight for the wine fridge and open a bottle. However, with the clock not yet

striking noon, even her permissive parents would have something to say about that. Holding back the tears that would
unleash a torrent of emotion, she said, "It does sound like an
amazing opportunity and I know you've always wanted to prac-
tice your Spanish in Spain. I'm going to miss you so much.
When do you leave?"

"Two days. They're heading to Costa del Sol soon and want
me to get to know the kids beforehand. I'm going to miss you
too. We'll FaceTime every couple of days, I promise," she said,
her voice wavering.

So this was goodbye then. Era hugged her friend, realization
crystallizing that she would face the summer alone.

With Alex gone, Era trudged downstairs in her pajamas to
pour herself a bowl of cereal, lunch of champions. Her mother
scuttled around distractedly, arms heavy with laundry.

Era cared little about her mother's mundane chores, but the
Gift sensed an anxiety, an urgency. Era stared down into her
bowl of Crispix and asked with mild interest, "What are you
doing? Packing to go somewhere?"

Her mother practically grunted in response as she threw the
clothes down on a dining chair. "Are you serious? Dad and I are
about to leave on our cruise. It's been on the family calendar for
months!" she responded, miffed.

She vaguely remembered seeing a note on the calendar a
while back and figured they were taking another long weekend
to Mexico. "Oh yeah, saw something but I didn't look at the
details. Where are you guys going?"

"Era, please, I've got a lot on my mind. It's our big European
vacation. We're going to be gone for 23 days—21 days cruising
and two days in transit. Why do we even update the family
calendar if you're not going to pay attention to it?" she scolded.

"Had a lot on my mind. Wasn't exactly concerned with the
calendar."

Her mother pursed her lips, her mind working to change

gears. Era looked down, as if she could stop herself from seeing what she always saw, a complete lack of concern. "I know you're going through a hard time. But don't worry, Cole will come around," her mother said, brushing off Era's feelings and the severity of the issue in the same breath.

"He's not coming around. It's over," she shot back.

"Oh, I don't think so. You guys are so perfect together. He's the one, I just know it."

Era stopped mid-crunch on her cereal. Era had prepared for any number of insulting remarks, but she had not prepared for this. Her mom saw a wedding in her mind, the satisfaction of giving Era away to Cole and knowing her obligation was dispensed. She only wanted them to be perfect together because then that'd be a wrap on having to mother her.

Her mom never wanted kids in the first place so of course she wanted to pass her off. Era had been an unhappy accident, one that continually rubbed against her mother's independence eighteen years later. Six years after that fateful day and she still couldn't escape the sting of the secret.

Era pushed away the ugly image, fists balled under the breakfast table. *Stop it!* she thought, *You're not an inconvenience.*

"Don't sulk. You'll end up with wrinkles. Why don't you go somewhere with Alex or Raquel?"

Yep, pawn me off.

"Alex is gone for the summer. Took a nannying job in Europe. I just said goodbye."

Era's mother's eyes darted with alarm. Era saw the picture in her mind, the one where her daughter crashed their cruise and complicated all their dinner and hotel reservations. She fumbled a second more before replying, "Oh I'm sure you'll miss each other but you can make other plans."

She wanted to be spiteful for once, at least pretend she wanted to go with them, that she was too fragile to be left alone in such a state for so long. She couldn't bring herself to do it. Instead Era sighed, "Yeah, sure. I'll find something to do."

"Use the credit card to go for a spa day with ah, another girl. Do some retail therapy. Whatever you need."

Money. Your solution to everything, Era thought. The trust from Grandma would be released soon. She'd threatened all those years ago to cut them out, but they assumed she'd leave her money to her son, Era's father. Instead, it had all gone to her granddaughter. Justice from the grave.

"Good idea," she said without enthusiasm.

"Call us if you need anything, we should have internet on the ship... well... except when we're in the Baltics, I heard the sea can still be rough even at this time of year—" and like that she bustled away, remembering something she forgot to pack.

Era shook her head, irritated but not surprised and dumped her milk into the sink. Sometimes she tried to justify the way they treated her. Her mom and dad were both only children, unused to the needs of anyone else competing with their own.

She tried to picture herself wanting a husband but not children, planning her future living the life of a DINK (Dual Income No Kids), and then having to abandon the idea and change course. Yep, she would do it for her own child. Her mother could not.

Selfish. Empathy exercise over.

Sometimes she thought about confronting her mom with the truth, but that was the problem with reading hearts. She already understood all the reasons her mom felt the way she did. There was no satisfaction to be had.

As long as she kept the secret, they had to keep up the pretense of loving her. And her mom and dad did try to be good parents on paper. The truth only reared its ugly head when something Era did or needed competed with their own interests or plans. Like when she came down with appendicitis at the start of her Dad's annual Christmas party with his business associates. They'd brought her to the ER and left her there, alone.

She pulled up the calendar and saw all the days blocked off, no different than the long lavish vacations they took every year, without her. A few years ago, they were relieved to finally not have to hire some nanny to stay with her, the idea of taking her with them never crossed their mind.

Era grimaced as she dropped her spoon into the dishwasher, thinking of the years she'd killed herself under the floodlights of the tennis court trying to prove herself as talented enough for her dad or the hours she'd spent learning makeup tutorials to impress her mom.

After years of feeling utterly rejected, she thought she had filled the emptiness with a perfect best friend and her true love. What a sick joke it seemed now.

Anyways, Era didn't really care that they were leaving. Relief flooded her as she climbed the stairs back to her room knowing that she could sulk in peace. Nonetheless, the rational part of her mind, the part she wanted nothing to do with at the moment, warned her of vague danger.

Her mind flickered to the wine cellar, remembering the way alcohol had called to her like a siren and decided immediately not to drink a drop, no matter what. She loved the thrill of a buzz but had read enough hearts to know that drugs and alcohol provided temporary relief but swept people away in an avalanche. New rule: no alcohol, especially without account- ability in the house.

As she pulled open the door to her darkened room, satisfac- tion filled her. Pleased with herself at her own maturity and self-awareness, she settled into her covers, unaware that she had avoided one pitfall only to plunge into another.

CHAPTER 18

THE NEXT MORNING, her parents removed themselves by an ocean. And took with them, the last vestige of accountability from Era's life. Her calendar yawned before her, empty white boxes that stretched into infinity—no tennis, no classes, no trips, no boyfriend to call. And so to fill the emptiness, she slipped into an endless rotting slumber.

Era didn't find her waking hours unbearable. She didn't feel much of anything besides a constant state of exhaustion and a strong desire to return to her dreams. Despite watching her future implode, terrible nightmares didn't plague her—at first.

Instead, her mind suddenly exploded with vivid and fantastic dreams that bettered her reality. In her dreams, she flew over rivers, she skied at breakneck speed next to Alex, and best of all, she made love to Cole.

And it was all better than being awake. Better than being alive.

The sun spun around her room—fourteen times, maybe more. But Era remained still, encapsulated in her own darkness, as if time had forgotten her.

Now at 2 p.m. she opened her eyes—sore and parched.

Unsteady. Like she wasn't sure how to be. By 4, she crawled back into bed. Her body too heavy to fight it. She didn't suffer. No, she wasn't *really* there. Not in the way people were supposed to be.

Barely slipping under the covers, she sank—*sank*, all the way —beneath the surface. Deeper. Deeper. Where nothing could reach her.

The snorkel pressed tightly against her face as she kicked through the vibrant coral, eager for a closer look at the young turtle feeding on some kind of sea plant ahead. The hollow sound of her breath echoed through the tube as she dove deeper to catch a better glimpse of the adorable creature. The pressure in her ears cleared easily, allowing her to blend into the serene underwater world by remaining still on the sandy floor. Brilliantly colored fish flitted in and out of an endless array of corals, letting her draw perilously close before darting away in a flash.

She kicked her way around the small island, pausing to marvel at a school of large, slender grouper fish weaving a tight line. They began in the light, glided under the dark of the small pier, and then spiraled back into the sunlight as a shimmering mass of silver. Immersed in the tranquil beauty of the ocean, Era felt as if she had slipped into a peaceful screensaver, leaving her life on hold. Completely absorbed in the moment, she lost all sense of time, unsure if she had been there for hours or days.

Finally, feeling the snorkel tangle in her hair, she let her face surface. The water burned with fire. Oil slicks shimmered, pulsing toward her pulled by the tide, and smoke choked the air. Her bliss transformed into panic as she scanned the shoreline for a clear path to swim back to the beach.

The hellish landscape crept closer with the waves. As Era swam away from the approaching flames, she realized she had drifted closer to the edge of another fire, and saw no clear path of escape. She screamed as the heat seared her face and arm, and jolted awake, drenched in a cold sweat. It was 3 a.m.

She gasped, sucking in gulps of the smokeless air, her hand gripping the arm that had blistered with fresh burns a moment before. Terror instantly transformed into an even greater panic, a sense of another presence nearby. The room radiated deep antagonism, reveling in her fear. Too afraid to speak, breathe, or move, Era lay still, paralyzed, her heart hammering. When she dared to move only her eyes, she thought she saw a blackness shimmering like a heat mirage near her window. She squeezed her eyes shut in frozen terror until a few seconds later when she got up the courage to look again. The room lay dark and empty.

A difficult task remained, how to fall back to sleep after waking up in the middle of the night having slept 10 hours already and pumped full of adrenaline. Yet somehow, Era drifted back into a fitful sleep, this time dreaming of endlessly wandering her school's campus. She couldn't recall where her classroom was, when she had last been there, or what she needed to turn in that day. Confused as to her schedule or where to go on this bizarre blended Cal and Emerald Prep campus, she heard the bell ringing obnoxiously, again and again, without knowing where to go.

"Era? Hey, it's me," the crazy sentence landing on her ears, making less sense than the mixed up dream. "I had to check on you–"

"What are you doing in my room?" Era spit out, reality taking shape in the form of Christopher next to her bed. It clicked that the bell ringing in her dream had been the doorbell.

Ignoring her question entirely, Christopher took in an exacting inspection of Era's frame, unobstructed by the covers she had kicked off in her fight or flight response at having an unwelcome intruder in her room. "You look terrible," he said, flabbergasted.

Her face appeared sallow, her complexion marred by blemishes. Greasy and matted, her hair hung loose, tangled in the sweat of her nightmares. Angular collarbones hinted at imminent malnutrition, while her eyes, wild and distraught, conveyed an alarming state of mind. It baffled Christopher to reconcile the image of the girl who once radiated perfect mental and physical health—her clever gaze, flawless skin, and toned arms—with the fragile soul laying before him now.

"How long have you been in here?" he asked, surveying the room. "Did you know you have spiderwebs stretching from tire to tire on your car outside? And here—" he said, slapping a parking ticket on her bedside table that read **Abandoned Vehicle** in bold red letters. At that point, he sought no response. He turned and strode out of the room, heading downstairs.

Era heard him banging around in the kitchen for about fifteen minutes before he came back up with toast, a bowl of yogurt topped with granola, and a protein bar. "This is the best I could do. You have almost no groceries here" –he put up a hand to silence her– "I wouldn't have come over to demand an explanation as to why you haven't returned a single one of my texts or calls, but then I spotted the webs on your car and realized you probably haven't left the house in weeks. I also haven't seen anyone else around. Consider this a welfare check."

He shot her an angry glare then grabbed her phone and plugged it into the charger. "Hey Siri, set alarm for 8 a.m."

Era looked past him into the mirror, equally shocked and self-conscious about her appearance. "My parents left for a long cruise right after graduation. Alex got a job overseas so she's gone too. I haven't really had anything to do other than sleep," she defended weakly.

Christopher paced over to Era's drawers, pulling out a workout outfit and tossing it onto the chair. "Sleep and death are brothers. But you're not dead yet. Get some calories in you. Drink some water. And take a shower for crying out loud. I'll be back at 8:15 sharp tomorrow."

He stormed out of the room leaving Era in a perplexed state of introspection. Sure, she had been sleeping a lot, but who cares? It was summer after all. Still, after finishing the breakfast, she registered the late hour, and reluctantly scraped herself out of bed to take a shower. She had to sit while drying her hair, she felt so lightheaded and her arms burned from holding the hairdryer over her head. She was weak as a kitten.

An hour or so later, she heard the doorbell ring again which meant she had to walk all the way downstairs. To her surprise, several bags of groceries sat on the porch. *Overbearing but thoughtful,* she thought and grabbed an armful. She trudged into the kitchen laden with bags, then had to sit down and recover for a moment before putting everything away. That night she made herself a spinach omelet for dinner and shuddered at the idea of the inevitable workout with Christopher in the morning.

True to his word, she heard the courtesy knock at 8:15 on the dot before he charged into the house, thankful to find her dressed and drinking a glass of juice at the kitchen island. He scowled at the unwashed dishes in the sink.

"Let's go," he said, waving his hand and heading back out the door without even a good morning. He offered no kindness, and no conversation as he took the lead, breaking into a light jog. The first few blocks demanded monumental effort; Era's feet felt as if they were cast in cement. After three-quarters of a mile, her throat burned, and stitches laced across both sides. How could this possibly be the same body that carried her ten miles around the Bay just a month ago?

She made it two excruciating miles before tapping out, bending over to breathe in shallow gasps, clutching her cramping calf. Christopher sat down on his heels next to her, rubbing with miraculous strength over the protesting muscle until it released.

After three weeks, it amazed her how quickly muscles could atrophy when not used; despite years of tennis and daily workouts, her lung capacity felt almost nonexistent. Hobbled and silent, she made her way back to the house. When she finally reached her driveway, Christopher spoke in a clipped tone, "See you tomorrow," then turned and jogged back toward his house. *Wow he really is pissed,* she thought as she stumbled through the door towards the sink to mix a huge glass of water with electrolytes. *Can't blame him. I'm a wreck,* she thought, catching a glance of her grey skin in the hallway mirror.

With the punishment of the morning behind her, Era did something she had not done for many days, she went outside and laid in the sun by the pool. Well, collapsed would describe it more accurately.

At lunch time, the doorbell rang again and a delivery driver handed her another plastic bag and a white styrofoam cup. A delicious smell wafted from the sealed brown paper bag, and inside—steak salad with a side of rice and a horchata. She couldn't help but smile remembering the time she ranted about her love of horchata in front of him. The man had a memory like an elephant and from the looks of it, wanted to turn her into one.

The next five days passed much in the same way. Christopher picked her up at 8:15 to run. He showed up and let the time pass in indifferent silence. Or maybe it was angry silence. Without words, the Gift could give her none of his thoughts. She might have entertained the suspicion that he was disgusted by her or hated her, except that he sent over food twice a day to make sure that she ate. She asked him to stop but he just pointed to his headphones and continued to ignore her. He didn't trust her to make the effort to cook anything.

On the third day, she came home from their run to find a cleaning lady named Rosa had let herself in with a bucket full of supplies and began helping herself to Era's dirty laundry and sheets.

They began to make some progress in rejuvenating Era's

body. After the third day, she managed three brisk miles on the dirt path. By day five, five miles.

Those days of quiet exertion, awkward at first, ended up being another gift from Christopher. The pain blocked out the negative chatter in her mind, allowing her to reflect on the dreams and the sleeping. Christopher's comment about sleep and death being brothers irked her in a most uncomfortable way. In her mind, she had just been very tired, hadn't seen anything nefarious about sleeping the days away. Who wouldn't want to go back to sleep, knowing indescribable experiences awaited them there?

Yet, with every strengthening step under the morning sun, the vigor of nature chastised her for retreating to a dusty bed in a dark room. She envisioned herself as a sickly patient in a hospital bed, wasting away while the world continued without her. The image shocked her, and she gasped, shaking her head to clear it. How could she have been so blind?

On day five, she FaceTimed Alex, heard how the twins were sweet but incredibly messy and endlessly fighting over toys. Era filled her in on the workout therapy with Christopher to which Alex gave a questioning look. She made sure to reassure her friend, explaining how they barely spoke, how cold their inter-actions were. Then she pulled up her email and wrote up a few sentences to her parents. Maybe they'd open it. After that, she left the house for the first time, alone.

She picked up the pho, the bag warm against her palm as she headed back to her car. It was never quite as good to go as it was to sit in front of a steaming ceramic bowl, letting the heat curl into her face. But she couldn't stand the feeling of being looked at by strangers, as if they could sense her pitiful state. Not yet anyway.

Now, she'd pour the broth from warped plastic, watch it mingle with noodles and herbs, and wonder vaguely how much cancer might be floating in her soup. Still, the smell seeped out, fragrant with licoricey basil and lime, and her stomach rumbled in spite of it all. She relaxed into the soup, a hug of comfort, a blanket she pulled tight around her frazzled nerves.

Until she saw Cole's face smiling over his bowl the last time they had been there together, chopsticks twirling pho into a wide flat spoon and a long noodle slipped down her throat, choking her. She frowned into her bowl, knowing that he probably wasn't thinking of her at all and she couldn't even get through a bowl of soup without his image assaulting her peace. This was why it had been so much easier to sleep the days away. Awake, she had to endure the memories that swooped down at her and ripped a small piece of her before she could bat them off.

On day seven, Christopher wrapped up their run by turning onto the path to his house, up to his home gym. He had her swinging kettlebells and doing push-ups and pull-ups—the nasty stuff.

"Let's go atrophy arms!" he barked at her between counting off reps, her triceps burning so badly they began to shake.

Era didn't want to give him the satisfaction of knowing he'd landed a solid blow to her ego, and replaced her acidic comeback with a groan of effort. He was right after all and quiet seemed to serve them both. After a thorough session of punishment, he dropped his weights with a clang and led her into the kitchen.

Motioning for her to sit at the kitchen island, Christopher began gathering ingredients to make them protein shakes. Era broke the ice with the words that had been forming in her mind for the past two days. "I think I'm depressed." Hearing it aloud felt strange, yet the words resonated with a truth that made the Gift sing inside her, the same Gift that had gone to sleep weeks ago, only to awaken in that moment.

Christopher's eyes softened as he looked at her with

newfound tenderness, his voice brimming with emotion. "Yes, I know."

"It never occurred to me that all the sleeping was a legitimate problem. I didn't see what it was doing to my body—until you showed up," she said thoughtfully, pulling the elastic from her tight ponytail and letting her damp hair fall around her face. "I'm not a coward. I don't want to run from my problems like that. Thank you for the literal wake-up call. Her Siri..." Her voice trailed off as she chuckled, trying to lighten the mood.

He grinned at her, his broad smile sending a tiny shockwave through her chest. In that moment, their usual rapport clicked back into place. He had given her the space she needed to emerge from her spiritual cave while doing his best to care for her physical body.

"You had me so freaked out. I'm no therapist but anyone could see you needed an intervention," he said.

"Thanks for being there for me." Her eyes beamed at him with admiration.

"Thanks for letting me," he said, and went back to making their shakes, all the while cracking jokes about how he mistook her for a zombie when he busted into her room a week ago.

They continued in the same way for a few more days, morning runs, followed by workouts in the gym, and protein shakes in the kitchen. Era skipped the festivities of the 4th of July for the first time ever, deciding to pass the night in Christopher's movie theater bingeing old shows. As Era began to feel more herself, she decided she needed to tie up a loose end if she ever wanted to prevent herself from accidentally unraveling again. That afternoon, she texted Cole.

Can we talk?

About an hour later, he finally texted back.

Sure if you need to. I'll come by around 8.

At least she didn't have to beg him to come in person. A phone call wouldn't cut it. Butterflies fluttered around in her stomach as she tidied up the living room and watched the clock. Finally, her phone lit up with a message asking her to come outside. Ouch.

How can it be like this now? she thought, her steps heavy and heart pounding. It seemed unfathomable that he wouldn't step inside her house, forcing her to endure the humiliation of having a private conversation with him out on the sidewalk.

Her heart pounded as she left the relative safety of her porch, her mind racing with thoughts of their month apart. She had hoped seeing him would bring closure to their relationship. But as soon as she saw him standing on the sidewalk in the orange glow of dusk, all of her intentions vanished. The warmth of his voice and the familiarity of his face washed away all other concerns. She threw herself into his arms, holding on tightly, never wanting to let go. He let her hug him, then he gently pulled away. The subtle movement reminded her once more that a chasm of distance still gaped between them.

"How have you been?" she began with some trepidation.

Cole stuffed his hands into his pockets. "I'm back home with my mom now that the semester's over. It turns out my dad is living in his girlfriend's beach house near that party you went to at the end of year. He took a lot of money out of the bank accounts and my mom is struggling to pay the bills since she isn't getting any alimony or child support yet. I picked up a summer job to help out," he said, anger and resentment taking him into his head and away from her.

"I'm so sorry to hear that. You're so loyal to your family, it must be hard being in the middle," she said, reaching into his heart. It killed him to hate his own dad.

"So what did you want to talk to me about?" he said, brushing past her sympathy, raking his hands through his hair.

"I haven't been doing great myself. My parents left on a long vacation right after graduation. Alex got a nannying gig with a rich family in Europe, and I've basically been on my own, not leaving the house and not really taking care of myself.

"You see after our... ah... talk, I didn't really know how to handle things. I missed a couple of days of school that I couldn't get excused and ended up screwing up my grade in history from a final paper that my teacher wouldn't accept after the absences. My GPA dipped below the contract threshold and I had my admissions to Cal revoked. The letter finally arrived yesterday. It's been the worst few weeks of my life," she said, summarizing her hell with the least emotion possible.

His face changed into a thundercloud as he ripped into her, "Are you seriously going to pin your screwed up grades and future on me? What the hell? As if I don't have enough going on without you dumping your emotional baggage on me."

The truth Cole struggled to face lay in his cowardice; he couldn't bear to see her suffer and felt immeasurably guilty for causing her pain. His powerlessness to support her and provide what she needed only exacerbated his anger, leading him to redirect blame toward her instead of accepting it himself. Era sensed this turmoil, aware that all he needed to do was *choose* her.

Era stood there, too stunned to speak; the man she loved never addressed her this way. Shock and pain buffeted her from either side.

Gathering her remaining strength, she responded to his

cruel accusation. "No, I'm not trying to pin anything on you. That's not at all why I wanted to see you. When we spoke last, you said you needed time to sort through what's going on in your life, and I get that. I know I lashed out at you and for that I'm so sorry. Hearing that you wanted to take a break—really hurt me. I didn't see it coming because I love you and holding that watch, you were telling me you loved me too. I still love you. You said you needed time, but the way we left things felt pretty final. Should I wait for you?"

That was Era's Gift. She could look past her own emotions and cut right to the heart of the matter. Cole might still love her, but the more important question remained. Would he allow her to sacrifice for him during his own dark time? She knew he loved her, more than he could show, and it killed him down to his marrow to think of a future without her, or of her with another guy. So the question came down to which side he would let triumph, mercy or despair.

Once again, despair won. The Gift saw it before he spoke and Era felt the riptide of sorrow pull her out to sea. His words had left the window of hope cracked open by a sliver. Now he shut it, letting them both return to their misery.

Her deepest fear came to life before her once again. No matter what she did, the people closest to her would always love themselves more than her. Somehow she always ended up as a casualty of other people's mistakes.

"No, don't wait for me. I know I said I needed time; I was trying to let you down easy. I don't need time. We ran our course. It's over." Just like that Cole crushed any surviving hope that Era had for a future together.

She walked straight from the sidewalk in front of her house to the stairs, barely making it to her bed before feeling the lights go out in her mind and slid all the way back through her escape hatch.

CHAPTER 19

THE NEXT MORNING'S run was particularly hot. Every time she slowed down, snippets of Cole's cruel words echoed in her mind—*Don't wait for me*—prompting her to push herself back into a grueling pace. *We ran our course,* she heard as she grunted and forced herself forward again. Finally, during her last sprint, with Christopher puffing beside her, the phrase, *It's over. It's over. It's over,* looped like a broken record, pounding in her head with each burning stomp into the dirt.

Feeling sticky and wilted, she chose not to follow Christopher into the house toward the gym. Instead, she strode over to the turquoise pool, shrugged off her clingy shirt, and dove smoothly into the refreshing embrace of the water. As her face broke through the surface, she heard a satisfying splash—Christopher's form glided beneath the surface. She gave him a good splash in the mouth as he came up for air, joking that he ruined her peaceful swim.

After several good dunks, they jumped onto floating loungers to relax in the morning sun. "Now that you've come back from the dead, I think you might be ready to re-enter the world," Christopher joked, flicking a bit of water onto her stomach. He stared up at the cumulus clouds passing overhead, his hands tucked beneath his damp hair and asked, "I've put together a trip with a few friends to my family's ranch. Will you come with me?"

Her knee-jerk reaction was no. Random friends she didn't know? No thanks. But the fear of him leaving her, even for a short weekend felt too much to bear. She knew she was using Christopher as a crutch but what other option did she have? And anyways, it might be good to change environments, get out of the house for a few days. Get away from the memory of Cole stomping on her heart outside her house and the resulting relapse. He was her safe place now; she didn't trust herself to be alone. She couldn't say yes too easily though, couldn't have him know that she would follow him anywhere.

She probed with caution, "What friends are you bringing? Not Dom and Julian I hope. Those guys are seriously players, and I don't need to hear them bragging about how much they can drink and who they've fought."

"No, not anyone from our school. It's actually a couple of guys from my hockey team, a few of the girlfriends, and friends of the girlfriends—nobody you've met," he said.

"Hockey team? You mean ice hockey?" Era asked in disbelief. Christopher nodded. "So, let me get this straight. You've got an entirely separate group of friends and probably an entire life outside of school that no one knows about. Hmmm….who does that remind me of?" she asked, scooping up another handful of water and throwing it at his face.

He laughed, blocking the water with his hands. "It's no secret. You never asked. The guys on my team drive from all over to the rink because our team is really competitive. It's a travel team so we play in tournaments all over, including Canada. We're state champions three years running."

"Huh," she said, taking in the new information on a guy she thought she had completely pegged. "I did always wonder how you were so fit" –her hand trailing over the line of his pec– "without playing any sports at school."

He grabbed her hand and pulled until her float touched his, "So you'll come?"

"Probably not. I'm still not 100% myself, and I don't know how I'll feel around a group of strangers who all know each other. Tell me about the ranch, the people and what you'll be doing, and maybe I'll reconsider."

"Ok, I promise I'll tell you everything about it... in the car. We've got to leave in an hour and a half at the latest to beat traffic and I bet you'll want to shower before we leave. Rosa already packed your bag—it should be here any minute," he finished with a self-satisfied smirk.

"YOU!" she screamed, this time jumping on top of him, knocking him off his float and into the water. She wanted to give him a good dunk but they had drifted into the shallow end and he had a definitive advantage with his feet planted. He grabbed her around the waist before she could attack him further.

"Sorry sorry! I know it's presumptuous, but it all came together last minute, and truthfully, I don't want to let you out of my sight. You're going to love it, I promise. If not, I'll send you home on the chopper," he chided.

"Chopper! You better be kidding." She shoved him again as he laughed. There was obviously no chopper. "Good one, har har," she mocked and then relented, "Fine, but next time I'm packing my own bag. That's just creepy."

"Alright! Let's make it snappy. I hate sitting in traffic and we have to pick up my friends Christian and Violet on the way."

He handed her a towel as they dripped their way into the house. As promised, her overnight bag sat on the guest room's coffee table. In the bathroom, her toilet kit, a blowdryer, and a tray of amenities had been laid out. *How does this guy communi-*

cate with his help? Telepathy? she thought, impressed and annoyed.

An hour later, she walked downstairs with her bag. He stood in the driveway talking to "Jeeves," and she made a mental note to ask for the creepy guy's name. He wore a black tank top, cargo skater pants, and black converse. Something about his still damp hair, styled in messy waves and black sunglasses did it for her. *This is not a good idea*, she thought, eyeing the way the tank hugged his rippling muscles.

"Era, this is Antoine. Antoine, Era. I thought you two should be properly introduced. If you ever need anything and I'm not around, Antoine's your man," he said as if Era would be sending the man to pick up her dry cleaning.

She smiled warmly at him and shook his hand. He struck her as a man of few words—tall and lanky, with sandy brown hair and a sharply pointed nose. There was a rat-ness to his face, maybe from his beady eyes or the narrow jawline. He looked decidedly French and mid-forties or so. And since he didn't actually speak, the Gift didn't show her anything else about him, leaving it to her imagination to fill in a backstory

Christopher opened the door to his truck for her and helped her in while Antoine loaded the remainder of the bags and gear into the back. His hands felt pleasant as he lifted her gently into the cab even though she could manage the jump on her own.

As he raced down the street, way over the speed limit, Era's house came into view, along with the place where she and Cole had stood outside. When she turned away and saw Christopher's handsome face, a pang of sadness hit her. She wished she could enjoy the moment without thinking about Cole. However, the time had come for brutal honesty. Her heart remained ripped to shreds and even if she felt the stirrings of something with Christopher, he could never be anything more than a rebound. Letting him help her recover was one thing, but leading him on when she knew her heart was still bound to Cole was another.

She should do the right thing for him, for both of them. She should put a stop to any further escalation of their relationship beyond friendship. Her life was messy right now. She needed him as a friend, couldn't afford to lose him to a complication. Like a judge swinging a gavel, she made her choice. She'd enjoy the trip and put back the old boundaries that served her so well with him over the past four years. *Survive to thrive,* she thought.

After settling into the idea of "just friends" again and bored with checking out strangers in the lane to their right, Era turned to Christopher with a playful expression. "Time to uphold your side of the bargain. Tell me *everything.*"

Christopher smiled beneath his glasses. "Sure thing. The Ridgewell Ranch is a land trust my grandfather bought back in the 50s. He wanted it for the water rights since it sits on several natural springs, a small river, and a dam. Since then it's been developed, part of it for ranching cattle, part for the vineyards, part for orchards, and the rest for us."

"Must be pretty big to contain all that," she observed.

"40,000 acres. Big enough for some industry and still plenty left untouched." Era whistled through her teeth at the staggering figure. "The main house where we'll be staying, built by my dad and finished a few years ago, has a pool—necessary since it gets really hot up there. Oh, and there's the BBQ area, which is my favorite. It's a little ways from the main house, featuring a Santa Maria grill and a fire pit, giving you the feeling of being outdoors without actually being far from anything."

"Ok, so big piece of land, big house, pool, and a place for rich people to play pretend camping, but what will we be doing out there?" Era butted in, making Christopher laugh again.

"There's lots to do. We have ATVs to ride and trails that go all over the entire ranch. We can go horseback riding if the group is up for it. There are a few really cool places to swim in the creek and rock jump. We can visit the vineyard. And we shoot guns–"

"Guns? You never said anything about guns? I don't know any of your friends and you think I'm going to be comfortable letting them shoot guns around me?" she asked, realizing she had been hasty in accepting the invitation before getting the details.

"I get it if you're not comfortable with guns, but let me explain. Shooting isn't some reckless redneck activity. The guys on my team are excellent shots; they know the ranch and how to handle firearms safely. We use guns on the property to protect livestock. Beyond basic safety, shooting has historically represented a privileged right of the upper class for centuries. Just think about Mr. Bingley and Mr. Darcy in your Jane Austen novels—they shot and hunted for sport because they were part of the landed gentry. Only those with land could hunt on their own property without the risk of poaching. Being a good shot was a mark of pedigree. Plus, it's really fun. Wait until you feel the thrill of hitting your first clay pigeon; it's a rush."

She had never really thought of guns and the connection either to the aristocracy or to the practical nature of running a ranch. In either case, she didn't have much experience with them and decided to keep an open mind. And she didn't exactly want to be mauled by a bear or a mountain lion or whatever else they were protecting the livestock from. She shuddered but didn't ask for the details.

"I'm not 100% sold on the idea. We'll see how it goes once I meet your friends I guess. Who exactly is going again and where is everyone sleeping?" she asked, her mind turning to more pressing social concerns.

"The house has five bedrooms. I stay in the Master. Christian and Violet will be in the second largest room because Christian's my boy. Benedict, he goes by Bene, and Celeste are another couple, they'll be in the third room. Chase is in the fourth room. And you'll be in the bunk room with the girls' friends, Kamila and Monica."

"Oh yay, a sleepover with two complete strangers. Hopefully, nobody snores," she said, leaning towards him and blowing in his ear. He jerked slightly and put a giant palm into her face, crushing her lips.

She nipped at the pad of his hand and he nearly swerved out of the lane with a yelp. "Guess it won't matter since I sleep like the dead anyway…"

"Ha! A joke! Era, you've really come a long way, haven't you?"

"Actually, I don't know how much progress I've really made. Last night I saw Cole and—

"You what—"

"I asked him to come over. Felt like there were some things we needed to discuss."

"And let me guess" —Christopher's hands flexed over the steering wheel, muscles bulging— "he screwed with your head and you're ready to tuck yourself in for an endless night."

"Yes, I mean, no. He did say some really horrible stuff to me. I can't lie about that and of course I'm kind of rattled. I did go straight to bed after he left but then I got up and ran with you," she said, not making as much sense as she hoped.

Christopher seethed with anger. "I still can't believe you saw him. He's not good for you. Look at what having him in your life has done to you. Even this morning! I thought you were going to drop after those sprints! Now I see where the motivation came from…" He took his eyes off the road for more seconds than Era was comfortable with.

"Just watch where you're going," she said, her hands motioning to the lane as he drifted right.

"You've barely started to get better and I won't sugarcoat it— you were in a scary state when I found you. You need to focus on taking care of yourself right now and forget about him," he rasped, his voice a mix of pain and fury.

Era realized then that simply deciding that she and Christopher should go back to being friends was not enough. She needed to make the line more clear.

She stared out of the passenger window, watching the road signs blur into a watercolor streak of whites and yellows. "You're right," she said, hesitating as she sculpted each word with care. "I need to focus on myself, on getting better. And... that's actually something I wanted to talk to you about."

Christopher's grip on the wheel relaxed slightly, but his jaw remained set, his profile betraying the tension within. "What is it?"

The neighborhoods zipped by as Era drew in a deep breath that filled the car with her anxiety. "About that night... in your room... it was a mistake." The words landed heavily between them, like stones into still water.

Christopher's jaw jerked toward her for just a split second, but he never took his eyes off the road. "A mistake?" There was a tremble in his voice that he couldn't quite disguise.

"Yes," Era continued, her heart pounding against her rib cage. "I'm... I'm too broken to start something new. And I don't want our friendship to change because of one night."

He tried to laugh it off, but there was no humor in it—just a cracked attempt at preserving some dignity. "That happened a while ago now. I haven't made a move have I?"

"No, and I really appreciate that. You've helped me a lot, were there for me when literally no one else was. But now that I'm getting better, I feel... something happening." The truth was mortifying. She felt so embarrassed, admitting her part in it while calling him out like this when he had been the picture of self-restraint. Still, he was the one that confessed his feelings for her at the graduation party. He pulled her back into his bed and kissed her until she saw stars.

"Sure, I get it. Friends," Christopher said in a tone that was meant to be casual but came off as brittle.

Era nodded, though she knew he wasn't looking at her. "I'm sorry I've waffled on you so much," she whispered. "But I don't want either of us to get hurt."

Just then, they pulled into the driveway of a stunning white Craftsman, where a cute couple—presumably Christian and Violet—sat on the porch with their bags. Their conversation screeched to a stop as Christopher jumped out of the truck to greet his friend with a high five, hugging the girl and grabbing their bags. Era smiled during the polite introductions but couldn't help noticing the twitch in Christopher's jaw.

CHAPTER 20

Two and a half hours stretched on as the previous conversation lingered, unacknowledged, between Christopher and Era. She did her best to ignore the waves of vexation radiating from him, instead focusing on getting acquainted with the new couple. Christian, a fellow defenseman on the first line with Christopher, sported a burly frame and soft brown eyes under a heavy brow. The boys acted more like brothers than friends.

Violet, on the other hand, exuded sweetness, though her reserved nature hinted at a more introspective personality. Her medium brown skin, hair, and eyes, were tied together by a natural beauty, a petite frame, and a beaming white smile. Coming from a family of doctors, she aspired to follow in their footsteps and become an anesthesiologist. Both she and Christian planned to attend Cal University together in the fall. Era saw the fleeting image of her and Cole replaced by this happy couple walking together on the campus of her dreams and felt her gut twist.

Violet also played tennis, recreationally not competitively. Alongside that, she enjoyed cooking—an unusual combination of hobbies for an 18-year-old girl. They might as well have been 35 year old soccer moms together.

Era liked them both. Christian was as loyal as a golden retriever and fierce when he needed to be. Violet was honest and humble and though tending to be a bit sensitive, had not a jealous or selfish bone in her body. The Gift could be extremely helpful in breaking into new circles and knowing with whom to align.

At long last, the truck veered off the road and through a grand wrought iron gate. Era coughed as dust billowed up from the oversized tires, prompting Christopher to roll up the windows. They bumped along a private dirt road leading to the Ridgewell ranch. Era smiled as the main "house" came into view.

The sprawling manor featured two stories and sat a hundred yards from the tree line. On one side, a gigantic porch wrapped around, disappearing from view, while on the other side, a pool overlooked the sunset behind the hills, serving as a stunning focal point for the back of the house. A massive outdoor living room attached to the rear boasted enough space for twenty or more guests to lounge or dine al fresco in the shade, beneath large fans that turned lazily overhead.

White climbing roses trailed along the porches, and bursts of tawny-colored dahlias dotted the meticulously manicured land-scaping. Era's fingers itched to cut the blooms and arrange them for the table.

They were the first ones to arrive, and Christopher instructed everyone to find their rooms and meet by the pool. She envisioned a cramped, childlike space when he referred to her accommodations as a "bunk room," but she discovered the area to be surprisingly lux. The bunks, set into three walls, resembled mini capsules. Each could easily pass for a solid wooden micro-apartment, complete with built-in storage, a personal item shelf, a reading light, and curtains for privacy.

In the center of the room, two sofas faced each other around a coffee table. The dahlias she admired outside were arranged simply in a vase on the table, next to a basket of snacks. Attached to the bunk room, an expansive bathroom featured four sinks, vanities, a walk-in closet, two Japanese toilet rooms, and a private steam shower.

Era unpacked her bag anxiously, hoping that Rosa had known her business. In fact, Rosa had done a better job than Era could have managed herself, especially without knowing all the planned activities or having been there before. She would need to write her a thank you note. She decided on the royal blue bikini, tortoise sunglasses, and a flowing white kimono before stepping out to explore the house.

The bunk room occupied the upstairs alongside the master suite and two additional bedrooms. A large bonus room awaited them, featuring a corner set up for live music with guitars, a drum set, a keyboard, and a microphone. The space also boasted a massive TV, cozy couches, and a wall adorned with artfully displayed gaming consoles

Downstairs, however, revealed an unbelievable space. The living room featured the largest sectional Era had ever seen, possibly accompanied by the biggest TV she'd encountered in a private residence. A quick peek beyond the living room revealed a cozy card and game room, a plush forest green space complete with a pool table and shuffleboard. Adjacent to that, a gym caught her eye, showcasing what appeared to be a sauna door at the back.

Era ran her hand along the soft fibers of the massive couch, past a modern fireplace done with smooth stucco and pitted stone, and stepped into the double-height kitchen. Sunlight streamed through large windows above, filling the room with warmth. The ceiling, beautifully paneled with wood, featured heavy reclaimed timber framing that accentuated the tall space.

Definitely elevated rustic, she thought, admiring the mix of modern and mid-century furniture. She loved how each angle of the house offered a different view: the tree line, the golden hills further in the distance, a small creek that wound through a field. Era imagined Christopher's mother pouring over each detail in every room—the candlesticks on the breakfast banquette table, the unique fixtures—thinking of ways to ensure her guests felt both comfortable and welcomed, while also providing an escape into this quiet country luxury.

Behind the primary kitchen lay a Butler's kitchen that twisted in several directions. Multiple dishwashers, appliance garages, coffee station, and even a walk-in pantry with a hidden alcove for a blender created a seamless space for making smoothies without disturbing the guests. The setup suggested that a significant staff must operate here when the house was fully occupied. Just as she absorbed this impressive sight, she nearly collided with a woman unloading glasses from the dishwasher into the storage pantry.

Heading back through the kitchen, she peeked around the corner to see another bedroom, an office, and a theater. How fun! Perhaps there was more but she wanted to get out to the pool. She fought back against the excitement of having this place as her fully staffed oasis.

As Era stepped through the doors, a ripple of giddiness surged through her, only to be extinguished at the sight of Christopher in the pool. He playfully bantered with a hatefully attractive blonde, her flirtatious laughter ringing out like music. Sunlight danced on the water, highlighting her sparkling hazel eyes as she reached for him, her voluptuous figure bobbing enticingly above the surface. Era winced at the bite of envy as she noticed the girl looked a lot like her—only with bigger boobs.

Scanning the pool deck, she searched for Christian or Violet, but her gaze landed on a newcomer lounging on a chaise, an empty seat beside him. Perfect.

She strutted up to him, flashing a confident smile as she

flicked the rolled towel down over the cushion. Now comfortably situated, she turned to face him and found herself starstruck. He sported a light golden tan, jet-black hair, and a toned, slender frame reminiscent of a surfer—*Definitely a forward,* she thought.

When he lifted his sunglasses to meet her stare, his eyes surprised her with their shocking blue hue, nearly as bright as the pool itself. When he smiled, equally delighted to find a stunning girl had taken up residence beside him, it felt as if the rest of him faded away, leaving only the brilliant white teeth of a Cheshire cat. Era was a sucker for a smile like that. Absolutely. Smoking. Hot.

Finally, he broke the silence between them, "Hi there, I'm Chase."

"Are all Christopher's friends hot? Who knew ice hockey was such a gold mine?" she mused aloud without embarrassment, calling out his clear genetic advantage from the start to lessen its power. "I'm Era."

He chuckled and beamed at her as if she had just told the funniest joke. Over in the pool, Era caught the turn of a head. Christopher definitely noticed. "How do you know the girls? I've never seen you out with them before?" he asked, intrigued.

"Oh I only just met Violet on the ride up. I'm a friend of Christopher's," she corrected.

"I see. Got it. You came up with Christopher," he repeated, connecting dots which were not there, not really.

Feeling the need to set the record straight she clarified, "We're neighbors, been friends since freshman year at Emerald Prep. And he's been helping me through a rough breakup... as my personal trainer."

The Gift pulsed with stars around him. *Opportunist,* it flashed. "Oh. I'm sorry to hear that," he said.

Chase wasn't the least bit sorry to hear that Era was single and Christopher was in the friend zone. He sensed this girl had something special about her and he wasn't about to withdraw from the game simply because his friend was the host. He had his own vacation houses to boast of even if they weren't quite as impressive as the Ridgewell Ranch. Their team was peppered with old money, though no one in their circle could best the Ridgewells for wealth.

Chase decided to pull out his full charm on this girl. He wanted her to think him gentlemanly, so he went inside to bring out a tray of glasses and a pitcher of mojitos. The chef had already been prepping them of course. Then he began stoking their lightning fast intimacy by retelling hilarious and oftentimes embarrassing stories of the team on the road.

Era, fully aware that this fox was calculated down to the last word, didn't care. He was handsome and funny, making her practically snort with laughter as he recounted the time Christopher's luggage went missing. He described how he knocked on door after door at the hotel, desperately seeking a pair of underwear from his teammates. To his dismay, no one would help him; instead, they tossed their dirty pairs into the hallway while laughing, which only fueled his frustration. In a fit of exasperation, he ordered a pack of Hanes on Instacart, a move that left Era in stitches.

She enjoyed herself enough to forget how seeing Christopher with that girl in the pool had made her feel like an interchangeable blonde. At this point, any further rejection felt unbearable, so she embraced the escape that the lighthearted conversation with this stranger offered.

"You guys enjoying the mojitos?" a startlingly close voice asked. Christopher stood behind her, sizing up the scene.

Era flipped away from Chase to face him, shielding her eyes from the sun. "We are. I'm already having more fun than I expected. Thanks again for inviting me." She intended the sentiment to sound genuine, but it came off as flippant.

"Glad to hear it," he said with his trademark courtesy. "I set up a tasting for us at the vineyard at 6, followed by dinner there." With that, he headed into the house, leaving Era to take his cue to get ready. She glanced at her phone and saw it was already 5 p.m.

"Hey while you have your phone out, send me your Snap," Chase said, wiggling his phone.

"It's @EraInBloom," she said, then saw her notifications light up thirty seconds later as she walked up the stairs. He sent a selfie from the lounge chair with kissy lips, real original. She would have to be careful with this peacock.

In the bunk room, Era had the pleasure of meeting Kamila and Monica just finishing their hair showers. Kamila greeted her as she stood in front of the 40 pieces of makeup and 30 brushes strewn across the vanity. Surfacey introductions concluded, Era jumped in the shower. After an afternoon of sun and mojitos, she didn't plan to do much about her appearance, but the contour crew insisted she get dolled up with them. She ended up with a full face of makeup and big waves in her hair. And while she didn't begrudge letting the other girls set the tone with their tight bodycon dresses, she drew the line at the platform wedges, opting for more sensible cowboy boots and a flowy babydoll dress.

During the impromptu GRWM (Get Ready With Me) video, which yes, Kamila filmed for her social profile, Era gained insights into the hierarchy among the group. Monica, a friend of Violet, appeared to be a typical insecure girl, harboring a crush on Chase, who showed no interest in her. Meanwhile, Kamila, a friend of Celeste, made some not-so-subtle comments about Christopher's yacht. It didn't take a genius to size her up as a golddigger. Of course, the Gift confirmed it with every third statement, showing garish gold hallows around her hands.

She excused herself from the foppery and stepped outside to explore the grounds. Enjoying the moment, she inhaled the musky perfume of the roses and savored the satisfying crunch of gravel beneath her boots. Turning a corner, she spotted Christopher at an outbuilding, presumably the garage, and made her way over to him. He rummaged for the keys to a remarkably styled golf cart, equipped with off-road tires and Napa leather seats across three rows.

Somehow, all nine of them managed to cram into a single golf cart, and off they sped down a tree-lined dirt road into the hills. The wind whipped through Era's hair, brushing against Chase's face beside her as they navigated the winding path. After several minutes, the hilly terrain opened up into a small valley, surrounded on all sides by vineyards that wrapped around the protected hidden meadow.

Kamila gasped and placed a hand on Christopher's arm to showcase her appreciation, her stack of David Yurman and Cartier Love bracelets jangling annoyingly. Of course, she had rushed to squeeze in next to the driver's seat. Yet Era found she didn't mind it now; the picturesque scenery surrounding them was too stunning to be tainted by thoughts of an imagined rival. If Christopher wanted her, she could have him—after all, he remained just a friend to her. She had no claim on him, she reminded herself, choosing to focus on the beauty of the moment instead.

The wine tasting unfolded like a magical experience. The sommelier poured glasses of white, red, and rosé, each glass corresponding to a specific hill of grapevines directly in their view. The tasting included a fantastic array of cow, sheep, and goat cheeses, accompanied by jams from the orchards and even local honey collected from the ranch. Era had never experienced eating and drinking the land until that evening. Even the bottled mineral water came from a natural spring on the property, adding to the exquisite experience.

After the tasting, a long rustic table appeared beneath string lights, nestled between the towering oaks. Dinner featured succulent steak and fresh vegetables, alongside homemade sourdough and berries topped with whipped cream. Nearly everything on the table hailed from the ranch or its surroundings, enhancing the ranch-to-table experience.

Christopher stuck mainly to his friends, which normally wouldn't bother her, but she'd be lying if she didn't admit that the lack of interest wasn't a little off-putting after spending so many days at the center of his undivided attention. Thankfully, Chase had a never-ending stream of stories. He'd even been to a few of the same French ski spots she liked which made for effortless conversation, even if he did lean in a little too close and touch her on the shoulder too often.

At the conclusion of the delightful evening, Christopher herded them back onto the cart and spun off at a harrowing speed back down the dirt path in near total darkness. Raucous laughter and chatter filled the night air from spending several hours dedicated to drinking and sitting around.

Era felt only a twinge of guilt at drinking since she had kept her promise to herself, not to drink alone, in her house. She thought she could keep herself under control even with her head buzzing pleasantly after the stout serving of Port she finished just before climbing onto the back of the cart, Chase beside her once again.

Back at the house, the gang decided to transport the party upstairs to the game room. Someone announced a round of karaoke on the Xbox was in order along with a round of shots. Kamila and Celeste kicked things off by screeching out a cheesy rendition of *Girls Just Wanna Have Fun*. Celeste swung her red hair around more than she actually sang. Next, Christian tried his hand at some old school rap. He couldn't quite keep up with the tempo but he knew the words, not terrible.

While Christian stumbled his way through some of the faster sections of the song, Chase leaned over and spoke softly into her ear. "You and I are up next. I was thinking– '*Rewrite the Stars*' —Zac Efron and Zendaya." Usually, she would have argued but liquid courage flowed through her veins and she actually knew the song, *really* well, as in she sang it in the shower regularly.

The rest of the intoxicated group was not ready for what was about to hit them. By the second line out of Chase's mouth, three people in the group had already whipped out their phones to record them. Chase had unbelievable tone and range. He could even make his voice sound just like Zac's. When her part came, Era's voice soared. She saw Christopher's awestruck expression as she sang and couldn't tear her eyes away from his as the song carried her away.

"It feels impossible. Is it impossible? Say that it's possible," she sang, reaching to him with a longing only the song's lyrics could unlock in her. Her harmonies melded with Chase's voice, transporting the small crowd to their Broadway debut.

By the end, everyone stood and hooted for them, clapping Chase on the back and high fiving Era. Feeling a bit light-headed from the unexpected emotion and the booze, she excused herself to get some air. Chase trailed her down the stairs, asking if she wanted to sit on the patio outside with him.

She grabbed a hard seltzer from the bar on her way out and followed Chase to a conversation set nestled around the corner of the deck, one she hadn't noticed earlier since it was tucked away from the pool area. The space offered a welcome respite of privacy, and a cool breeze—exactly what she craved in that moment.

Taking a long swig from the bubbly can that burned the back of her throat, she sighed and let her head fall all the way back onto the cushions. "Wow, you're amazing. Have you always been able to sing like that?" she asked, noticing the brightness of the stars above them.

"No, you're amazing. I had a feeling about you, the moment you threw down next to me without even a hello. I can see why

Christopher is working so hard for you," he confessed without exaggeration.

Era shifted on the sofa but didn't take her eyes off the stars nor acknowledge the compliment. "He's not working all that hard. He's barely spoken to me since we got here and he looks a little distracted by other possibilities, doesn't he?" she pointed out without emotion.

"He's an idiot if he's going to pass you over for that social ladder-climbing gold digger," Chase scoffed.

"I knew it!" Era said, raising her can in triumph and chugging the can to the bottom.

Chase paused to laugh at the gesture and then continued, "You're worth ten of her. I haven't met anyone like you before and I wouldn't let you slip through my fingers. You and I" —he got up from his chair and moved next to her on the loveseat— "could be great together. You just need a little help getting over whatever his name was. I can help you forget about him."

His hand reached out, tucking a stray strand of hair behind her ear, his hand lingering on her neck. Chase glanced down at her lips and dipped towards her until she could smell the trace of mint on his warm breath. Perhaps her reaction, a beat too slow after drinking so much, made him think that she wanted to be kissed. But as he tried to close the last few inches between them, she pulled back slightly, looking quizzically into his face. That's when she saw his eyes dart toward an entrance that had escaped Era's notice—French doors leading somewhere obvious.

A rush of adrenaline cut through her buzz, and everything became crystal clear. He had lured her outside to the private entrance of his room, a clever way to sneak her in and out without anyone in the house seeing!

Just then, Era spotted Christopher's frame outlined by the pool lights behind him. His shock and anger at finding them together in the dark, Chase's hand still touching her neck, were unmistakable. Searching for her own escape, she stood up too quickly and stumbled directly into Christopher's arms.

He made a comment to Chase about his guest being over-served and supported her the rest of the way to the bunk room. She had drank way more than she had meant to and the last fizzy cocktail sent her over the edge. It felt good to have his strong arm supporting her up the stairs.

She slumped down on the bunk room couch and looked up at him with slits for eyes. "Can you take off my boots?" Her lips puckered and beckoned to him.

Shaking his head and sighing, he knelt down in front of her to oblige.

"What made you come looking for me anyway? Weren't you busy entertaining your new blonde?" The unkind words popped out of Era's mouth like so much bottled truth. The alcohol stirred her emotions and flattened her walls.

"You've got to be kidding me? You have to know that I am not interested in Kamila. Why would I bring you here if I was?" he asked, the vulnerability of his admission to liking Era, blunting the stab of her planned retort, especially after their talk.

"Oh, well you've barely spoken to me and she is pretty. I thought that after our conversation you were just moving on. Really fast," Era said, her voice small.

Christopher rolled his eyes and yanked off a boot, "I'll admit I didn't take hearing that you saw Cole well. You can imagine why. And us being friends? Well, I'm pretty used to it at this point, even if you outed yourself when you told me you felt something. But what's going on with you and Chase? It looked like he was about to take you into his room when I found you."

"I know you don't *really* like Kamila. Seeing you in the pool with my lookalike was more than I could handle. So much rejection..." she said, losing her train of thought with the delicious relief as he pulled off the second boot.

"And Chase?" he asked again.

"Oh yeah, I figured out what he was trying to pull right when you showed up. Trust me, no way in hell was I going in his room—the crafty devil," she said, then yawned, "I'm so tired, can we finish this tomorrow? Can you take off my socks too?" she smiled, sleepiness tugging at her eyes. He peeled them off her and pulled her up from the sofa and into an embrace good night which lingered longer than a friendly hug.

"You have no competition. Remember that okay?" Christopher spoke into her ear. This man even understood her double standards. She wanted to be "just friends" and somehow keep him all to herself, and he got that. Era couldn't help but pull him a little closer when he said that to thank him for calming her insecurities. His eyes were glinting in the soft light and her body thrummed with energy at being so close. She laid her head on his chest for a second before he pulled away and left her in the bunk room.

As her head rested on the pillow, she replayed Chase's words and Christopher's rescue in her mind when the light flicked on. Even with the privacy curtains pulled shut, the brightness offended her tired eyes. Someone rustled around and Era squinted through the curtain to see Kamila, who at long last, shut off the overhead lights, only to flick on the one in the bathroom before going in and shutting the door with a creak then a slam.

She could have overlooked it if the light intrusion stopped there, but Kamila proceeded to come in and out of the bathroom multiple times to retrieve forgotten items from her bag. She bustled about the bathroom for at least half an hour, turning the faucet on and off, generally making a lot of noise. Then, Monica finally made her way back into the room as Kamila finished and took her sweet time rummaging around the room as well.

Era barely kept herself from screaming at them. Needless to

say, she didn't sleep well and woke up feeling frayed, toxic, and with a raging headache. Knowing she had no Advil in her kit, but that Christopher always kept his well stocked, she tip-toed her way over to the Master to try and swipe a few of his. She didn't seem to wake him when she opened the door, her hands skillfully releasing the knob lightly so as not to make a sound. In the bathroom, she unzipped his Louis Vuitton travel bag and found the tiny Advil bottle, picking it up in the palms of her hands to muffle the sound and began to slink back out.

This time her luck ran out. "Can I help you?" a raspy voice called out. Christopher rolled towards her and gave her an accusing look.

"Rosa didn't pack me any Advil and I really need some" — she held up the bottle as if showcasing Exhibit A of her evidence — "that and water," she finished, hurrying towards the door.

"Here, I have an extra bottle of Fiji," he said, motioning towards the side table of the bed and grabbing his phone to send a message. "You're killing me with this wakeup call. It's 8 a.m. and I didn't go to bed until 3. The guys and I started a game of poker after I put you to bed... I mean you went to bed."

It was too awkward to refuse so Era walked over to the bed for the water. She stood bickering with him for a minute about how he did not "put her to bed."

"I didn't get any sleep either. I was trying and Kamila came in and started her 13 step skincare routine or something in the bathroom, flicking the light on and off. She took forever! And when she finished torturing me with her absurd lightshow, Monica came in and started banging around. Also, Kamila talks in her sleep in case you wanted to know. So that was fun," she said, realizing they had been chatting for a while and she should probably let him get up to use the bathroom.

As if on cue, Era heard a knock and Christopher called to someone opening the door. He then jumped up to use the bathroom and brush his teeth while the ranch chef brought in coffee service, for two. *This guy is unbelievable,* she thought, *he opens his eyes and starts commanding the help.*

The chef smiled, flashing broad teeth without judgement as he set the coffee tray on the bed. On it sat a large insulated french press, two beautiful rustic mugs, Laguiole spoons, sugar, cream, and two almond croissants. "Good morning, sir. Would you like anything else?" the chef asked Christopher as he returned.

"No, this is perfect. Thank you Charles," Christopher said with sincere gratitude. When they were alone once more, he got back into bed, and looking up at Era casually said, "You'll have coffee with me won't you?"

She couldn't help but look past his CEO-in-training tendencies of ignoring boundaries, expecting his command to be obeyed without debate, and bursts of charisma. She could see he had no immediate bad intentions. Plus, her head pounded— Advil and coffee would do the trick. She looked at the croissants and nearly salivated they were so beautiful. "Cream until you see it hit the top, and no sugar please," she said as she plopped down on the bed.

Era felt like garbage, but truthfully, laying in bed with Christopher drinking coffee while the rest of the house slept quietly was kind of dreamy. Or maybe she was still a little buzzed from getting almost drunk the day before. In either case, they were bantering for three quarters of an hour before the thought hit her, *This could be us. This could be what 'us' is like.* She pushed the thought away, remembering her solemn decision to keep him as a friend, no matter what fleeting thoughts or emotions came flying her way. Her situation hadn't changed at all.

"What were you thinking about just then?" he interrupted her thoughts, "Your face changed. What were you thinking about?" he repeated.

Damn this guy is too perceptive for his own good, she thought, impressed he had caught the minute lapse in her facade. "I was thinking how good sitting here with you like this is and how cute your little Louis Vuitton toiletry bag was in the bathroom," she replied, sticking as close to the truth as she could and then lobbing a spike of highly effective misdirection at him.

"What!? It was a gift someone gave my Dad that he handed down to me. I did *not* buy it," he defended, tossing a pillow and nearly spilling her coffee. "We are good together though, aren't we?" he continued, his smoldering eyes latching onto the more important half of her statement. She saw the air crackle around him as the Gift roared to life, showing her his vision of them, naked together in that moment and with his arm around her protectively in the distant future.

Era wanted that present and that future despite knowing she was too broken to have either. "So good," she said as she leaned toward him and gave him a tight squeeze, tucking her face into the side of his neck before standing up and heading back to the bunk room for her clothes and a shower.

CHAPTER 21

A BELL RANG DOWNSTAIRS. The rooms stirred with noise, doors opening and closing. The Ranch crew gathered downstairs for a spectacular breakfast. Platters were laid out with scrambled eggs mixed with veggies, freshly made almond croissants, and a sliced tropical fruit salad of pineapples, kiwis, mango, dragon fruit, and watermelon.

"Thanks Charles. Yeah thanks Charles," the group repeated as they scooped heaps of fruit and eggs onto their plates. Hanging out with Christopher was a delicious affair.

During breakfast Christopher gave a little safety meeting to the group about the day's itinerary. "So they're bringing around the ATVs now. We'll cut East first and then circle around. Make sure to watch out for any big ruts and the trail does get tight in a few places. It's going to be fun but don't push it too hard. Oh and Kamila, you're going to want closed-toed shoes," he said, motioning down at her delicate leather sandals disapprovingly.

"We'll have lunch at the swim spot and then head back. Dinner is out at the grill. We'll take the guns down there with us and shoot for about an hour and half before dinner at 6."

"Alright! Let's see who can catch air on those woompties,"

Christian hooted, ready to ignore everything Christopher just said. They headed towards the garage where the ATVs beckoned. Everyone was pumped up for the day's activities and itching to get out there, despite the earlyish hour and the all-around hangovers.

"Get my back for me?" Era asked, turning around in front of Christopher and lifting up her hair.

"I'm surprised you don't have it slathered all over already," he teased, "But the sun is really strong out here so it's a good call." Christopher squeezed the lotion from the bottle and then tugged at Era's bathing suit straps, sliding his big hands all the way underneath. How thorough. Next he lifted her tank and did her lower back even though it would be a while before she took it off to swim.

"I don't really want to get my hands oily, maybe you should finish me off," Era said cheekily, turning around and spreading her arms into a T. Christopher raised an eyebrow before squeezing a generous dollop into his hand and then painting his fingers across her chest and arms. Era's tank dipped low but not quite low enough so Christopher pushed the straps off her shoulders. His hand slipped down her bare but modest cleavage, sliding his fingers just under the fabric of her bikini top to make sure she was protected even if things slid around a bit.

He pushed her tank up now and continued working his way down her body, strong palms massaging her stomach. Unsure how far he would take it, Era decided to keep quiet and look away unaffectedly while he finished her stomach and then began unbuttoning her shorts.

She bit back a smile but didn't look at him when her shorts hit the ground and he used his hand to part her legs slightly. She caught Chase's greedy eyes staring at her from a distance where Monica sprayed his back. She gave him a little nod, as if to say she noticed the extra attention he received.

Just then Christopher's hands glided up the inside of her legs and a little gasp escaped her mouth. "Oops sorry," Christopher said.

"No worries, you just caught a ticklish spot, that's all,"

"Do you want me to do the back?" he asked.

"Might as well," she squeaked and Christopher moved behind her, massaging sunscreen over the bottom of her full round cheeks and down her legs. He definitely put some extra love into rubbing it all the way in. Chase's mouth dropped into an "O"'

Of course, Era ended up getting her hands greasy anyway since Christopher insisted on her reciprocating. She enjoyed the application, spending a moment too long on the lines that ran down the side of his abs into his shorts and had a little fun tugging his shorts down in the back and getting a good look at the round top of his bum. Somehow it had escaped her that he had a seriously incredible backside, maybe even better than her own! Era might not have been a "butt girl" but she couldn't help enjoying the sturdy shapeliness under her hands. "Mmm hockey," she joked, giving him a good pinch.

"Ok, friend," he said, grabbing her wrist.

"What? Friends can appreciate each other's bums." The flirty friendship damn started showing its cracks.

She hated rubbing sunscreen onto hairy legs but obliged on that front too. And wowza did he have thick thighs.

Holy Hockey, she thought, smearing the lotion around them as he clenched against the tickle, making sure to give him a squeeze above the knees to break the tension and nearly got kneed in the face. Afterwards, she went inside to wash her hands and found Chase, mixing a protein shaker.

"If you need to reapply, I'm your man," he said, winking at her as he flexed the arm holding the shaker.

"Shameless," she replied, flicking her wet hands at him rather than using a towel. Era knew not to trust him, but she couldn't help her attraction to his confidence.

The chef tied up a cooler to one of the ATVs, presumably their lunch when Christopher called her over. "Do you want to ride with me or solo?" he asked.

"I've seen enough ATV accidents while traveling to know that these things are dangerous. I've also never seen most of your ranch. The only way I'm getting on one of those, is if it's with you," Era said, watching Kamila's face fall with disappointment beside her.

Monica piped up from behind him, "I'm with Chase. No way I'm going alone either."

"Alright, Kamila, that means you're our solo rider today. You'll be on the one with the lunch cooler, over there," Christopher said without deliberation. They strapped on their helmets and were off in a kick of dust and exhaust towards the larger hills to the East.

The morning was warm but not yet hot. Wind blew exhilaratingly across Era's face as they flew through the meadow, first in the line of vehicles. She had to keep her body pressed to Christopher's to prevent her helmet from bouncing off his back when they hit a bump. She began to embrace the feeling of safety she felt near him, winding her arms around him and grasping the front of his shoulders. Even though the ATV's engine made for a noisy ride, she couldn't help but relish the peaceful stillness within her and the feeling of closeness beyond proximity to Christopher.

What a beautiful piece of land they have, she thought as she took in the passing landscape. She imagined Christopher, the steward of everything as far as the eye could see and beyond. It was truly a magnificent place, destined for an incredible owner.

They wound through the hills, the path narrowing and the thickets of chaparral creeping up until it closed into a tunnel overhead. The shade provided a welcome respite from the baking sun above and the heat of the engine below. An encroachment of rock at the top of a tight squeeze followed by a particularly washed out section of hill reaffirmed Era's decision to ride with Christopher who took them down the bumpy decline with expert finesse. He circled back at the bottom to guide his friends down and warn them to slow down.

While waiting for the others to make their way down, Christopher stretched his aching hands, letting them rest on top of Era's thighs. As Kamila pulled up the rear of their caravan, she caught sight of Christopher's hands and took her eyes off the outcropping. Her vehicle caught the rut of the washboard and tilted onto two wheels, causing a jagged protrusion of granite to slice into her leg.

Kamila yelped as the ATV rocked downwards, then bounced her like a ragdoll, her teeth clacking as she went straight through the washboard instead of picking a line to traverse across it. Era watched Kamila look down in horror, at the bright red running from her leg down into her sock, and then back up to Christopher, expecting him to rush to her. Christopher dismounted and approached to inspect the damage, but Christian and Violet beat him there with the first aid kit.

"Don't worry," Violet said, jumping into action immediately with the kit in her hands. "I'm not a doctor yet but I can fix you right up. Christian, give me a water bottle." Within a few minutes, Violet had the cut disinfected and bandaged up. It wasn't deep but it was long.

Era's Gift could see Kamila's emotions going haywire as she bounced from fear, to worry, to vanity about the cut, to anger that Christopher didn't seem all that alarmed, to gratitude that Violet believed it wouldn't scar, and back to vanity once more about wearing a bandage for the rest of the trip. Era shoved her hand to her mouth to keep herself from smiling and turned away to retrieve her water bottle.

Monica graciously switched with Kamila so she could ride with Chase and they were off once again. She looked over to see inky undulations dispersing off Kamila towards her—hate. Era enjoyed imagining her as an angry octopus waiting to pop out of her cave.

What a sore loser, Era thought, unconsciously moving away from the disturbance that only she perceived. Kamila didn't understand that what she saw, or thought she saw, between Era and Christopher was just close friendship. She would have to watch out for her. She had been burned too many times by girls to underestimate what jealousy could do.

They cut their way through a grove of walnut trees, the ground pockmarked by an endless field of squirrel burrows and then over a hill thick with red-barked Manzanita trees. At the bottom, a creek chattered through the wood and hushed to fill a delightful prize that beckoned to her sunbaked, wind-whipped face.

A crystal-clear pool, adorned with Scarlet Indian Paintbrush and Pitcher Sage along the margins, sat nestled among large boulders that appeared either driven or placed along its edges. Noble old Live Oaks encircled the pool, spreading their gnarled arms over the water, creating ample shade for canopies of fern fronds to link together and cast an even cooler shadow. The air dipped a full fifteen degrees near the shaded pool compared to the scorching midday sun.

Era peeled herself off Christopher's back, their combined sweat plastering her tank top to his shirt. She relished the stretch of her back as she stepped down onto the soft dirt, her feet and legs still thrumming from the jolting vibrations of the ATV. Within minutes, everyone had dismounted, shedding sweaty garments to leap into the inviting water.

Bene and Christian scoured the water's edge for frogs, returning triumphantly with a giant toad, which they lobbed directly at Kamila, perched on a smooth slab near the pool. She squealed, turning to Christopher with an exaggerated pout, complaining that she didn't deserve to be teased after his "little activity." Christopher swam over to offer her pointers on riding the ATVs, prompting her to insist on riding back with him for safety.

What a crock of crap, she thought.

Not wanting to incur anymore of her wrath than necessary, Era paddled over to Chase, flipping over on her back like a starfish to enjoy the rays of light filtering down through the branches overhead. He rolled to his back beside her, their eyes gazing at the blue sky before he spoke, "Hey I wanted to apologize about last night. I hope you didn't feel pressured or anything. I swear I didn't know you were drunk. You hold your liquor well."

Mildly annoyed at what was quite possibly the weakest apology she'd ever heard, she decided that dwelling on it would spoil the perfect moment.

Era kicked her feet and replied, "I definitely felt like you set me up outside your bedroom, but since nothing happened, let's forget about it."

"I didn't set you up, I swear! Okay, I mean once we were out there, the thought obviously occurred to me, but that's not why I took you there," he whispered, warm light reflecting off his ice blue eyes.

Era's Gift showed her that he was lying, strangely, it was not a lie to her but a lie to himself. He sincerely believed what he said. Likely his intentions were muddled from the abundance of alcohol. She would give him a second chance.

"Anyways," he continued, "You gave me the impression that you and Christopher were just friends–"

"We *are* just friends!" Era responded in a harsh whisper, not wanting to alert anyone to the fact that their conversation had turned the corner into something more serious.

Chase shook his head with an impish grin. "If that's the truth, then I wish I had more hot friends that looked like you who need help rubbing sunscreen on their booty."

Era gasped and splashed him as he ducked under the water to pinch her butt.

"Ow!" she yelped as he got a handful of her left cheek and she felt her heel connect with something. Chase broke the surface with a hand on his jaw where she had given him a sound kick. "Not sorry about that," she huffed indignantly.

"Neither am I," he said, flashing his smile at her like brights from a car in the dark. She couldn't be mad at him, he was handsome enough to get away with almost anything. Unfortunately, he knew it.

Once everyone tired of swimming—of doing flops and flips, and holding their breath for obscene lengths of time under the water, Christopher and Christian set up sheets and laid out the picnic chef Charles had packed for them.

There were cold turkey and avocado sandwiches, mediterranean style pasta salad with olives, feta, and garbanzo beans, and more fresh cut watermelon. *How in the world did this guy make breakfast and lunch for all of us before 9am?* Era thought, impressed with the hiring chops of the Ridgewell family.

Chase and Bene were discussing a past game against their rivals, and the shooting preferences of their star forward. Bene apparently was the goalie which explained his stockier frame and slightly odd personality. Monica, Celeste, and Violet were all talking about a birthday party they were going to together and coordinating outfits for the Catalina Wine Mixer theme. Christian looked for another frog.

Era felt the weight of being an outsider in this circle, and sitting alone without conversation only amplified her fatigue. She laid flat on the cool sheet beneath the luxuriant ferns, closing her eyes to the world around her. The soft rustling of the leaves above and the gentle hum of nature enveloped her, offering a momentary escape from the foreign social dynamics.

Noticing her attempt to sleep on the ground, Christopher announced that they should head back to the house so everyone could grab a nap before shooting. He added that there would be no alcohol until after shooting—a Ridgewell Ranch rule.

The ride back passed quickly. Era rode with Chase while Monica volunteered to be the solo rider in place of Kamila. Meanwhile, Kamila wrapped her arms smugly around Christopher, relishing the attention.

"Ugh, I can't wait to lay my body down. I'm so exhausted after last night," Era complained, hugging onto Chase as they sped through the dust.

"Really? I thought you got to bed earlier than almost anyone else."

Era and Chase rode at the back with good distance until the next rider so she could speak freely. "I went to bed first, but Kamila is the worst roommate. She kept me up forever and then I ended up waking up early with such a bad headache that I had to get up for Advil."

"Sorry to hear that," Chase said, the Gift radiating the hot lie back at her. She knew he was only sorry she hadn't slept in his room and exultant to have an excuse to get her out of the bunk room tonight. Era immediately regretted mentioning it and didn't say anything more, choosing to turn her attention to drinking in the last of the epic views.

As the path continued, several orchards came into view, with mature avocado, lemon, and pomegranate trees filling the air with a heady fragrance that enhanced the unforgettable pleasure of the ride. Giant oaks with splayed fingers stood alone amidst undulating golden meadows where cattle eyed them and horse paths wound through like water finding the path of least resistance. Finally, they found themselves surrounded by blonde hills of grass, already dried after the spring rains.

The cresting sea of golden hills triggered a memory for Era, something just out of reach until there. It materialized, slapping her like a broken branch in the invisible wind. She recalled the golden watch and the words inscribed on it, a red-hot brand on her heart: "I have loved none but you."

She blinked and saw the words, burned charcoal into the grass of the hill. Then his voice, Cole's distinctive low timbre, mocked her with cruel irony, "I don't need time. It's over."

Her stomach dropped, and a wave of nausea gripped her as the main house came into view. This asinine vision gleefully sought to shatter the day's happiness, reminding her that after her visit to fantasy ranch, she would return to her ruined life. Stumbling toward the house, she wanted, needed to sleep, burdened by the weight of more than just a single night's deprivation dragging at her every step.

CHAPTER 22

INSIDE, Era lugged her body, aching with exhaustion and grief back up to her bunk and shut the curtains. She was desperate for the pull of dreams and the dreams were happy to oblige, colors and voices materializing the moment she shut her eyes. So close to the first burst of a dream, a grating voice shattered her vision, pulling her back to a bedraggled consciousness.

Kamila complained loudly, of her ugly cut and her shoe ruined by the blood. "Those are my brand new Golden Goose sneakers. I'm so freaking mad. Monica, can you please go find the cleaning lady and see if they have something that can get this out?" she bossed and then stormed noisily into the bathroom.

Not wanting her only window of rest to be ruined once again by Kamila's rude clamor, Era climbed back down from her bunk to look for another bed elsewhere. *This house is gigantic, I'm sure I can find a quiet couch somewhere,* she thought, beginning her quest.

Bene and Christian were of course, not sleeping, and so were sitting on what would have been the perfect sofa in the game room playing something hockey related on the Playstation. The living room couch was too central and staff or someone else would end up disturbing her there. Downstairs, she nearly resigned herself to a pilates mat in the gym when Chase spotted her creeping around.

"She's on the rampage about her new shoes getting messed up isn't she?" Chase spoke quietly.

"There's no hope for me in that room," she said, totally defeated.

"Well, I'm not tired and can't nap in the middle of the day anyway. It's quiet in this corner of the house. Why don't you sleep in my room?" he asked, as Christopher came around the corner, overhearing the last snippet of conversation.

Christopher froze mid-step. Era waited for him to speak so the Gift would show her what he felt. Shame sprang on her unexpectedly. He'd caught her outside of Chase's room, twice, in less than 24 hours. Still, she was too tired to play petty mind games. She wanted a bed, now.

Turning to Christopher, she acknowledged him briefly, "Oh hi there, Kamila is raging out about her ruined shoes so I am going to crash in Chase's room." She turned to head through the door. "See you at 4."

Before she could take the step, Christopher's iron grip grabbed her arm, spinning her around. "You know you can sleep in my room if you need to. Come on," Christopher said, his insistence finding little resistance from her exhausted state.

"Friends don't let friends sleep in other friend's rooms right?" Era said sleepily as they trudged back up the stairs.

"He's not your friend. And I don't want you in his room. I want you in my room," he replied with bare honesty.

Era gulped, her sleepiness wearing off as a dose of adrenaline hit her bloodstream. "I'd rather be in your room too. Not for that reason, but because I feel so much safer around you than anywhere else. But" —she paused as they stepped through the door of his room and the door clicked shut behind them— "I realized something on the ride back here. This place is so amazing and you're so amazing, but I'm a mess and my life is a mess and—" she choked on a sob with her last word, unable to finish as her brain taunted her with that hateful mantra, *It's over. It's over. It's over.*

"See this is exactly why I wanted you to come in the first place. I know you're still in a bad place," he paused and wrapped his arms around her, "And it's ok that you're still hurting. I won't leave you alone." She sobbed now, and wrapped her arms around his neck as he picked her up and lifted her into his bed.

"You really are overtired and all the alcohol you drank could be making you feel even more depressed. Sleep. I'll come back to wake you up." He kissed her gently on the forehead and left the room. But she was already underwater, the dreams crashing over her by the time the door clicked shut a second time.

Two hours later, Christopher knocked on the door and peeked in to let her know they would be heading down to the "campground" in 30 minutes. Two hours of sleep had refreshed her, and though she couldn't remember the fitful dreams, she caught brief glimpses of faces that melted into one another— Cole, into Christopher, into Chase, into her dad, into Mr. E.

Still, thirty minutes hardly seemed like enough time for a girl to shower and get ready, so she needed to hustle. The thought of using Christopher's shower felt a bit naughty. What if he needed to come in for his toiletry kit? Just as she wrapped herself in a towel and began frantically drying her hair to be ready on time, she heard him knock on the door.

Era jumped into a pair of jeans, boots, and a corseted top that covered her shoulders, providing protection from the butt of the gun. She dabbed on a bit of concealer, tinted brow gel, mascara, and bronzer while her mind drifted back to the branded image in the grass. It was hopeless to try and forget about it.

Sudden horror gripped her as she realized something unsettling: the Gift had always shown her images connected to other people, revealing their truths. It had never displayed random visions, and she feared that such experiences might resemble symptoms of schizophrenia or some form of psychosis. A chill ran through her veins as she heard Christopher's voice cry out, "Time to roll!"

Rejuvenated by her nap but now shaken by the awareness of an incomprehensible shift in either her power or mental stability, Era thought for the first time in a long time of that day so long ago, when the Gift had come to her. She thought she was going crazy then too.

Era moved ponderously through the next fifteen minutes. Christopher remained preoccupied with preparing guns, ammo, transportation, and various other tasks, too engrossed to notice her distracted state.

It was Chase who eventually broke the spell. "Era, Era? Did you take a sleeping pill this afternoon or what? Because you look like you're sleepwalking on Ambien."

His voice interrupted her dazed muddled thoughts, where she had been revisiting past visions in her mind and examining them for clues. "Gross. No, I don't take pills."

"Well you better wake up if you're going to shoot because I wouldn't trust you with a gun looking like this," he said, the honest observation rousing her more effectively than if he had shook her awake.

"You don't need to worry about me."

With that, Christopher pulled her, Kamila and Violet aside. Monica was already an accomplished marksman.

"I know you ladies are all somewhat new to shooting so I'll explain a couple of things to you. Rule number one, keep all the guns pointed down range and never point a gun at anyone, even if you think it's unloaded, and especially when loading the guns.

"Rule number two, always make sure to brace the guns, even the handguns. The shotguns kick hard and the handguns kick too, so pay attention when we show you how to place your hands and where the shotguns sit on your shoulder unless you want a huge bruise tomorrow.

"Three, keep your headphones on the whole time or you're going to be half deaf for the rest of the night."

Christopher put a reassuring arm around Era's shoulders. "You're going to do great. Do you want to try the shotgun first?"

"Sure. Walk me through everything. I've never shot any kind of gun before so don't assume I know anything.".

He started off with an overview of the 20 gauge shotgun that he'd selected for Era based on its lesser recoil and lighter weight. The lesson was kind of hot. He pressed his body against hers in order to demonstrate how to position the smooth wooden butt against her shoulder and to aim using the sight. The smell of his delicious cologne and the anticipation of feeling the first kick of the heavy gun gave her the jitters.

He gripped the handle of the plastic clay thrower and placed the bright orange disk into its cradle.

After shifting the weight of the gun and checking to make sure she braced it properly into the crook of her shoulder, she yelled, "Pull!"

He turned slightly, the muscles in his arm shifting under his fitted shirt as he wound up, and then—snap—his arm short forward in one fluid motion, launching the disk into the air. The clay pigeon spun fast, slicing through the sky in a perfect arc, dead-center in front of Era, then dropped slowly, giving her the best possible chance of hitting it.

"All yours," he said, his voice low and full of confidence.

She lined up the sights with the flying orb and squeezed, the sharp crack of her shot slicing through the air as the orange disk shattered into tiny pieces.

"I hit it on my first try!" she shouted triumphantly, lowering the gun to crush Christopher in a hug. His joy at her natural talent for the sport radiated from him, and she knew he would be bragging about his expert lessons later that night.

Since Christopher was the best skeet shooting teacher, she moved down the line to Christian to work with rifles while the other girls waited their turn for shotgun lessons. Rifle shooting was fun. She lay down on a blanket and found the target pasted to a cardboard box 90 yards away. The sight reminded her of looking through a microscope, of getting it settled in just the right spot and then, "Wham!" The rifle kicked like a mule on her shoulder, the sound deafening, thumping her eardrums even through the earplugs.

Christian dropped his binoculars and looked over at her. "Damn Annie Oakley. You can come hunting with us anytime," he said, his voice barely audible through the earplugs and headphones. Christopher had been right. Shooting was satisfying.

To complete the arc, she fired handguns with Bene. Era had spent the least amount of time with him since coming to the ranch. He was something of a gentle giant but with a wicked sense of humor. As he taught her how to check the glock to know if the chamber was loaded or not and how to hold the gun properly, he used the opportunity of their first private conversation to dig for information.

"So I heard Chase tried to put the moves on you last night, even though you're obviously spoken for by my man Christopher," he said, casually popping bullets into a revolver with meaty hands.

"I am *not* spoken for!" Era replied with too much emotion. "We're friends and I just got out of a long relationship. Something he knows all about. Sorry if you got the wrong impression," she finished, smashing a clip into the silver glock and setting it down on the folding table in front of them.

Bene chortled and reached over to check the gun. "You're spoken for in *this* group. Only Chase would try to snatch a girl from his teammate. Anyways, Chase has a girlfriend or something like it. The worse part is, he knows how much Christopher likes you. We all do."

"WHAT!?" she bellowed, true fury igniting in her chest. "Bene, I know we barely know each other, but I'm begging you, tell me exactly what you're talking about." Era turned her Gift on him, blue waves emanated from her and then found purchase like a grappling hook before pulling his truth out.

Because in this case, she needed to not only know what he knew, but she needed him to *say* it or else she would not be able to confront either Chase or Christopher with any of the knowledge.

Bene already wanted to confront her with the truth, but with the Gift's pull on him, he crumbled like a granola bar. Details that a guy would not typically share in Era's experience came flooding out.

Christopher had been talking to his teammates about Era since right before she mentioned having a boyfriend, over a year ago. Apparently, he was about to ask her to Junior Prom when she devastated him with the news. He thoroughly hated Cole since he saw him at the football game, even more so after they met. He'd even had a tracking device installed on Cole's car to make sure he stayed away from Era. The last of this news had her nearly bursting into flames with rage but she kept silent until Bene finished dishing out the choice details.

Last night, Christopher, Christian, and him had stayed up late playing poker and Christopher had retold the story about finding her with Chase outside his room. He told them about how he had kissed her the night she stayed over and how he wanted to help her get over her ex because he'd wanted her for four years. Oh and for some reason, he threw in how Kamila and Christopher had a brief fling at the end of last year although nothing came of it.

She looked down at the handguns and said calmly, "I don't think it's a good idea for me to touch these right now," and stormed off.

She headed over to the Santa Maria grill where chef Charles had a massive tri-tip on the grate which he raised slightly above the too-hot fire with the turn of a crank.

"Hi Charles. Do you have anything to drink over here?" she asked, ripping off her headphones. "I just had my trust completely broken and I don't think I can manage the night without something stiff."

He looked back at her calmly, slightly taken aback by the inappropriate level of honesty yet equally sympathetic. Blunt truth was a weapon Era knew how to wield with precision. "Let me mix you up a quick whiskey sour. Anything stiffer and the boys might get a bit suspicious," he said, giving her a wink before heading over to the bar, stocked for the night's dinner with nearly a full spread for the nine of them.

Era sat at one the chairs set up around the unlit fire pit, mulling over her options while everyone else continued shooting. Part of her wanted to figure out how to get home tonight and away from the two-timing flirt, the possessive blabbermouth, and the jealous rival who was likely looking for the nearest opportunity to get her payback. Why hadn't she driven her own car? Her Jeep could handle the dirt roads on the ranch and she probably would have taken the precaution to drive if Christopher hadn't sprung the trip on her at the last minute.

She was decidedly stuck. Thankfully, she only needed to make it through until the morning. She walked back for a refill, seething once more about the tracker on Cole's car. Who knows maybe Christopher called in a favor at Tesla and had them upload

Cole's location to him directly? She thought it best not to underestimate what the Ridgewells would do. She had seen it herself when she read Christopher's heart at the party—he would do whatever it took to get what he wanted. It hadn't occurred to her what that revelation implied if she was the object of his desire.

When the shooting party concluded, the guys strolled over, debating and bragging who among them was the better shot. They weighed the merits of different shooting styles, each asserting that their strengths would make them the best hunter of wild turkeys, pheasants, or boars.

A long table had been set up between the now-lit fire pit and the Santa Maria grill. Garlands of olive tree branches ran the length of the table, interspersed with bud vases filled with wildflowers. Each place setting featured a menu card and an aromatic sprig of rosemary, adding a rustic yet elegant touch. String lights hung between the old oaks, casting a warm glow and giving the entire setup a magical ambiance.

Era took the head of the table, opposite Christopher and motioned to Chase to sit beside her. She wanted the least amount of dining companions so she could get the truth out of him without Christopher nearby. As they dug into their heirloom tomato and burrata salad, she leaned in close to him.

"Chase, I would love to hear all about your girlfriend," she said, licking the balsamic glaze from her fork. "Monica will be devastated to hear her efforts have been in vain."

His eyes blazed before shooting over to Benedict. He knew immediately who outed him. "He told you, didn't he?" Chase asked, his nostrils flaring. The Gift showed her guilt and anger flashing blue and red, blue and red, and then gray, sadness. "Bene needs to learn to stop getting into other people's business."

He cleared his throat and continued more calmly, "There is a girl that I have been seeing on and off for a while, over a year actually, but she's not my girlfriend. If she was, I would have brought her here with me."

The explanation reminded Era of his D minus apology from earlier. He purposely edited the truth in order to appease without mentioning the part that really mattered. His honesty capped out at a bare minimum.

Era gave him a frosty glare. "It doesn't matter to me who or how many girls you date. Just don't insult me with your lines about what a special unique snowflake I am, on a group trip, with friends that know you're seeing another girl. If I had kissed you, you would have made me look like an idiot. Thankfully, that wasn't ever going to happen.

"You're lucky to have Christopher as a friend. He never mentioned this girl to me, even after you tried to undermine him. Your manners are nothing compared to his."

Come to think of it, Christopher did get some points in her book for keeping Chase's confidence when he could have easily assassinated his character. That put him at a plus one and a minus ten. She'd deal with him later.

"I know I am. Christopher is a really great guy actually, so long as you don't cross him..." Chase paused and the Gift showed her a warning bell. "This girl Marine, that I've been dating on and off, well, it's super complicated," he finished, trailing off. The gray sadness wrapped around him once more. Era decided that rather than letting her pride cause her to over-react to a guy she had met only recently, she would do her best to help him.

Era took a breath and softened her tone considerably. "Tell me about her," she coaxed.

"You want to know about Marine?" The question left his mouth, but his voice cracked slightly, betraying his doubt. When Era nodded, her eyes dilated and let the Pull flow out to him.

He set down his fork, unsure how to proceed, his brow furrowed in thought. "She and I met at the beginning of last year. At first things were perfect. She was my first. After a couple of months, I felt pretty serious about her and was getting frustrated that I couldn't compete with her ambitions. She just didn't prioritize my feelings the way I did hers. But this was the first girl that ever got me. She saw all my flaws and loved me anyway.

"I tried really hard to hold things together but after six months, I couldn't take it anymore and we broke up for the first time. Every couple of months we try to start over and then it falls apart again. Then, during one of our breaks, I found out she had gone out with another guy, at least ten times. Not that I haven't gone on dates, but I haven't been able to get over what felt like her starting a whole new relationship with someone else.

"We're toxic for each other, fight all the time, and now she kind of brings out the worst in me. I hate it," his breath came out in a whoosh, the catharsis from expelling his bottled up truth showed as his jaw relaxed and his hands dropped to his sides.

Era put a hand on his shoulder, soaking up the truth from his soul. There was more to the part when he talked about being loved despite his imperfections. She saw that he had not been loved properly in his life, that his family was harsh and cold, critical and demanding. He longed for a love that was safe and unconditional and had been thrown over for superfluous reasons. He felt his love wasn't good enough and it also explained his natural charisma, a skill he had developed to win the intimacy of others since he had to work so hard for even basic approval from those closest to him.

We're exactly alike, Era marveled, blindsided by the eerie similarity of the secret they both kept and the adaptation each had developed.

When she spoke, her body became a tunnel through which wind blew. The words meant only for him poured out of her with a tingling sensation. "Sometimes people don't have that much love to give. She gave you all she had, the problem is, she doesn't have very much. That capacity could grow if she saw the value of love, if she was willing to let go of some of her other loves to make room for it. Until she does that, Marine will never be able to put your needs before her own.

"I promise you that there is another girl out there that has more to give and who will accept every part of you, even the bad. Don't let the bondage of her being your first, keep you from finding someone who can go the distance with you in life.

"We didn't get to choose our families, the people who were supposed to teach us what love could and should be, but we do get to choose who becomes our family someday. Who cares that we're young? It's not too early to find 'the one.' You'll never regret leaving behind a person who refuses to put you first—to put love first."

As she spoke, Chase felt the wisdom of her words mending wounds that had long laid open. He felt the guilt at leaving Marine behind melt away, replaced with the certain hope that a bright jewel remained for him to uncover. The truth freed him and he knew with conviction that he'd never go back to Marine after today. And even though the words of the Gift were for Chase, Era needed to hear them too.

While experiencing this deep healing, he looked at the beautiful girl before him. He saw that her rebuke earlier hadn't been jealous or petty, but that she had been concerned for her good name. He liked that about her and he wanted a girl in his life who'd take care of her reputation. He also saw that she was not broken like him, and that he ardently wanted someone more whole to love him, to teach him how to love the way nobody taught him in his life.

Her understanding and the way she could step outside herself and see the situation with such perspective, to reach out and want to help him, made her a thousand times more beautiful. Suddenly, Era was the bright jewel he longed to uncover and whereas before he considered stepping back and letting Christopher have her, at this point, he prepared to double down on his efforts to win her. This was no longer a game for him. He wanted her more than anyone or anything.

Chase had no idea that Era could see his heart mending before her very eyes, and witnessing that little miracle, healed a small part of her too. *Trauma bond,* she told herself, but there was something more to it. She connected with him in their shared understanding of broken family life and tumultuous love. Knowing him like that brought him out of the realm of stranger, of acquaintance.

He looked quietly into her eyes, and took her hand at the table, giving it a grateful squeeze. "Thank you," he said. "What you said really helped me see things differently and I needed that."

Their conversation ended as the table began stirring to wrap up the dinner. Era glanced across the table to see Christopher's eyes on her and Chase's hands. She didn't really care. Helping Chase had trumped her anxiety at provoking Christopher's jealousy and she had felt the change in him with her words.

The Gift revealed that it now also healed. Era began to grasp that she had only begun to experience the power of what this Gift could do and what its purpose was in her life. She had accepted its presence as merely something to wield to her advantage, yet the Gift proved to have a breadth and depth that went far beyond unlocking the secrets of others and aiding her in manipulating those around her for immediate gain and advantage.

She looked up at the night sky and felt that in choosing to help Chase rather than allowing her rage to proceed unchecked, she had unlocked a piece of her own mystery. Her fears about a mental break vanished and she took a deep breath, her chin tilting towards the vastness above, and spotted a shooting star springing across the blackness, filling her with much needed peace.

The peace didn't last long as the party streamed back towards the main house. This time they gathered on the living room sofa, nearer to the kitchen with its many possibilities for a night of intoxication.

Wanting to reassure Christopher after he spotted her and Chase touching... again... she jumped onto his back as they made their way through the house and spoke, her lips touching his ear, "I'd kill for a good Cab. Do you think you could pick out something nice for me?"

He set her down and she grabbed his hand as he unlocked what she initially thought was a closet door, leading her down a flight of stairs into a cavernous, temperature and humidity-controlled wine cellar below. Surprised to find such a place in the house—since basements were rare—Era marveled at the rows of bottles that lined the walls, each one a promise of exquisite flavors waiting to be explored.

She found it difficult to stay angry with him. Who cares if he tracked Cole's car? Cole broke her heart and who picked up the pieces? Christopher did. So what if he had told his friends that they kissed one time? It would be different if he had bragged about something more serious, but he likely mentioned the kiss in the context of his feelings for her.

The only part that irked her was that he had made her feel stupid for being jealous of Kamila, when in fact, something had happened there. The Gift had shown her that he was being truthful about not having feelings for her, but that didn't mean there wasn't history. He should have owned up to it. It was a lie of omission. A lot was getting past her these days, she was really losing her touch.

Era held onto his hand as he scanned the wall of bottles, squinting at the labels until he found it, a rare vintage from a famous Napa winery. She didn't dare ask too many questions for fear of placing the price tag and not being able to enjoy the bottle without guilt. She knew he wanted to spoil her.

Loosened up after the wine tasting and not thinking about either the implications or the repercussions, she wrapped her arms around his neck. "Thank you for always taking such good care of me," she said, pulling back to look into his eyes and laying a soft sensuous kiss on his cheek, much too near his mouth.

His hands rested on her hips as he looked back at her, touched by the sudden show of affection and gratitude. Then she grabbed his hand again and led them back upstairs so he could cork the bottle and pour her a glass of the liquid gold.

In the living room, the group argued about what to do. Christian wanted to play beer pong, none of the girls did. "Ew, save that germy game for the frat house. No thanks," Monica said with a bratty attitude.

"How about Truth or Dare?" Kamila asked, flipping her hair trying to look sexy. Several heckles went up—rejected.

Christian burst out in response, "Grab a guy and go upstairs if you're looking to get some. This isn't junior high." Era threw a hand over her mouth to keep from spitting out her wine, as she choked on a stifled laugh. No sense poking the bear.

"What about King's Cup?" Celeste suggested, her enthusiasm bubbling over. Era noticed a strange orange hue around her red hair—a sign of malicious intent. Not good.

The group erupted in approval as Bene hopped over the couch, embarking on a quest for the cup and returning with a Baccarat pitcher. "Better be careful with this one. It's the biggest I could find, but it looks fancy," he said, gingerly placing the thousand-dollar crystal glass on the coffee table. Christian tossed him a deck of cards from the game room to set the stage. "So, who hasn't played before?"

Era and Monica raised their hands, prompting Bene to fan the cards in an unbroken circle around the cup. "I won't go

through every single card, but each one does something different. For example, pulling a 4 means 'whores'—I mean ladies—
drink. A 10 is categories; you think up a category, like animals,
and it kicks off a mini-game. You say 'zebra,' and the person to
your left has to come up with a different animal until someone
repeats or can't think of one, which means they drink.

"We'll fill you in as we go. Oh yeah, and if you break the
unbroken line of cards on the table, you drink. Pull a King, and
you pour the rest of your drink into the Cup. The person who
pulls the last King drinks the Cup and ends the game. Let's play
already," Bene concluded, rubbing his hands together.

Era knelt beside the coffee table. Kamila and Celeste pushed
in in to claim seats on her left. The orange hue enveloped them
both, and Era realized they were scheming against her. Pulling
Christopher down next to her, she sipped her delicious wine,
bracing herself for the game to begin.

Christian went first, coming up with a Jack. "Never have I
ever... crashed a car." Kamila, Bene, and Violet all took a drink,
their bashful faces making Era giggle.

Good one, Christian, she thought, feeling hopeful that the
game might actually be fun. Next, Violet pulled a 5 and had to
"jive." She stood up and started to Cat Daddy, an old-school
dance, while Era held her sides, laughing at the guys trying to
mimic her moves. Kamila, nursing her bandaged leg, sipped her
drink instead.

Christopher drew a 9 and had to "Bust a Rhyme." He kicked
off with "tinkle," and only Era managed to come up with "wrinkle" before Kamila's attempt at "hinkle" earned her boos and a
drink.

When Era picked the first King, outrage surged through her
as she realized she had to pour her treasured glass of wine into
the King's Cup, knowing it would be tainted with everyone
else's drinks. Christopher laughed beside her, patting her thigh.

Bene artfully pulled his card, maintaining the unbroken

circle around the cup. A 10 appeared, and no one was surprised when he chose NHL teams as the category. Monica ended up drinking after mistakenly naming the Blue Jays instead of the Maple Leafs.

Next, Kamila pulled an Ace—waterfall. Bene fidgeted about explaining the rules. "Whoever pulls the Ace starts the waterfall. When that person starts drinking, everyone else drinks and doesn't stop until the person on their left stops. So Celeste can stop anytime after Kamila, and so forth. No cheating, no baby sips."

Era quickly realized that Kamila and Celeste had sat to her left intentionally. Almost last for the waterfall, she braced herself for the challenge of chugging room-temperature red wine.

Why is it always the girls?

Christopher filled her cup, and they began. Of course, Kamila and Celeste took their sweeeeet time putting their cups down. Era's eyes watered and her stomach clenched, especially when Bene prolonged the torture as well. As the last few dropped their cups in unison, Era lowered her glass to find it nearly empty. Yikes.

Pick me twins, Era thought as the girls laughed and avoided eye contact with her.

Celeste pulled a Queen and became the Question Master. The game sounded simple enough, ask any question to anyone. All that person had to do was remember to direct a new question at someone else and not be drunk enough to get tricked into answering the question.

Celeste turned to Era to kick things off. "Who do you like more, Christopher or Chase?" she asked with outright devilry.

Era's face burned as she heard the boys laugh and choke on their drinks. Christopher stiffened beside her.

So they want to play like this, huh? she thought, anger coursing through her and working to decide if she'd let it pass or give them a taste of their own medicine. The girl was too stupid to realize she had insulted Christopher, her host, with the grasping little dig.

She decided to let it slide and turned to Christian. "Who was the best shot today?"

Who turned to Chase, "Are you a theater kid or what?"

Chase smiled the grin of a cobra ready to strike and asked Bene, "Why are you such a gossipy lackey bitch?"

The tension wound like an overtightened guitar string ready to spring and cut someone at any moment. Within ten seconds, a cutthroat spirit descended upon the game.

Bene puffed out a breath, a look of pure disgust in his eye and turned to Kamila, "How's your leg?" Era could tell Bene and Chase would be having words later no matter where this game went.

Kamila nearly fumbled the game and answered him, her vanity could hardly escape the concern about herself. She caught herself just in time and cocked an eyebrow at Era, turning her face into a mock frown. "Are you still sad about your boyfriend dumping you?"

Era's eyes popped open in shock. This girl had a real problem. She shot back, "Are *you* sad you'll never step foot on Christopher's precious yacht so long as I'm in the picture?"

"Nope, sorry Era, you can't answer the question," Christian called out.

Kamila laughed but the emotion didn't reach her eyes, which darkened at Era even as she went along with the break in energy.

Era pursed her lips and took a long slow sip of her wine, happy to have that little exchange over. She didn't dare look at Christopher. She knew it was rude to bring up his name, but after everything she found out tonight, she felt compelled to fight back. Regardless, she reached over and laid a hand across his bare back, offering her touch as an apology.

Next up, Chase drew the second Jack. "Alright, let's lighten it up here. Sorry, guys, but you're playing this card all wrong. The Jack is the Rule Maker. My rule is that if anyone touches, they have to drink," he declared, grinning, "and anyone can enforce it." Era pulled her hand back.

The game continued, the laughter growing louder and more chaotic. Like all card-based drinking games, the hardest part involved keeping up the momentum which meant needing to yell at every third player when their turn came up. The group's increasing intoxication became evident as the category game managed to make it through fewer participants each round.

Chase relished giving out drinks based on his rule, targeting Christopher and Era whenever they laughed and touched shoulders or exchanged high fives. Era threw him the evil eye after the third penalty, earning herself a pleased smirk in return. He remained the only one truly paying attention.

Three-fourths of the way through the game, justice struck when Kamila pulled the final King. She took one look at the mishmash of the King's Cup and screamed that there was no way she'd drink wine, beer, and White Claw mixed together or risk throwing up on Christopher's couch.

Deciding the game had been fun enough, Christopher grabbed the pitcher and walked over to the sink to dump it. "No one is throwing up in my house. Thanks, guys," he said with authority before departing, as many others did for bathroom breaks.

Era got up from her seat on the floor, her legs numb and flopped down on the wonderfully soft couch. Chase followed suit, tucking into the corner seat next to her so that her head nearly rested in his lap.

"I like looking at your face upside down," he said, "Your cat eyes look even more sneaky from this angle."

"I am not sneaky looking!" Era protested, smashing a throw pillow into him, which he deftly blocked.

"And I can see your long lashes," he said, his fingertips closing her eyes and tracing over her face. "Come for a night swim with me. Or a jacuzzi. We can have it heated up in ten minutes. What do you say?"

She looked up at him, letting her eyes squinch and sparkle with danger, "Okay." Era knew herself to be a shameless flirt, especially after five-ish drinks and an emotional day. The care-free side of her personality was bursting to come out and play.

"Okay, what?" Christopher asked, his head popping up above her on the other side of the couch.

Standing on the couch in front of him, she winked and said, "Night swim. Want to join?" Then, she vaulted over the side and bounded up the stairs to find another bathing suit.

Word spread quickly, and soon everyone was cannonballing into the pool or sinking into the steaming spa. Only Kamila, with her bandaged leg, pouted on a lounger beside the jacuzzi.

The sensation of the hot jets felt incredible on Era's muscles, tense after the ATV ride, as she sipped her drink. Celeste had mixed a round of Cranberry Vodkas, and as Era looked down at her cup, she noted its strong flavor, reminding herself to slow down.

Chase sat across from her, grabbing her foot and delivering the most incredible massage. She stared out into the utter blackness of the night stretching out all around them, relishing the lack of man-made light, and the blanket of quiet.

"Listen," he began, "about what you said earlier—calling me out for saying you're a unique snowflake. You really are. I'm going to show you I mean it if you give me another chance." He cleared his throat before continuing, "And I don't want you to think I'm trying anything, but if you need a quieter place to sleep tonight, my room is available. I swear I won't try anything. I'll even tell everyone I crashed on the couch... I'll sleep on the couch if that's what you want. Even if it's the middle of the night and I'm asleep, you can come in whenever."

Era shook in head in disbelief. "How very chivalrous of you." The offer was fraught with double meaning but the Gift showed her that he told the truth, even if his intentions weren't entirely pure. He imagined them pressed together, sleeping. "I don't think that's a very likely scenario," she said as Monica splashed into the water next to Chase. The Gift lit up in an off-kilter way with a decided pink glow. Monica reeled, highly intoxicated and intent on making her move on Chase, oblivious to the moment she crashed. Seizing the distraction of Monica's entrance, Era slid into the heated yet refreshing pool.

As Christopher came through the doors with his own fresh cocktail, he set his drink down at the edge and dove in beside her, splashing her tied up hair.

"Jerk! Never get a lady's hair wet in the pool if she has it up. I thought you had perfect manners!" Era huffed.

"I have perfect manners do I?" he said with a grin and an arched brow.

Gosh, this guy catches everything, she thought, spinning in the other direction, preparing to swim away.

Before she could kick off, Christopher wrapped his arms around her waist, pulling her back to face him. "What were you and Chase talking about?" he asked, pausing in that deep way that made everything he said feel so serious and catching her off guard once again.

Knowing truth to be a better offense than a lie, she replied simply, "He told me I could sleep in his room if I wanted and promised he wouldn't try anything." Rather than reacting with anger or jealousy, he tugged her closer, her legs wrapping around his waist as naturally as anything in the world.

"And what did you say?" he asked, his voice low and heavy in her ear, setting off a string of firecrackers down her spine.

"I didn't say anything. Monica jumped in looking like she wanted to take a bite out of him, so I took that as my cue to 'gtfo' out of there."

"Please don't sleep in his room, Era. Sleep with me," he purred. "In my room, I mean. You know I would never touch you unless you wanted me to." His voice held a teasing warmth, and Era could see steam rising from the water, even though the temperature chilled her enough to make her shiver.

The conversation felt bizarre, especially with her sworn friend, her legs wrapped around his waist with his arms supporting the rest of her weight beneath the water. Gazing into his emerald eyes, she saw her own desire reflected back at her. Era wanted to tell him she did want him to touch her, right now, yet she somehow remained silent.

He bit his bottom lip, and she caught the movement, threatening to break her resolve when an ominous presence loomed behind her. Looking over her shoulder, she caught a glimpse of Kamila's hateful, glowing eyes fixed on her like a lioness in the night. Instinctively, she unlocked her legs.

The situation stirred a feeling of déjà vu, and she recalled the time she awakened from a nightmare, to the sense of a presence in her room. Thoroughly creeped out by the memory, she fidgeted to get off the watery stage.

Era grabbed a towel from the basket and wrapped it like a shield around herself, using the bathroom as an excuse to escape. Wobbling her way into the house, the quick exit from the water accentuated the heavy, clumsy feeling in her limbs after so many drinks. Celeste had probably added an extra shot to her cup, hoping she'd get completely plastered and embarrass herself in front of Christopher.

She realized she might be very drunk and a self-preservation safety mechanism began to kick in in her mind. Era struggled up the stairs to grab her bag from the girls' room before making her way down to the Master. She knew time was running out before she needed to pass out.

Her subconscious guided her through the motions of brushing her teeth and washing her face. She pulled her bikini loose, letting the pieces drop, forgotten, to the floor. Strangely, even though she knew her pajamas lay in her bag, she found herself in Christopher's closet, surrounded by neatly folded stacks of his shirts and boxers. Helping herself to a shirt, she reeled over to the large couch and fell onto it, pulling an over-sized throw blanket over her body. Sleep enveloped her without delay.

When she awoke, disorientation struck as she found herself on the couch in the living room. Panic surged; she had napped far too long. Glancing at the clock, she realized only an hour remained until their friends arrived for dinner, and she had nothing prepared. Era hurried into the kitchen, spinning the oven's temperature control to 425 and tearing ingredients from the fridge and pantry.

"Babe, please help! I need someone to chop," she called over her shoulder, mentally prioritizing her menu tasks.

Cole appeared around the corner, a grumpy expression on his face. "I'll help, but only if you promise not to yell at me if all the carrots aren't cut perfectly."

"Yes, I promise. Just start with the rosemary and garlic; I need those for the spatchcock chicken."

Era and Cole worked in tandem, preparing dinner for the night. She teased him about some of the uneven cuts, but laughter and conversation flowed as they worked like a team.

No one arrived for dinner, and she couldn't recall anyone being expected. Instead, she enjoyed a quiet, blissful evening with Cole, the two of them alone in their apartment. He looked so handsome, his face alight and brilliant, reminiscent of another memory.

They settled on the couch, his hands cupping her face as he gazed into her eyes. "I have loved none but you," he said, leaning in for a kiss. Suddenly, his expression shifted, confusion replacing affection as if her lips had betrayed her silent truth. "You kissed him?" he accused, his face twisting into an eerie ugliness. Shame and confusion engulfed her, the weight of his words hitting home. She looked down, grasping for an explanation only to find Christopher's shirt and boxers clinging to her body.

Cole stood up, rage exploding from him so that Era shrank away, wanting to curl into the corner of the couch. A part of her recognized that she'd had everything with him, and ruined their perfect life. As he turned to leave, his bags sat already packed by the door, like they had been waiting for his inevitable departure.

Era was shattered, every fiber of her being cried out for him to stay, to forgive her, to try. She woke with a silent whimper, sweating, heart racing, and shaken to her core. Across the dark room, Christopher's silhouette, barely outlined by the fluffy covers beckoned her. Without hesitation, she felt her way over and climbed into bed with him, tears still drying on her clammy skin.

He stirred from deep sleep, gathering her into himself, his heavy arm resting like a weighted blanket over her frazzled nerves. As he tucked her in closer, his hand brushed her cheek, feeling the last tear lingering there. Now more awake, his husky voice broke the silence. "It's okay. I'm here."

Her heart leapt for him in that instant; he didn't ask, "Are you okay?" Of course, anyone who slips into someone's bed in the middle of the night, crying, isn't okay. Even in his sleep, Christopher possessed an intuition that surpassed any guy she had ever known.

The simplicity of his statement struck her, making her feel like a Jenga tower toppling after being poked in just the right spot. Who cared if she wasn't ready to love again or if she couldn't forget about Cole? Here stood a superb man, and even if she felt unworthy of him, she wanted him. And he clearly wanted her.

I don't want to be friends anymore, she thought, discarding the resolution made during the car ride. Her will had reset, and she surrendered to the refuge—and the pyre—that was Christopher. Turning to face him, she cupped his face in her hands, pulling his mouth to hers. He responded eagerly, rolling over her, his hand winding into her hair. Their kiss unfolded slowly and deeply, until he sensed that Era's hesitation had completely dissolved. Her hands glided down his smooth back, nails raking gently around his sides until her fingers hooked into the waistband of his boxers.

Christopher broke their kiss, his lips trailing toward her ear, where his hot breath and wet mouth tortured her. "Tell me you want me," he said, his voice ragged and husky.

"I want you. Always," Era admitted, her fingers tugging at his hair. The pyre was lit. Era moaned as Christopher peeled her shirt off, his lips sliding down the length of her body. He slipped her shorts down, and she kicked them into the abyss of the covers. Despite the copious alcohol still swirling in her system, his kisses sent electric zaps across her stomach and down her legs.

He looked up at her, their eyes locking in a final moment of consent before his mouth claimed her, and she felt the fusion of his being with hers. It differed from her experiences with Cole; yet, with her eyes closed, the space between her pleasure and his person seemed to vanish entirely.

The ecstasy built to a crescendo, suddenly not enough, and she found herself pulling him up to her, craving the true union of their bodies.

He hovered above her, his eyes shining in the dark, hungry and wild. Just as he positioned himself to join them eternally, flashing blue and red lights startled her, reminiscent of a speeding driver caught off guard by sudden sirens behind them. Her palms shot up to brace against his chest, muscles clenched.

"No, wait. We can't," she burst out. Christopher looked at her, puzzled, and leaned in to kiss her cheek before rolling away. Frozen, she still expected the impending doom of a "tap tap tap" on an invisible glass window around her. Christopher pulled her close, but instead of feeling safe, she longed for the protective barrier of her clothes against the too-intimate feeling of all his skin against hers.

Mercifully, he didn't press for an explanation. Gosh, she could learn to love this man. Ignoring the desire for her clothes, she offered him the trust of her naked body and forced herself to drift off to sleep.

CHAPTER 23

WHEN ERA AWOKE in the early morning hours, the awareness of her nakedness felt immediately unbearable. Instead of rummaging for her clothes, she listened for Christopher's breathing, still heavy in sleep, then stole out of bed and into the closet with her bag. Dressed in her own pajamas, she slunk out the door with feline steps, tiptoeing down the stairs to the gym, where she could shower in the private bathroom.

Hot steam smothered her, exacerbating the poisoned feeling that throbbed in her head and tingled in her limbs—a hangover compounded by two days of relentless partying. The sound of water bouncing off the tiled floors echoed in her ears as a flood of thoughts assaulted her. The dream clung to her mind, achingly fresh, both painful and perfect, leaving her in greater agony. And in her torment, what had she done? She had run straight into Christopher's arms. In the moment, it felt so right, but now, under the harsh light of day, she recognized that she had used him to console herself.

Sober now, she understood the flashing lights indicated disapproval of their night together. The thought of that close call brought a wave of anguish, yet she felt relieved to have stopped them from taking it too far. She would only be beating herself up even more this morning if she had indulged further. Even though Era wanted him more than ever, she knew she deserved him less.

There was nothing left to do but backpedal, avoid him, and once they got home, stop seeing him. Era needed time to ensure she wouldn't attempt to use him that way again. This agonizing decision would undoubtedly confuse and anger him, but she was too ashamed to reveal the true reason she needed space. If there was going to be a chance for them in the future, she needed to wait until she wasn't so screwed up.

Era hid in the gym for the rest of the morning, only emerging when she heard a chorus of voices gathering in the kitchen. From that point, she made sure to stay in the company of Violet, Christian, or even Chase, engaging in light conversation and drinking cup after cup of coffee.

She didn't fool Christopher; however, with all the arrangements for their departure demanding his attention, he lacked the time to pull her aside for a heart-to-heart. He didn't want to create a scene either, resolving to wait until they were home to discover why she had bolted from his bed.

Era's plan proved effective, at least temporarily. They all exchanged goodbyes; Chase wrapped her in an inappropriately long hug, lifting her onto her toes and kissing her cheek. The group broke up into their carpools. Era even offered to sit in the back of Christopher's truck with Violet on the way home, an offer that Christian happily accepted, grateful for the extra legroom.

Once Christian and Violet were safely dropped off back at the white Craftsman, Christopher and Era still had an hour together in the car. As they reversed from the driveway, Christopher turned the music down and dove straight in. "So what's going on?" he asked, not beating around the bush. This boy had the makings of a leader; he showed no fear of confrontation.

Era hesitated, contemplating how much to reveal. "I could tell you, but you're not going to like any of it," she admitted, still uncertain about sharing the real reason behind her turmoil.

"Are you upset about what we did? Do you remember?" he interrupted, panic creeping into his voice…

"I do remember, although I was pretty drunk when I went to bed. I went upstairs to your couch because I knew I was going to pass out. That drink Celeste made must have had at least three shots in it; I barely made it up the stairs after getting out of the pool," she retold, skirting around the main issue.

Era observed Christopher's anxiety, palpable ripples in the air around them. This was another one of those moments when she wished she could turn off the Gift; she didn't want to see how her selfish choices affected him now.

His hand raked through his hair as he focused on the freeway ahead. "I don't know what to say. I asked you last night what you wanted, but maybe you were too drunk to know." His uncertainty hung in the air, unsure if he should apologize for touching her; except he wasn't sorry.

"I don't think I was that drunk by the time I woke up. I had a nightmare and woke up really rattled. I didn't realize it at the time, but I think that last night was me trying to erase that feeling, and what happened felt too fast for… um… us," she finished, aware that she hadn't explained herself properly.

"Tell me this. Was the dream about him?" he asked.

"It was."

Jealousy and outrage flared in the car, filling her nose with the acrid scent of burnt plastic. They sat in uncomfortable silence for the rest of the drive home. Thankfully, the quiet meant no new damning revelations from the Gift; she couldn't handle stewing in his painful emotions when she was already tortured enough by her own. After what felt like an eternity, Christopher finally dampened the unbearable tension by turning on some music for the remainder of the drive, though their silence remained.

The final parting posed her last hurdle. As expected, Christopher mentioned their usual workout for the next day.

"Can't do it tomorrow," she heard herself say. "Have some things piling up from not getting out much these past few weeks." The blatant lie sounded almost true.

He sucked his teeth and gave a cold nod, grabbed her bags from the back of his truck, and walked her to the door.

"Thanks for driving me. I'll call you." She hugged him and felt his body turn to stone in her arms.

Walking into the empty house alone, a deep sadness washed over her. She knew she had lied to his face twice. She wouldn't call. And she would be alone, again.

CHAPTER 24

ERA WOKE up half an hour before her and Christopher's usual workout time, determined to leave the house before he could poke around and catch her in a lie. The problem was, she had nowhere specific to go. After taking a few random turns, she headed toward the beach.

As she sped down the coastal highway, Sage Beach came into view. This popular spot would likely be as deserted as her soul, this early in the morning. The steep steps deterred everyone except teenagers and college kids. The cove didn't connect with any other beaches, leaving it free of dorky beach walkers, and making it a perfect refuge where Era could tuck herself into the cliffs.

Spreading out the blanket she kept stashed in her car, she lay down, ready to catch up on some reading and soak up the morning sun. Yet, she couldn't bring herself to open the book. Instead, she found herself mesmerized by the undulating current, imagining the hidden secrets beneath the surface. Two hours slipped by in this way, allowing the moving yet unchanging picture to free her mind to wander over many thoughts: Cole, school, Christopher, her future, her past, her broken dreams.

Nothing felt settled or clearer than before, but after two hours on the hard sand, she needed to stretch and escape the strengthening sun. Following her mom's advice, she decided to indulge in some retail therapy at a nearby boutique before heading home.

Chase had been Snapping her since leaving the ranch, sending pictures of the white and green leather passenger seat in his Maybach with a caption reading, "Wish you were here," along with a selfie of him lounging by his pool. Era responded with innocuous replies, a picture of her morning coffee and a glimpse of the yellow bodycon dress she tried on at the boutique. Christopher had texted, but she hadn't opened his messages, letting the small circle hang ominously next to his name.

On the third day of her morning wave ritual, Era mulled over the unread messages and the conflict of wanting to be with Christopher while knowing it to be radically imprudent. Far out on the horizon, she spotted dark blue ripples moving and reforming into a number: 218. Looking down at the book in her bag, she thought, *No, it couldn't be,* yet she picked it up anyway and turned to the page.

The words of the third paragraph sprang up at her like a jack in the box: "Look away from him, and let him be." She flinched and threw it away from her into the sand.

The foreboding message struck her, and in that instant, she looked back up at the horizon to see a water cyclone spinning, reaching down from a cloud so black it couldn't have been real. Instinctively, she understood that whether or not she recovered from her long funk, dating Christopher would bring only destruction.

The Gift had expanded its power decisively. She had initially questioned her sanity upon seeing the vision at the ranch, but this time, the vision connected to secret knowledge. She had never read the book in her bag and had no way of predicting what was written on page 218.

The dark cloud dissipated, leaving Era to feel only the baking sun on her shoulders. She picked up her towel and tote, making her way to the narrow stairs when a familiar face approached, flanked by two strangers.

Dread and nausea swept over her, tossing her into the rapids. Her leaden feet fused with the sand at the bottom of the stairs as recognition dawned on his face.

Cole approached, accompanied by two guys she had never seen before. His lips moved, likely mentioning her, and when they reached her, the two strangers continued to the sand while Cole stopped in front of her.

Era braced herself for the incoming chitchat, praying she could keep her composure. It had only been six days since he had ripped her heart out, leaving an unhealed wound in her chest that throbbed without ceasing.

He stepped off the last stair, standing uncomfortably close. "Hi Era. Early beach day, huh? How have you been?" Oddly, he seemed happy to see her. How could he be so flippant after his cruel words?

As her initial shock wore off, anger bubbled beneath the surface, recalling the nights she had woken up gasping and sweating from nightmares, and the destruction she had faced since their breakup.

"I've been fine. Just got back from vacation at my friend's ranch this past weekend—wine tasting, ATVs, and shooting guns. It was good to get away," she replied, pointedly ignoring the fact he hadn't actually asked what she had been doing.

"Sounds like a lot of fun. Who did you go with?" he asked, taking the bait.

"My neighbor Christopher and some of his ice hockey buddies. I met them all up there; it was a fun group," she elaborated, knowing the sparse details would sting. Cole's smile remained frozen, but it was clear her words hit him in all the right places.

"You went on vacation with that guy? Whatever, Era. At least be real about it. I saw the two of you in the jacuzzi. He's not trying to be your friend. Hope you're taking care of yourself," Cole warned, brimming with jealousy.

"You don't know what you're talking about," Era said, raising her hand in a stop gesture. "He's been the only friend I've had. If you don't recall, my life has been a literal hell, one that you put me in. Christopher sent food every day when I was too depressed to get out of bed. And when I didn't answer the door, he cared enough to go all the way into my room to check on me when he noticed I hadn't moved my car in weeks. He even forced me to start working out with him, which has helped me feel like a normal human being. I know I'm not your problem anymore, but you should at least be happy to hear someone's been there for me."

"You're one to talk. I've been going through my own hell, and now I have to hear you've already moved on. You've got a new guy busting into your room, working you out, and taking you to his family's ranch. Are you guys together? Have you hooked up?" he asked, his hands clenching into shaking fists.

Era had wanted to make him a little jealous, but she hadn't anticipated his directness. She found herself in a tough spot, wanting to respect their past relationship without incriminating herself. Despite her current hatred for him, she felt he deserved honesty. On the other hand, what she had shared with Christopher felt like it belonged to him alone. Finally, she sighed and let the simple truth fall from her lips, "We're not together. But yes, we did hook up."

The air expelled from Cole like a punch to the gut, and he covered his eyes with one hand, as if blocking out the truth could make it disappear. The Gift stirred within her, sensing his awakening. Nothing in their previous conversations had brought him out of his protective shell until now. His heart seemed to leap at her, wild with possessive fury. He had never faced the reality that she would move on, especially since he truly loved her. Licks of flaming agony appeared around him and a popping sound like the small sappy explosions of a campfire flung burning bits of jealousy at her.

"You didn't," he said at first, disbelief lacing his tone. The words burned Era with a wicked intensity. She felt acutely ashamed, knowing her actions were further marred by alcohol. His line of questioning grew intrusive as he spoke the words she could never be prepared to hear, "When did this happen? Did you have sex with him?"

Oh gosh, there it was. The painful question hung between them like a ten-thousand-pound weight, crushing guilt ready to smash them both. "We kissed three days after you broke up with me. This past weekend it went further, but we didn't have sex," she muttered, the words burning like acid vomit coming out.

"Three days?" he roared. "What was that at your house then? You ask me to come over to talk, tell me you love me, and ask if I should wait for you," he scoffed, continuing, "You couldn't wait a week! And you're telling me you seriously hooked up with this guy, even though you didn't have sex with him, what... one day after we spoke? You're unbelievable. It sounds like you have a lot of secrets and our relationship meant nothing to you. I don't even know you anymore," he spat.

His perspective on the timeline convicted her actions even more harshly. She hadn't connected the dots the way he had, leaving her repulsed by her own choices.

"I know. I've felt horrible about it. I haven't been making good decisions, drinking too much, and feeling depressed. I haven't spoken to him since we got back. It was a mistake," she admitted, laying herself bare before his wrath. Era recognized his anger as justified, unwilling to shield her shame behind excuses.

Though Cole still fumed, he stopped yelling, which felt like progress. Tears brimmed in his eyes, fighting to spill over until Era stepped into him and wrapped her arms around him. "I'm so sorry, Cole. I would give anything for things to go back to the way they were. I miss you so much."

At that, a tear slipped down his cheek, and he hugged her back. "Promise me you'll stay away from him," he said, shaking slightly as he melted into her embrace. One touch and he experienced the way they snapped back together, perfectly aligned like magnets. It was maddening.

"Okay," she replied to Cole's demand. "Goodbye, Cole." With that, she turned, her legs carrying her up the stairs on their own. Her mind drifted a mile away. She never looked back, feeling his embrace like vines that grew quickly and attempted to wrap their bodies together once more. She needed to put as much space between his physical body and hers before losing herself all over again.

CHAPTER 25

Coming home, shaken after her run-in with Cole, proved difficult in the empty house. She tried FaceTiming Alex, but as usual, she didn't pick up. She checked her email and saw a message from her mother. They had fallen in love with a charming village in the French countryside. Her dad decided to work remotely from an Airbnb for a few extra days while they explored lavender fields, ruins, and vineyards. Good for them.

A Snap from Chase caught her attention—thank goodness for a positive distraction. He was on a large boat, asking if she wanted him to pick her up on the way to the Island. He planned to take some friends out to stay overnight, anchored in the harbor. Era knew that the marina in Emerald Beach was out of the way for him. He must really want her to go.

If there was one thing she had learned, it was that vacations made for perfect distractions. She snapped back a picture of a weekender bag on her bed, surrounded by her outfits, bikinis, and accessories—and her unmentionables.

Chase responded with a little present emoji and the words, "Kamila will not be on board."

That sealed the deal; she agreed to let him pick her up locally at 11 the next morning. Still, the troubling visions and harsh conversation with Cole lingered in her mind. Thankfully, her to-do list of packing, planning, and emailing her mom occupied her thoughts.

The next morning, as she grabbed her belongings plus a tote and headed out the door, she noticed white paper sticking out from under the mat. Era gawked at the substantial envelope with her name on it, then recognized the handwriting instantly. She darted to her car with it, slamming the door closed behind her, her pulse hammering in her ears. Once seated in the privacy of her black Jeep, Era pulled her finger through the sharp edge of the sealed package.

It was a letter from none other than Cole. She gulped painfully, her mouth suddenly dry. The letter read:

Era,

I've been miserable all day since seeing you. I can't begin to describe how painful it was to hear that you've already moved on with someone else. I'm not writing to guilt you about that, but it was a shock. I hope you meant it when you said you were sorry it happened and keep your promise to me to stay away from him.

I know that I'm partially to blame for the terrible place you've been in these past weeks, and I'm so sorry that you've had to suffer at my hands. I want so much to be there for you, but things aren't better for me

and every day is a battle to get through. I'm
sure if nothing had gone wrong in my family, you
and I would be together right now. Instead of
making happy memories with you, I'm fighting to
protect Cassia from being traumatized by the
breakdown of my family.

I do still love you and hope someday to
have a second chance. You can call or text me
anytime you need to talk. I promise I will
answer every one of your messages from now on.

None but you,
Cole

Era screamed in the car as she read those final words, smashing
her palms into the steering wheel, tears blurring her vision as
she clutched the gold watch in her hands. He had included it
with the letter, and she hadn't expected an inanimate object to
fracture her so completely. She threw the letter and the watch
into her tote and sped recklessly to the marina, determined not
to let his words destroy her once more.

Era sat at the dock, the muggy air clinging to her, heavy with
the scent of salt and anxiety. Nearby, the stench of sea lions
basking on the transom platforms of docked boats mingled with
her mood. Then she saw it, a handsome black yacht gliding
toward her. She knew little about boating, but this vessel
appeared to be at least fifty feet long and stunning. Even if it
paled slightly compared to Christopher's yacht—one she had

only seen from a distance—it signaled that Chase's family possessed not just money, but wealth. And style.

"Hi, I'm Justice," a dark-haired guy with honey-colored eyes called as he threw a bumper overboard to cushion their approach. He helped her aboard, pulling her safely over the narrow but anxiety-inducing gap of water.

"Nice to meet you. How do you know Chase?" she asked, intrigued. He looked older—perhaps in his early twenties—with a muscular build that surpassed the younger hockey players. His long hair fell in waves around his face, and his bronze skin contrasted with a tight black T-shirt. He flashed a million-dollar smile, momentarily knocking Era off balance.

"Chase is *my* little brother," he replied, clarifying that he was not defined by his relationship to Chase, but the other way around.

Era flashed him an amused smile before saying, "Well then, thank you for having me aboard. Your boat is gorgeous."

Justice offered to take her bags to a cabin below, and as she turned, she was greeted by a stupefying sight: Christopher stood before her, looking sexy and preppy in a white button-down shirt, sleeves rolled up over strong forearms, navy chinos, and dark sunglasses. Overcoming a wave of vertigo and a choking sensation, she moved to hug him.

"Didn't think you'd get rid of me that easily, did you?" he whispered as they embraced.

Chase appeared, looking a bit sheepish, and gave her a playful hug, lifting her off her feet and spinning her before setting her down. He introduced her to the rest of their small party: Justice brought along a brown-haired girl named Grace, who he liked but wasn't dating yet. And then she met Priscilla—Cilla for short—a chirpy blonde with a warm demeanor.

Afterward, Era followed Chase for a quick tour of the boat. The main level featured a sun deck at the front, a kitchen and dining area in the center, and a spacious aft deck for their group. Below, a well-appointed bathroom with a shower and a cute little window overlooking the water greeted her at the bottom of the stairs. To the right was a master bedroom boasting a king bed, while to the left was a cozy second cabin with two double beds and little room for much else.

"It'll be a little tight for the six of us. Listen, I'm sorry I didn't warn you Christopher would be joining us. To be honest, he kind of invited himself at the last minute," Chase explained, his wide eyes begging her forgiveness.

"It's okay. The guy has zero boundaries, so I'm not surprised," she said, surveying the layout again. "Where exactly do you have me sleeping?" she asked, raising an eyebrow.

"Wherever you're most comfortable. Justice is trying to snag the big bedroom, but if you want to stay with me, I could claim it. I know this is like the fourth time I've offered, but I seriously respect you. I won't try anything. A room with me might be less awkward than other arrangements, if you know what I mean. I saw the way you hugged Christopher, and it looks like something's weird there," he finished, presenting his case for cohabitation, cool as a cucumber.

Dammit, he was astute about how the other options were potentially worse. What was she going to do—share a bed with Priscilla, a random girl she just met or, worse, with Christopher in front of Chase?

Her heart hammered in her chest, her stomach dropping as if the ship had crested a twenty-foot wave, even though they were motoring through the no-wake zone of the harbor. That thought felt too complicated to tackle now. She pushed it down and made her way back up the stairs, bracing herself for close quarters with yet another group of strangers and a jilted beau.

The open water greeted them with a brisk wind and a touch of chop. Chase captained their trek to the island, about two hours off the coast. Justice stepped up as an excellent substitute host, mixing a round of the island's trademark drink—a twist on a White Russian that featured crème de banana and a generous topping of whipped cream. They called it "Buffalo Milk." Eww. Era politely declined; she had enough trouble with alcohol-fueled decisions lately.

The boat sliced through the water smoothly, minimizing the bounce of the chop until Era felt soothed by the irregular rhythm of the jostling. Christopher sat up with Chase in the captain's chair while she made conversation with Cilla and Grace. Both lived in suburbs close to the city, an hour away, and neither shared similar interests or hobbies with Era, making it unlikely they would become anything more than acquaintances.

She caught snippets of conversation between Christopher and Chase, but she did her best to focus on the proximate company. That is, until she overheard a distinctive word— "Snap"—and the Gift went haywire.

Christopher's heart squeezed with pain and jealousy. Era saw the memory of him checking his phone repeatedly, waiting for her reply, and seething with frustration. Chase appeared cocky yet slightly guilty. He had slipped up in mentioning the ongoing Snapchat conversation with Era since leaving the ranch. Nope, nevermind. It hadn't been a slip. Era bristled that Chase had rubbed their private communication in Christopher's face. Though he didn't know that Era had entirely ignored Christopher since he dropped her off. He stood up and went downstairs without looking at her.

After a few minutes, unable to bear the tension, Era followed him down to the cabins. She felt marooned on this tiny floating island and knew it was time to face her fate. She found him in the main cabin, where Justice had suspiciously stored her bags.

"Looks like I've got to beg you to stay out of Chase's room for a third time, don't I?" Christopher chided angrily as she entered. Era opened her mouth to reply but froze at the alarming and rather sickening sight before her: the letter—her letter—lay in his lap.

She took three swift steps towards him and snatched it off his leg. "Are you seriously reading my letter right now?"

Christopher showed no sign of remorse for snooping through her purse. "You saw him... again... after we..." he sputtered. Anger mixed with devastation washed over his features.

"I ran into him at the beach, a total coincidence," she said, momentarily confused as to why she was justifying herself when he had invaded her privacy. He had no right to question her about information he had obtained illicitly.

A flicker of relief passed over his face before he pressed on. "He's hurt you so much. Why would you make him any promises?" His hands tore at his hair, his voice tight with frustration. "Promises about me?"

"No, you're right. I don't owe him anything. He caught me off guard, and when he asked me to promise him, I said 'okay' and walked away. I didn't mean it. That's not why I've been avoiding you. I've been processing what happened, struggling to figure out what the right thing is to do," she explained. The overwhelming emotions and the stress of tackling too many subjects at once was throwing her off. She took a deep breath, steadying her focus.

"Era, by now I'm pretty sure you've figured out that I would do almost anything for you. I'll wait for you, take care of you, let you bounce me around between the friendzone and the friends with benefits zone. I let you throw me aside when you need more time to sort yourself out. I've been going crazy these past three days without hearing from you, and I would have given you space if you really needed it, but I can't get past the fact that you were talking to Chase, sending him cute good mornings and pictures in beautiful yellow dresses.

"Do you know how that makes me feel? And then to find out you apologized to your ex about hooking up with me—ugh," his voice trailed off, filled with anguish and exasperation.

Era wanted to respond, but she sensed he wasn't finished

and wanted to let him get it all out. The conversation left her stumbling for a way forward; should she defend herself regarding the letter, rage at him for reading it, console him, or apologize for messaging Chase while ignoring him?

He turned his gaze to her, eyes brimming with a vulnerability that made Era's legs quiver as he spoke. "I've never held back from you. I've always been straightforward, telling you exactly how I felt, no matter the risk of rejection. And there's something special when we're together. Our bodies feel like they're meant for each other. But you're so wrapped up in your grief that you haven't considered how you're hurting me. So your heart was broken, and now mine is broken too."

She didn't cry. His words piled up in her arms like rocks, pushing her down, sinking her with guilt. She reached for him, but he brushed past her without wanting to hear a single word. The door to their intimacy slammed shut, replaced by a cold and alien distance.

The boat had reached the protected cove and began to drop anchor a short distance from shore. Overwhelmed by the thought of staying there for another second, Era charged up the stairs, grabbed a paddleboard and leapt into the water without thought or hesitation. She paddled to the shore and climbed the tallest nearby cliff to sit and think. The cerulean water and bright cloudless day would have made for a glorious sight; except that today, Era felt as dangerous as a wildfire and a thunderstorm combined.

Why did I leave the stupid letter in my open tote bag? she thought, frustrated. It was likely he had seen it easily without even trying to poke around in her things. She could have passed off the harmless Snaps to Chase, but the letter? No, it contained too many excruciating details for Christopher to overanalyze

The worst part about this whole situation revolved around Cole's letter, which clearly indicated his desire to reopen communication, promising to answer her messages anytime. He felt jealous of Christopher and horrified at the idea of her moving on. He said he loved her!

But it was too freaking late. The misery of the past few weeks had begun to subside, and she found herself seeing Cole's lack of mettle. It hurt to admit, but he behaved like a coward, untrustworthy with her heart. His cowardice led to selfishness, and he acted first out of self-preservation. Now his words opened up a clear path for reconciliation, and perhaps that realization frightened Christopher more than anything. It likely explained why he hadn't wanted to hear her speak, believing a reunion with Cole was on the inevitable horizon.

Christopher's eyes flickered in her mind, exposed and raw. Part of her knew he would never shy away from her, no matter the challenges he faced. The undeniable pull of his desire for her filled her with warmth, even in the wake of her actions. The fact that she could hurt him only meant that his heart still stood all the way open to her. And just like that, his was the heart she wanted. A part of her, still deeply sleeping and hiding from reality, began to awaken. He had stirred her once from a dream in her room, and now he opened her eyes to a future she longed to grasp. He had won her—won her with his broken heart—and now she yearned to heal it.

When she looked up, the Gift fiercely disagreed. Thunderclouds gathered over the yacht, and a swirling whirlpool threatened to pull the boat under. Alarm shot through her, and she inhaled sharply. But she scowled at the picture and pushed the fear away. It merely served as a warning, one she didn't care to heed. The moment she upheld her previous decision, to secure Christopher's heart for herself, the vision blinked away, returning the cove to calm emerald waters and sunny skies.

Delirium and euphoria swept over her as she dug the paddle into the water, paddling back to the boat, panting and glistening with sweat.

"How was it?" Justice called, eyeing her body as he helped haul the board back onto the deck.

"Cathartic," she replied, toweling off before grabbing a surprised Christopher's hand and dragging him back downstairs to the cabin. She shut the door, seeking as much privacy as the ship could offer. "Everything you said—everything—is so right. I don't deny any of it. I knew I was hurting you, and I'm so sorry for it. Please forgive me—"

"Are you going back to him?" he asked, assuming she merely sought to apologize.

Era grabbed his face, her heart racing. "I'm never going back to him. How could I, when all I want is you?"

His hands hung limply at his sides. "You do?" he asked, sounding unconvinced. "How do I know you won't change your mind? Maybe tomorrow you won't."

"I've wanted you since that night in the jacuzzi at my house. I didn't think you deserved my torn-up life. Now I don't care about any of that. You know what you're getting yourself into with me. If you want me, I'm yours—today, tomorrow, always."

His hands lifted slowly to her face as she finished her declaration, astonishment followed by bliss filling the bubble around them. She leaned closer, and he crashed his lips into hers. The joy of opening her heart in that kiss felt glorious. Her heart sang for him, and she Pulled him with the Gift until their mouths transformed into doorways leading to the most secret chambers of each other.

Not long passed before the kiss ignited that same frenzy as before. The wave of emotion dashed her against him like a storm-battered boat finally thrown into the rocks, every point where they met a thrilling connection. He tore away from her lips, the separation painfully tangible for both of them.

"It's true then."

"Yes, it's true."

"I do want you, every part of you," he declared, his eyes alight with intensity.

"Mmm, good, because I'll expect every part of you," she replied, rubbing his earlobe, suddenly annoyed that they were stuffed on a too-crowded ship. "I just wish we could get off this boat and be alone somewhere else."

He chuckled, "That can be arranged. Come on."

"No way, let me guess, you already sent out a telepathic message in the last five seconds and a chopper is about to appear in the sky."

"Better," he said, grabbing her hand and leading her back up the stairs. She felt a mix of shock and anticipation upon seeing a massive yacht approaching. "After you left, I decided I was over being here, so I called our captain to pick me up. Looks like my departure just got an upgrade."

"Christopher, come on! How do you have the whole world at your beck and call at any hour? This is insane!" Era stood on the stern in anticipation, and looked out to see Antoine putter across the water on a small dinghy to transfer them. Chase came around from the sundeck on the front, shiny with tanning oil, a confused look on his face. Once he glanced down and saw Era and Christopher's hands linked, he put the pieces together and visibly deflated.

"Hey, man, something came up. I can't stay the night after all," Christopher said, reaching out to give Chase a high-five, his tone casual. "I'm gonna give Era a ride home, don't think she's feeling up to being out here for a whole night."

Chase turned to Era, bypassing Christopher and spoke to her directly, "We just got here. Why don't you hang out for a little bit before you head back?" he suggested, his tone light but his eyes sharp.

"Can't man, I've got to get back," Christopher replied, speaking on Era's behalf and handed both their bags over to his assistant.

She cast her eyes down to the ground; she felt pretty crappy about bailing on him after he'd gone out of his way to pick her up.

"Such a shame. We were just starting to have fun." He looked over at Christopher, and then back to her. They locked eyes and she felt a flutter in her chest, but she held his gaze.

"I'm so sorry to bail on you. Thanks for picking me up."

"Of course," he said, a hint of warmth threading through his voice. "Just remember, I'm not going anywhere. Whenever you're ready for some real adventure, you know where to find me."

He shot her a grin that felt both reassuring and teasing, a flash of something deeper smoldering. As Christopher offered his hand to pull her onto the dinghy, Era glanced back at Chase.

"Take care, Era," he added, his tone shifting, revealing the sincerity beneath his playful demeanor.

She nodded, a mix of gratitude and uncertainty rolling through her. "You too, Chase."

With that, she took Christopher's extended hand and stepped onto the bouncing craft, feeling the weight of his gaze on her back, the subtle tension drifting in the air like the salty breeze.

And just like that, Christopher and Era found themselves alone on his family's yacht—well, sort of. The captain and Antoine, a last-minute crew member, shared the space.

Christopher led her on a second tour. The absurdity was not lost on her. Four levels, five staterooms, indoor and outdoor dining areas, a jacuzzi, and a sauna sprawled before them. Era spotted her bag tucked away in the closet of the second-largest stateroom.

"I guess you finally won't have to wonder where I'll be sleeping tonight, will you?" she teased, grabbing his side.

With a mischievous grin, he scooped her up and tossed her

onto the bed, landing on top of her before capturing her lips in a kiss.

"I think we should celebrate. Come for a swim with me," he suggested, his voice low and inviting.

"You mean, while the boat is moving?" she asked, disbelief mingling with excitement.

He guided her through the back glass doors, calling over his shoulder to Antoine, "Champagne for two, please. We're celebrating."

"We are? What's the occasion?" she replied, her curiosity piqued.

"This is better than skating the rink holding the state trophy. You–us–our anniversary. Today marks the first day I can officially call you my girlfriend," he announced, stepping into the bubbling water.

"I guess it does." She looked him over, the boy she had watched grow into a man before her eyes, now hers. It felt surreal. She had always been a reader of hearts, yet never predicted he would be the one to steal hers.

'Pop!' The sound of a champagne cork startled her from her navel gazing. She set her tote down on the nearest chair and slipped into the swirling water beside him.

Their glasses clinked together, the sprightly bubbles tickling her nose before sliding smoothly over her tongue. It seemed impossible that her life could turn around so completely in such a short time, but she knew why it had—he had made it so.

Wrapping her arms, legs, and lips around him, she surrendered to the moment, unwilling to let him go. Suddenly, the ship lifted over a large wave, jostling her purse and spilling its contents onto the deck. The gold watch tumbled out, gleaming ominously—a stark reminder of broken promises and unhappy endings.

CHAPTER 26

ERA LAY beside her perfect new boyfriend, savoring every detail of his face. The soft moonlight streaming through the cabin's window highlighted the curve of his earlobe, the strong jawline, and the thick lashes resting like fans above his high cheekbones. As she pressed her face into his neck, her fingertips ran across the contours of his chest. He stirred slightly but soon slipped back into a peaceful state. Happiness enveloped her.

She closed her eyes and let the gentle rocking rhythm of the ship lull her to sleep. However, the inside of her head looked very different from her reality as she fell deeply into a net of nightmares. Her dreams pulled Era through a stream of chaotic, carnal sex with Cole that intertwined her memories and insecurities in a way that only dreams can, whipping her violently from intense pleasure to excruciating misery.

She awoke in a weird mix of shame and confusion. It took a minute to calm her racing thoughts. Christopher had no idea of her distress, greeting her with a beautiful, drowsy smile, looking tantalizingly disheveled.

"How did you sleep?" His scratchy voice held a concern that made it hard to resist pulling him on top of her. But last night, as their chemistry heated up, she had decided to take it slow. She didn't want slow, not really, but her confidence remained shaken.

"Next to you—perfect," she lied, planting soft kisses from his lips to his chin and down his neck before jumping out of bed for a shower. Inside, however, guilt gnawed at her for enjoying the fantasies she wouldn't, couldn't, shouldn't pursue with Christopher. She lathered the shower gel onto her shoulders wishing she could wash away the sickening feeling that she had cheated on him after just one day together.

Once dressed, they walked from the boat, safely docked back at the slip, to the main house. Christopher made her breakfast before driving her home—a distance so short it was laughable. Upon arrival, Era found her parents finally back from their cruise. She greeted them cheerfully, eliciting a smile from her mother who asked with unthinking presumptuousness, "Did you and Cole get back together or something?"

Era breathed deeply through her nose. "He's old news. I have a new boyfriend, Christopher Ridgewell. Actually, he helped me through my breakup with Cole—"

"Oh that's nice honey. I wish you'd give Cole another chance though, he's such a nice boy. I bet the shopping helped too. I saw the credit card," she chirped, quickly changing the subject to their trip.

Era gritted her teeth and braced herself for the next few minutes of mindless prattle.

Her joy overshadowed her mom's out-of-touch response. She let her mother rattle on about the details of random strangers she would never meet and the minor inconveniences and sub-par dining experiences they endured on their lavish vacation.

When she went upstairs to unpack she had a message from Christopher.

Come back. I miss you already.

The man was nothing if not emotionally available. She sent a
swift reply.

I love that you miss me but my parents are
finally home. Don't want to make them feel like
I'm running out on them. See you for dinner
and a movie?

It felt good to return to the comforting routine of spending
every free moment with someone—especially since she had
nothing but free moments right now.

The next few days settled into a delightful rhythm. Era woke
in Christopher's bed, they worked out together in the morning,
shared breakfast, and then she occupied herself at home for a
few hours before returning. Rinse and repeat.

After several days, Christopher mentioned that his parents
were returning from vacationing in Sun Valley, Idaho, and he
wanted her to join them for dinner.

Excitement coursed through her. Although she had spent so
much time in their home, she had never met them. The thought
of their scrutiny unnerved her; who could possibly be good
enough for the heir to their empire? It felt as if she were being
evaluated by some American royal court.

She spent the next day FaceTiming with Raquel as they tore
through the sites of their favorite brands, lobbing links to
dresses back and forth until she found the perfect outfit. Well,
Raquel found it, bless her.

Later, she got her nails done with her mom, who, of course,

gushed embarrassingly to the nail techs about her daughter meeting the parents of her 1% boyfriend. *Sheesh, pick a horse already,* she thought with irritation at the flip-flop over which boyfriend she supported.

The pressure steadily increased with each passing hour until she stepped out of her Jeep, onto the familiar driveway, and walked up to the door.

Era smoothed the minimalist champagne House of CB dress and adjusted the vase of black and white anemones, freshly cut from her garden, for Christopher's mother. Taking a deep breath, she rang the doorbell and heard the chime echo down the halls inside.

Antoine opened the door with a nod, creepy silent as ever, and led her down the familiar hall to the outdoor living room where hors d'oeuvres spread out next to a lighted fireplace. When Christopher spotted her, he stood from the outdoor sofa, where Era caught the tail end of their conversation, business of course.

"Lovely to meet you," Laura, Christopher's mother, greeted her first. "I'm Laura. Your dress and these flowers are absolutely gorgeous. I can see why my son has raved about you." Warmth and genuine adoration radiated from her as she leaned in for a polite hug. Laura, dressed in a simple camel sheath with black heels, embodied understated wealth and taste. At around late thirties, she looked remarkably youthful for a mother of a college-bound son, her ash brown hair and brown eyes complementing her fit figure.

Christopher's father approached next, offering a firm handshake. "We're glad to have you. I'm Caspar." The Gift revealed his cautious yet optimistic nature, a father eager to like her but wary of the intrusion into their guarded life. Era didn't hold that against him.

"Thank you for having me. I've heard so much about the both of you and have wanted nothing more than to hear about your plans for Christopher" —she said, addressing Caspar before turning to Laura— "and compliment you on the stunning design of the ranch house."

Laura's face lit up with excitement as she began to share details about working with designers to select fabrics for the kitchen banquette and the exquisite mid-century vintage candlesticks adorning the table. Apparently, they were truly mid-century vintage pieces from Denmark.

In minutes, she had the two of them in the palm of her hand, hitting the sweet spot of their most preferred subjects without coming off as too familiar.

As she settled on the outdoor sofa beside Caspar, Christopher chatted with his mother out of earshot. "So what's the plan for Christopher with the family business?" Era asked, making sure to keep her tone light and casual as she navigated the conversation. "It seems he is one hundred percent invested in its success and speaking from my experience as his classmate for the past few years, I believe you to have a bright mind at your disposal."

"I agree," Caspar replied, his eyes steely but benevolent. "We've always instilled a strong work ethic in him and I can tell he is cut out for the business though it's not easy, let me tell you." He paused and swirled the honey-colored liquid in his glass. "I plan to let him finish his studies, then start him as a VP in one of the departments. But shhh... don't tell him I told you that," he added with a conspiratorial grin, clearly testing her with the little bit of confidence.

Era saw his pride and concern for Christopher's future as he sipped his Scotch. "He'll have to work his way up and prove he can handle real responsibility before I hand over anything."

"If I may make a suggestion," Era chimed in.

Caspar's eyebrows rose, a mix of delight and surprise at a young woman boldly offering business advice to the CEO of an empire. "Of course."

THE GIFT OF RUIN

"Consider putting him in acquisitions. He has an exceptional gift for perception. I believe he can sniff out the true intentions of anyone, something business school can't teach."

"Is that how he finally won you over?" he asked with a teasing tone.

Era feigned shock but couldn't help but smile. "Yes, well, that and patience."

"If you worked for me, where do you think you'd fit in?"

"Talent Acquisition. I excel at reading people," she replied confidently. "And I have a certain knack for detecting dishonesty. But—" she lowered her gaze demurely, "I see myself owning a business, not working for someone else."

Caspar raised a brow and leaned towards her. "Each unit of my business is worth hundreds of millions. It would take quite a while and a lot of luck to create a company from scratch that rivaled even a single sector. You might reconsider joining the Ridgewell family someday." His words were sincere but she could read down to the depths of his unsaid meaning. He didn't take her seriously and thought it would take little time or convincing to get her to do just what he wanted, given the right enticement. Everyone had a price.

"Are you offering me a job?" she asked, only half kidding and wanting to cool down the contentiousness. She knew if she stayed in this family, he would expect her to work for them. Caspar believed in keeping everything tight to the vest.

However serious, their little exchange cracked the door of familiarity, and Era and Caspar continued their witty banter as he probed deeper into her background. She mentioned only details that would impress him without coming off as too showy—her best friend's job as an Au Pair in Europe, her tennis ranking, and her vigorous workouts with his son. She touched on her London friend circle, hinting at exciting travels while avoiding any implication of being a golddigger. Finally, to align herself with Laura's interests, she spoke of her passion for hospitality, especially in growing and arranging flowers, cook-ing, and hosting parties.

By the end of their conversation, Caspar appeared convinced he stood before his future daughter-in-law. In his eyes, there existed no possibility his son could find a more excellent accumulation of the beauty and gifts that he would have wanted to collect in a trophy wife in his younger years

Era marveled at the construction of what he believed formed the "right type of woman" for his son. As he had enough wealth, he cared little about money or accomplishments. In fact, if she had said she wanted to study medicine or any similarly demanding career, she would have lost favor in his mind. To him, only refined manners, a proper upbringing in a sensible family, domestic interests, and a moldable discreet personality mattered. Money provided the rest.

Era witnessed how he envisioned a role for her in the fami-ly's future endeavors, knowing she needed only an undergrad-uate degree before fitting seamlessly into a position under Laura. Caspar, a firm believer in keeping family close, believed that anyone near the family should be woven into the business. He had known about Christopher's infatuation with Era, and expected them to be a lasting pair.

The Gift showed the pride he took in his son for securing Era after four years, crediting her with desirability and worthi-ness since what else could have caused her to ignore his son's affections for so long. He knew wealth attracted women.

Within fifteen minutes, Era marveled at how willing Caspar was to bring her into the fold. He loved and trusted Christopher that much. Despite recognizing the future he planned for her in a gilded cage, the vision of their familial acceptance drew her with an unshakeable appeal. They would absorb her, shape her identity yes, but she would never again feel like an outsider, unwanted. An inconvenience.

"So where are you going to school in the fall?" he asked, as

Antoine signaled that dinner was served. Era welcomed the interruption, glad to postpone that particular question and avoid popping the bubble of admiration. Losing her admission? Not a good look.

At dinner, Era had the pleasure of further conversation with Laura. They exchanged an array of questions, from favorite authors (Sowell for Era, of course) to her decision to pursue tennis in high school. His mother, so full of warmth and genuine interest, pressed for every detail about Era's weekend at the ranch, her and Christopher's rivalry in school, and even the impromptu dinner Era had hosted. She inquired about the menu! Era preened and glowed. By the end, Era found herself enamored with both Christopher and his mother, the latter a singularly remarkable lady.

Crème brûlée with raspberries topped off the meal, after which Christopher and Era excused themselves for some one-on-one time, retreating to the pool table in the game room. He itched to hear her impressions of his parents, while she took a moment to breathe, tempering visions of her potential future with the sober reminder that fairytales rarely unfolded as hoped.

"So?" he asked, pecking her on the lips as he ushered her into the room, then walked to the small bar to mix them a drink.

Era's voice caught in her throat as she began, "I think I'm in love..." She saw his hand, stirring ice into tumblers, freeze. "With your family." His hands resumed movement as he turned, carrying Old Fashioneds over to her, a smile lighting his face.

"I'm sure I'll get the full rundown later. I can say definitively that they like you. I've never seen my dad engage with a girl I brought home for that long and with such interest."

"Who did you bring home?" she asked, her eyes wide in exaggeration.

"Meh, nobody important," he replied and clinked their glasses in cheers.

"You're really lucky, you know. Your parents invest so much in your future, and they genuinely care about what you have to say. I mean your mom showed more interest in my life than my own mother ever has."

As she stirred her drink, she snuck a glance at him, her eyes a bit dewey. Though she thought she had long accepted her parents' neglect and made the best of it, moments like this made her feel hollow, reminded her of that pesky desire to be part of a real family. Now, she desired Christopher—and all of them. A vision of herself as a permanent member of the Ridgewell family unfurled, a dangerously hopeful thought.

"I know how lucky I am," he said, reaching into the bar drawer to pull out a rectangular black box. "I noticed the watch in your purse and hope you throw it out. But it wouldn't feel right to ask you to do that without replacing it first."

He opened the box to reveal a stunning gold smart watch bracelet adorned with diamond links. Exquisite and practical, Era absolutely loved it.

"Now you can't say you didn't receive my messages either," he teased, fastening the band around her wrist and kissing her open palm.

Era treasured the watch, but what moved her even more was how Christopher found every every little path into her heart, never overlooking the smallest opportunity to show her what she meant to him. Overwhelmed by the waterfall of love she felt throughout the night, she buried her face in his neck and kissed him, her heart brimming with gratitude.

Feeling too self-conscious to stay the night with his parents home, Era returned to her own bed, allowing Antoine to drive her. As she climbed the dark stairs to her room, a glimmer on her wrist caught her eye. Glowing green eyes looked up at her from the watch face, jealous and sinister. Anger flared within her, and she shook her arm, frustrated that the Gift tainted the meaning of the thoughtful present with devious implications.

It took just a week for Era to grow comfortable sleeping in Christopher's bed even when his parents were home. They didn't mind; it aligned with their family philosophy of keeping those in their inner circle close. Era soon abandoned the charade of returning home, preferring to spend her time with Christopher, at his family's beach club, and even helping Laura with fabric swatches for her latest project or running her errands.

Before long, Laura began off-loading extra Celine purses and other luxury items onto Era. Christopher invited her to be his date for a gala in D.C., heavily underwritten by the Ridgewell family's companies. They boarded a private jet, with a suite at the Four Seasons booked for them.

Christopher linked his card to her phone and watch so she could pay for whatever she needed—dresses for their dates, gas, food—anything. Era felt no discomfort with this gesture; having grown up in a comfortably wealthy family, she understood it satisfied his desire to take care of her. She wouldn't think to abuse it, knowing that the amount remained negligible compared to their wealth.

As Era immersed herself in this new phase with Christopher, she noted the opulence surrounding them. The luxury of the private jet and their lavish hotel suite underscored a seriousness in their bond that felt remarkably adult for two eighteen-year-olds. She embraced the extravagance without discomfort, realizing that their relationship had evolved beyond typical teenage infatuation. Wrapped in this cocoon of wealth, Era felt a sense of belonging, aware that she and Christopher shared a connection that held the promise of forever.

Just a month into their relationship, Christopher joked about taking her out for their "first anniversary." Celebrating a one-month milestone seemed silly, yet Era began to reflect on the time they had spent together. They had fallen into what felt like the most serious adult relationship of her life.

Still, one aspect remained untouched: despite their closeness and desire, she hadn't gone back on her wish to wait before sleeping together. Sex clouded everything, and though she wanted to cross that line several times, each instance brought forth memories of the way her soul had fused with Cole's and restrained herself. She knew that act introduced the potential for pain, pain she had only recently been able to push out of her mind.

If only she could talk about it with him. He never brought up the subject, never pushed even in their most passionate moments, and simply enjoyed all the other ways they could be intimate. But how long would he wait before he pushed for more? More importantly, how long would he wait before he pushed for the reason behind why not? She couldn't give him one and it didn't feel right.

CHAPTER 27

CHRISTOPHER PULLED out all the stops for their one-month anniversary celebration. Antoine, mute as ever, drove them to the City in a Mercedes Sprinter van, the new limousine. Plush leather captain's chairs filled the luxe interior, complete with a bar and even a bathroom in the rear. Era smirked at the thought of the trouble she and Alex would have gotten into if they had driven this luxury hotel on wheels instead of a Jeep.

Era chose a pale silvery dress to accentuate her summer tan. Laura had gifted her a stunning pair of vintage Prada heels and lent her a diamond and white gold drop pendant necklace to complement her watch. Christopher's broad shoulders looked sharp in a black single-breasted suit. She peered behind his collar, spotting the magical label—Prada, of course.

At dinner, no menu graced the table, a telltale sign that a fantastic experience rather than just a meal awaited them. Caviar unveiled under a smoke-filled cloche, salmon nigiri torched table-side, and a Wagyu served on a hot stone set the stage.

But as the final course arrived, Christopher's body language shifted, becoming skittish. The Gift fell dormant around him, a troubling sign she hadn't anticipated.

Era suspected that the Gift was remiss to show her more about him when she had so forcefully rejected its warnings to stay away from him. As such, her appetite for dessert shriveled as her anxiety skyrocketed. She didn't want to be caught unprepared for some kind of news so late into their evening together.

"As much as I would happily celebrate any day with you, our one-month anniversary isn't the real reason I took you out tonight." Era's heart raced, a swell of adrenaline coursing through her. What could he possibly have to say?

Oh my gosh, if he pulls a Cole right now I will literally die, she thought.

He opened the lapel of his jacket and pulled out a piece of paper from the inside pocket. "I can't take all the credit for this; my dad had the most to do with it. This is for you." He handed her the paper, but she struggled to open it, feeling the weight of déjà vu settling over her.

"My dad's lawyers wrote a letter to Emerald Prep and resubmitted the paper you wrote for Mr. E's history class. The administration wanted to avoid litigation and agreed to give you half credit, which bumps your grade up to a B-. Then my dad pulled a few strings with Cal, and they reinstated your admission. You're going to school with me after all. Can you believe it's only two weeks away?"

Her brain stalled at "litigation," and she stared at him, mouth agape, before processing his words. He had threatened to sue the school—and it had worked! "Christopher, you didn't!" she nearly shouted, jumping out of her seat to hug him. "Oh my gosh, we're going to be there together. I've never been so happy in my whole life. Thank you."

To continue the celebration he led her upstairs where a trendy lounge awaited. A DJ spun music while a young, vibrant crowd danced, enjoying bottle service of champagne and vodka.

The moment they found a pocket of space, Era seized Christopher by the collar and pulled him close, swaying her body with the beat. His bright eyes sparkled down at her, filled with warmth and desire.

He was a net of safety that caught her free fall, swaddling her in protection from all the evils of the world—including herself. How could she not fall in love with this man? She wanted to give him all of herself in that moment, to hold nothing back. Overcome with euphoria, she kissed him deeply, ready to surrender her heart. He returned her passion, letting the moment build without breaking the kiss. When she finally came up for air, she saw fire burning all around them.

I don't care. As long as I can have him, let it burn, she thought.

CHAPTER 28

Now, two weeks didn't seem like enough time to change the complete direction of her life. Many arrangements needed to be made, but the most critical loomed large: she had to petition the housing department to place her and Alex together as roommates.

Somehow, Caspar made a few calls to sort it out, endearing him to her even further. In fact, she hadn't been kidding when she confessed to falling in love in the pool room. She really was beginning to love Caspar and Laura while simultaneously falling hard for Christopher.

Era shoved down the memory of the exchange with her own parents over the news. No surprise, they had figured out a way to take credit for it.

"I knew I raised the kind of daughter who could figure things out," her mother had said before changing the subject to some "renovations" she planned once Era's room was vacated, as if Era's entire life trajectory hadn't been redirected in the blink of an eye.

"Don't make us look bad. Focus on your grades, not parties," her Dad had said, a visible mushroom cloud of jealousy blooming around him at the knowledge that Caspar had accomplished it all. No congratulations, no joy, just an enthusiastic shove out the door. Era kept her face serene through the conversation, reminding herself that the trust from Grandmother's inheritance kicked in on her next birthday and she wouldn't need his approval, or his money after that.

All these preparations would have been distraction enough, yet something shifted within Era. She couldn't pinpoint the exact moment the changes took hold, the feeling of being sucked out, much like a swimmer caught in a riptide, unaware that their efforts to reach shore were futile against an invisible current.

Two days before leaving Emerald Beach for the dorms, Era soaked in the early morning quiet of the Ridgewell house. She carried two steaming mugs from the kitchen and began heading back up to Christopher's room, until she felt the twang of a chord humming through her, a song long-forgotten. Despite not wanting the help to see her in pajama shorts, Christopher's baggy shredded hockey tee, and wild hair, she stopped in her tracks across the room from the glossy black piano.

That thrum vibrated through her again, and her fingertips tingled, as if telling her she could let that beautiful tone out, if she only touched the keys. She crossed the room and set the mug down on the little table next to the couch and let the object pull her in, the tone taking up texture and shape in her mind.

She had never played an instrument, did not even read music, but as she looked at the contrast of the bright black and white keys, her hands reached out as if wanting to hold the melody she heard. When her fingers touched the smooth surface, the entire piece burst into her mind.

The sound rang out, as familiar to her as Happy Birthday. She saw with perfect clarity the intricacy of the music, not only how to play the notes but the theory of their beauty. The math and scales wove together in her mind, until she saw the cohesive piece hanging before her, an intricate tapestry, embroidered with a detail that only a master could create.

She began to sing, lyrics bursting from her soul, as if the secrets of her heart were pouring out of her mouth. It must be a dream. Only a dream could feel like this, where the potential of an untapped mind rose above physical limitations.

Her voice soared with grace, with a simultaneous ease and power that lifted her into an ecstasy above the notes. She heard the words from a distant place and realized that the Gift sang a love song to her. Her voice personified its beauty as it told her how it protected and guarded her. It begged her to trust and to give herself over to a love that would never fail her, a love that was forever.

Her cracked heart seized in that line. Failure. That pain she knew well, the pain she believed she could never escape. It would always find her in the end. But this promise, could she trust it? God, she wanted to believe.

Her fingers traveled over the keys, with the dexterity of a ballerina, her ligaments stretched to accommodate the complex shapes in the melody. Her voice drew the song to its close and her burning eyes gave up a single tear.

When it ended, a sensation like wind rushing back into her fingertips returned her to the present moment, only to realize she wasn't alone. Christopher stood nearby, recording her with his phone. "That was unbelievable. I didn't even know you could play." His eyes danced with pride and disbelief.

Era knew that this new development would be more difficult than the secret knowledge of the Gift to conceal. She tucked a stray hair that dropped from her messy bun behind her ear, smearing the tear away with the motion and gave him an embarrassed smile.

"Hope it's not cold," she said, handing Christopher his coffee.

Upstairs in the shower, she had a private freak-out. The truth of the song and the feeling of releasing that beautiful melody with her hands held an undeniable power. After collecting herself, she planned a way to keep Christopher from asking her parents when she started taking lessons. She would have to cover her tracks and get him to delete the video. She couldn't do it herself. He was too smart for that, and it'd end up drawing his attention and his suspicion with it.

The only problem was, she thought she'd have more time to do it.

The next morning, she woke up to 47 text messages. Bewilderment battled with alarm. What could be wrong? A death? Some major world event that took place during the night? She swiped the intricate pattern into her phone to unlock it and knitted her brows to see the compilation of names texting her— five from Alex, several from distant cousins, three from random classmates, and an old fling in London. All connected to her. She started with Alex's messages.

> Babe, you're probably going to kill me when you read this but yesterday Christopher sent me a video of you playing the piano and singing in his house. It was the most effing incredible thing I've ever seen. And when I said it was impossible, he sent ANOTHER video of you doing karaoke at his ranch with some hot dark haired guy. So I thought what the heck and made a social media account for you and posted the videos.

> I swear I did not think they were going to blow up like this, but here's the link.

> OMG Era you already hit a million likes.

> Call me as soon as you wake up.

> Hello? Wake up, you're famous!

She was living in a bizarre reality. Visions and levitation and reading people's secret desires and playing instruments of which she had no training or knowledge was one thing. But to have one of her inexplicable Gifts be thrown up on the internet for the world to see and comment on? New nightmare, unlocked.

She scrolled and gasped as she saw Cole's name in the string of texts.

> Wow, just saw the video of your song. Really beautiful. Can't believe you never shared that talent with me. What else don't I know?

Ugh, annoying. Then she noticed a Snap from Chase.

> I didn't realize we were such a power duo. Heard you're joining me in the fall at Cal. Can't wait for our encore.

. . .

That did it. "Wake up!" She shoved Christopher awake and slammed her thumb down on the FaceTime icon next to Alex's name. Time to murder her best friend.

Alex picked up on the first ring. "Can you believe this?"

Era ignored the joy on her friend's face. Not an ounce of remorse then. "No, I can't! What the hell were you thinking?"

"Don't be mad. Everyone loves you! Have you seen the comments?"

"No, and I don't want to. You know how I feel about social media. Promise me, no more videos!"

"Okay, I promise. But the Rule is dead, remember? Fresh start? Oh, and good morning, Christopher! Your girl's a star! See you tomorrow. Can't wait to grab the better side of the room before you get there!"

Era took a few breaths to let the knee-jerk murderous rage settle and her heart to slow. Yes, the Rule was dead but her desire to be in control of other people's reactions to her wasn't.

Christopher scrolled and scrolled and scrolled through comments next to her until she couldn't take it anymore and slapped a hand over his screen. "Got it," he said, trying to keep the mood light and put his phone away.

If it were *anyone* else, she probably would have made them take it down and stormed over to unleash the fury of the Pull on them if they refused. But this was Alex. Her survival instincts roared within her, but the agony of tearing the thrill of a viral video away from her proved too cruel. Man, she loved her friend too much. It'd likely be the death of her.

"Gym sesh?" she asked Christopher as she flung back the covers and jumped out of his bed. She needed to work out the bees buzzing in her head. She pictured Alex arriving early to obsess over setting up their new dorm room. Her feet snapped into the tight leggings as she dressed.

What's done is done, she thought. Maybe Alex had just unwittingly ruined her life, but Era missed her best friend so much she didn't care. She would be together with all the people that mattered most to her in the world. What harm could two little videos do anyway? They'd be forgotten in a day.

CHAPTER 29

THE BIG DAY should have marked a monumental shift in her life. Era felt like a rehabilitated animal released back into its natural habitat. Her parent's thoughts would stop pounding her self-esteem, the double life shattered, and her relationships could grow, unfettered by old limitations. And going from one to fifty thousand students meant she could find her people, and spread her wings.

She stepped outside her house in Emerald Beach and into a new chapter that felt more fabulous, more Gifted, and more free.

Yet unease crept in as she hugged her parents goodbye in the driveway and climbed into her Jeep, where Christopher waited in the driver's seat. She looked over at his soft waves and proud eyes and wanted her heart to gush. But the cab felt muffled, the sounds hushed. Her Gift slumbered somewhere deep, refusing to awaken in his presence, taking with it that fourth dimension of noise and color that she had grown used to around others.

She didn't want to dwell on it, to spoil the day. She turned to wave at her parents but they had already turned away and hurried back into the house. Her Jeep shifted into drive and then they departed, Antoine following in Christopher's truck, packed with all the belongings one could stuff into two small dorm rooms…

"Are you sure you don't want to stop and pick up at least a few things before we get there? I don't even have a lamp?" she asked him, worried and hating the feeling that she would be showing up so unprepared.

"I told you, my parents have a designer friend with a store in the City. As soon as you're unpacked, I'll take you over there and you can pick out some awesome stuff for your room. You'll love it, I promise," he said with a soothing pat of his hand.

Hiding something, hiding something, hiding something, the Gift blared a little siren at her without showing her the whole picture. Rude. She gave him a side-eye but at least she knew he had some kind of plan. Surprises were not something she was used to, but she'd have to learn to deal with them. The Gift worked only sporadically on Christopher now that she'd chosen him over the warning of the visions. It was a small price to pay to have him in her life.

Cal University lay an hour north of Emerald Beach, two and a half hours if traffic was terrible, which it usually was, even on weekends. As Era stepped out of the Jeep, a rush of exhilaration surged through her. The sun cast a golden glow over the sprawling campus of CalU, illuminating the red-brick buildings adorned with ivy and bustling with students. She caught sight of palm trees swaying gently in the warm breeze, their fronds rustling like excited whispers.

A chorus of laughter echoed from a nearby quad, where groups of students gathered, animated and vibrant. She watched as a cluster of freshmen, wide-eyed and bright with anticipation, lugged boxes and dorm essentials, their faces a blend of joy and nervous energy.

Era saddled herself with two giant duffels and followed

Christopher through the doors of the dorm to find her new room. The building featured an X-shaped design, with four wings jutting out from a central common area. Two wings accommodated girls, and two housed guys, each set up as two-bedroom apartments connected by a central living room, kitchenette, and bathroom.

She walked through a mostly empty living room and kitchenette to a white door with a paper taped to it bearing her and Alex's name. She turned the knob and a wave of blue hit her.

"WHAT THE—?"

As she stood frozen in the doorway, her breath caught in her throat, utterly astonished by the transformation. She knew how plain the dorms at CalU were. She'd stayed in Cole's room more times than she could count. What she saw before her could not possibly be called student housing

What was once clinical white walls had been transformed into a sanctuary. Modern and bright furnishings in vivid blue tones filled the room from floor to ceiling. She took a tentative step onto the soft, plush rug, her sneakers sinking into the luxurious fibers. Her eyes were immediately drawn to the neon signs above the beds—one glowed "Era" in soft blue light above her own bed. The other flashed Alex's name. No one had ever given her such a gift, a gift that showed how well her friend knew her with each thoughtful detail.

Her fingers skimmed across the monogrammed pillows, perfectly placed on the lofted beds. The elegant "E" stitched into hers made her feel at home. The framed artwork on the walls sported cheeky phrases like "Get Ready With Me" and "#Rush" worked seamlessly into the modern, contemporary theme, as if a marketing mind had designed the room...for...an influencer.

Omg, I told her no more videos! she thought, circling the room.

Era admired the gold hardware that adorned the furnishings, catching the light and adding a subtle touch of glam. The soft scent of warm vanilla lingered in the air from a candle flickering on the desk, mixing with the faint, sweet perfume of English garden roses carefully arranged in a vase on the small table. She inhaled the delicate scent, and peered out the window, taking in a prized view of the park-like canopy of trees outside.

Every detail—the calming blues, the plush rugs, the chic gold accents, and the fragrant air—came together in perfect harmony, a far cry from the dull dorm room she had expected. It was more than just a space; it was an experience, one filled with personality, elegance, and surprise. Era had only to unpack her personal items into the dreamy retreat.

Alex appeared in the doorway and Era spun to crush her into a hug.

"Babe, how did you do all this? I don't even know what to say, it's incredible. And you're probably still jet-lagged from yesterday," Era said, working to keep herself from bursting into ugly tears. The room was like looking at a painting of her friend's love for her, and Era felt overwhelmingly undeserving of it.

Alex cocked a sneaky eye to Christopher. "Laura designed it, sent her team in to install it, and he" –Alex waggled a finger at Christopher with a wink– "paid for it. I simply gave some inspiration."

Era leaned over and smooched Christopher who beamed with satisfaction at her, then grabbed her friend, crushing her into a hug. "My girl!" she squealed, touched by the grand gesture on both their parts. She stepped back and took her in. "You look so tan! And did you get me a present too? This is already too much," Era asked, spotting two gifts on the coffee table, one wrapped with a blue ribbon and the other with a white one.

"Oh, those aren't from me. They were at the door when I got here with your name on them."

Era picked one up, turning it in her hands, "Huh, these are Greek letters." She opened the one with the blue ribbon and found an Owala water bottle with a sorority's name printed on the side and a handwritten letter inviting her to join their recruitment process. The second contained a charm bracelet and a similar invitation. "You know this is all your fault right?" she said looking up at Alex who couldn't hide the pleased look on her face.

"Come on, what did you think we'd be doing the first week of classes, studying? You saw the sign right?"

Era narrowed her eyes and pursed her mouth at the #Rush sign. "I haven't even had time to think about that. I'm still kind of processing even being here." But she knew it was game over. She'd do whatever Alex wanted at this point. She looked over at Christopher who smirked with his arms folded in the corner. "Tell me you're not rushing too."

"As much as I'd love to stay your dormmate forever, I think I'd rather live in a Frat house with a private gym and a team of chefs. Plus, you know… parties."

"What are you talking about—dormmate?

Christopher laughed and took her hand. "I'll show you. The Ridgewell family connections helped me make some arrangements for us." As she followed him down the hall, the unfamiliar panic rose up from her stomach again. Why were surprises so horrible?

They turned the corner to the adjacent wing. Christopher opened the door on the right and dropped his bag inside. Era's mind raced to piece it all together and then saw Christian stand up from underneath a desk where he had been crouching to plug in the charging base of a Roomba. Era's mind continued to short-circuit, unable to process the facts before her as Christian crossed the room to pull her into a hug with his giant arms.

Then it clicked and the realization hit Era like an invisible blast of wind, knocking her back a step. They were going to be neighbors? *My boyfriend is top level creeper,* she thought, doing her best not to give away how weird and forced the arrangement felt.

Not that she didn't want to see Christopher every moment, but after the break up with Cole, she had a new appreciation for space and independence, and a healthy suspicion of codependence. She chalked it up to another thing that lay out of her control and combatted her alarm bells with the thought that at least now she could hang out with Christopher without ditching Alex.

"Hey guys!" another voice called from the second adjoining room. Chase walked around the corner and beamed a great white smile at her. He high-fived Christopher as Era, too shocked to even smile back, stood paralyzed. He leaned in to hug her, but unlike Christian who crushed her with heartiness, this hug felt like a jaguar rubbing its black haunches across her. His head dipped just a little lower and she felt the grip of each one of his fingertips across her back as his entire chest pressed into hers.

Era snapped out of it and plastered a grin on her face. *This is a joke. He's messing with me,* she thought now. And then, like an episode from the Twilight Zone, a fourth voice echoed her name.

"Era?" it asked. She nearly blacked out from the shock.

Cole stood in the doorway balancing a giant bin, head swiveling from her to Christopher. If only the Gift provided more practical abilities, like turning her invisible, so she could run shrieking from the room and escape this absurdity. Panic bounced around in her head like a wild bird trapped in a house. Her throat constricted, choking her.

Please no. Don't let him be the fourth roommate, she begged the gods silently, unable to swallow let alone speak.

"Hi, I'm Chase," Chase said, ending the stare down between Christopher and Cole, then motioned to the other guys. "This is Christian and Christopher. Woah guys, we should call ourselves the 4-C Club or something," he cracked, but the joke fell flat.

Christopher continued to glare at Cole, wrapping a protective arm around Era. "We've met."

"Oh no way! How do you guys know each other?" Chase asked, totally oblivious.

"Actually I know Cole" –she turned to face her ex– "hi."

"You helping him get settled in then?" Cole asked, struggling to mask his resentment.

"Well, yes and no. My room is around the corner. Christopher got my grade amended and my admission reinstated, so I go here now too."

"Yeah floor buddies!" Chase gloated, still not reading the room.

Cole's expression shifted, his emotions cracking the facade he'd built. Era gathered her wits before making a run for it. "And about that, I need to start unpacking. I'll see you guys later."

"Let's talk later," Cole said as she brushed past him.

Era's eyes went wide and didn't respond as she chanced a glance over her shoulders and saw Christopher's clenched fists. She had only been on campus for twenty minutes.

She hugged the wall. The hallway narrowed, a dark tunnel that trapped her and the thoughts, the thoughts like bats that swooped down at her. *None but you. Promise me you won't see him anymore. What else don't I know? Let's talk later.*

She stopped breathing, trying to block out the attack. It hurt so much to see him, to hear his voice. And then the guilt smothered her because it shouldn't hurt so much right? Not if she was happy with Christopher.

Era turned into her room and collapsed onto her picture-perfect bed, finally allowing a breath to whoosh into her burning lungs. Alex jumped onto her bed without hesitation, wrapping her arms around her, stroking her hair in consolation.

"What's wrong?" Alex asked.

"It's Cole. He's here—lives here," she hiccuped. The truth spoken aloud sent the room spinning. "He's Christopher's roommate. I can't see him everyday. Can't. He's going to ruin everything."

Could the world truly be this cruel?

The following days felt surreal. She used only the stairs at the back of the girls' wing, never the elevator, never anywhere near the boy's room. But to her relief, everyone seemed busy enough that she avoided any run-ins.

Alex insisted they rush the sororities, twisting Era's arm into recording cringey videos each day to share on her social pages. "Trust me. People love #Rushtok. We can't let your momentum fizzle," Alex argued, insisting that managing Era's social media would look great on her résumé one day.

Era relaxed her reins of control. She couldn't bring herself to put a damper on either Alex's resume padding or her enthusiasm for the sisterhood. And so she agreed, with a few stipulations, so long as Alex knew she'd get the bare minimum of participation from her.

Alex ran with the account, edited and uploaded everything, going so far as to impersonate Era to increase engagement. Era didn't care so long as she didn't have to do anything. But while she could hide from the growing online fame by ignoring the apps, classes were another rub. Even in the stadium-sized classes, whispers surrounded her, eyes trained on her every move. The Gift heightened her awareness of the chatter; it wasn't in her head.

Adding to the chaos, Christopher's mom, Laura, showered them with gifts daily. As a former Cal graduate, she fully supported Era rushing Greek life and her growing influencer status. True to the Ridgewell family's penchant for excess, she sent boxes filled with Nikes, accessories, dresses, makeup sets, and stacks of athletic wear.

Once their outfit-of-the-day and unboxing videos gained traction, Alex approached Era again. "Let's upload those travel reels from our private albums," she urged. The idea made her want to puke, but after a call to Raquel, acquiesced, aware of Alex's vision for a branded empire.

Era floated along, pretending she didn't feel overwhelmed by the suffocating closeness of her boyfriend, her ex, and the boy with a crush on her, along with the peering eyes of strangers that followed her every move. Only months ago, she kept her reality hidden, but now, everywhere she went, strangers recognized her, one girl even casually brought up her friends in London.

The rush process sucked up every minute. Sorority girls bombarded her with intrusive questions about her relationship with Christopher. The conversations at the different houses attempted to be warm and genuine but Era could only feign excitement for so long when she could see how they tallied her up. Social media followers—check. Legacy family from a good zip code—check. Face card—check. Body—check. Neckline low, but not too low and hemline short but not too short—check.

But while the girls sized up Era, she in turn took the opportunity to see if she could thrive in an environment with so many girls on top of each other.

For the first time, Era longed to be ordinary. She wished to enjoy movie nights with Christopher instead of navigating the throngs of admirers and critics alike. Instead she avoided his room entirely and found herself surrounded by throngs of girls who admired and dismissed her, an all too familiar danger

Campus life, too, proved unexpected. Large demonstrations erupted weekly, protesting various issues. Conversations with students revealed a mix of hot topics—wars, climate change, and politics—but rather than civil discourse, she encountered the stench of self-righteousness and downright hostility at every turn. Freshmen tried to remain objective, but by sophomore year, everyone became an expert. Her hope of finding students whose minds weren't poisoned with political hatred shrank.

Era had mistaken college for a chance to be herself, yet she quickly learned that conformity reigned supreme. Manners had vanished, sacrificed at the altar of a poorly-dressed army of social crusaders.

CHAPTER 30

ONE SAVING grace amid the madness was that Era shared several classes with Christian, who had become a protective big brother figure. He walked with her to class and insulated her from the attention.

Cultural Economics, taught by the renowned Professor Dr. Travata, was the largest class they attended together. Two hundred kids filled the stadium seats in the lecture hall, creating a distracting atmosphere for Era as she felt the weight of their judgmental gazes, some even gesturing to her while pulling up her videos on their phones to show to other classmates.

Her hyperawareness faded as Dr. Travata quoted a quirky turn of phrase from the book in his hand. The Gift kicked on like old machinery humming to life in a way she hadn't felt in some time and watched as his skin turned a sickly gray, his eyes a glowing green. As he set the volume down on the table, the book sank with rot, mold bursting forth from its pages and falling to the ground in a stinking heap of maggots and crumbling ash.

Startled, Era returned her gaze to the professor, whose smile revealed sharp, rotten teeth as he exhaled a cloud of mold spores into the air. She nearly choked, squeezing her eyes shut. When she opened them, everything appeared normal again; just rows of students typing notes as he spoke. Era wondered if it was too late to switch classes.

In high school, subjects had been relatively straightforward. Sure, teachers had some freedom in selecting books for AP Literature and a few topics in AP Psychology could get controversial, but she never sensed any attempt at brainwashing. Yet, here a professor preached as if from a pulpit, purporting obvious lies as truth, and no one questioned a word he said! How could she be the only one able to detect the glaring errors in his argument?

With class dismissed, Era followed Christian out of the building, lost in thought over the strangeness of the lecture, when she spotted a familiar figure sitting on a bench. As Cole stood up, Christian glanced at her, asking for permission to tell him to eff off without saying a word.

Era laid a reassuring hand on Christian's shoulder. "It's okay; it's probably time for me to talk to him anyway. I can't avoid him forever. I'll see you later." She made her way over to the bench, motioning for Cole to sit beside her.

"Why have you been avoiding me? You get back into school and don't even tell me?" Cole launched into her, barely giving her a moment to collect herself.

"I haven't been avoiding you. Obviously, I'm not seeking you out. I'm with Christopher now, and I've been rushing and going to class—"

"I noticed that. The guy you promised to stop seeing. The guy you kissed three days after we broke up. Now you're here with him."

"You had no right to ask me to promise that." She meant every word, but even amid their argument, the sound of his voice stirred old intimacy between them. She recalled their souls bonded to one another, and this time her own soul loathed that connection. The torture of sensing their bond and hating herself for it added to the affliction she felt at seeing his face up close, still handsome but now cruel. She longed to be free of her attachment to him.

"I know. I guess it doesn't matter now anyway. This whole situation is bizarre," he said, his eyes shifting from angry to aching. "When I saw you at the beach and wrote you that letter, I thought you would at least respond."

Era clenched her teeth to hide the grimace.

If she could pull anyone using the Gift, he could do the same to her. She had given him that power the night their souls fused, and now he wielded it, drawing her to himself forcibly with his pain.

Era paused, remembering the moment she sat in her car, pulling the gold watch from the envelope and feeling the inscription under her fingertips: 'None but you.' She felt the scream of rage she'd let out, contained only by the glass windows of her Jeep. She recalled the dream of them in their off-campus apartment, cooking dinner together happily. When she looked back at him, she no longer saw the awkwardness but the boy she had loved, the one still hurting.

In that moment, her logical side crumbled. Even though he had broken her, she found herself trapped in this twisted reality, attending college with him, living so close she could feel his heart beating through the walls when she tried to sleep. His voice scrambled her brain, making it difficult to remember her resolve to push him away.

Her tone softened, "You hurt me so much. And the idea of being back in touch, well, it was too hard." She puffed out a breath and bit the inside of her tongue. "I don't know what dark forces conspired to make us neighbors while we're trying to move on—"

"I haven't moved on. I don't have a new girlfriend. My family is still a nightmare but I feel the same about you."

"Cole, please don't. You're not going to make our situation any easier. I still care about you; you know I do. Can we just be friends? That's the most I can offer."

Era hated that he still held so much power over her and knew why he had it. For a moment, she considered that sleeping with Christopher might transfer this power away from Cole. She likened her attachment to Cole to being infected with chickenpox—it never truly left the system, only lies dormant, resurfacing later as shingles, nerve-endings firing pain from ugly pustules. His influence floated forever in her spinal fluid waiting to attack her in her weakest moment.

"Friends?" He spat the words out like a bite of rotten fruit. "Sure, we can be friends, but that means you have to stop ignoring me. And when things don't work out with your rebound, I'll be here."

"How can you say any of this to me? You crushed me! You told me to move on, so I did. Now you're just waiting for me? You nearly ruined my life. It's better if we forget..."

"How can I ever forget the feeling of being with you?" He reached for the hand pressed against her face, catching the tear that fell down her cheek. "You and I are meant to be together. I know it."

As Era turned away from him, her body frozen, she locked eyes with Christian across the square, his jaw set and arms crossed tightly over his chest. He hadn't left after all. He'd seen everything. His judgment of her actions ignited a line of guilt between them as he spun away and stormed back toward the dorms.

She looked back at Cole. "Friends don't need to touch," she said and marched away, longing for a quiet place to hide. With Cole out of sight, she found herself heading toward the library —a perfect retreat to plan her explanation to Christopher, who likely would hear a damning version of the story from his best friend.

The library served as the sanctuary Era hoped for, sparsely populated so early in the semester and filled with the musk of millions of dusty pages. She wound through the tall shelves to a remote corner where solitude awaited and settled onto a rolling black footstool. Leaning her head back against an even row of crinkly plastic bindings, she closed her eyes when three distinctive sounds thudded—thump, thump, thump. Opening her eyes, she found three books strewn across the floor.

Alarmed, she scanned her surroundings, noticing no stir of air in her secluded corner. Rising, she glanced around the back of her aisle to ensure no one had accidentally knocked them off the shelf from a row over. As she approached the haphazard pile, she noticed with a quirk of her head that the top book was written by Thomas Sowell. Despite his status as a literary genius and an American intellectual treasure, Era had a hard time finding his books stocked in libraries. Upon closer inspection, she discovered all three books belonged to Sowell, and to her delight, she had yet to read any of them.

When she bent down gleefully to collect them, time slowed down. Her body felt like it moved through glue until at last, her fingers brushed the first cover, unleashing the force of a thousand collective words that crashed into her mind, knocking her to the ground. She lay immobile atop the pile, their ideas blossoming within her like wisdom from a sea of lotus flowers.

Her mind attempted to understand what happened. *Supercharged photographic memory?* She didn't need to see the pages to memorize the words; touching the work allowed the author's thoughts to flow into her. The ideas intertwined with critical analysis, revealing immediate truths and errors.

Picking herself up, she unzipped her backpack with trembling hands and stuffed the three library books behind her Econ textbook. Her hand hesitated on the class book, and then, two snakes—one black and one white, their iridescent scales shimmering like rainbows—slid up her arm, accompanied by the sound of angry whispers that raised the hair on her neck.

A furry reddish-brown centipede coiled around her wrist, crawling along her vein. Era froze in shock and horror, unsure how to deal with three potentially venomous attackers. She attempted to shake the centipede off when it bit her painfully. Stifling a scream, she reached for the white snake with her free hand, which hissed and snapped at her fingers, forcing her to recoil.

Heart racing and sweat forming on her brow, the three threats slithered toward her neck, while the nefarious lies from the Econ book echoed around her. She was at their mercy; the slightest movement would prompt the snakes to sink their teeth into her skin and continue their ascent up her body. The room darkened around her, trapping her in blind panic. What a way to go—her obituary would read, "Young girl killed in library by exotic poisonous snakes. Investigation ongoing."

The creatures crept over her jaw, and at that moment, she could hold her breath no longer. Feeling her doom imminent, she exhaled, and a stream of light poured from her mouth. The vermin met the spear of truth as light from those other books filled her mind and the aisle, countering the whispers. The rainbow snake hissed, its scales drying and eyes sinking into its head. The three menacing creatures collapsed into dried exoskeletons on the ground, exploding into puffs of dust.

Unable to suppress her reaction to the horrific vision, Era screamed and fled the library, ignoring the beeping security gates that sounded as she passed through with her three stolen items. After a moment to calm her nerves, she surveyed the mundane scene—students ambling around or chatting in pairs, small groups seated in the shade of large oaks on the grassy lawns. Not one of them could fathom her life, and surrounded by so many people, she felt utterly alone.

She rubbed her unmarked forearm, still burning from the

bite and then glanced at her backpack holding the four books that changed her. The drama with Cole and Christopher paled in comparison to whatever unfolded here. If only she could decipher what was happening and why. Perhaps then she could make sense of her life. As it stood, carrying the Gift grew to a heavier burden, a bigger secret and an isolating force with each revelation.

She trudged back to the dorm, wondering what misunderstanding, wildcard event, or unexpected development from the surprise pack the Gift had become waited for her there.

CHAPTER 31

TO HER GREAT RELIEF, only Alex occupied the room when Era returned, engrossed in her laptop while flicking through her phone. Era barely had time to toss her backpack down and sink into the couch before Alex switched into business mode.

"Girl, you won't believe it! We have two DMs from music agents. I looked them up, and they're legit. A couple of brands want to do paid ad collabs on your account too." She tossed her phone over to Era, who glanced at the messages. As Era clicked from the DMs to her profile, she saw Alex had posted over thirty times.

"What is all this?"

"I told you I was going to use videos from our past trips. You have so much fabulous content and people are eating it up. Check out how many comments you got on the Maldives post!"

Era groaned, shutting off her phone. "Look, Alex, I love that you're so passionate about this, but I don't enjoy having every person on campus stare at me. Cole stalks me outside my classes now, and Christopher will be miffed that I spoke with him—thanks to his spy Christian watching us. Not to mention, I haven't spent time with him since rush started. And I think I need to switch some classes. Now, with my profile gaining traction, I'm worried people see me as some jet-setting bimbo. It's only been a week, and I feel like I've aged a decade."

"I know, I'm sorry. I've known all this time that I had this incredible friend, and I finally get to reveal you to the world. Don't worry about the social stuff; I can handle it. You just have to wear this red suit tomorrow night because I have a paid partnership offer. If you wear it, we can put #partner under the post and increase your cred."

Era's eyes widened, her mouth forming a silent 'O' in disbelief. "Look I know I should be more excited about all this. I'm just not adjusting all that well. Everything is so different from how I pictured. Like I'm here and it seems like everything has worked out, but something's still off. I feel like my life is this runaway train and I have no idea where it's taking me."

"I'd feel sorry for you, but babe, you've got freaking everything. Rich handsome boyfriend, dream school, best friend roomie, internet fame and a hot bod," Alex said, counting up the blessings on her fingers. "What more do you want from the universe?"

"Okay, okay. You're right. The stress is overshadowing my gratitude."

"Go get your man next door and smooth things out with Cole. Oh, and babe, I booked my friend's studio next week for you and Chase to record something new together. It doesn't even matter what you sing; people are dying for another post with him."

Era resigned herself to being managed, despite her reluctance to flaunt her musical ability with Chase. He always complicated things, and she had enough problems. What bothered her more was the feeling that Alex had crafted a new identity on her behalf. No matter what she did, escaping her double life felt impossible—now, the false persona existed online. Even worse, school hadn't turned out to be the bastion of freedom

and self-expression she'd hoped for. Instead, she found herself
loaded with more secrets than ever.

A knock at her door snapped her out of her thoughts. When
she opened it, she found Christopher standing there, serious
and somber. "Hi, babe," she said, pressing reassurance into him
with her lips. "I haven't eaten dinner yet and I'm starving. Want
to take me out?"

Ever the picture of discretion, Christopher waited until the
truck door shut before bringing up the subject that hung in the
air between them. "Christian told me Cole waited for you
outside class, that he touched you... and you didn't stop him
either. Please explain what's going on before I go back to my
room and kick his ass."

"I didn't appreciate him ambushing me after class. There's
not much to say. His ego is bruised, especially since I told him I
kissed you three days after we broke up and then ignored his
letter. I told him all I could offer was friendship and that friends
don't need to touch."

"Ha! Friends! You mean the way you and I were friends
before we became more than friends? I've seen how he looks at
you. It would never work."

Era sighed, exasperated, and grabbed his hand, bringing his
knuckles to her lips. "You were never just a friend to me. As for
Cole, I prefer space to move on, but that isn't happening with
him living in your suite. I'd rather feign friendship than endure
his presence as an enemy every time he sees us together. I want
peace and I want you, without anyone making things difficult
for us."

"Fine. I get it. I won't kick his ass unless he puts his hands on
you again. But Era, you have no idea how infuriating it is to see
him looking at me and know he's thinking about you. I try to
forget, but I see that vision of you in your bed the day I found
you, and I know he's the one responsible for that. It makes my
blood boil."

"Shh," she grabbed his face, bringing their foreheads together, her nails raking over his scalp from forehead to the back of his neck. "Yes, you found me, you took care of me, and that's why I'm here with you while he's alone in his room full of regret. You're everything I want."

His hand slid up to hers, fingertips tracing along her arm and sending goosebumps down her skin. He kissed her roughly, expelling the last remnants of his fury, eager to claim her and erase Cole's touch from their minds. Though Christopher knew Era belonged to him, memories of the night she had traded a near kiss with him for a night of sex with Cole plagued him, a step she had yet to take with him.

He dragged his lips and teeth along her jaw, ear, and neck, above her collarbone, eliciting purrs as she squeezed his scalp, clutching his thick hair. "No one touches you but me," he breathed, his mouth nearly covering her ear.

She lost it then. Though Christopher had always been passionate, this intensity felt different. The Gift revealed his desire to possess her, much like Cole had in their most secret moments. Christopher wanted her body because he wanted her soul, and that kind of total want intoxicated her. It nearly killed her not to give herself to him completely in that moment, their desire raw and unencumbered by distracting hesitation. Still, they sat in his truck, on campus.

With a whimper, Era straightened, looking at him with wide eyes. She knew they had taken another irrevocable step toward each other, that she teetered on the edge of a deep well, so close to falling. Would that plunge lead to drowning again? Unsure how long she could maintain her balance, the abyss gaped before her like a hungry mouth. All she knew was that she longed to be alone with him, as far away from campus as possible. The only problem? She had committed to sorority rush events through the weekend until Bid Day.

He took her to a hole-in-the-wall sushi place, where she

momentarily forgot about all the crazy–ex-boyfriends stalking her, evil professors, millions of strangers sharing her cherished memories, and now hidden knowledge absorbing through her skin through supernatural osmosis. Nope. In this moment, all she wanted to think about was not dripping soy sauce down the front of her dress and avoiding brain freeze while devouring an entire bowl of creamy green tea ice cream. And when thoughts of any bizarre nature tried to creep in, she marveled at some lovely detail of Christopher's face, his angular jaw as he chewed or the perfect outline of his nose to swat the interference away. Christopher spoke animatedly, but Era's gaze remained fixed on his sparkling white teeth and luminous eyes.

Ah, he's so beautiful. How did I ever resist him? I might not be there yet, but I need to stop holding back. I should let myself fall in love with him, she thought. Only Christopher could transform such a chaotic day, making her forget every worry and turn jealousy into understanding, pivoting from conflict to passion in an instant.

"What are you thinking about?" he said, interrupting her daydreaming.

"Only that I want to keep you forever," she replied.

"I wouldn't want you thinking anything else. Stay with me tonight. Christian will be at Violet's; her roommate went home for the weekend."

Era agreed, knowing the situation would likely become awkward as hell with Cole and Chase in the suite next door. She decided it better to rip off the band-aid rather than give up sleeping with him because of the strange roommate arrangement. All she wanted was the safe refuge of his arms, even if it meant cramming into a small bed.

They walked back to their floor, pausing for a quick kiss in the common area. "I need to prep for tomorrow and get ready for bed, then I'll sneak in, okay?" she said, continuing down the hallway while he ducked around the corner.

Back in her room, Era took a hot shower, changed into cozy sweats and a soft tank top, then vaulted up into her ridiculously high bed. Part of her couldn't face any more drama today, so she delayed heading to the boys' room, instead opening her social page for the first time in days and scrolling through the comments.

The posts garnered an astounding number of likes and interactions; however, what stood out were the people dragging her for wanting to join a sorority. The comments ranged from cautionary tales to sweeping judgments, painting her as a stereotypical, slutty dumb blonde. *Ouch.* Many assumed horrendous reasons for her vacations featured in her posts.

She didn't want to stand in the way of Alex's grand marketing scheme, but she recognized that this profile shaped her reputation, and she would bear the brunt of the judgment. If she wanted to avoid being labeled as shallow garbage, she needed to step up and use her voice to say something.

"It's about time," a voice from across the room chimed, tinkling like faint bells.

Era screamed, flinging her hands up and sending her phone flying through the air to clatter noisily onto her desk. Three immediate thoughts registered when she saw the figure casually propped up on Alex's bed.

First, the unearthly tone of his voice signified he wasn't human. Second, his glowing face, hands, and golden hair reminded her of how the Gift revealed certain people with pure hearts, even small children. Third, beauty and power enveloped him so strongly that she felt a wave of terror. She covered her eyes, wishing the vision would disappear like the others had.

"No, no, that's not going to work. I'm not a vision of the Gift."

Lowering her arm, she looked at him again. The initial shock wore off slightly, and thankfully the glow receded to only his eyes, allowing her to focus on his words. He sat on Alex's bed, still. Statue still, wax museum still. His chest didn't rise, his eyes didn't blink. It didn't seem wise to contradict this—whatever this was—so she simply asked, "How do you know about the Gift?"

Swinging his legs over the side of the bed, he faced her. "Because I know all things, and in my realm, there are no secrets. You humans believe your thoughts are private, that secrets exist. You don't realize any of my kind can hear your every thought, your desires, know all of your memories. We see deeper and further than you can into the hearts of men."

On some level, Era had awaited this conversation for years—the one where she could openly discuss the Gift with someone who understood. Yet she never anticipated that the first person would not be a person. It felt rude to ask 'what are you?' So instead, she braced herself and asked, "Who are you?"

"I am Michael the Archangel, Captain and Prince of the Angels, and Guardian of the Church. Oddly enough, I have a message for you, and though I've conversed with humans before, they typically held more integral roles in the war."

"War, what war?" asked Era stupidly.

"The war for souls, of course." Michael placed one hand across his breast and lowered his head solemnly. "Souls fall to hell like snowflakes in a great storm, every day. My army fights to rescue as many as we can."

As he spoke, fat flakes began to fall, and instead of being in her room, they stood on a vast plain. The wind carried faint moans and screams, and she saw each flake melt upon contact with the ground, forming rivulets that flowed away from her in every direction.

She felt a thump as her body returned to her bed, and knew that what she had witnessed was no vision. They had traveled somewhere and back in an instant. Growing more frightened, she looked at the stranger again and asked, "Why are you showing me this?"

"A very good question. I believe I should start at the beginning of your story. About a hundred and forty years ago—"

"A hundred and forty years ago! My story?"

"It's rude to interrupt. Again, yes, a hundred and forty years ago, Pope Leo XIII was allowed to overhear a conversation between the Master and the Prince Below. I'll paraphrase: the Prince of this world bragged about his ability to destroy the Master's Church, to which the Master challenged him to try. The Dark Prince claimed he needed more power over those who serve him, and more time, 100 years to reign. This request was granted, and Pope Leo, upon hearing of the impending dark power, received a special prayer to combat this new evil, should people call on me for assistance. It is known as the St. Michael prayer. You've heard it but don't know it yourself, so I'll recite it for you. I advise you to remember it."

St. Michael the Archangel, defend us in battle, be our defense against the wickedness and snares of the devil; may God rebuke him, we humbly pray; and do thou, O Prince of the heavenly host, by the power of God, thrust into hell Satan and all the evil spirits, who prowl about the world, seeking the ruin of souls.

"If you've been doing the math with me, you'll understand his reign is over even if the crafty devil did get himself two extensions. But it's been an ugly century and the battle scars still bleed. The Master calls upon you for the next great offensive. What you have experienced are mere trifles of the Gift. You'll understand everything in time. The Master doesn't reveal everything to mortals at once."

If I throw myself from here to the floor, I can get that door open with two more steps. I can make it, she thought.

Michael paused his long-winded sermon and gave her a dark look. "You're kidding right?" You're not jumping anywhere, unless you want to finish this conversation in the Plain of Souls."

Era sucked in a breath and straightened her back. He really could read her mind. But just in case, she gave him one more test. *I want to trust you, but this is a lot. What was the name of my first pet?* she thought.

"Mr. Pickles," he answered, adjusting the epaulet on his shoulder.

Finally, she addressed him, her voice sounding feeble compared to his. "I don't understand what this has to do with me."

"Because you keep saying 'NO.' Even when the Gift gets stronger, you still choose to ignore the messages. The Master doesn't force anyone to serve Him; you are free to do as you will, though I am here to tell you that it is always unwise to resist His plan. As it stands now, you should not be here, in this school, or with Christopher. Neither is part of the plan and you know this. Alex will stay with you; she will fight with us.

"You must let go of the idea of what you thought your life was supposed to be. It's time to follow a new path."

"Let go of my hopes and dreams for my own future? To do what? Fight in some war? Why would your Master pick me?"

Era, forgetting the new arrangement, went back into her thoughts, *This can't be happening right now, not to me. I don't care enough to give up my whole life for some crusade.*

"It *is* happening. As to why you were chosen, *that* is something even the Angels cannot know. But you know what they always say, 'His ways are above our ways.' I certainly wouldn't have picked you. I find you to be a particularly flawed human yet here we are." The angel slapped his knees and stood up. He easily stood seven feet tall.

"But back to the matter at hand, when I first spoke, you were thinking about your profile. It's time to say something that matters. You can't really think that all of these videos are reaching millions by accident can you?"

"You're doing that?"

"I tinkered with the algorithm."

"How could you do that?"

Michael laughed, a tinkling sound that sounded like a combination of wind chimes and a harp. "All human knowledge, all science, all computing power in the world until the end of time could not approach the knowledge I possess. As an inanimate rock stands an unfathomable distance from a living tree or a dog from a human made in the Master's image; so far, does an angel transcend a man in the order of creation.

Era's mind blossomed with understanding at his words, the Gift hard at work unwrapping his full meaning. Even with the help, the concepts were hardly comprehensible. She had simply never contemplated angels and now she faced their amazing share of creation's glory.

He smiled at her warmly, looking into her thoughts once more. "I will be with you, and you have my invocation. Use it earnestly to call on me, and I'm at your service."

At that, he imploded into a tiny wink of light, along with the life she knew before that moment. Nothing prepared her for this revelation. She grabbed her keys and stumbled out to her car, seeking solitude without disruption, leaving her phone where it had landed when she flung it into the air.

Inside the locked box of her Jeep, her mind whirled— Michael the Archangel, a war, no secret thoughts, the order of created things, Alex will fight with us, Christopher and school are not part of the plan, particularly flawed human, let go of what you thought your life was supposed to be, souls fall to hell like snowflakes, a new path.

Everything laid out before her felt overwhelming, its implications weighing heavily on her chest and making it difficult to breathe. As she rocked back and forth, she saw no way out, no way through, and most importantly, no way back.

Her mind momentarily stopped spinning, and a single thought crystallized: Christopher, with someone else. The image scalded her, a searing heat splashing across her face as he leaned over another blonde, kissing her slowly.

Regardless of everything the Angel said, one truth resonated: there was no way to return to her previous life. She unequivocally believed in the Master, in Angels, and in a plan for her. Now that she'd heard the truth, could there be any other explanation? But more importantly, would she serve? Era felt unprepared to forsake her life or her relationship based solely on knowledge. Perhaps, in time, she could figure out the rest.

For now, Era prepared to take the first tiny step. She would let her true voice echo on her profile, come what may, and she had exactly the words in mind.

"ERA! What are you doing out here?" The shock of Christopher's voice nearly made her black out in fright. He stood outside her window, visibly angry, searching for an explanation for her absence from his room. She hadn't forgotten that he expected her; but their plans to cuddle paled in comparison with the supernatural announcement that her entire life should change course.

How did he think to look for her here? How did he even know where she parked? Suspicion crept in as heat radiated from her wrist, like the watch's battery might explode. She instantly realized the watch he gave her contained hidden tracking software. It appeared that the Gift had turned itself all the way back on and illuminated the blindspot Christopher had enjoyed since the day she ignored the vision of the sinking ship.

Stepping out of the car, she faced him carefully. "Scared the daylights out of me. I needed a moment of privacy to think. How did you know where I was parked?"

"I saw it parked here earlier," he replied, black vines of guilt sprouting around him, even though his face remained composed. An hour ago, she would have believed him, but the Gift revealed the truth.

An excellent liar, she thought, impressed. The Gift offered her an image she winced to see—Christopher speaking to someone on the phone about purchasing a watch with undisclosed tracking capabilities, agreeing to a price of two thousand dollars for the install.

All fun and games to have a rich boyfriend, until they use their money against you, she thought. But Era was too practiced at seeing the truth and hiding her reaction to it. *Never show your cards.*

The instinct to protect her hidden knowledge remained too strong, she'd have to swallow the sourness of his betrayal. Boyfriend or not, he wasn't entitled to know her whereabouts at all times. She would let the watch die and hide it in a drawer somewhere, regretting its loss, as it was the most beautiful piece of jewelry she owned.

"My bad. I should have let you know I'd be coming over later than expected. I forgot to bring my phone when I came out here to grab something."

"It's okay. I was just worried " He put his arm around her and guided her back toward the dorms. "Is something else going on? Everything okay?"

Ha! What a question! The sheer magnitude of secrets swirling around her was absurd. Where to begin? The closeness she felt earlier, the image of standing at the edge of the gaping well returned, but this time, she took a safe step backward. Sticking to her old habits under interrogation, she spoke as closely to the truth as possible.

"After my shower, I got distracted scrolling through my profile—the one Alex manages—and some comments started to get to me. There's a lot of negativity, and people don't hold back with their judgments."

"Aw babe, I'm so sorry. You're so stoic about those kinds of things that I didn't think any of that bothered you. I know it's been a tough first week of classes. Christian told me how hard it is shielding you from all the attention. Next time, come to me instead of running out here by yourself. It's not safe." They rounded the final turn toward his room.

She saw the door there and stopped in her tracks. She didn't care that Cole was somewhere on the other side of it, but going inside to be with Christopher, felt like a slap in the face to the Angel's premonition—that her relationship was doomed and her affections misguided. Sleeping with him in his room could draw down the ire of who knows what.

The realization struck her—when the angel mentioned there were no secrets in thought or memory, it meant he or any angel would know everything that happened in Christopher's bed. A sensation of knowing they watched her entire life without her having any awareness of it, slammed into Era. An image of Jim Carey in the *The Truman Show* talking to himself in the bathroom mirror while the whole world watched flashed in her mind. She shuddered.

What should she do? Enter Christopher's room, where invisible angel eyes could pry, and possibly hook up in front of invisible witnesses? Or sleep next to him while keeping things as PG as possible?

Two steps from the door, Era turned to Christopher. "I can't tonight."

"What do you mean? You were fine with coming over an hour ago."

"I know."

Don't say it's because it's weird. He'll think it's because of Cole. It's so weird though.

"I just need to get some good sleep in my own bed tonight."

Christopher frowned. "It's not because of *him* is it?"

"No, I'm over that. But as much as I love what hockey has done for these shoulders over the years" —she smoothed her hands over the top of his solid frame– "they don't exactly leave much room for a guest in a twin bed."

He cracked a smile, but he wasn't buying it. He walked Era to her room and kissed her goodnight, all the while working to piece together the dodgy details of the night.

A wave of fatigue hit her and no matter how much she tried, her brain wouldn't offer her a way to smooth things over with Christopher. As she pulled the soft duvet up to her chin in her own room, she pondered how this relationship might work, regardless of the larger problems waiting for her tomorrow. Yes, tomorrow she would think about everything, and with that, she drifted off to her favorite sanctuary: sleep.

CHAPTER 32

ON FRIDAY MORNING, Era opened her eyes to a brightly lit room with a hangover-like headache. The night's dreams had not been kind, waking her more than once, heart racing, sheets twisted around her legs and torso like a boa constrictor. Swinging her legs over the edge of the bed, she noticed four books piled neatly on her desk, with her phone perched on top.

Ugh, it's like Angel homework. As if I need any more items on my to-do list, she thought begrudgingly. Era picked up the phone and began recording.

She titled the post: Freshman Economics at CalU is brainwashing students. Here's how they're doing it.

"Here's what they're teaching us," she said and showed the first book from Professor Travata's class, which she threw straight into the trash along with a dangerous quote.

"And here's what they'll never show us," she continued, holding up three Sowell books in succession, and a quote from each that refuted the first.

In less than ten minutes, she had filmed the clip, overlaid the text, and added background music. She wrapped the video with a cheeky grin directed at the camera.

After posting it, she took a quick shower and headed to the cafeteria to meet Alex for a late breakfast. The day ahead looked easy, with only one class at noon, followed by a full afternoon and night of slideshow presentations at sorority houses. Inside each house, Era surrendered her phone, allowing her to forget about the morning's post, which quietly picked up steam.

The house tours intrigued her, especially as she disliked the co-ed housing situation she currently found herself in, the one which allowed Cole to worm his way back into her life. Yet, she already had a best friend in college. Era knew she could forge friendships with the sorority girls she met without living with them and adhering to their rules and expectations.

Sorority life presented a double-edged sword; it could offer a remarkable experience but also risked exposing her to hurtful dynamics, threatening her college experience. She anticipated that at least one girl would envy her, especially given the spotlight now shining so brightly on her. She was torn between not wanting to disappoint Alex's dream of joining a top sorority and knowing that if things went south in the sisterhood, they were sure to turn on Alex as quickly as they'd take her down.

Christopher had his own fraternity rush commitments, and after returning late Friday night, exhausted beyond words, Era sent him a goodnight text before turning her phone off. With thirty unread messages awaiting her, she felt too tired to sift through them, pushing the world off until tomorrow.

By Saturday morning, Era could no longer ignore the train barreling toward her. As she turned her phone back on, it rang immediately. Not wanting to answer an unknown number, she let it go to voicemail, reading the message live as the caller spoke. "Hi, this is Amber, Associate Producer from *Good Morning America Weekend.* I'm calling to invite you to be a guest on the show as soon as possible—"

"Hello?" Era interrupted, picking up mid-message. "Yes, I'm the one who posted about Sowell's books. No, I hadn't heard anything about the best-sellers list. Tomorrow? I'm not sure I can make it; I have some events here at school. A flight at 11 a.m.? I don't know if I can get to the airport that fast. You'll send a car? Okay, I guess so then. A 5 a.m. call time for hair and makeup? Wow, that's early. You can send the details to my email. I'll see you in the morning then. Thanks. Bye."

Alex, wide awake and watching her with wide eyes, asked, "What just happened? You're flying somewhere? Now?"

"A producer from *Good Morning America* invited me to be on the show tomorrow. I have to pack; a car is coming for me in an hour. Also, check those books I posted about yesterday. She mentioned something about a best-sellers list. I have no idea what she's talking about," Era replied, already out of bed and picking through her drawers.

Alex's face fell. "So I guess this means you're withdrawing from Rush week then?"

Era dropped a pile of underwear and moved to sit in front of Alex, taking her hands. "I don't know if you know this or not, but I'd do almost anything to make you happy. You're one of the most precious gifts in my life. But I've been meaning to talk to you about my hesitation with Greek life. While it looks fun, it also seems dangerous. You know my track record with girls; I feel like I would be setting myself up, and you by association, for disaster. I don't want to stop you from going for it, even if the timing is off for me. Please keep going and get the bid of your dreams. I have this strange feeling that something exciting is about to happen. I can't quite explain it, but I sense our biggest adventure is about to start."

"Don't worry about me. I'm with you until the end. I support whatever you need to do. If you need to ditch me to go be on TV, then get out of my way because I'm picking out the outfit," she joked, laughing as she began rummaging through their closets. Eventually, they settled on a white shorts and blazer suit with a cream top underneath.

"You're going to look like a hot ass weather girl in this," Alex declared, wrapping up the coordinating jewelry and pumps and stuffing them into the suitcase. "You finish packing and getting ready. I'm going over to Christopher's to explain everything, so you don't have to waste time running him through the whole story."

Era admired Alex's determination as she frantically assembled her toiletry bag while brushing her teeth. Moments later, her proud boyfriend, still in pajamas, ambled into the room to congratulate her and wish her luck. He would have booked a last-minute ticket to accompany her, but like Alex, he was tied up with Rush events all day. Era headed downstairs with her bag, barely reaching the curb before a black Escalade pulled up and a well-dressed driver stepped out to open her door.

As the driver merged into traffic on the way to the airport, Era googled the first of the three Sowell books, gasping in disbelief. There it was on the Amazon list at number one, with the other two books she recommended taking the second and third spots. It was no wonder the show sprang for a same-day business class ticket and insisted on booking her for the show the next day. This phenomenon extended far beyond a single post.

The whirlwind of rushing through the airport engulfed Era as the mingled scents of fresh coffee and Cinnabons wafted through the air, tempting her. Even with TSA Pre-check she was barely going to make it. Twenty minutes until they shut the door.

Brightly colored advertisements flashed overhead, vying for her attention against the backdrop of the dull hum of conversation and the rhythmic thud of rolling suitcases on tiled floors. Era maneuvered through the crowd, her heart racing with the electric thrill of anticipation, only to be met with the cacophony of announcements echoing from the overhead speakers—urgent calls for passengers to board, reminders about gate changes.

An agent waved at her from the entrance of the jetway, urging her to hurry. Era heard the woman scan her ticket and pick up a phone nearby, then heard the click of the door shut behind her. She just made it.

When she finally settled into her seat, she felt the aircraft rumble to life beneath her. Her entire life could be summed up in that feeling, strength and deafening noise as an entity larger than herself pinned her in place and elevated her into the air with an incomprehensible power.

Once the ride smoothed out and quiet returned to the cabin, she took out her laptop, eager to check if the producer had sent any instructions to her email. One message in particular caught her attention. The sender's name appeared as garbled, colorful characters, like a text mistake in an AI image from ChatGPT, and the subject line was so specific it creeped her out: "Open these attachments during your flight to NYC." Assuming it referred to the package Amber had mentioned during their conversation, she opened the email, only to find a blank message with a zipped file attached.

This better not be some kind of ransomware, she thought, hesitating before clicking the attachment. As the file unzipped, she discovered over three hundred documents, each simply numbered from 1 to 304. She chewed the side of her tongue and selected all, allowing every file to open at once.

In that moment, Era felt a sensation akin to her fingertips fusing to the keys, accompanied by a pulsing energy that surged from her hands, pumping through her arms and chest, all the way to her eyes. Terror paralyzed her as the familiar creeping movement overtook her, and without warning, the pulse exploded into light across her vision. A bomb detonated in her mind. If three books in the library had dropped her to the floor, absorbing over three hundred at once felt like a suicide bomber detonating a jacket.

The attachments were all books—collections brimming with

millions of ideas flooding her consciousness. Blinking away dryness from staring, Era felt an elegant thesis form in her mind, synthesizing a century's worth of economic theory.

It became clear that Michael had sent the ultimate preparation package for her interview tomorrow. Come what may, she could now hold her own against any PhD. She signaled the flight attendant and ordered a ginger ale to sip, ready to contemplate the powers of angels—especially now that she understood they did mundane things like send email and play with algorithms. What else could they do?

CHAPTER 33

THE FOLLOWING morning proved to be a rough one for Era. Her 5 a.m. call time felt more like 2 a.m. due to the time change. Her bloodshot eyes burned with heaviness, and her stomach churned in protest at being jarred awake at such a rude hour.

Era donned the white shorts suit, grateful for the forty-five minutes spent in the stylist's chair, where she could close her eyes and sip an extra-large coffee. Amber, chipper for the hour, buzzed around her, explaining when her segment would be filmed and what to expect. She handed Era a list of pre-written questions that might come up.

With little left to do, Era sat in full hair and makeup for nearly two hours, watching the crew scurry around off-camera. Finally, a young man in a headset approached her, leading her to an area near the set while she was "on deck."

"You're going to do great. Just keep your focus on the person interviewing you, not the cameras, and act naturally," he advised before nudging her out under the bright studio lights.

Era crossed the stage, sat down in one of the modern bright yellow chairs, and greeted the interviewer—a middle-aged man in a gray suit with horn-rimmed glasses perched on his nose, his salt-and-pepper hair neatly combed. She felt surprisingly at ease, responding to his questions about her viral posts and, ultimately, the inspiration behind her latest book critique.

Era dropped her shoulders and lifted her chin, as she prepared to diplomatically defend her bold stance. "I have to be honest—initially, my best friend Alex posted the first two videos without me even knowing, and I was fine with letting her manage the profile. But as things started escalating, I realized my online reputation should match the things I care about in the world.

"I'm only a week into my studies at Cal University, and I've found myself diametrically opposed to some of the incontestable theories being taught in the economics department. In class, I've been surprised to see no one else willing to challenge what's being said. So, I felt it necessary to put the truth out there."

When the interviewer pressed her about her qualifications to criticize a published academic at such a prestigious institution, Era asserted her plan to release an essay refuting the theories in her professor's book, using the three Sowell texts she had posted among others. She made a commitment on the spot to utilize her return flight to write the essay.

The interviewer leaned forward, adjusting his glasses. "One last question, Era—why do you think your post inspired so many people to pick up *Basic Economics*, a book that's been around for fourteen years and didn't even hit the bestseller list when it first came out?"

Era tilted her head, a thoughtful pause stretching before she answered. "I think it's because Sowell doesn't just present ideas —he uncovers how data can be twisted to fit narratives. He doesn't shy away from asking the hard questions, the ones people are too afraid or unwilling to investigate. It's like he's saying, 'Let's trust the facts to speak for themselves, whether we like what they reveal or not.' And people respect that."

She crossed her legs, her hands resting on her lap. "Take my economics class," she continued. "We're taught certain theories as if they're gospel, but no one's challenging them or even looking deeper. Sowell's work shows us how to step back, question the data, and expose contradictions—because facts without proof are opinions."

The interviewer nodded, intrigued. "So, it's about trust in his approach?"

"Exactly," Era said, her voice steady. "Sowell trusts his readers to handle the truth, no matter how uncomfortable. And that trust, that honesty, it resonates. People are tired of being spoon-fed conclusions—they want to see the whole picture and decide for themselves. Sowell gives them that window."

Era leaned in, feeling the camera zoom in on her face. The Gift cracked open the man's heart to her, revealing his skepticism and disenchantment with having to report on topics he found tiresome. But he knew it would be career suicide to apply his own critical thought. Anyways, he cared little for academic subjects, preferring to focus on the cut of his jacket and his next contract.

The Gift spun him around in her mind until she saw his intentions and his memories more clearly than he ever would see himself and then she let the Gift tug him to her, hand over hand, until his heart was pressed against her every syllable.

"You're a fairly wealthy man content to live in the insulated bubble of your profession. You don't see that your country is declining like the latter centuries of the Roman Empire, with technology accelerating that decline within the next fifty years. Instead of obsessing over the tailoring of your clothes or worrying that the network is interviewing your younger replacement, you should work for something that truly matters. Because no matter how much money you make or if you add another two bedrooms to your high-rise apartment, you'll never be happy here.

"I posted what I did because academia is diseased. They're churning out graduates that have been pounded into homogenized ideology. There are no diverse viewpoints, no critical thinking, no free debate. Try talking to the kids protesting on campus, destroying buildings, tagging graffiti on the walls. It's pointless. But the disease isn't limited to just university campuses. People are simply less happy, less fulfilled by the lives they lead.

And you know, that's *Basic Economics*. There has never been enough to satisfy anyone completely, and that is the real constraint. As we continue to cram ourselves into populous cities, you will feel this dissatisfaction more acutely. I believe our coming revolution will involve a devolution from urban centers that hurt family life, brainwash our youth, contribute to our decline in health, and create hotbeds of prejudice against free thought. This shift will result in smaller, tight-knit communities. I'll lay all of this out in my podcast beginning next week," Era concluded.

She shifted her gaze from the interviewer to the main camera, the Gift now Pulling on a million shimmering souls behind the lens. She could feel her words drawing them to her, through her. The interviewer stammered as he realized he had lost control of the segment, inadvertently plugging her nonexistent podcast before abruptly cutting the broadcast short.

Afterward, a man with a clipboard tugged Era offstage. "Whoa, bet they didn't know when they booked you that you'd drop some Red Pill theory on them. You're either delusional or a visionary—either way, that was brave."

She was still reeling from the sensation of touching so many souls at once, their faces and hearts, a vast undulating sea of anxieties and hopes. The speech she gave echoed in her head with a voice she barely recognized as her own.

She hadn't expected any of that to come out of her mouth, nor had she ever considered leaving the urban sprawl of

Emerald Beach for anywhere else. The Angel had said that the plan would be revealed to her in due time, and unbeknownst to her, it had been made known to her and the millions of viewers of *Good Morning America* simultaneously. Still, after reflecting on the idea, accompanied by the illumination of her intellect after ingesting the brilliance and wisdom of so many great minds, it made perfect sense to her—even if she remained personally unconvinced about moving anywhere else.

Era paced off stage, her heart still racing from the adrenaline of the moment, thinking about the paper she had committed to publishing by tomorrow and the podcast she was starting. It had only been 36 hours since the apparition.

The next few days passed in a blur. Era caught a same-day return flight, writing and posting her essay in its entirety from the air. The paper garnered immediate attention, getting picked up by *The Economist*, with snippets quoted in an article about her appearance the next day in the *New York Times*. When she returned to campus, everyone had seen the *Good Morning America* segment—even those who had never watched an episode.

The YouTube clip and the broadcast shattered network records, breaking every previous benchmark by tenfold. She received an immediate thank-you and an invitation to return to the show in two weeks, along with a slew of requests from local and national news channels, talk shows, and podcasts.

The three Sowell books flew off the shelves, going entirely out of print. Her words struck a chord; many were now expounding on the idea of toxic cities being at the root of an array of societal ills. The comments poured in, centered around the inexplicable feeling of being moved by the message, of being seen by Era in a way that sparked everything from admiration to tears and pledges of loyalty. It was a strange phenomenon indeed.

Back on campus, Alex received a Bid Day invitation to

become a pledge for Theta Omega Gamma, the undisputed top sorority, despite rumors that the girls had been highly offended when Era dropped from recruitment. Christopher, likewise, matched with his first-choice fraternity and officially became a pledge. Everything happening would have been amazing—a dream come true—except this was never the case with Era.

The on-campus blowback had just begun, and the shift in her housing decision would lead to Era and Christopher's first blow-out fight. It was a Tuesday afternoon when he pulled at the thread of their unraveling.

CHAPTER 34

ERA DROPPED BY THE BOYS' room right after dinner. It was already a little messy, unwashed cups sat on the kitchenette counter, heaping laundry hampers waited to be washed, and the lingering scent of last night's pizza box still hung in the air. Cole sat on the couch, his eyes glued to ESPN while he tapped away at his laptop. When he noticed her, he closed it and stood up, greeting her with a hug that was a touch too warm for her liking.

Era let him wrap his arms around her shoulders, nervously glancing behind her, half-expecting Christopher to appear at any moment. "Um, hi," she said, patting his back lightly.

"Christopher's not back from dinner yet. You can hang out with me until he gets here," Cole offered too eagerly.

"Actually, I was looking for Chase. Is he here?" she asked, taking a half-step back from Cole's oppressive closeness.

"Yep," a voice from the door to the right answered. "Hi beautiful." Chase stepped towards her, lifting Era her into the air with his signature hug. Cole's eyes went wide at the display.

In that instant, Cole connected the dots as to why Chase kept asking so many questions about his and Era's relationship

—he had been mining him for information about her. It hadn't occurred to him that Chase knew her in more than a superficial way, that she could have inadvertently captivated both Christopher and Chase in the short time since their breakup. Era felt the Gift bloom with Cole's resentment towards Chase, and recognized the urgency to separate them.

"Can I talk to you really quick?" she said, grabbing Chase's arm and pulling him out the door to the common sitting area between the four wings on their floor. Once they were away from the boys' suite, she jabbed him lightly in the arm. "Are you seriously going to pretend like you don't know Cole is my ex and flirt with me in front of him? Do you have a death wish?"

Chase laughed, a carefree sound. "Of course I know. He's practically retold your entire relationship to me after only a week of encouragement. I know A LOT more about you now."

Era felt blindsided by this invasion of her privacy. She had anticipated potential friction between Chase and Christopher, but this roommate dynamic with Cole added a dangerous layer of complexity. Cole knew her so intimately and he had unknowingly shared their private moments with his direct competition.

Part of Era wanted to believe that her new relationship with Christopher would diminish Chase's interest. Instead, it seemed to intensify it; he saw her as the ultimate prize, relishing the chase. The irony of Chase's name only fueled her frustration. *DAMMIT*, she thought, anger boiling within her at the thought of being constantly hindered.

Gathering herself, she shot back at Chase's teasing demeanor. "I hope he makes your life very interesting now that he knows you've been milking him for information about me. Cole's been acting a little unhinged lately, so you better watch your back. What did he tell you, anyway?"

"Now that wouldn't be any fun would it?" he said.

"Fine, be a butt. Anyways, the reason I wanted to talk to you is because Alex wants us to record at her friend's studio tomorrow. Are you free at 4?"

Chase spoke through his dazzling smile, his face doing the Cheshire Cat disappearing act again, "I'm at your beck and call."

At that moment, Alex and Christopher appeared, walking together down the hall before spotting Era and Chase sitting side by side on the loveseat.

"Perfect timing, Alex," Era called. "Would you mind filling Chase in on the details for tomorrow?" Alex grinned and led Chase away, diving into her ideas for their recording session.

"What details?" Christopher asked, sliding in beside Era and burrowing his face into her neck, nipping her lightly.

Era giggled as his lips tickled her collarbone, her hands gripping the line of his jaw. "Mmm, we're going to sing something tomorrow in a more official studio."

"Is that so?" he replied, inching his lips up the side of her neck. "And when can I get on my girlfriend's schedule for a private session?" His words were jealous and hot at the same time. They had spent minimal time together since school started, and she knew he felt somewhat neglected.

"Alex can pencil you in, she's scheduling my whole life these days," she said, tugging at his shirt playfully. Inside, she grappled with the implications of rejecting the Angel's wisdom regarding her relationship.

Christopher pushed her hair away from her ear and kissed the soft skin behind it before responding, "I could send for the boat. We could throw a party there."

Era squealed with delight at the suggestion but trembled with anticipation and anxiety as she envisioned the bed in Christopher's stateroom. "That sounds so fun, but I think we should focus on campus life right now. We just need to get better at syncing our free time."

"Speaking of campus life, babe, there's something else I've been thinking about. I know you decided that the timing wasn't right to join a sorority, but I don't like the idea of moving into the fraternity house at the end of the year and leaving you here with *him*. There are condos off-campus that I could set you up in so you don't have to live here after I move out—"

"I am not moving off campus. Parking is terrible here. Do you realize how inconvenient that would be? I'm sure I should be thanking you for offering to buy me a house or whatever, but I'm not going to rearrange my entire college experience because you're worried about my ex. I'll be fine."

Christopher's eyes darkened as Era spoke. He clearly hadn't anticipated her rejection, his inner conflict evident as he wrestled with the desire to join the fraternity while also protecting his relationship with her. He knew sharks circled around her, her undeniable magnetism serving as chum in the turbulent waters of college life.

"Just think about it, okay? If parking is the only issue, I'll get you a driver." Of course, Christopher had no qualms about throwing money at any obstacle in his path.

"I'm sorry, but there's no way I'm living in an isolated condo while you go off to a big fraternity to make friends because you're worried—what? I'll cheat on you with my ex?"

"I overheard him talking about you with Chase. I'm pretty sure that snake has been asking all about you since they became roommates. He said you were terrified at the idea of talking to him again and that you still cared about him. He even mentioned what you two shared—um, physically—and implied that there was no way you'd stay away for long."

Christopher paused, swallowing hard. "You don't understand. I was physically ill hearing him say that. And I know you told me that it's over between you two, but it doesn't seem like it. Even if you think you're done with him, I saw what that breakup did to you, and it's been what? Three months?"

Just then, Era's phone, face up on the coffee table in front of them, lit up with a text from Cole. Christopher's face twisted in agony as if that single message validated his entire argument, and stood up from the couch.

Era knew she was being unfairly condemned by a text message she had no control over receiving. Chase and Christopher were both prying, eavesdropping asses. She still hadn't forgotten her latent anger over the diamond tracking bracelet which had made her feel like a chipped dog. Even Christian had no right to spy on her and then report back to her boyfriend. The rampant lack of respect for her boundaries from the 4-Cs reached a fever pitch in her mind, causing Era to spiral into a rage she would later regret.

"That's enough. I have no control over people sending me text messages. Stop acting like it's my fault Cole is trying to win me back. You're right; we did have something special, and it was really difficult getting over it. It's even harder when my boyfriend keeps throwing it back in my face, reminding me of how pitiful I was after what should have been a painful but private breakup."

She glared at him even harder, knowing the crash of words about to hit him might sweep them both away, but unable to stop it. "So thanks for being there for me, but stop using it as a crutch to cover your insecurities about us being together. If I ever did go back to him, it would mean you and I were never real anyway, so you should stop worrying about it. Also, since I've seen you look at my naked wrist multiple times, I should say that I don't appreciate being tracked like a pet.

Next time, send a request to my phone if you want Find My Friend privileges instead of taking them without asking." Her eyes glowed like embers and she watched her words find their mark in the most vulnerable spots of his chest.

Her last accusation caught him off guard, diffusing the anger she had stirred by her stinging rebuke. His teeth gritted as he lowered his voice, wary of anyone nearby who might overhear. "Anyone close to my family is at risk of kidnapping for ransom.

We all wear something that sends our location to a security team in case of an incident. I didn't want to scare you, so I didn't mention it when I gave you the watch."

Unfazed, Era's razor-sharp tone sunk into him again. "What a convenient excuse. Don't lie to me. If only this 'security team' has access to my location, how did you manage to find my car the other night on this huge campus? If we're going to be together, you should know one thing right now: it's pointless to lie to me."

As Christopher stormed away down the hallway, Era heard the Angel's words echo in her mind—*not part of the plan*, whatever that was. It was difficult not to sabotage what she already knew was doomed to fail. But nobody had asked her what she wanted. And that part sucked most of all.

She slunk off to her room, feeling sullen and dejected, yearning for the comfort of her covers to shield her from the inescapable conundrum in which she found herself. The old temptation to sleep away her problems was rearing its ugly head once again.

This time, however, she fought to resist the temptation to sleep. Instead, she forced herself to confront her situation. Here she was at her dream school (though the dreaminess was diminishing quickly), after overcoming a serious bout of depression. Though her heart still ached from the summer's heartbreak, it was healing—thanks to Christopher. Yet, the Angel's words echoed in her mind, suggesting that she would have to give up everything. The chilling warning regarding those who ignored the Master's plan haunted her. Even the word "Master" sent a tremor through her stomach.

Despite the doom and gloom of the prophecy, exhilaration coursed through her at the prospect of being part of something greater—a fight against an unseen evil. She had seen real evil before; people harbored dark secrets in their hearts, memories that twisted and coiled like snakes. She had learned to cope with existing alongside such people, viewing the Gift as a protective fortress against those who might do her harm. It had given her the unique ability to sidestep the predators of the world.

Even those who weren't necessarily dangerous but consumed with despair, fear, insecurity, or mental illness—she had always managed to pivot around them. It had never occurred to her to help or fix anyone; intervening seemed too risky. She had viewed the Gift as a survival mechanism at worst and a ladder to help her climb to the top at best. The biggest exception had been at home. Without the Gift, she could have deluded herself into thinking her parents loved her "in their own way." But facing the truth meant confronting the harsh reality that they simply didn't.

So, what if this evil force was responsible for turning ordinary people, like her parents, bad, or twisting those who were already bad into monsters? Did she care enough to meddle in such matters? Why was this her problem? Her life was good now—why should she sacrifice everything to face a darkness she didn't understand?

Even if she could write a blank check for her life to the Angel, one major sticking point remained—she couldn't fathom a reason to give up Christopher. She recalled the first bag on her doorstep, the meal he sent when she was so unplugged from reality that she stopped eating. She remembered the way he had understood her, really the first person perceptive enough to do so, during their conversation at his party. She placed a hand on the back of her neck and rubbed the sensitive line that ran into her hairline, thinking of how he'd found the spot that made her weak, turning her around and holding her hair up to kiss her there. He made her feel alive, fully awake.

Era realized that their argument would be inconsequential in the grand scheme of things, heard the sound of an invisible clock ticking down the seconds of their relationship. Whatever was coming for her, she wanted to take as much of Christopher as she could. Determined, she padded quietly out of her room and down the hall.

The boys' suite was, of course, locked. When she tapped on the door, a surprised Cole answered. She brushed past him, not giving him more acknowledgement than a simple, "Hi," and "Thanks," before slipping into the room across from his.

She climbed under the covers next to a sleeping Christopher. When he awoke with a start, feeling the covers shift, she placed a calming hand on his chest, which he clasped without hesitation. His eyes, filled with a mixture of sadness and apprehension, softened when she nestled her head into the crook of his shoulder and pulled his arm around her. The Gift faded to grey around his unspoken thoughts; clearly linking itself to the "plan" the Angel revealed. But she didn't need it to know him intimately in that moment, to know he offered her forgiveness even before she apologized.

She climbed on top of him, tucking her feet behind his knees, letting the weight of her body connect them once more. He relaxed and began trailing his fingers gently up and down her back. As their breathing synchronized, she brought her face close to his, kissing him softly before sinking beside him, allowing drowsiness to wash over her.

Era awoke the next morning with Christopher pressed firmly against her in the small bed, warmth radiating from his body. Needing to pee badly and unwilling to brave a morning run-in with any of the boys, she slipped from beneath the warmth of his bed and crept out, evading the notice of any early risers.

Once safely back in her room, she closed the bathroom door, relishing the lingering warmth of Christopher's embrace and the innocent look of his sleeping face, all soft lips and long eyelashes waiting to be kissed. It took all her strength not to run back to him and climb under the covers again.

As she lathered the scent of fruit punch shampoo into her

temples, she played back the night's memories in her mind. It had been so innocent yet profoundly meaningful. The part that she loved the most was that he had taken her back into his bed completely unresolved after their fight. She knew he would forgive her without question, that he provided a safe haven without conditions, and that he always gave without asking for anything in return. She knew she fell a little harder for him then, that she wanted and she needed him more.

"All couples fight, right?" she said, speaking to her reflection in the mirror as she squeezed out her hair and toweled off.

As she rubbed moisturizer down her legs, her brow furrowed in thought. *And I did say some pretty harsh things to him yet he still comforted me without question. Why were we even fighting? Because he wants to buy me a house, to shield me from being hounded by my obsessive ex? Because he wants to protect me against the possibility that someone could target me as an extension of his rich family? And what did I do? I weaponized his concern for me and called him insecure, pitting him further against Cole.* Era groaned, her heart heavy with regret, and saw that her reaction and her words had been callous and uncivil.

Sometimes having access to knowledge of the most vulnerable part of people's hearts equaled a temptation to aim for them in a fight. She resolved to speak with him again, soon, and ask for forgiveness. He had his own apologizing to do, but that didn't excuse her treatment of him. Era finished getting ready and hurried off to make it to the earliest class in her schedule, wishing she didn't have to leave the conversation until later.

CHAPTER 35

THE MORNING UNFOLDED warm and sunny, the true summer weather of California. Era settled into a seat beside a pretty brunette, a fellow freshman, clad in a chartreuse sweater. "Hi there! Are you a Poli Sci major or just taking this for general ed?" she asked, hoping to break the ice.

"General ed for now. I've thought about declaring for this department, but I wanted to feel it out first. I'm Arabella, by the way," she said with an openness that Era was immediately drawn to.

"I think you were wise to choose Public Problems as a litmus test for the Political Science department. The syllabus is crazy— homelessness, global warming, corruption, bankrupt pension systems, educational inequality. Expect some contentious discussions," Era said, noting Arabella's shyness.

As the professor quieted the room, his voice rose with authority, launching into a lecture about homelessness. The AC must have turned on full blast above her as a freezing chill enveloped her, bringing with it a dank musty smell. Only a few minutes in, the vision began—lights dimmed, obscuring the students around her, and a portal of purple light opened behind the teacher. As he spoke, creatures emerged, climbing or flying toward the nearest, most vulnerable targets.

One winged beast, dripping with a putrid slime that clung to its furry yellow skin, landed on a girl's shoulder, digging its sharp claw into her flesh. Era winced as she watched drops of blood leak from the wound. The creature leaned in, revealing double rows of jagged teeth, ready to bite behind the girl's ear. The sounds of soft gulping and slurping filled the air as these horrific beasts feasted on her classmates.

A few students swatted at the winged monstrosities, but instead of retreating, the creatures sank their teeth into hands and arms. Though the students showed no visible pain, their bodies began to slump in their chairs, growing weaker, their skin taking on a gray pallor the longer the beasts feasted and poisoned them. Era's stomach lurched at the sickening sight. She grabbed her bag, and prepared to make a swift exit when the vision dissolved, the lights brightening around her.

"Please break into groups of ten to discuss the prompt on the screen," the professor instructed. Era stood up, flustered, glancing at the girl two rows away, who sat unscathed with creamy skin and a rosy complexion except for two barely visible red pinpricks just behind her ear. Unsure whether to make a scene, she stood up on shaky legs and followed Arabella to form a mixed group of mostly upperclassmen and a smattering of freshmen.

A junior kicked off the discussion in the wrong direction, but Era chose silence. Her opinions, sharp as shards of glass, waited behind her teeth, biting into the pressure of the moment. Instead, she leaned in, letting the voices wash over her. Nine hearts, beating in mismatched rhythms, swirling thoughts and fears that flowed into her as though her skin had become the surface of a river.

The conversation spiraled. Words wrapped around each other like dancers in a waltz gone wrong, tugging in tight circles, their logic folding over itself. Era tuned into the unspoken, feeling the collective pulse of their minds. Her vision sharpened.

Before her, the thoughts of her classmates took shape: a network of hexagonal cavities, filled with a black, tar-like substance, hardened in jagged lines. Every crystallized cell, a belief, sealed shut. And creeping across this web, a thick, organic growth—the spongy black mold of conformity, festering and multiplying. She coughed at the smell of rot, the decaying spores wafting towards her.

Era did not hear the voices of adolescents. What she heard was something darker—a whispering undercurrent, carrying the weight of centuries of conditioned thought made perpetually new. Something ancient, a hum—soft, grinding, like the endless churning of machinery that never stopped. She strained her Gift, letting it stretch toward the unsettling shape, a repulsion she couldn't quite touch but couldn't escape either. The hum—no, not a hum—an otherness, ancient and sentient— made her skin prickle, goosebumps crawling up her arms.

Her eyes darted between the five students who dominated the conversation, their words spoken in unison as if rehearsed, like a finely tuned orchestra playing a score no one had questioned for years. Three guys, two girls—each a reflection of the same mold, their minds shaped by the same false truths. As Era studied them, a sick realization settled deep within her. These were the same tired arguments, recycled and reshaped, each student locked in the same pattern of thought, dancing to the same monotonous tune.

One student, a squirrely guy with a half-grown patchy beard hiding his weak jaw, launched into a tired position from "the consensus of experts." But all Era could hear was more of the same—a world where alternative viewpoints were marginalized, where opinions were presented as facts. The conversation smothered like stale air.

Her eyes caught the faintest details in their thoughts: their experiences, their memories, each one filling the black cells that formed the hive mind. Fear masked as logic. Emotion turned into a justification. They spoke with such confidence. Years of lectures, of reading distorted books, and hearing those distorted clanging arguments repeated by the mouths of their peers, cured those black cells until each was seated deeply into the hive mind. Era felt a sick rush of dread as she watched the circle close in on itself.

How could she not have known this was happening when she visited Cole? She had been on campus plenty of times even if they kept mainly to his small circle of nerdy friends that spoke endlessly of crypto and stocks. But on second thought, she reminded herself that he had made her blind to everyone else. She hadn't seen because she hadn't cared.

Then, a voice pierced the static. A broad-shouldered junior, his sun-kissed skin and blonde highlights betraying his laid-back, surfer exterior, spoke out. His words were unexpected, a break in the chain of thought.

"Perhaps the homeless problem in the City won't improve as long as we keep paying high salaries to the people in charge," he said, his voice steady. "What incentive do they have to solve it? Solving it would make them irrelevant."

The room seemed to hesitate. A girl scoffed, slamming her voice down like a hammer. "You can't be serious. No one would sacrifice the people they help for their own job security."

The hive mind snapped back, eager to smother the intrusion. But Era's attention sharpened. She turned her focus to him, the surfer bro who dared speak his mind. There was something in his gaze, something that didn't fit with the rest of the group. She reached out, her Gift unfurling like a quiet storm, and peeled back the layers of his thoughts.

Beneath the surface, Era found something unexpected—a storm of anger, frustration, and resignation. This wasn't just an opinion; it was a man who had been punished for thinking differently, a young soul scarred by an environment that demanded conformity. Memories flashed through his mind: the shouts of his peers during an assembly, a paper graded unfairly, his scholarship hanging by a thread after daring to speak his mind.

Era felt the burn of that injustice deep within her. This was the price of free thought. The punishment for a single step away from the prescribed path.

She watched as the girl with pink-streaked hair, desperate to protect the circle, shot him down. But Era saw through the facade—the freedom to speak, to think, to exist without fear of reprisal, was slipping away from him, and the others, one stifled voice at a time.

The conversation moved on, but Era couldn't shake the image of his frustration, his quiet revolt. And then, the girl turned toward her.

"What's your opinion?" she asked, mouth frothing with the certainty of her own righteousness. As if she stood a chance. "You're published, right? Surely, you have something to contribute."

Era's heart sank. This was the moment the hive was waiting for, the moment it could either swallow her or spit her out. They were sniffing for weakness, for a crack in her defenses, hoping to expose her as a dissenter.

Era forced herself to smile, refusing to be baited. Her voice calm, she replied, "I'm still forming my opinion on this matter. After all, I'm just a freshman."

The girl rolled her eyes and moved on. Era allowed herself a moment of relief, the tight coil of tension in her chest loosening.

Her thoughts turned inward as she moved on to another group of ten students. The hive mind hummed louder now, a buzzing that echoed in her ears, demanding homogeny. The older students, those indoctrinated by the years spent in this intellectual prison, controlled the flow. Their arguments were based on faulty premises, but it didn't matter. The hive had already made up its mind.

Era recalled a Sowell quote: "It is usually futile to try and talk facts and analysis to people who are enjoying a sense of moral superiority in their ignorance."

Era felt a deep frustration build within her, the truth pressing against her chest like an avalanche waiting to break free. She remained silent, her lips tingling to expose the lies, to challenge the system. But she didn't. Not yet. The Professor called time, and the room emptied. Era slipped out the door, her body tense, her mind racing.

She emerged into the crisp air of the quad, grateful for the fresh air, but the weight of what she had witnessed lingered like a shadow. This wasn't freedom. Not here. Not in the place she had hoped would be different.

Emerald Beach had been a cage, and now, even here, she was being held in a different prison. And the guard towers stood manned, 24/7.

Her next class, statistics, felt like a breath of fresh air compared to the tension-filled lecture halls. A sanctuary of quiet focus, where numbers were the only thing that mattered. Afterward, Spanish became an unexpected oasis. The room buzzed with talk of travel and culture, the air lighter, the conversations less heavy with social agendas.

And then, the back shelf. It wasn't much—just a stack of reference materials, an afterthought in a corner. But Era's fingers skimmed the spines, each title offering a whisper of something new. She ran her hand along the paperbacks, feeling a strange attraction toward a particular volume. She opened it and found herself drawn into the words of a 16th-century mystic.

The rhythm of the verses unlocked something inside her,

and soon she was speaking the words of the woman who had lived centuries before her, "Muero porque no muero," a phrase that sang from her lips as naturally as her own name. She left that class feeling like she had unlocked a piece of herself, eager to show off her newfound fluency to Alex one day.

By 3:30, fatigue hit. She was drained, yet there was a sense of excitement bubbling under the surface. That's when Chase's Snapped a picture of his passenger seat with a caption:

> Get in loser. Serestrom Hall. 10 minutes.

Era raised an eyebrow as she looked up to see him pull up, bouncing in a two-tone Maybach GLS600. Blue and white headlights flashed like neon, and the thumping bass of a hip-hop track vibrated through the air, punctuated by the weird creaking sound of a mattress in the background. It was absurd —ridiculous and hilarious. She nearly burst out laughing, stifling the sound, not wanting to give him the satisfaction of knowing how much she enjoyed his antics.

Ever the performer, Chase stepped out of the car with exaggerated swagger, bouncing his arm in time with the beat. He walked around to open the door for her, a self-assured grin plastered across his face. Era couldn't help but roll her eyes and smile, feeling a rush of affection mixed with the absurdity of it all. This was Chase. Always entertaining. Always performing.

Her abs burned from laughter. "Gosh, I needed that, you have no idea." Chase wrapped an arm around her shoulders and slid a kiss across her cheek, as if they were in Europe instead of California. *Already pressing his luck—great,* she thought.

He guided her into the passenger seat, even reaching over to buckle her in. Just as she opened her mouth to tease him, she spotted the console and gasped. "Matcha! How did you know I was crashing and not to bring me some hot milky coffee or sparkling drink before we sing? Were you really a theater kid or something?"

Chase laughed as he settled into the driver's seat. "I did some acting and singing when I was a kid, but that was ages ago—before ice hockey." He gestured around her form before adding, "You look good in my car, Era," prompting her to lightly slap his arm. She let the Gift glide over his intentions once more; he had known about the tea from Cole and was ready to leverage every bit of information he had gathered.

"Just drive. You know there's going to be traffic, and I thought I'd use the ride to grill you on what the eff you've been saying to my ex behind closed doors." Chase snorted and sped off toward the studio.

"Cole's not a bad guy. He told me a bit about his family's drama, and it's some real shit—excuse my language—stuff. He mentioned that you don't like people swearing in front of you either." Era raised an eyebrow but appreciated the apology about the language; it was true she didn't normally allow men to swear casually in front of her.

"No real surprise that it took seeing you with Christopher for him to realize that, drama or not, he was stupid for letting you go. Anyone can see you were bound to be snatched up immediately. I mean, if Christopher dumps you, I'm ready to pick up the pieces anytime," he said, his voice lilting.

Era nearly scalded herself on a sip of tea, turning to him in disbelief. "Chase, you can't say those things! I get it, you're a brazen flirt, but take it down a few notches, please."

Chase tilted his head toward her, keeping his eyes on the traffic ahead. "Anything for you."

The SUV squeezed into a tight space against the wall of the studio lot. When they stepped out, Era fully appreciated Chase's outfit for the recording session: a loose-fitting beige sweater vest, gold chain, Lululemon dress pants, and styled, messy hair. He looked like a snack. Era was grateful that Alex had taken on the role of her personal stylist. Inside, she'd have a complete outfit and makeup for touch-ups.

Stepping into Studio A, they spotted Alex, who had set up a small table with makeup and hair tools. The room invited creativity, showcasing an array of Persian rugs and warm fleece-covered chairs. Instruments lined the wall—acoustic and electric guitars, keyboards, a small upright piano, and percussion instruments. In the center stood two microphones with filters attached, facing a desk equipped with multiple screens connected to a computer and another keyboard.

Alex shook her foot, eager for Era to sit down so she could begin touching her up. Unperturbed by the obvious impatience, Era wandered around the room, studying each instrument, wondering why she felt neither drawn to nor inspired by any of them. As she paused at the desk, she moved the mouse to wake up the computer. Electric vibrations surged through her, like a million electric ants crawling over her skin. Each shock converged to form a total picture of musical science: loop, tempo, reverb, samples, quantize, pitch correction, and the list went on and on. Immersed in a world of possibilities, she hunched over the keys, relieved when the crawling sensation dissipated, only to be replaced by the sound of a beautiful song, carried on the wind from a distant place.

"Ehem, any day now Era. We need to get you camera-ready before we can record anything," Alex said, weirded out by Era's quiet moment with the still computer.

Lifting her head, her unfocused eyes cleared as she pushed back from the desk. Era walked over to the chair, her gaze lingering on his, her lips curving into a faint smile and said, "I have an idea for a song. Can you pull that keyboard over to me?"

Alex began curling Era's hair as Chase wrote down the lyrics Era wanted him to sing while she played the notes for him on the keyboard. They discussed timing for call-and-response lines and a few harmonies.

Once Alex finished her look, the real magic began. Era sat at the computer, composing a complex track. She laid down beats, looped instrumental riffs using various instruments, sang vocal samples, and even created a sound effect by tapping a BIC pen on the table. Her work on the violin was particularly elegant, especially since she hadn't touched one since a musical workshop her school hosted in fourth grade. That time, she had produced only one harsh screech and abandoned the bow immediately. Alex and Chase watched, mesmerized, as Era demonstrated astounding prowess, transforming and layering sounds into an instrumental piece that imitated a full orchestra.

As the track looped, Era stood and walked over to the pair of mics, where Alex could record her and Chase singing together. And if witnessing Era produce a hit instrumental that sounded like cinematic pop with a euphoric crescendo in mere minutes impressed, then hearing her lay down the opening vocals on an original song felt like front-row tickets to a private concert. Her words struck at Alex's core, covering every inch of her skin with goosebumps. She captured it all through the phone's screen mounted on a tripod.

Era heard *"The Next Thing"* in her mind so distinctly that she could visualize the notes and rhythm. The song narrated the story of someone never happy, misled to believe that by reaching the next milestone, they would find happiness. Thus, they became trapped in a never-ending cycle of tragedy. Chase's voice in the song personified the "next thing," beckoning her to chase him, telling her how close she was to having all she desired.

As she sang, Era knew she needed to pull her audience through the tiny lens of the camera. However, seeing Chase there and experiencing him pour himself out to her made it easier to turn her full force on him instead.

They sang a breath apart, facing each other, allowing the words to come alive in her voice as they hit their fortissimo notes together. His hands lifted, and she brought hers up to meet his, intertwining their fingers, voices, and souls.

His voice rang out, "Come to me, I'll be your Next Thing. If we found each other, there'd be nothing left to search for," and he meant it. The strangest part of the song? All of his lyrics held the unlocked secrets of his heart. She felt his heart as a physical heat, a fire threatening to melt them together even as she sang back that it would never be enough, that her heart would remain restless forever. A deeply private moment for them unfolded, one neither would forget.

They finished the final note in crushing harmony, breathless. As emotion from the song scattered, Chase awoke from the moment with a colossal grin, grabbing Era from the other side of the mic stand. He lifted her off the ground in a half turn, enveloping her in arms that wrapped around her small frame, his breath hot on her neck.

Era's hands rose to Chase's face, as if to say, she couldn't believe what had just happened before regaining her composure and detaching herself from him to return to the computer.

Alex never paused the video, planning to launch an entire series of behind-the-scenes clips if the song succeeded. After hearing them nail the vocals in a single take and feeling a tear trickle down her cheek, the tightness in her throat assured her it would be a success.

Within the next hour, Era mixed the track, playing back the finished product for the first time. The video continued to roll, capturing their reactions. Alex couldn't contain her pride or excitement, throwing her arms up and jumping out of her seat. Chase, overwhelmed, grabbed Era's hand and brought his forehead down to her knuckles as the melodic, emotional track filled the small studio.

"You're going to be a star, you know that, right?" Chase said as the room fell silent. "And I can only hope you'll take me along for the ride." Alex stood up and walked over to the tripod, finally stopping the video.

"I hate to be a buzzkill after the magic we just made here, but Era, you've got to get over to Studio B to record your podcast in fifteen minutes. We're doing double days!" she exclaimed while packing up their equipment—always straight back to business.

Chase looked longingly at Era, suddenly reminded that outside this room, she belonged to someone else, that her heart wasn't open to him the way it felt only moments before. As they hugged goodbye, his cheek brushed against hers, and she sensed his disappointment. Unable to stop herself from consoling him, she stroked the back of his hair, feeling a twinge of guilt at letting the Gift draw them together, again.

"See you on the floor, beautiful," he said, taking his leave as Alex hurried her into the next session.

CHAPTER 36

Era recovered from her momentary whiplash, sobering up and focusing on the task ahead. The second studio featured four velvet armchairs and mics arranged around a glass coffee table, behind which loomed a giant green screen. Two cameras stood on tripods, ready to record, bright lights blazing onto the set.

The gravity of what Era knew she was supposed to talk about as well as the reach that she knew her words would have, hit her with an unexpected weight. Her previous statement on the show—that dismantling city centers could lead to greater personal freedom and happiness—haunted her. Even though the lights felt blinding, corners of her vision began darkening, collapsing into a tunnel around her.

Creating this podcast meant that she would never be accepted at Cal University or any other traditional workplace. While she yearned to detach from societal approval, this notion felt foreign after years of carefully cultivating her reputation and planning her future. So much of her was screaming out that she had to hide the Gift at all costs. This would expose her, leaving her alone forever. Her soul was being drawn and quartered, each anxiety a horse that yanked her limbs in a different direction.

"Hey, I'm so sorry, but do you mind if I have a moment to mentally prepare—alone?" she said, her face tight, her fingers gripping the plush chair for dear life. Alex nodded and slipped out of the room, leaving Era to face her thoughts. An idea struck her, and she began to recite the words, "St. Michael the Archangel..." Instantly, a figure blinked into existence, sitting in one of the velvet chairs as if present the entire time.

Panic seized her; this being wasn't Michael. A beautiful child with wavy brown hair and golden eyes sat across from her. His garment, woven like a story, resembled stained glass windows. As she gazed at his youthful but intelligent face, Era felt an uncanny familiarity with the figure. It was like encountering a smell that triggered a deep nostalgia from childhood that you couldn't place, a memory from so far back in your unformed mind that it can't be grasped. Instinctively, she bowed her head; the angel mirrored her gesture.

"Yes, it's fair to say you know me, as I've been with you since your conception in your mother's womb. I am your Guardian Angel, and it is my honor to meet you in this realm. Michael has tasked me with speaking to you."

"Wait, you've been with me every second of my life?" Era asked in disbelief, yet she knew this child could never lie.

"Yes."

"So what? Protecting me? Guarding me? Every moment of every day?" Her mind spun in slow motion, struggling to comprehend the implications of such a relationship. When the angel smiled and nodded, she accepted the truth, yet the logical side of her brain resisted. The idea of an intelligent being following her every moment and purely in service to her was irreconcilable. She rejected the thought—it was akin to having a slave! "How could I ever repay you for staying with me my whole life? For keeping me safe?"

At that, the child's face blazed blue hot with an unforeseen wrath, and his voice boomed, "Praise Him!" The impact of his words knocked her flat to the floor.

That moment tipped the scales. Sprawled on the floor, the curtain of time drew back. She saw her potential future if she chose it: a divorce from Christopher, unable to reconcile their ambitions, and blurred faces of children caught in the fallout of a messy public split. She would fall into a demanding career in music that would transform her into a sexualized false idol to the masses. The Gift would leave her, slowly diminishing until she doubted if it had been real or a fabricated story in her own head.

This stark revelation awaited her if she continued on her current path. The last remnants of disobedience and resistance dissipated, punched out of her by the angel's words. In their place stood a conviction of the lowliness of her desires. Era recognized the futility of her goals compared to the wisdom of the child before her. She no longer needed to understand the plan's endgame; she simply knew she was called to work for something greater than herself—and she would answer that call.

The angel approached her as she picked herself up, handing her a thick stack of papers. "This is your work for the day. I'm happy you've chosen to serve."

"Is this written by the Master?" she asked.

The angel laughed, "Not exactly. These are your own thoughts, informed by wisdom and knowledge, of course. You will see."

The angel handed Era the papers, which vanished upon touching her hands, all the words and arguments tucked safely into her memory. He spoke the truth; the words felt distinctively "her."

Sitting in the chair, she prepared to record, basking in pure bliss. For the first time in her life, she knew she was right where she was supposed to be, and it felt good. Peace rained down on her, the first true peace she had ever experienced.

When Alex reentered the room and began recording, words streamed effortlessly from Era's mouth in a torrent of enlightenment. With the Angel's blessing, she overcame her imposter syndrome. Still, making a public statement weighed heavily on her—shouldn't she advocate for people to move from urban centers while living anywhere besides the City, in the dorms? Pushing past her perceived hypocrisy, she continued to lay out her logical argument.

"Many of us live in cities or larger urban sprawls because of the Industrial Revolution. The invention of the cotton gin created a new pathway out of poverty for uneducated individuals, allowing them to earn more from unskilled factory labor than trapped as tenant farmers. As more people flocked to centers of industry for employment, opportunities expanded for enterprising individuals to grow their wealth through commerce, services, and the sale of goods. Machines replaced the need to employ the majority of able-bodied men and entire families to produce enough food for society. Modern cities were born. Hang in there with me. I'll get to part where this matters to you.

"So think about it. The entirety of the human experience changed just 250 years ago. Before that, most people lived in the country and worked in agriculture. Then, a global shift occurred, resulting in more people living in cities. Perhaps this trend would have continued indefinitely if not for the invention of the computer in the 20th century, opening new avenues of connectedness.

"Let's examine what the reorganization of modern society has brought us. Among the majority, we see isolation within dense population centers. It's not uncommon for someone to die in an apartment complex, their body remaining undiscovered until the stench alarms neighbors. I couldn't tell you the names of more than one or two people on my block, despite the fifty or so people living there. I don't even pay attention to who lives within fifty yards of my house.

"Furthermore, we observe an explosion of mental health disorders, a decline in physical health and fitness, a massive rise in obesity, and an increase in divorce rates and children raised in single-parent households whose parents were never married. Who can definitively say that humans born today are happier than those from 300 years ago? From where is our modern happiness derived? Is it from consuming poisoned food or swimming in plastic-riddled oceans? Is it because we can enjoy tacos, dim sum, and chicken tikka masala all in one day?

"I urge you to consider what technology makes possible for modern humans. We can live together on a smaller scale, form true communities, and enjoy greater freedom. Consumer culture in cities has created an endless cycle of want and unhappiness. We don't need more junk in our lives. We need fresh air, time in our days, and time in our years. Are you building something lasting that matters? Or are you scrolling through life, idolizing others on social media, and filling shopping carts that drain your disposable income?

"Where will your accumulated possessions end up when your life is over? Will they even make it to the landfill? Picture the fate of every single item you own in 100 years—they will rot back into nothingness. Stop striving for passing things. It's time to embrace the gift technology has given us: the ability to live closer to nature and one another in true community. We can connect without living so closely that we become strangers.

"Cities are nothing but oppression factories now. Who can speak or think freely in a city? Who can foster true community there? Who can live amongst so many without becoming an expendable possession of someone else?"

Era's argument against urban living unfolded like a flower, each point igniting exclamatory bursts of inspiration. As she spoke, Era was transported to the times she described—distant country villages, early factories manned by children and families in hazardous conditions. She looked upon the countless souls on the other side of the camera, living unfulfilled, dead-end lives, unaware of the alternatives.

Alone on one side of the rope in a million-man game of tug-of-war, Era felt the Gift Pulling with all its might. Words flowed uninhibited by her personal filter; her pupils dilated, and warmth spread through the room as she filled the air with an unnaturally sweet perfume. Listening to her own voice, she caught the tinkling sound of angels, a supernatural quality that wouldn't be perceptible in the playback of the video.

Finally, she stated her conclusion and made her last appeal, promising viewers she would lay out the logistics for breaking free from diseased, depressing cities over ten podcasts. When the live stream ended, Alex rushed over, tears in her eyes. "Era!" she exclaimed, throwing her arms around her neck. "This is going to change everything for us, isn't it?"

"Yes, it is," Era replied, squeezing her friend reassuringly. "And I need you now more than ever. You'll play an important role in what happens next." She held Alex tightly, grateful for a friend who had always loved her more than anything else. Alex never batted an eyelash at the idea of living double lives in high school, traveling the world as minors with an international group of friends, or forsaking a normal life to embark on a completely untested theory. No matter the price, Alex remained by Era's side, both recognizing the other as irreplaceable treasure.

Alex sniffled and wiped a tear from her cheek, crying for the second time that day. "I thought what I saw in the music studio was life-changing, but what you did here was earth-shattering. What if people take your advice? What if we do? Where are we going?" she asked, voice trembling. "I thought I'd be moving to sorority row, and instead, I'm following you out into the desert or something. Please say we're not moving to the desert. You know I hate the heat."

"Don't worry; I have no plans of moving to the desert. I can't even claim to understand how this will all play out. Regardless, I know you're meant to be by my side, and I can't imagine anyone else I'd rather have there," Era finished, pulling Alex's hair back into a ponytail and letting go.

Still a bit teary, Alex smiled. "As much as I'd like to sit here in our group therapy session about how we're all doomed to be mentally unstable and repressed because we live in the City, we'll incur extra charges if we don't wrap it up. Anyway, I have a huge video file to edit and market, so let's get out of here." Ever the pragmatist, she began packing their belongings into the duffel bag and rolling luggage she had brought to the studio.

That night, Era dreamed of a little house nestled among green hills, surrounded by flower-filled pastures. She wandered through a field of chest-high dahlias and fragrant sweet peas until she encountered a modern-looking, shiny black road that abruptly cut through the meadow.

Curious, she stepped onto it, feeling its glassy firmness beneath her feet. Admiring her reflection in the sunlight, she soon noticed the road had turned scaly and vibrated slightly. It dawned on her that she wasn't walking on a road at all but on a gigantic black snake, the same one that had crawled up her arm in the library.

As she stood on its body, the muscled column rose before her, quirked its head menacingly, and stared at her with red eyes. She wanted to scream but she knew in that instant, she was alone. Awakening with a start, her chest and hair soaked in perspiration, she immediately searched for Alex in her bed, only to find the covers crumpled and empty.

Grumbling after checking her phone—6:20 a.m.—she knew sleep wouldn't return. Instead, she jammed her feet into slippers, grabbed her robe, and headed into the suite's living room to make coffee and look for Alex. She found her on the couch, a blanket draped over her and a laptop perched on her knees.

"Good morning!" Alex chirped, strangely enthusiastic after what clearly had been an all-nighter. "I got the song and podcast posted last night, though getting the song uploaded onto all the different platforms for maximum reach took the longest. Since I recorded the entire session, there's a lot of opportunity to break it into chunks and release those as part of an ongoing strategy. I'm still working on the content calendar. Oh, and we've hit three million views on the song, and it's only been up since 10 p.m. last night. I'm skipping my classes today. Call me whenever you're free, and I'll keep you updated."

Omg, we're really doing this.

CHAPTER 37

AFTER GETTING READY, Era knocked on the boys' door, kissed Christopher, and then walked out with Christian toward their Thursday morning class, Cultural Economics. The campus buzzed with a whole new energy for Era. Heads turned in her direction, and students called out as she walked by—no longer whispering or glued to their phones, but openly watching the latest releases on their phones from the night before. She might as well have worn a shirt proclaiming, "Queen of CalU."

As they approached the Economics building, Violet joined them. Clad in a periwinkle leggings and tank set that complemented her creamy skin and brown hair, her eyes sparkled with enthusiasm. She linked arms with Christian and Era.

"Girl, sorry I've been so caught up since the semester started. I know we haven't had a chance to hang out, but oh my gosh. You're shooting to stardom *and* stirring the pot before midterms! And that song with you and Chase... wow," she exclaimed, fanning her face as Christian glared at her, "it was riveting and hot. You guys have some serious chemistry!"

"Okay babe, she's Christopher's girl remember?" Christian interrupted, clearly unenthused about the feedback he knew to be true after seeing it himself last night. "See you at lunch?" he said as they neared the building entrance and prepared to part ways.

Violet turned to Christian, standing on her tiptoes to peck him on the lips. "You bet." She then faced Era and winked mischievously before giving her an unexpected hug. Violet's enthusiasm for Era's music revealed a refreshing lack of jealousy. Era liked that girl more with every interaction.

"Thanks, stop by my room anytime. We should catch up," Era said, hoping Violet would take her up on the offer.

Cultural Economics with Dr. Travata presented a different challenge altogether. The lecture focused on how city centers fostered freedoms and income potential for minorities. The arguments lacked depth, relying on flawed research and manipulated data samples, yet Era refrained from correcting the evident bias in front of the large class. Toward the end of the lecture, the professor unexpectedly turned his murky eyes toward her, saying, "I'd like to speak with you after class if you have a minute."

As class concluded and students filed out, Era approached the professor's podium with determination. He remained calm as he stuffed a few papers into his bag before silently exiting the room. Beneath his feigned professionalism, seething anger simmered. Dr. Travata entered the adjacent empty classroom, shutting the door behind them—an inappropriate move that aimed to avoid any witnesses.

"Young lady, I'm sure you understand why we need to have this conversation. Your aggressive language outside of class creates an unsafe learning environment. Several students have approached me, expressing discomfort in sharing their opinions for fear of public humiliation via your prominent social media accounts.

"If you wish to continue in this department, you must publicly apologize and recant your position. If this were just about me, I wouldn't intervene, but your divisive actions have demonized the entire department—" At the mention of "demon," the ugly face from her previous vision jumped out at her, and she did her best not to recoil from him. She steadied herself to respond, feeling the dual earthly and unearthly presence of an enemy before her.

"No one feels safe expressing themselves in your class if they disagree with the biased garbage you're force-feeding impressionable minds as facts. I mistakenly believed college offered a place for rational thought, not a brainwashing camp where your rhetorical assertions replace independent thought. Your pseudo-moral superiority and narcissistic compassion for minorities during today's lecture are dangerously misguided. Those same notions have resulted in decades of failed policy. I fear for my classmates who, while studying at this university, will never encounter alternative viewpoints or consider the consequences of your so-called 'solutions.'"

Dr. Travata's lip trembled as horror and hatred filled his gaze, her words striking at his most sensitive and unacknowledged insecurities. Recognizing her as a worthy opponent, he abandoned any attempt to debate her on intellectual grounds and resorted to his only power play. "I do not care about your irrelevant freshman opinions. You will publicly apologize, or I will pursue your expulsion with the Dean," he hissed.

Era squared her shoulders, unfazed. "Go ahead and try. If any due process remains at this school, you'll embarrass yourself even more. And remember, I can shine a light on you that millions will follow."

She knew before he stormed off that he would pursue the unfounded "hostile environment" case against her. The Gift revealed that her disagreement with his teachings merely threatened his intellectual authority. Having read her paper, he recognized it as a potential blow to multiple theories he had developed with graduate students over the past decade, and its popularity jeopardized his chances of publication.

She exited the building with her phone in hand, knowing that she needed to get ahead of this, which meant leveraging the Ridgewell influence. About to hit Christopher's name and fill him in, Cole approached her.

"Hey, I was hoping I'd catch you. I promise I didn't come here to wait for you. My Tax Accounting class starts in fifteen minutes in the building next door. Congrats on the song. 30 million views huh? I guess I never knew how musical you were," he added with a half-smile.

"Oh wow, it's that high already? Alex manages everything, and I haven't called her for an update yet," she replied sheepishly, feeling clueless and unconcerned about the song from the night before.

Cole smoothed his hair back nervously before continuing, "Well, I'm sure you have a lot going on, but I was wondering if you wanted to grab breakfast tomorrow before class. I noticed you don't have an early class, and I imagine it feels weird sitting alone on campus right now."

Damn if that's not the truth, she thought, eyeing him and reading his intentions. Everything she saw looked fuzzy, out of focus. The Gift had only ever retreated when she ignored its warnings. Could it be telling her something now? She couldn't recall ever going against it where Cole was concerned. Anyways, the idea of breakfast seemed innocent enough, and she hated eating alone now more than ever. "Okay," she replied, "Friday *friend* breakfast it is."

"Great... and Era, you know you can talk to me about anything, right? I'm here if you need anything," he said, standing closer than would normally be comfortable with anyone else, yet strangely calming for her. His soft voice and proximity sparked that familiar fluttery feeling in her stomach.

She looked up into his honey-brown eyes for a beat too long

before distraction arrived in the form of a bicyclist whizzing past them, snapping her back to reality. Era fidgeted for her phone before dismissing him, "See you tomorrow then. I need to make a call. Have a good class," and walked off before he could try to hug her goodbye, which he clearly expected.

Christian had likely already headed to his next class, but she wasn't taking chances that he might be hiding in the bushes somewhere. She appreciated his protection, even if he could be overbearing at times. She wondered how much of it stemmed from Christian's loyalty and how much from Christopher's encouragement as she tapped Christopher's name on her phone.

Christopher picked up on the second ring. Furious at the way the professor spoke to her, he assured her he would speak to his father to get their lawyers on it right away. No one would kick his girl out of school, especially not this school.

When Era finally headed back to her room, Alex sat in the living area with their two suitemates, Ami and Graciela. Ami, average height and Japanese, had silky black hair that hit below her shoulders and a medium build. She was slightly better-looking than average, with high cheekbones on her wide face and full lips, although her nose appeared somewhat flat and her figure wide through the hips and thighs. Era found her to be a little cold around her even though she knew Ami felt intimidated by her popularity and association with a known corporate heir.

Still, she knew girls who used this defense mechanism were usually insecure, and insecure girls always ended up posing a threat to Era. Also, Era had overheard her on the phone lamenting about the heavy workload to her parents, when in reality she knew Ami was more focused on the college social life. All she talked about was getting into the best parties, and how many likes her posts from trendy restaurants in the City got. Basic as hell.

Graciela, their fourth suitemate, was short and curvy, but

not heavy. Dark lips framed her naturally lined smile, complemented by full black lashes and perfectly tanned skin. Her garishly long nails changed colors and designs weekly, and she preferred wearing skimpy workout sets wherever she went, though she never actually worked out. She was friendlier but still a bit skittish around Era, and the messiest of the four. Her stuff constantly spilled out in the shared space, her room a bomb of laundry.

The four of them hadn't seen much of each other lately, everyone busy with rushing, making TV appearances, or enjoying the start-of-year parties. Era knew the two girls had been hanging out often, dining at famous foodie spots and posting everything to impress their friends back home. They seemed nice enough, even if Era was in no hurry to bring them into her inner circle.

Graciela and Ami crowded excitedly around Alex's laptop, engrossed in metrics on the song and the podcast. No doubt, Alex planned to bombard Era with the details the moment she entered the room.

"Hey guys," Era said, her tone flat as she set her bag down and sat across from them. "What's the word?"

"Oh, so happy you could join us," Alex began sarcastically. "Thanks to my digital marketing prowess, your song has several hundred thousand downloads and three million streams on Spotify alone. That means you made somewhere in the neighborhood of a quarter million dollars today. Or you made $125,000, since Chase will claim half the song. You two probably should have worked that out before I uploaded it, but oh well, live and learn, right?"

Era stared at her, beginning to sweat as the room suddenly felt stifling hot. She dashed to the window and threw it open, sucking the fresh air into her lungs.

"Babe, you're a smash hit," Alex continued, unfazed by Era's apparent panic attack, too practical for any nonsense. "I expected nothing less after hearing that song. What surprised me more was the number of YouTube views on the recording of your podcast. You made another thirty grand from the five million views that already racked up there."

At that, Graciela and Ami lost their composure, stood up, and started whooping. "Girl, you better be taking us all out to celebrate! Are you going to end up playing at Coachella? Because that would be awesome. Please tell me you're planning on performing live. I've always wanted to go backstage," Ami shouted, jumping around the room.

"This is really something special," Graciela observed with a smidge more decorum. "And Alex, you're going to receive some unbelievable job offers because what you did here single-handedly is almost as impressive as that song. Era is lucky to have you."

Era took one last gulp of cool air from the window and turned around. "Yes, I'm lucky to have her. She's incredible, and I'll end up getting all the attention even though she's equally amazing behind the scenes. Thank you, babe; I know how hard you worked and that you stayed up all night to put it out there." She pulled Alex in for a big hug and then allowed Graciela and Ami to offer their slightly awkward hugs before excusing herself to the sanctuary of her own room.

Not one to get overwhelmed easily, this was one of those rare moments. Campus suddenly felt small and bizarre; she wanted nothing more than to escape to the ocean and enjoy anonymity among the soothing crash of the waves. *That's it!* she thought. In an instant, she rushed off to the 4C suite, ready to hit two birds with one stone.

Thankfully, the first bird opened the door when she knocked. "Chase! Just who I hoped to see!" she whispered enthusiastically, tugging him by the hand into his room and shutting the door.

"If you want to be alone together, I don't think my room is

the best place for us. I could make other arrangements..." he crooned seductively, pushing his full lips together and raising his eyebrows while holding onto her hand.

"Stop it! I'm not here for that kind of alone time. I need to discuss business. We should have gone over this before we recorded the song—well before I wrote it and you helped me sing it. That's why I'm prepared to offer you 25% of the royalties. I'll take 50% for writing and production and 25% for half the vocals. You'll get 25 for your vocal contribution. I'll pay Alex from my cut. How does that sound?"

Chase considered for a moment before replying, "I feel like I should consult a lawyer before agreeing to anything, but I have to admit, it does sound like a fair deal. Okay, done."

"Great. For the record, my phone is recording this conversation. I'll need you to send me an email confirming our agreement, and I'll have an attorney draft a legal contract for us to sign," Era stated, all business. "You're going to make a pretty penny off this song."

Chase smirked at the statement, then his face froze into shocked astonishment at the next. "Alex thinks you made over 60 grand today."

Chase choked at the mention of a real dollar amount. "You're kidding? Holy crap, this is amazing! We're amazing," he shouted, grabbing her around the waist and crushing her into his usual bear hug. Era giggled and hugged him back. "We absolutely have to celebrate now. I'm taking you out."

"I can't tonight," she deferred politely.

"Tomorrow then? Saturday?" he pressed.

"Saturday might work better, but we'll celebrate as a group. Let's invite my suitemates, Christian and Violet, and Christopher obviously—"

"You do realize Cole will want an invite, or else he'll cry about it like a little baby?" Chase chimed in. Blegh, an accurate prediction she hadn't considered.

Era chewed her lip, mulling it over while fiddling with the band at the top of her leggings. "What the hell. He should be there too, I guess. Can you set it up?"

"I'd love to. You're my duet partner for life. And Era..." he paused, taking her hand and twirled her around, "Tell your girls to dress sexy. We are pulling out all the stops," he swaggered with unnecessary bravado.

The door swung open mid-twirl, revealing Cole in the doorway, with Christopher standing in the living room behind him. "What are you pulling out all the stops for?" Cole asked innocently. See-through ice daggers flew through the air from Cole to Chase when he thought she wasn't looking.

Real original, she thought, resisting the urge to roll her eyes at the Gift's trite imagery.

"Chase will fill you in. We're all going out on Saturday to celebrate the song's success," she summarized over her shoulder while approaching the true prize of the day. Christopher stood motionless, turning his suspicious gaze from his friend as she walked toward him, her eyes raking over him with unconcealed desire.

She hadn't forgotten her professor's threats or how Christopher had jumped into action on her behalf. Now, he stood before her, soaked in sweat in a loose muscle tank and athletic shorts, exuding manliness and strength. Gratitude and chemical attraction merged into an irresistible aphrodisiac. She could have eaten him. Instead, she placed a hand on his damp chest and pushed him straight back into his room, locking the door behind her.

"Hi, to you too," he replied, a hand curling around her waist. Era leaned into him, inhaling an aroma that was musky but not funky. She stood on her tiptoes, lightly kissing him, tasting a hint of saltiness. "I didn't think I'd find you in such a good mood after our earlier conversation, but I'm glad to see how much faith you have in my father's lawyers. They're the best money can buy, after all," he said smugly, giving her bottom a playful squeeze.

Era squealed and batted at his hand. "Today has been a roller coaster. I've got a professor threatening to get me kicked out of school, and I also have a hit single likely debuting on the Billboard list tomorrow. Alex said it already made a quarter million dollars on the first day."

As Christopher reacted to the news and tried to congratulate her, she cut him off. "But what I'm most excited about is seeing you."

Christopher pressed Era closer, kissing her more deeply. This time, she really tasted the salt on him and felt the rough stubble around his lips. "As weirdly hot as this is, I think I should let you hop in the shower. But first, I wanted to ask you a favor," she said, tracing her finger along the outline of his pec that barely fit inside the tank.

"Whatever you want, as long as you don't stop and make me take a shower."

"I know I shouldn't ask, but today has been surreal. I feel like I need to clear my head and could use some time back at the ocean. That's where I do my best thinking," she paused, looking up at him, desire mixed with vulnerability. "Could you call for the boat tonight so we can stay there instead of on campus? I thought we could celebrate, just the two of us."

He considered for a moment before grabbing his phone and dialing the captain. "Yes, I was wondering if you're on call tonight and if there are any previous engagements. Oh great. Can you bring it up to the City harbor? My girlfriend and I would like to stay the night. We should be out early for our morning classes. Yes, that would be great. See you at 6 then."

Christopher ended the call, looking at her with a smirk. "Sunset cruise and dinner on the boat at 6:30 work for you?"

Era threw her arms around his neck, then stepped back.

"Yes, I love it, but babe, you're dripping. Get in the shower. I'm going back to my room to pack a bag."

Christopher slapped her on the rear as she turned to leave, prompting her to turn back and shove him, her hand hitting the wall of his stone abs. "If I don't stop touching your body, I'll never be able to leave," she said over her shoulder before slipping out of his room.

Era made her way back down the hall towards the girl's wing of the dorm and felt a cattle prod hit her as she rounded the corner into the common area.

Her face.

Above her face, printed in large bold letters, a paper attached to the bulletin board read: **STOP HATE SPEECH.** Below her picture, lines. As she stepped closer, she read the last bit of print. "Sign the Petition for Expulsion."

Cowards! she thought and ripped the paper off the staples, crumpling it in her hand and throwing it into the trash. She knew she'd have opposition, but the attack felt personal. Some invisible enemy sought to turn her neighbors against her.

Back in her suite, Ami and Graciela told her not to worry about the stupid flyers and then cheered at the news of their Saturday celebration. They ran off like chickens to squawk around in their room, pulling out dresses and tossing shoes through the door into the living room. Alex had finally crashed and snored softly, buried in her blankets. After gathering a few essentials for her overnight bag, Era spent a quiet hour alone on her laptop, reviewing the craziness unfolding online.

She began with the song. Unsurprisingly, many girls were already in love with Chase, some assuming they were together or had something going on, while a few others were already outing her relationship, naming Christopher. She liked and commented on the top posts, skipping over any criticism, before moving on to the podcast.

The podcast downloads exceeded her expectations, fueled by

a few celebrity mentions, but the YouTube video of her speaking amassed the greatest views: 5.3 million and counting. The comments though, had turned into a battleground.

Many users volunteered to join whatever community she established, while an even greater number wholeheartedly agreed with her. The haters had a loud voice in the comments, and lots of responses. Her critics mainly focused on logistical difficulties or the economic repercussions of her ideas, but few attempted to refute her premises.

Feeling caught up on the state of the union, Era clicked open a new tab. A tickling feeling in the back of her mind kept coming back. She started typing in the search bar: saint michael the archangel. Before she could hit enter and see the results, her phone rang on the desk beside her.

"You ready to go?" Christopher asked as she picked up.

Era glanced at the time and realized she was late to meet him. She slapped her computer shut, tossed it aside, and grabbed her bag, hurrying out to the corridor to meet him.

Behind her, the laptop opened back up, its glow filling the room. And the search results on her unfinished tab populated, waiting for her return.

CHAPTER 38

"WE'LL FIGURE out who's putting those flyers up and stop them, okay? Christopher said, rubbing her hand.

"How? We don't even know who's behind it?"

"Everyone we know is keeping an eye out for people putting them up. We'll get to the bottom of it soon."

Era sighed and did her best to enjoy the drive out to the marina. And sure enough, as the miles between her and campus increased, so her anxiety over the present difficulties decreased. Mostly because Era loved the feeling of being driven in Christopher's truck—the care that he took of her, his presence that she had all to herself in the small comfy space. She rolled her window all the way down, holding Christopher's hand as he maneuvered through traffic, never letting go. The warm, dry air poured over her skin, dispelling the stuffy atmosphere that threatened to suffocate her on campus.

She glanced over, admiring how the wind lifted light and dark streaks in Christopher's hair and the exquisite line of his profile. Sometimes, she wondered how she had never allowed herself to appreciate him in high school until realizing he had grown about two full inches since the beginning of the year, filled out his frame with muscle and become her Christopher. Naturally, all these changes made him endlessly more attractive.

He caught her staring and smiled, his perfect white teeth making her stomach flip. She let go of his hand, gliding her fingers up the back of his neck and tugging at his hair slightly. He turned into a parking spot and kissed her, his lips a promise of things to come.

Onboard, Era spotted the captain's familiar face alongside Antoine, who nodded at her. The captain and Christopher chatted informally about the route for their cruise, settling on a northern path showcasing cliffs and estates perched atop grassy lawns, invisible from the streets above.

As they sat on the aft deck before a delicious charcuterie board, Antoine approached. "Would you like some champagne to celebrate this momentous occasion?" The Gift struck her with a surprise blow she had not often experienced in her life. Era realized that Christopher's personal butler had never spoken to her directly, so she had never read him.

Now, however, she saw threatening red eyes hidden within a black cave—his hostility towards her fueled by his suspicion that she posed a great threat to the Ridgewell family, one he served with ancient devotion. His bland expression made it impossible to reconcile his entrenched enmity with his unaffected demeanor. She knew for certain he couldn't be trusted.

"Yes, that would be wonderful. Thank you, Antoine. You always come prepared, even on short notice. Christopher is lucky to have someone so attentive," she replied.

"Well, Christopher didn't exactly find me. I have been with the Ridgewells for thirteen years, since he was only five years old," he corrected gracefully.

"I'm sure they appreciate your loyalty!" she remarked before he finished pouring Christopher's glass, then went off to assist the captain in preparing to embark. She turned to Christopher inquisitively. "I had no idea he had been with you for so long. Must be weird ordering around the same adult you knew as a child."

"It was strange at first. I always had a nanny when I was little. Antoine worked mostly for my dad, but since he was around so much and traveled with us, he did things with me as well. When I turned 14 and outgrew a nanny, my dad hired a new assistant, and Antoine transitioned to help drive me to hockey and manage school tasks, trips, stuff like that. He takes care of the house and the boat now, although he drives up every week to restock my fridge, swap out my laundry and sheets, and get my truck washed. I could send yours too if you want it done with mine," he finished, as if having a servant take care of basic college tasks was run of the mill information.

She felt a bit annoyed. Doing things for yourself was supposed to be a rite of passage. Hopefully, having a servant to baby him wouldn't hold him back from growing up.

Era rolled her eyes and shook her head. "Nothing your family does surprises me anymore. I guess I should thank him for keeping your sheets clean. I doubt many freshman boys do the same once a week. Eww," she gagged, thinking about how crusty the beds on campus probably were by midterms.

The yacht glided slowly as they exited the marina before picking up speed in open water. They sat side by side, snuggling on the banquette, looking out at the serene coastline while the spray of water danced around them. The rushing sensation around her felt fantastic, soothing her anxieties.

They feasted on king salmon, mussels served on the half shell with tomatoes and melted cheese, exquisitely roasted carrots, and fresh-baked bread. They finished the bottle of champagne after the first course and switched to a bottle of Screaming Eagle Sauvignon Blanc from Oakville. Christopher gave her a sly side-eye when he brandished the label, easily worth over $4,000. "There's something I've been meaning to ask you," he began, pouring the pale honey liquid into their glasses.

Era stiffened, searching with the Gift for his intentions before he could say anything more but all she found was wall, wall, more wall, fuzz. Finally, a clue—she saw the word "Friends" floating around him, but like the other images, it appeared blurry, shrouded in fog. Now she knew for sure, the more she resisted the Gift's directive, the more its clarity faded. All she could do was steel herself against the icy sensation in her blood and silently dispel the PTSD from a perfect dinner suddenly taking an unexpected turn.

She envisioned the gold watches in her mind, "None but you," and another, dead in a drawer hidden inside a pair of socks, reminding herself that disappointment could come for her happiness at any moment, like a thief in the night.

"I know I still haven't made things right since the watch incident—which I noticed you haven't worn since. I wanted to offer a small truce." With that, he took out his phone and typed something. Era's phone buzzed a second later with a notification to accept his Find My Friends location-sharing request. "I thought it only fair to entrust my location to you. If you want to reciprocate, that's up to you. I won't ask for it or expect it. I'm sorry I took that choice from you."

Era's eyes welled up with tears, and she nodded as she leaned in to kiss him. "I understand why you did it, which is why I came to you afterward even though I was still angry. I wish your family having money didn't mean you have to worry about things like that. I know you wanted to protect me, but I hated that you did it in a way that made us unequal."

With her lecture over, she picked up her phone, accepted his request, and fired off her own, hoping she wouldn't regret it. "There," she said. Christopher heard the buzz on his phone and responded by pulling Era into his lap. With the spat behind them, they could move past the incident with trust restored and a better understanding between them.

Neither had room for dessert, so instead, Antoine brought crystal snifters of Port. The syrupy, thick dessert wine smelled heavenly to Era, her guilty pleasure. She had learned to love Port while flying with Alex in business class. The flight attendants often offered it alongside fruit as the last course. No one cared about the drinking age over international waters, and as long as Alex and Era conducted themselves well, she never met with any objections when ordering alcohol on a transatlantic flight.

After two hours of cruising, the yacht stopped in front of a particularly beautiful vista, and Christopher suggested they head to the top deck for a better view. Era stood up, wobbling slightly on her heels before kicking them off and following him up multiple flights of stairs.

An invigorating wind blew at the top, alleviating the dizziness she felt after navigating the rocking enclosed stairs. She stopped behind Christopher, laying her head on his back and sliding her hands up his short sleeves to enjoy the view. Without thinking, her hands moved downwards, slipping under the hem of his shirt, nails tracing across the indents on either side of his abs. She felt him shudder under her touch, then spin around to have his turn putting his hands on her body. She relished the luxury of having the open water all to themselves.

Perhaps they had privacy from the outside world, yet two others remained on the yacht with them. Antoine climbed the stairs with purposeful heaviness, allowing them to hear his approach before asking if they wanted another glass of wine or a cocktail. Era ordered a margarita as Christopher snickered beside her. "What? We're celebrating, aren't we?" she pouted, upset he spoiled her fun with his judgment.

"Yes, of course we are, babe, but you've had champagne, wine, and port, and now you're switching to tequila? Remember we have class in the morning. I don't think you want to go too hard. Tomorrow my frat is throwing a big party. We can get crazy then," he pointed out, ever the disciplined CEO-in-training, thinking beyond the impulses of the moment.

Era quirked her head and grabbed his chin, placing her thumb over his plush lips before kissing him. "My class isn't until noon. Last one, I promise." He turned to putty in her hands; he could deny her nothing. She took the glass with her downstairs to their room and settled in, changing into lounge clothes that would double as pajamas. Her days of retreating into the closet to change had long passed, and she caught Christopher's eye as he admired her lacy bralette and scalloped briefs before she stepped into joggers and pulled the tank over her head.

Christopher walked up behind her, running his hands over her shoulders and drawing lines down her back. "You know how beautiful you are, don't you? I don't think I've ever seen such a perfect figure." His hands grabbed her waist, trailing down her backside and then her thighs as he knelt behind her, worshiping the curves of her body. Christopher hooked his thumbs into the waistband of the pants she had just put on and pulled them down to her ankles, then stood and removed the tank top. "How about you sleep in this?" he asked, running his hands over the panties and bralette.

That was it for Era. The freeing quality of the alcohol, the heady presence of the man she practically loved, and the privacy they had both longed for overwhelmed the remaining hesitation that plagued her since their fight and the other supernatural events. Even if it proved impossible to forget the two angelic visitations, she was as close as she could get.

Era felt bombarded with a stream of thoughts. *Perhaps sleeping with Christopher would bring her Gift back into focus; surely,*

she wouldn't feel any more butterflies around Cole if she committed.
She batted that thought away, only for another anxious line of
thinking to take its place: *Our time together may be short. Shouldn't
I enjoy the happiness we have together now?*

She countered this with the idea that sleeping with him now
and then facing separation would be even more painful. Ultimately, her mind turned to imagining how much he must love
her, how long he had held onto feelings for her through rejection and disappointment, and how the last thing she wanted to
do involved disappointing him further. This line of reasoning
tempted her to act on what her body already craved.

In the blink of an eye, they were both naked and perilously
close to consummating their relationship when Era caught the
acrid smell of sulfur and phosphorus, as if someone had lit a
match in the room. She jolted out of the moment, scanning for a
fire or hazard. Then she spotted it—a black shimmer in the
corner, the source of that unsettling smell.

She knew Christopher wouldn't understand why she let
them get so close, only to change her mind at the last second.
Talking about her true reasons was out of the question, but she
hated that she'd have to rely on the Cole heartbreak longer than
she felt. Even that reason would eventually lose its potency. For
now, she rolled over onto the bed, tucking the covers over her
shoulders as if to guard against the menacing presence that had
interrupted the moment.

The pain in Christopher's eyes struck her as he spoke. "Are
you okay? I'm willing to wait as long as it takes... But it seemed
like you really wanted to, and then something happened at the
last second." Perceptive as ever, that man.

She squeezed her eyes shut, and when she opened them, the
last remnants of the smell and shimmer vanished.

Sticking closely to the truth, she returned his gaze. "I really
do want to. It's hard to explain why I panic at the last second
like that. Surely, when the time is right, that won't happen."

"I'm glad that you stopped then. I don't want you to feel that way our first time together." His understanding and patience began breaking down her barriers for a second time. Yet when she glanced back at the spot where the shimmer had been, she knew she wouldn't be able to relax, let alone enjoy her moment with him.

CHAPTER 39

As Christopher predicted, the morning proved rough for Era. She awoke to a half-full glass of melted ice and a lime, remnants of a margarita, next to her bed. Her mouth tasted metallic, as if she'd eaten foil dipped in acid. Staggering to the bathroom, she brushed her teeth, groaning as a wave of nausea swept over her in the hot steam of the shower. She let the water pelt her, matching the regret she felt about the night before.

How did she never learn? Once again, she had drunk too much, toyed with Christopher, and made herself feel like garbage. Above all, she forgot that if she and Christopher couldn't have a future together, she only increased the impending heartbreak by entangling their hearts. She moaned again in both physical and spiritual agony.

"Tequila did ya in, did it?" Christopher called as he entered the bathroom. Unable to conceal her body or shame from him, she turned and faced away, quickly rinsing off the soap and grabbing her towel from the hook. She arranged her face into one that looked ill but not distraught and hurried into the other room to dress.

Though earlier than she would have chosen to wake up,

Christopher had an 8 a.m. class, so they needed to be back on campus before then. Era thanked him again for the incredible date and watched him walk briskly down the tree-lined path to his business class when it hit her—she had promised to meet Cole for breakfast.

With a groan that sounded somewhere between a sob and a whimper, she spun on her heels and trudged off to the food court-style cafeteria. Her stomach roiled and sloshed with the coffee she'd already consumed. Perhaps something greasy would help soak up the alcohol and see her through the morning.

On her left, her eye caught the unwelcome sight, more signs with her face on them. Even from afar, she could see ink scribbles across a few of the lines. So now people were joining the petition. Just great.

Cole waited for her at a corner table, coffee and a book open in front of him. "Woah, you don't look so good," he commented as she slumped into the chair.

"Thanks, just the pick-me-up I need to hear," she replied. "Do you mind grabbing me a coffee and a breakfast sandwich? I need to lay my head down on this table for a minute." She dropped her head into her folded arms.

Cole laughed and set off as her errand boy. He returned with her coffee, just how she liked it: no sugar, cream to the top. "I stopped by your room, and Ami said you didn't stay there last night, so I wasn't sure if you'd remember our breakfast. She's very friendly."

Era looked up, eyebrow raised. "Is that so?" The statement felt uncharacteristic of Cole, leading her to suspect that Ami had been more than friendly with him for that observation to surface.

She tried to rake him over to no avail. The Gift no longer cooperated at her beck and call, at least not with Cole–or Christopher.

The breakfast helped distract her from the hangover. They caught up on his family drama and topics rooted in reality rather than social media. His parents had reached a temporary custody agreement for his little sister, though the money fight still loomed. Era consoled him, reminding him that the situation would work itself out eventually, validating his right to feel angry.

In return, she explained the threat her Economics professor posed. He scowled, visibly upset and assured her she could come to him if she needed anything. Era was too polite to mention that she would seek help from her current boyfriend if she needed any.

The first threads of their tenuous friendship formed, and Era allowed for a brief hug before heading out to her late morning Poly Sci class. She spotted Arabella's silky brown waves in a spot close to where they had sat together the week before and took the seat next to her again.

Arabella smiled as Era sat down. "I wasn't sure if you'd be back. Thought you'd be out promoting your number one single," she said.

"Honestly, I've been too distracted to think about it much. I went out with my boyfriend last night and have been nursing a massive headache today."

"Might have missed this then." Arabella picked up her phone and did a quick search of the Billboard Top 100 before sliding the screen in front of Era. Sure enough, there it was, Era and Chase's song sat at number one on the list with a slew of heavy hitters below them in second, third, and fourth place. She let out a loud gasp that caused several students in front of them to turn in surprise. With barely a moment to collect herself, the professor walked in and began yet another pathetic lecture. At least they didn't have to break up into groups; she could simply zone out.

By the end of class, major news channels had picked up the

sensational story about her song, sung by an unsigned independent artist, recorded by a musical prodigy, and released from a dorm room of Cal University. As she walked back from class to talk to Alex, she spied two local news station vans outside the building, waiting for her. One cameraman was getting close and personal with one of her Stop Hate Speech fliers on the light post.

She ducked around to a back entrance before taking the stairs two at a time to get to her floor. She threw open the door to her suite, breathless, and charged into her room, promptly shutting the door to keep out any prying eyes.

Alex sat on the bed, engrossed in a phone conversation. When she saw Era, she excused herself and hung up. "Hey there, I have lots of updates, but we should discuss the big picture before diving into details. There are some... ah... money aspects we should probably discuss," Alex began.

"Yes, I realized I lacked oversight in planning the song's release without discussing compensation with you and Chase first. I'd like to give you a 10% cut of the royalties on revenue for anything you help me release and market, and for managing the business and accounting side of things. Also, I want you to hire an assistant. I'll allocate a budget of $30 an hour. I can't have you pulling all-nighters and skipping class. Actually, there's a girl I have in mind—Arabella. I'll put you two in touch, maybe invite her out with our group on Saturday to get to know her. I've already worked out the details with Chase. He's getting 25% of the royalties on the song since he's a co-artist but didn't write or produce it. I'll need you to cut the checks," Era dictated as Alex whipped out her laptop, jotting down notes.

"We'll need to create a statement for the press. Craft whatever you think works best. Let's avoid mentioning my relationship with Christopher to keep his last name out of it. I don't want any reference to my musical background or family," Era continued. Alex typed furiously, nodding as she absorbed the information.

"Got it. Don't mention that you've never taken piano or violin and your own best friend had no idea you could play. Check."

"I've got enough to worry about without your conspiracy theories right now."

"Okay, okay. Don't act like it's not weird though. Something is up but I'll let you tell me about it when you're ready," Alex said, letting Era off the hook way too easily.

"Um, whatever. Oh, and I'm not talking to those local news hacks out there." She motioned toward the two vans stalking the building outside their window. "If we do an interview, let's secure a spot with a late-night show in the City—no traveling—and get some compensation for it. Same split as on the music royalties. Christopher's lawyers will send you and Chase a contract and a non-disclosure agreement to sign. If any record companies offer deals, the answer is no," she finished.

"Gosh, you're good at this. Vision, purpose, and something to say. I can barely eat or sleep. I'm shaking with excitement," Alex said, taking a long sip of her coffee.

"You should grab a nap then. No more coffee. Christopher's frat is throwing a huge party, and I need you there with me." Era took a beat, a deep appreciation for her friend washing over her. "One more thing, this will be a wild ride. No matter what, you and I stick together."

"Ride or die," Alex replied, winking. "Now leave me alone. You've dropped this massive to-do list on me and said we're going out tonight. I need to write this statement, release it, and send emails to the late-night show before I can even think of sleeping. Bye!" she said, flicking her hand toward the door.

The crew assembled at 9 p.m. for a pre-game drive. Christopher brought the Sprinter van, allowing all ten of them to squeeze in and cruise around the City before the party. Christopher, Era, Christian, Violet, Chase, Alex, Cole, Ami, Graciela, and Arabella—who had accepted the last-minute invite from Alex—piled into the livery vehicle, which permitted them to drink alcohol onboard. Technically, only Cole was over 21, but it was better than a limo; it had a key feature—a bathroom—and felt less garish than a party bus.

Era's hangover had just begun to subside around 3 p.m., and now she found herself partying again. It was difficult not to get swept away by the energy. They kicked off with shots to celebrate Era and Chase's song hitting number one, then passed around beers and hard seltzers. By the time they arrived at the party, Era's head felt light, her headache long forgotten.

They entered like royalty. Kids moved out of the way, many taking out their phones to capture their arrival. Era walked in front with Chase, wanting to avoid drawing attention to her relationship with Christopher, knowing that videos would surface online within minutes.

The setup exceeded her expectations for a frat party. Instead of the big house party she had imagined—having never attended one when Cole dated her—it resembled a club more than anything. The production value impressed her: giant steel structures loomed overhead with mounted lights and effects, colossal speaker columns filled the corners, and platforms stood ready for the DJ and for girls to dance under rainbow-colored spotlights.

As she followed the boys through the thick crowd, they climbed the steps to a couch that had been dragged up onto a platform beside the DJ booth. Their group received a designated VIP area to party front and center. Though pretentious, Era was grateful to avoid the sweaty mass of kids.

Just then, the DJ announced, "Give it up for Cal University's Billboard number one hit artists, Era and Chase!"

The party went absolutely crazy, screaming and whistling for them. Era and Chase stood on the platform, phones pointed at them, recording. After a brief dance, Era retreated to the couch for a drink. Ami and Graciela busied themselves pouring another round of shots, which Era eagerly downed before grabbing Christopher and dancing with him behind the screen of their friends.

Era swept her hands over Christopher's shoulders reassuringly and squeezed him into a tight hug as their bodies moved with the music. It helped, but she could tell his defenses were still up. Era battled nervousness herself, so many eyes, so many phones pointed her way. No room for wrong moves. She took another long gulp off her vodka tonic.

Within half an hour, she transitioned from nervousness to euphoria, allowing the frenzy of the crowd and the calming effects of the alcohol to carry her away. Though she typically avoided shots, tonight's celebration of her success made them difficult to resist. As the buzz intensified, she spent more time with Chase, as partygoers continually asked for them to pose together.

It wasn't until after midnight that she felt Christopher pull her toward the couch. "Babe, no more shots, okay? It's crazy in here, and I see everyone pushing drinks on you," he warned over the loud music.

"Tell that to Ami! She's the one handing them out," she replied with an uncoordinated flick of her wrist.

"I already told her to stop. And I get that everyone wants to take pictures, but tell Chase to keep his hands to himself, or he and I will have words tonight," Christopher stated flatly. Era glanced down and noticed he sipped water with ice.

"It's no big deal. He's just a peacock. He loves the spotlight, and he knows photos of us together promote the song," she said, dismissing his valid concern and caring more about avoiding a fight that might sour the night.

"Fine. But I did warn you," he replied, getting up. "I'm

heading to the bathroom." With Christopher's seat vacant, Cole slid in beside her.

"You having fun?" he asked.

Era chugged a third of her drink. "I was, until Christopher got all jealous and insecure. He thinks Chase is being too handsy, which he isn't. It's all for the cameras."

"I think I have to agree with your boyfriend on this one. Chase is a flirt, and I've overheard him talking. He doesn't think you and Christopher will last now that you're rocketing to fame. After he tricked me into telling him all about you, it's obvious he wants to be the one to fill the void," Cole finished. The warning sounded flimsy and hypocritical, and she didn't care to think about it at the moment.

Just then, another shot landed in Era's hand as the DJ called for a toast to their song before playing a hastily mixed version laid over a dance beat. She stood up to down the shot, and as Chase's arm wrapped around her waist, she felt his hand casually rest on her backside. The cheap tequila hit her stomach like a rock, and her mouth and eyes watered as she struggled to keep it down. The cramping feeling refused to subside, and the metal trusses overhead tilted as she swayed to the side. The flashing lights turned from exciting to disorienting, and when she scanned the crowd, Christopher was nowhere to be found.

Era swiveled around and spotted several unfamiliar faces mixed with Christian, Violet, her suitemates, and Cole. Arabella and Alex had headed off into the crowd with Chase after the shot. Her legs felt distant, yet she managed to walk to Cole, leaning on him heavily for support. "I'm not doing well," she managed to say into his ear.

Cole shouted something to Christian, then grabbed her waist and led her out of the party, pushing through the crowd. Era sensed she wasn't stumbling and she could hear her own words, clear with only a hint of her actual level of intoxication. Still, she teetered on the brink of a blackout. Time sped up and slowed down. Events blurred together—flashes of her getting in and out of a car and then riding what felt like the world's longest elevator ride to her dorm's fourth floor. She barely remembered walking down the hall or entering her room.

With a start, the lights flickered back on in her head though her brain seemed to be filming in clips instead of full video. And she was as blank as a robot accepting commands. A flash—Cole rummaging through her drawers.

"Turn around," he said. Without a thought, she did so, and heard a zizz sound as her dress fell to the floor. She felt the release of pressure as he unhooked her bra and watched it fall onto her bed.

"Sit down," his voice commanded again and she sat, topless but too drunk to feel exposed. "Arms up." Like a marionette, her arms lifted, and he slipped a long shirt over her head.

When her head hit the pillow, it floated away from her like a balloon. As her eyes closed, the last sensation she remembered was lips pressing against hers before darkness enveloped her.

CHAPTER 40

ERA WAS GETTING USED to waking up to terrible confusion and regret at this point. She looked around the room, bewildered, struggling to understand how she had returned home. A glance down revealed a strange shirt she never wore as pajamas. Slowly, the flickers of memories came back—snippets of a car ride, an elevator, Cole in her room, and then...the feeling of lips against hers. Had she kissed him back?

Oh my gosh! What have I done? she thought, her hand flying up to her traitorous lips. Agony ripped through her confusion like a serrated knife as the truth sliced into her conscience. Grabbing her phone, she noticed ten messages from Christopher and one from Alex, who now slept beside her.

Quickly, she fired back a response to Christopher, explaining that she had gotten sick from the shots and that Cole had been the nearest person to help. She passed out so fast she hadn't even thought to check her phone. Reaching for the ibuprofen in her drawer, a packet of electrolytes, and her water bottle, she knew the only reason she didn't have a headache yet was because she was probably still drunk.

Knowing she was in a disastrous state to talk to Christopher and that he might be storming over at any moment, she quickly changed into her workout set and fled the room, half-drunk. She texted him again, informing him that she intended to sweat out some of the alcohol from her system with a run. Perhaps he would assume she hadn't been too wasted last night if she was already out exercising. Nothing could be further from the truth; this workout served as her sweat penance, one she wouldn't soon forget.

She set off at a jog, her leaden wobbly legs protested, every tendon and muscle crying out for mercy but she had to distance herself from the dorms. Fortunately, campus remained quiet on Saturday mornings, and few paid her much attention as she panted beneath the excruciatingly bright sun.

As she ran, her thoughts swirled in a lazy susan of doubt. She replayed the night's events, questioning, *Did he really kiss me? Did I kiss him back? Could I have dreamed or imagined it? Did anything else happen? What if I told Christopher? What would he do? Would he suspect something happened?*

After half an hour of endless rhetorical questions bombarding her, Era was sweating out tequila as a few decisions crystallized in her mind. First, she would avoid Cole like the plague. Their disastrous friendship had officially ended. On that note, she was pissed that she had to feel so guilty over something she didn't even want or provoke.

If she brought it up with Cole, he would deny knowing how intoxicated she had been. She cursed her ability to remain high-functioning while drinking, knowing it to be a double edged sword. She also knew she couldn't tell Christopher; she would pretend it never happened. No way around it—she would eat her regret.

Era understood the hearts of men, and Christopher's trust would be irreparably fractured, even though she knew he would forgive her. The ripples of his distrust would echo indefinitely.

Her punishing run continued up a long steep climb, a perfect place to perform her atonement. Blood throbbed in her temples as she forced her uncooperative limbs into higher gear, stitches stabbing both sides and a tight burning in her throat. At the top, she ducked behind a large tree and retched, the release cathartic, before collapsing onto a grassy lawn and bursting into thick sobs.

Era didn't feel like any leader who inspired people to sell their homes and leave their jobs to follow her. Lost and alone, she felt isolated under the weight of the truth and the tasks demanded of her by knowing.

If ignorance was bliss, knowledge was misery. Why would anyone choose her for anything? What was she other than a selfish, binge-drinking excuse for a girlfriend?

Era lay on her back, her limbs splayed, the damp grass soaking through her clothes. Then she recalled something terrible—she had promised Chase she would go out with him tonight to celebrate. Everyone was invited. Round three of drinking and partying. The thought churned her stomach. This commitment taunted her as another punishment, forcing her to drink despite feeling poisoned.

On top of the physical illness, she recognized the mental trial that lay ahead. If she stayed silent about the kiss, which she intended to do, she would spend the entire night enduring Cole's phony, opportunistic friendship.

How had she gotten into this mess? What did this music and all this distraction have to do with the message she needed to share? It seemed to introduce so much temptation, pulling her attention away from her true goal and back to the boys she needed to leave behind.

Money, she thought. It all came down to the money. Everything she envisioned would require significant funding, and having more of her own would expedite the process. The royalties would serve as seed money for her venture. She'd get her inheritance from Grandma's will in a few more months, but that wouldn't be nearly enough. Grateful for the insight, she gained perspective on the chaos unfolding around her and how best to harness it.

With a heavy heart, she trudged back to campus and texted Christopher to meet in the common area. The last thing she wanted was to have any kind of conversation with him while Cole lurked nearby.

"What the hell happened? I couldn't have been gone for more than twenty minutes. People stopped me all the way to the bathroom to ask about you. When I finally got back, you were gone. How could you leave with *him* without telling me? Do you know how that made me feel?" Christopher asked, trying not to raise his voice but not doing a great job. Disgust and fear trembled in the air around him.

Era pushed her flattened hands into the air, as if she could deflect the undulations in the air that only she could see. She didn't want to delve into Christopher's pain, pain she had caused, which would only deepen if she confessed the truth. Images of all the scenarios he envisioned flickered in her mind —Era sleeping with Cole or, worse, Cole taking advantage of her back at the dorms. Era spoke to the Gift in anger, *So now you want to show me what he's thinking?*

"I drank way too much. You called it; the shots were a terrible idea. I wish I had listened. Everything hit me at once, and I felt like I would either throw up or black out. I had no choice but to ask Cole for help. Alex was somewhere else, and you were gone. I barely made it to my pillow."

"He's been looking for a way to weasel back into your life. He must have enjoyed that you had to lean on him instead of me in your time of need. Did he touch you?" he asked, his voice sending a blast of freezing air over her. The molecules in the air between them stilled like outer space. What would fill the void? Truth or lies? If she chose to lie, she needed her guilty conscience to perform convincingly in front of the most perceptive guy she'd ever met.

Dodging the question would come across as guilt, so any response along the lines of, "Oh, you're so paranoid," would reveal something had occurred. No, she needed to maintain her poker face and lie boldly. He sensed something was up, so she'd have to give him a bit, something he could be upset about without exposing the darker truth.

"No. He did grab some pajamas for me and saw me change. I was so tired and out of it that I didn't think twice that it wasn't ok," she lied, knowing her guilt-laden tone would convince him, especially since he had removed her clothes himself instead of merely watching her take them off.

"That asshole!" he yelled, fists clenched, ready to storm down the hall and toss that scheming punk out the window.

"I know. I had time this morning to reflect and realized I made a mistake trying to be friends with him. He'll never respect my boundaries, will always feel entitled to special privileges in a way that would make us more than friends," she admitted. "I'm so sorry for how I made you feel last night. I'm going to rein in the drinking too. Can you forgive me?"

Although still visibly angry, her apology, promise, and humble request for forgiveness softened him. Relief welled in his eyes as he accepted her watered-down version of events and wrapped his arms around her, whispering into her hair, "You have no idea how worried I was. My mind went to some terrible places."

Era soothed him by running her hands through his hair, wanting to calm him, and showered his cheek with kisses. With the rift mended, Christopher headed off to the library for some reading. She wished she could share her Gift with him; she had already "read" all the books for her classes, including related materials in the library. Nothing remained but to wait until it was time to get ready for their night out, although she realized she should offer to help Alex with answering messages or something. Era shuffled back to her room, determined to make herself useful.

To her ire, Cole sat across from Ami, laughing and eating tacos. "Oh hi! Can't believe you actually worked out after last night. I can barely move. I'm so hungover, I ordered lunch. You want one?" Ami asked, her tone grating Era's ears with fake innocence.

Era narrowed her eyes at the pair of them, the Gift revealing Ami had bought extra tacos specifically to entice him to hang out. He, in turn, attempted to read her expression, gauging what she remembered from the previous night, fully aware she might not recall the kiss. Both of them disgusted her, and she was irritated she had to hide her revulsion.

"None for me. I'm trying to avoid the freshman fifteen," she said, walking off to her room and shutting the door behind her. Inside, she found Alex sitting on her bed with a laptop, a phone, and an iPad laid out around her.

"What the eff is that about? Why is Ami eating tacos with my ex in the living room?" Era asked with a huff as she vaulted up to her bed.

"Chick's a snake, that's why. She's totally got a crush on Cole. I noticed it last night at the party. What happened to you, by the way? Why'd you take off?" Alex asked calmly, her focus still on the screen as she typed.

Era sighed and rearranged the pillows beneath her, punching one of the throws. "Too many shots, that's what happened. You had gone off with Chase, and Christopher took forever to come back from the bathroom. I nearly vomited on the seven people live streaming me all night and started feeling myself black out. I had to ask Cole to take me back."

"Woah, that's crazy. I had no idea. I thought the party was too much for you and you bailed. But I thought it was weird for you to leave without Christopher. Poor guy was a wreck. Chase, Arabella, and I had a good time after you left."

A sadness stirred in her when Alex threw Chase's name out there, but let it slide since she hadn't finished her story. "I know. I feel so bad. Anyway, Cole was cool at first, but once he got me back to our room, he got me some pajamas and then totally undressed me like a creep. He's seen me topless a thousand times, but this felt skeezy. My memory isn't great, but I have a clip in my mind of him tucking me in, then I felt him kiss me before I passed out. More of a brown out than a blackout. I told Christopher he 'watched' me change but left out the kiss, which I plan to pretend never happened. I'm no longer playing 'friends' with him," she finished, watching as Alex's eyes widened, finally tearing away from her computer screen.

"So we're taking this one to the grave, are we?" Alex asked.

"You're the best."

"I know."

They agreed to watch out for any more sneaky behavior from Cole and to keep Ami from getting too friendly with him, especially in their suite. After taking a nap, Era awoke to Alex poking her, urging her to make a "Get Ready With Me" post. Alex had a jewelry sponsorship lined up that needed promotion. Era whimpered into her pillow; it promised to be a long night.

CHAPTER 41

THE TEN OF them gathered outside the dorm at 8 for dinner. Two black Escalades arrived to collect the group—Era, Christopher, Chase, Alex, and Arabella in the first, while Christian, Violet, her questionable roomies, and her ex climbed into the second.

Era opted for a structured black dress exuding mature elegance with its asymmetrical lines, and Alex dazzled in a pale pink ensemble that draped alluringly over her bust and flared below her cinched waist. Arabella sported Dior dress shorts paired with a lacy top, flattering her dark hair and slender figure. Ami and Graciela both wore tight mini dresses that screamed "college girls." Chase, ever the peacock, flaunted a silky button-down unbuttoned to showcase his smooth chest, while Christopher chose a conservative tailored look. Christian and Violet coordinated in safe black outfits. Cole didn't look half bad either.

Era, relieved that the split meant Cole rode in the other vehicle, glanced between him and Christopher, hoping for no confrontation. It proved difficult to maintain an anxious mood with Chase's infectious excitement bubbling behind her. He thrived on the high of their recent musical success, and Era didn't want to rain on his parade. She pasted a smile onto her face and vowed to keep Christopher close throughout the night. Their first stop, Nobu, served two purposes, sushi, and a place to be seen. Oh, and an outrageous bill. Next, the black SUVs whisked them away to the Social Club, where they strolled in, no hassle, even though Ami and Graciela kept breaking the strict no-photography rule by snapping pictures every five seconds. They dispersed into the main bar area while waiting to enter the private back club through the kitchen. Era sent Christopher to the bar with her order for a club soda with lime, when she spotted a familiar face approaching.

"I had a feeling I'd see you in here again. You look incredible," said Jesse, the tall, dark, and handsome bartender who played host tonight. Ami and Graciela's eyes glued to him as he leaned in to embrace her.

"You look perfect, as always," she cooed, sizing up the dinner jacket that built a beautiful triangle from his broad shoulders to his trim waist. "I can't believe I'm the only one who gets to admire you in person—don't they know looks like yours belong on TV?" She smiled and gazed into him, admiring the sweep of dark lashes. The Pull ebbed out of her, his eyes dilating and he reached for her hand before she realized the slip and dammed the channel.

His focus cleared, and he answered, matching her charm, "I wish they did. I think your table's about ready. Why don't I take you over?" Jesse looked over her party, noticing Christopher's return from the bar and nodded to him. "Hey there. Good to have you with us," he said before turning back to Era. "Take my number for next time. That way, you can work with me directly." With swift hands, he grabbed Era's phone, held it up to her face to unlock it, and texted himself from her number.

Christopher followed a step behind as Jesse led them from the room using his hand at Era's lower back to guide her through the kitchen toward the secret club entrance. After passing through what looked like refrigerator doors, they entered the tiny club, dark yet crowded—though not too crowded.

A DJ occupied a booth slightly elevated above the bar and dance floor. The space only fit around a hundred people. The low ceiling created a cozy, exclusive vibe, free from bottle rats and riff raff. Here, everyone belonged to the top echelon of the party, music, or movie crowd—a vibrant tapestry of youth, beauty, and power. Even Christopher's business connections couldn't have gotten them in; they enjoyed this privilege because Chase and Era were hitmakers. Their names had been absorbed as fresh blood to the scene.

They settled into a booth sandwiched between a group of trust fund babies on one side and some minor celebrities on the other that Era recognized vaguely as actors without being able to place their work. Christopher leaned closer, and as he began to say "Babe," the Gift roared around him. Era braced herself for a potential argument with him in front of their friends.

He leaned in, speaking into her ear over the loud music. "What was that about? He broke into your phone! And why does every guy think he can put his hands on you?" he asked, putting his hand in the spot where Jesse's had been.

Era sighed, exasperated. "He knows me from before and doesn't know you and I are together. His job is to network and make guests feel important. That's just how things work; it's nothing personal," she explained, her eyes already darting around to size up the room, hoping he'd drop it.

His jaw clenched, and his voice came out low and sharp. "Fine. I know you have a slick answer for everything, but I can't help feeling like there are too many things making me jealous and upset. We're fine one minute, then something complicated happens. There must be a reason it keeps happening." Christopher's keen instinct sensed an underlying connection among the contentious events.

"Give it time. You know it's crazy right now. You don't need to worry about a bartender or anyone else," she assured him, guilt gnawing at her as she spoke. "Come here," she added, leaning in to kiss him long and slow, choosing to ignore the closeness of the group.

He remained stiff even though he did kiss her back. She never kissed him in front of Cole, something neither of them ever acknowledged and her doing so now demonstrated a vote of confidence in them. He got it. He got everything.

When Era opened her eyes, the Gift did something she had never experienced. Her hearing sharpened, and despite the loud music, every conversation around her became crystal clear. Unfortunately, this acute awareness meant she now felt the hearts of her entire group simultaneously.

Across the booth, Cole barely concealed his annoyance at witnessing the private moment and seeing the gold watch from Christopher glint on Era's wrist instead of his own. Ami, noticing Cole's distraction, simmered with bitter jealousy, viewing her as a heartless temptress unwilling to let Cole go.

To her right, Chase's initial pleasure at watching Era and Christopher bicker morphed into despair at seeing their kiss, a stark reminder of the intimacy he lacked with her. He continued his conversation with Alex, deciding that Era's friend would serve as an excellent placeholder, a way to stay close to Era without relying solely on Christopher. This thought riled Era considerably.

Seated next to Christopher, Christian bristled, noticeably bothered. He had noticed Jesse's hand on Era. Offended on his best friend's behalf, he recognized their argument and appreciated Christopher's backbone in standing up for himself. He was sure Christopher would end up getting played by the combination of her smooth talking and his own readiness to overlook any of her faults. It was interesting to see Christopher through his friend's eyes. Christian was happy for his friend to finally bag his dream girl, yet didn't like how much power that gave Era to disappoint him.

Finally, Era turned her attention to Alex chatting with Chase, alarmed to see Alex forming a deeper attachment to him than a simple crush.

What an absolute disaster, she thought. Era knew she needed to do something before everything spiraled out of control, inevitably leading to more misunderstandings with Christopher.

As she pondered where to begin, a round of drinks arrived at the table. Era decided to nurse hers, determined to avoid a repeat of last night's debacle or this morning's hangover. The girls soon wanted to dance, and made space in front of the booth to enjoy themselves. Grateful for the moment alone, Era sat on her phone while Christopher and Christian chatted.

A group of guys at the next table partied hard. One, perched atop the back of his seat connecting their booths, leered at Era. Finally, after ignoring his obnoxious overtures, he leaned over to goad her into a conversation. His gross warm breath blasted across her face.

"Don't you smile?" he asked, the question as tasteless as the giant yellow diamond embedded in his flashy watch. His criticism of her detached attitude only fueled her irritation. She flung back a combination of a sneer and a smile and looked back down at her phone.

He leaned closer and bellowed in her ear, his breath dampening her face, making her gag, "Congrats on your one hit wonder. Now get off your phone and enjoy the night. You think you'll stay on top forever?" Then he reached into the pocket of his cardigan and taunted, "I know what will get you in the mood," and slipped a small, hard object into her hand.

She glanced down at the flat red pill, with a heart-shape

pressed into it. It was almost passable as a piece of candy should the recipient be so naive. Then she looked up, into the dark night of the guy's soul, someone who routinely carried drugs with him and used them freely to soften up girls to make them easier targets.

Era met his gaze, recognizing the darkness within him. "No, thanks," she replied with tight lips, dropping the pill into the cushions of her seat and standing to head to the bathroom. She shuddered in disgust as she squeezed through sweaty bodies in this den of darkness. Her revulsion mounted as she opened the bathroom door to find a girl exiting the handicap stall, and caught sight of two others snorting lines off the flat steel top of the toilet paper holder.

The room smelled funny, like someone had lit a match even though there was no sign of a candle or a cigarette anywhere. Caught staring, Era felt the girl's grip on her arm as she yanked her into the stall.

"Shh, don't say anything," she whispered, her long brown hair framing her bony collarbones. It was clear the group relied on alcohol and coke, their bodies alarmingly thin. "The manager doesn't like girls bringing stuff in here. Want some?"

"No, thanks. I've really gotta pee," Era said, squeezing her legs together, faking urgency while sidestepping the girl and ducking behind the nearest stall door. She waited for their giggles to fade before emerging, now livid with the drug pushers. The club became a dungeon, triggering her claustrophobia with menacing faces, the temptation to drink and drown it all out swirling around her. No safe corner existed where she could hide.

Suddenly, her phone buzzed in her hand, which it never did because she always kept it on silent. Era glanced down at the message, puzzled by the unfamiliar combination of characters instead of a number.

Don't you think it's time you left?

The warning was clear. And it clicked. Michael. It had to be him.

Angels texting now... great, she thought. She grabbed her purse from the booth and headed toward the entrance, planning to text Christopher from the kitchen and give him five minutes to meet her before leaving. She couldn't be there right now. The club's walls closed in on her now, as if angels were squeezing into every unoccupied space, cramming into the air between the sea of heads and the low ceiling. There wasn't any air left. She began to spiral into a full-blown panic attack.

As she maneuvered through the dance floor, she spotted the back of a blonde head in the corner and started making her way over. She didn't want to get any more flack for her Irish good-byes. She'd let Alex know she wanted to leave and give her the choice to stay or go.

As she moved closer through the crowd, a pair of arms snaked around Alex's waist and—oh—Chase bent his head low —and kissed her. Unsure whether to intervene or let it be, Era hesitated, vexed with frustration at them both. How could Alex be so easily duped? Anger flared at Chase for using her friend, but then an impossible sight caught her eye to the left.

Ami ground against Cole, and his hands cradled her hips. Era's stomach turned, possessiveness sinking its teeth into her. It didn't matter that they weren't together, he was still hers because he still loved her. And she had never seen him touch another girl. It felt like a betrayal, especially after kissing her only two nights ago.

The vision of her soul, fused to Cole and touching Ami by association sickened her. No matter what she did, a part of her was tied to him, and was affected by all his actions.

It didn't make sense. It wasn't fair. And it sucked.

Scanning the crowd for Christopher, she looked back at Cole and nearly gagged. Now they were kissing—an unrestrained, sloppy makeout on the dance floor. Hot fury surged through her and she took a step towards them, wanting to call him out for being a traitor. But before she could act on that impulse, Cole turned and caught sight of her, sensing her presence.

He started toward her, but not before Era saw Ami's face change from disbelief to horror at the obvious insult that Cole had left her to chase after his ex. Era's righteous anger morphed into panic at seeing him move towards her, prompting a full sprint out of the club.

She moved with speed through the crowd and then the exit into the kitchen. There she ducked behind a rack filled with heavy pots, and watched Cole search for her before heading out toward the main bar.

Whimpering in utter defeat, she texted Christopher, grateful that, despite everything, she'd had only one drink and could take care of herself tonight. But ten minutes passed with no answer. Unable to stand it any longer, she took one last cautionary check for Cole's reappearance and emerged from her hiding place, dashing towards the back exit when Christopher burst through the doors.

"What's going on?" Christopher asked, concern etched on his face when he saw her.

Era's voice trembled. "I can't be here. Some guy handed me Molly, and when I tried to escape to the bathroom, a girl yanked me into a stall where her friends were doing lines of coke. I've been hungover all day, and being in this tiny shoebox of a club, that is only going to be fun if I drink, is a toxic environment for me right now. Please, can you take me home?"

He ran his hands through his hair, frustration mounting. "Yes, I'll take you back, but I swear, it's happening again. I keep having this feeling like you're not telling me everything, like there's something else going on." His eyes pleaded with her. "Era, please, I hate feeling this way. If there's more, can you trust me enough to tell me?"

Era longed to tell him everything right there in the club kitchen. But how could she explain her ability to read hearts or that Chase was kissing her friend to get closer to her? How could she articulate the pain of seeing her first love betray her with someone she had to live with? She couldn't confess her guilt over Cole's stolen kiss or the angelic message urging her to leave. And she certainly couldn't explain a prophecy that their relationship was doomed to fail, and that nothing but a messy divorce and custody battle lay in their future together.

She was a sherpa of secrets trying to climb Mount Everest. How would it ever be possible for her to be completely honest with him or anyone else? She felt certain that the affliction was hers alone. Era opened her mouth to come up with something to say to him, but couldn't muster the strength to lie, and instead, tears flowed down her cheeks.

Christopher crushed her to his chest, rubbing circles on her back as she cried. He knew that she wasn't revealing the whole truth, but he thought she would, given time. His patience and understanding were daggers in her heart, causing her to choke on a sob. He stroked her hair gently and murmured soothing words until she quieted.

"Let's get out of here," he whispered. "I'll take you home, and we can talk or not talk, whatever you need."

Era nodded, grateful for his understanding. She wiped her tears and followed him out of the club, relieved to escape the noise and drugs. As they walked to the black SUV, guilt nagged at her for holding so much back. Christopher trusted and loved her, and she wanted to be open with him, but some secrets were too big to tell.

She climbed into the car, exhausted, and laid her head in his lap, falling asleep as they navigated the traffic that plagued the City, even at night. When she awoke, she thought she was dreaming to see the path leading to the Ridgewell's oversize door before her. He had brought her home! To Emerald Beach! Tears sprang to her eyes. She had never felt so grateful or so impressed by Christopher's intuition.

Though emotionally drained, when the comforting sight of his room came into view, a silky nightdress laid out on the bed waiting for her, her heart brimmed with love. She wanted to let her heart love him fully, despite the inevitable pain of separation looming ahead. She let him undress her like a child, slipping the nightgown over her head, then gathered her into his arms under the soft covers, tucking her close.

CHAPTER 42

WHEN ERA AWOKE the next morning, bliss wrapped around her, warm and soft as the blankets. She lay gazing out the large windows, watching the sunlight transform the bay into a shimmering mirror, occasionally disturbed by ducks that charged before ripples on the surface. Christopher's chest rose and fell in a regular rhythm that calmed her, and the knowledge that she was far from the menacing forces at school allowed her chest to relax in a way she hadn't felt since moving.

She studied his face as he slept, his perfect face, still her face. Even the small scar on the underside of his chin, where the hair didn't grow quite right, appeared beautiful. Each hair of his eyebrows and the straight line of his nose captivated her; she wished she could hold onto this picture of him in her mind forever.

In him, she saw the true definition of a man—someone who would use his strength to love her unconditionally, take care of her, and sacrifice his happiness for hers. She wanted to scream and shout at the heavens that they were wrong for trying to separate such a beautiful love.

Even during their fights, he won pieces of her heart, always seeking the truth so they could grow together rather than apart. His goals always focused on clearing obstacles threatening their relationship because she knew one thing for certain: he loved her. He had patiently awaited the right moment to say it, ensuring she was ready to hear it. Even in his silence, he prioritized her best interests.

Tears streamed down her cheeks as her heart swelled. Christopher stirred, alarmed at the sight of her crying, thinking she must still be upset from the night before

Rolling toward her, he wrapped his strong arms around her, comforting her gently. "Hey, it's okay. You're home now."

She gulped the sob that hitched in her chest at the word "home," for that was precisely how she felt beside him. But he didn't deserve to deal with anymore crying. She endeavored to calm herself and reassure him that she wasn't upset about the night before.

"It's not that. I'm just so happy to be here, home, with you. I didn't even know this is where I needed to be, but you did," –she opened her heart and felt a rush of power stream out– "I love you, Christopher."

He sucked in a breath through his nose, stunned by her confession yet bursting with joy to hear those words. His eyes brimmed with tears as he cupped her cheek and replied, "I love you too, Era. I've waited years for you to let me love you, and I promise I'll never take your love for granted. You know me. I could never love anyone as much as I love you."

When he kissed her, fireworks exploded behind her eyes. The undeniable connection between them blazed. When he paused to look at her, she trembled, the intensity of her emotions evident in her involuntary movements. At that moment, she pushed out every thought interfering with her desire for him and embraced the present.

Christopher wrapped her into his arms, reluctant to let go.

This moment had long been his dream. He had always known he loved Era, but never imagined how incredible it would be to hear those words from her lips.

As they kissed and basked in the afterglow of their confession, Era's stomach growled loudly. She realized she hadn't eaten more than a few bites of fish at Nobu the night before.

Christopher chuckled as he rolled out of bed to grab her a sweatshirt and sweatpants. "Looks like I'm back to my full-time job, keeping you fed," he said, dodging a pillow she threw at him from the bed.

Downstairs, they enjoyed breakfast with Christopher's parents, recently returned from a summit on real estate consolidation. Laura greeted Era with a smile like honey, abandoning her half-made coffee to hug her then kiss her son.

Caspar set down his iPad and smiled at them. "How is the young couple this morning? I'm glad you brought her by so soon after the 'misunderstanding,'" he said to Christopher, nodding with a serious expression.

Era jerked slightly at the comment, realizing that Christopher bringing her there might not have been entirely altruistic.

"Oh, give the girl a minute to wake up," Laura butted in. "What would you like for breakfast?" She called out to the chef, "Karl, can you bring over a coffee service? The kids have had a long night."

"Now sweetheart, tell me all about school. It seems you've had quite an eventful start to the semester." Laura's eyes lit up with genuine interest and Era melted at the endearment. Her own mother never addressed her so sweetly.

"Is an omelet okay? Some protein would do you good after being out all night with those worthless druggies," Laura continued, and Era realized Christopher must have filled her in on more details than she ever imagined sharing with her own parents. She mentally noted to discuss boundaries regarding sharing information with him later.

Era launched into her tale, recounting her experiences with academic bullies and professors, her appearance on *Good Morning America*, the impromptu recording of her hit song, and the release of her first podcast. It felt surreal to hear herself retell all these extraordinary events woven together.

Laura let out little gasps and sounds while clutching her cup of coffee but didn't comment until Era finished. For the first time with a mother figure, Era didn't feel rushed or talked over, like someone waited for an opportunity to jump in and redirect.

When the polite break in conversation appeared, Laura reflected, "You certainly are a force to be reckoned with. How are you doing with all these big changes in your life?"

Era appreciated Laura's focus on her, not on the money, not on her next steps. "It's a lot, and really fast. I don't like the feeling of losing my privacy, that's something I always protected and it's uncomfortable being so exposed."

"Now that, I can understand. Marrying into this family, everyone seems to know everything about me, the moment they meet me. Not a lot of room left for me to change their mind once they've already formed their idea of me, or our family. Just don't let any outside influences pressure you to rush into making any big decisions. Freshman year is all about finding out who *you* are and what *you* want," Laura said, wrapping Era in her gentle empathy once more.

Ooh, that one hit a little closer to home than Era expected. "Yes, I am trying to figure out what *I* want and I think that may be the hardest part of all of this."

"Well, isn't it fortunate you have my son to lean on. For someone so young, he is already a rock. I know it."

So do I, Era thought wistfully, as she admired Christopher giving input to his father on an upcoming investment opportunity. "It is," she finally responded.

Caspar paused his discussion with Christopher to pipe in. He must have been listening in while talking with Christopher.

"You've done some real good, exposing the bias at CalU; however, the situation with Dr. Travata is unfortunate. My best defense lawyers have drafted a response to his accusations—which are totally frivolous—and sent it off to the board. It's harassment and intimidation.

"Off the record, I'll make it clear that Ridgewell Enterprises will rescind funding for the AI technology upgrade to the business school if they don't drop the case against you immediately. Perhaps you could delay any further agitations until we get this matter resolved."

His unspoken directive hung in the air—stop stirring the pot while I clean up your mess. Era thanked him more than once for stepping in on her behalf, though she knew she was just getting started; her most controversial statements awaited her.

True to Christopher's penchant for being unapologetically generous, especially when it came to practical matters, Antoine announced his package arrived just as they wrapped up breakfast. Christopher went to retrieve it and returned, handing Era two retail bags with a kiss on the cheek and asked, "You want to go for a run?"

Beneath the tissue paper lay two complete outfits—Lululemon sets (one for working out and one for lounging afterward), a hat, sports bras, underwear, a pack of socks, and coordinating HOKA running shoes. He was Christmas every day. And it wasn't just the gifts she appreciated; it was that he constantly thought of her, remembering her shoe and bra size. He found ways to show her he was programmed to take care of her. A little thing like not having an overnight bag wouldn't deter him from wanting to spend the morning with her.

She leaned over and kissed him near his ear, whispering, "I love you," watching goosebumps rise on his neck before hurrying upstairs to change.

They made their way along the Back Bay under the dappled shade of the canopy arching over the path. The familiar yet overly sweet and pungent smell of coastal sagebrush surrounded them. Each time her foot found the next patch of dirt along the trail beside the untouched blue waters, profound tranquility descended on her.

How had she escaped her hometown to her dream school only to have it turn into hell and long to return? If only she and Christopher could remain in the Ridgewell house high on the cliff, shielded from news vans and the machinations of duplicitous people and hateful professors.

Era reflected on why the fantasy of escaping back to Emerald Beach appealed to her. She saw herself assimilating into his family, finding her home with them. She wanted it. So. Freaking. Bad. She wanted that perfect little breakfast like Groundhog Day for the rest of her life. She wanted to lay in bed with Christopher in the morning and hear "I love you" forever and ever. And she knew she could have it and that she couldn't. If she thought about that for even one more second, she would crumble to nothing.

Instead, she turned her attention to school and realized that campus reminded her a lot of middle school now. Her deep-seated aversion to being hated still needled at her, triggering her flight response. Years of the Gift had filled her with a sense of self-determination, of real power. Usually, the formula was so simple. Search a heart to find what a person wants, what they fear—then drop the breadcrumbs and assuage the fear in bits and pieces. It *always* worked.

And when her more subtle approach didn't work, she could bring out the big guns—the Pull. But even the Pull didn't work on those who either deeply feared or hated her. Unfortunately, as the numbers of people that admired her grew, so did the numbers of those suspicious and hostile towards her. Her control seemed to be increasing and decreasing in equal maddening measure.

Era's fear walked alive and well in her mind. She saw how a single enemy could upend her world, whether it be a middle school nemesis or a high school teacher. She knew she shouldn't care, shouldn't be afraid, but after living in a home where she carried the invisible burden of knowing she was an eternal inconvenience to those who ought to love her, the idea that those outside it should also be against her, crushed her. If she couldn't find a way to get her own mom and dad to love her, she'd make the whole world love her instead. It was easier said than done.

Determined to confront her adversaries, she recognized Dr. Travata as the first of many hurdles she must overcome on the perilous path ahead. An uncomfortable conversation with Alex awaited her, and she knew she could no longer delay recording her next podcast. Tonight, she would return to the studio—to face the music, literally.

As they circled back to Christopher's house and slowed to a walk to cool down, Era expressed her desire to return to campus as soon as possible, thanking him for bringing her home. Within an hour, the two were in the back of the comfortable Sprinter van, Antoine at the wheel.

"It's too bad we had to rush back," Christopher lamented as the van drifted into traffic. "The weather is perfect for a beach day."

"I'm sorry, babe. The little escape was exactly what I needed, but I have things to take care of today that can't wait until tomorrow," she said, picking up her phone to call Alex. "Hey, can you book both studios again tonight? I need less than an hour in Studio A and maybe two hours in Studio B. No, we don't need Chase. Don't even mention it to him. Let's head over at 2. See ya."

Era couldn't help but notice Antoine stiffen at the mention of the word "studio." He clearly paid attention to her conversation, and from the Gift's previous insights on his personality, she sensed his discomfort about her taking on more public positions, especially after Caspar's suggestion.

Could he know about the conversation from this morning? she thought. She hadn't seen him in the room. Era wanted to strike up a conversation with him to gauge his feelings, but Christopher began talking her ear off about his plans for the week and the Frat's upcoming parties, straining her patience.

Silent as ever, Antoine dropped them off at the dorm and drove off, leaving Era to ponder her concerns. The Gift being unusable to her on people who didn't speak in her presence annoyed her every time he came around. Inside her suite, she was grateful that only Alex was there. She still debated if she could stomach a confrontation with Ami about the situation with Cole.

As Era entered, Alex chastised her, "Girl, you've gotta stop dipping out like that. Remember when we used to leave together? I feel like I'm constantly trying to track you down. I even sent a Find Friends request for your location; it's too stressful not knowing if you've left or if you're being held hostage in the bar somewhere."

"I know, I'm sorry. I had a bit of a freak and then I spotted Cole and Ami kissing and kind of lost my mind. He actually saw me and started coming after me, so I hid in the kitchen," Era explained, omitting the dirtier details.

"Get the heck out of here! Era, I'm so sorry. He's been acting like such a piece of crap lately. And *Ami* is officially cut from the group; we knew she was up to something with him," Alex said, comforting Era with her loyalty before turning back into the practical one. "I'm sure it was hard seeing him with another girl but it was bound to happen sooner or later. Maybe it'll help you both to move on." The words were true if difficult to hear, the wound still too raw.

Era chewed her cheek before continuing, "I saw something else on my way out. You and Chase kissing—"

"Ha! Of course, you would see. I swear you have eyes in the back of your head. He's so hot, and wow, is he a good kisser too. We've been talking a lot about the song and the marketing plan, and we've just sort of clicked, you know? I know he comes off as a player but I think he really likes me," she finished, while Era cringed.

"I have to tell you something that is really difficult for me to say, and I know you won't want to hear it. But here's the thing, you're more important to me than anything, and I can't let a guy hurt you because I was afraid to tell you the truth. Chase is playing you—"

"What? There's nothing going on yet! We only kissed. How could you possibly think he's playing me after one kiss?"

Era shifted on her bed, working through the best way to explain without crushing Alex's ego or revealing too much. "Well, first off, he told me he liked me back when we were at the Ranch, the first weekend we met—"

"You weren't even together with Christopher then!" Alex interrupted.

"I know, I know. He told me he liked me, and I thought he'd give up after Christopher and I got serious, but he hasn't. Recently, he said he's waiting for things to not work out with Christopher so he can have a chance. Cole warned me that Chase said something similar to him. He's using you to get close to me without going through Christopher," Era stated matter-of-factly.

"That's such bullshit, Era! First Christopher, who you knew I liked for a long time before you two got together, and now Chase? You don't even like him—why do you care if he wants to like me while waiting around for you? Does everyone I like have to like you?" she shouted.

Era's heart sank at the thought of hurting Alex. "Listen to yourself! You deserve better than a guy who's going to use you as a placeholder. Yes, Chase is hot—smoking hot—but don't you think he knows that? That's the only reason he can get away with confessing his feelings for me and going after my best friend at the same time."

Just then, the door, which had been ajar, swung open, revealing Christopher, his mouth agape as he caught the tail end of Era's statement. "I freaking knew there was something else going on last night that you wouldn't tell me! So Chase confessed his love to you, did he? Is there anything else I need to know?"

Both Era and Alex jumped at the intrusion. While Era's first instinct was to feel guilty and defend herself, she forced herself to gather her emotions before replying, "We're having a private conversation in our bedroom. I'm sure you didn't mean to eavesdrop, but this doesn't concern you."

Christopher's eyes blazed with anger. "Are you for real? My friend is telling my girlfriend he loves her, and that's not my concern? If he's trying to get with you, why are you off singing with him? You told me he's all over you just to promote the song!"

Era stood up and closed the distance between them. "I shouldn't have to explain anything to you when you're barging into my room and listening in on a conversation with my best friend. You have no boundaries sometimes!" she retorted, her voice heated. "Now we need to be at the studio in thirty minutes, and I don't have time to hash this out."

She watched anger radiate from him as visible steam, dampening her shirt. Even though she felt justified in not having to explain everything, she knew her words hurt him. Moving closer, she softened her tone and laced her fingers through his. "I don't feel anything for Chase—you know that. I'll make it clear to him that I won't tolerate any unwelcome touching. You've never had anything to worry about."

Though still fuming, he nodded and left the room, her words easing some of his tension.

Turning to Alex, who seemed further wounded by having to listen to Era promise her boyfriend that she'd keep Alex's crush at arm's length, Era continued, "You can do whatever you want. I won't tell you what to do or judge your decisions."

Alex met her gaze, a serious expression on her face. "I planned on it."

CHAPTER 43

THE RIDE to the studio was tense, filled with unspoken words as Era and Alex sat in silence, letting music fill the void between them. Era's first stop at the studio involved remixing her song into an uptempo dance track, aiming to reclaim it from the hands of DJs who gave it the hack treatment at the party the other night. They were in and out in under forty-five minutes, with Alex recording the process for content to keep the momentum going on Era's social media.

Next, they moved to Studio B for her podcast recording. Era took a seat, her eyes fixed on the chair where she had seen her guardian angel during her last visit. She wondered where he was now and struggled with the idea that he was somewhere nearby.

"Are you alright?" Alex asked, walking over to her with a bottle of cold water. "Do you need a moment?"

"I'm fine. Ready when you are," Era replied, steadying herself and smoothing the silky top Alex had chosen for her. This podcast episode would shift from persuading her audience to laying out the logistics of organizing and executing her plan— because the time had come to move the spokes forward.

First, she proposed a radical idea: society needed to reform into more homogenous communities. People who shared fundamental truths—often, but not always, those who practiced the same faith—should live together. She suggested establishing central "towns" of no more than 500 people, with essential services like hospitals and law enforcement. Surrounding this core, additional groups of around 500 could form, creating communities of roughly 3,000.

Next, she explained that this restructuring could only succeed if people embraced technology comprehensively. All work that could be done remotely, should be, utilizing enhanced connectivity technology. Shared neighborhood gardens could foster food independence through aquaponic gardening, indoor greenhouses, and orchards. Education needed a complete overhaul, relying more on tutors and AI for practical subjects to prepare the next generation for a world reshaped by technological exports, offsetting the economic shrinkage as people spent less, borrowed less at high interest rates, and entire sectors of business faced collapse.

The shift would also require improved infrastructure, particularly greater access to water in remote areas, along with regional airports to facilitate the movement of people and goods. She wasn't calling for isolation but rather advocating for deeper community ties in daily life and maximum connectivity in business.

She reminded listeners how the pandemic had shown them they could live without many of the frivolities they once deemed essential. They had all survived without highlighting their hair, eating in restaurants, shopping in stores. A large-scale adoption would disrupt banking, retail, services, and so many more industries. This restructuring would birth a new nation, and like any birth, it would come with pain and labor.

By the end of her monologue, Era felt drained, her throat parched from speaking so long. Alex cut the recording and dimmed the overhead lights. "That was some heavy stuff. It's hard to even imagine people following your plan, yet part of me wishes they would. And I can see how the world you envision would be a better place to live," she remarked, sitting beside Era on the plush chair, energized by Era's passion.

"Lots of people will recognize the wisdom of the plan, but they'll have to take the leap, and it won't be easy. I didn't get into all the things I can see going wrong, but I know that eventually, if we can convince enough people to do this, life for everyone will improve. I'm still uncertain exactly how it will all come about, or how long it'll take. But it'll happen," she murmured softly, drowsiness beginning to overtake her. "Can you drive us back? I'm so wiped I can barely keep my eyes open."

Back in the dorms, a relentless stream of nightmares attacked Era in her sleep. Rather than one terrifying story, she endured what felt like an endless year of horrors that melded into one another. Sometimes, the monsters from her Poli Sci class swooped around her as she ran across campus, tangling in her hair and scratching her scalp. At other times, she found herself inexplicably in bed with Christopher, indulging her deepest fantasies—only for him to morph into a lifeless body, pus and fluid oozing from his eyes and gaping wounds across his skin.

In one vivid moment, Alex attempted to stab her in her bed, while in another, Cole and Chase conspired to drug her, intent on exacting their revenge for spurning them.

In the haze of her disjointed dreams, a phrase escaped her lips, "St. Michael the Archangel," and with that invocation, she awoke drenched in sweat and tears, the early morning light barely breaking on the horizon. Never had she felt so grateful to be awake, yet the haunting images lingered, refusing to relinquish their hold on her mind.

Shaken but resolute to sort through the mess in her life, Era decided today would mark the beginning of definitive change. She started with a Snap to Chase.

> Need to talk. Meet me at the library, 11am.

Why is this so hard? Era thought as Chase strolled up. She braced herself for an unusually rude greeting, opting to remain seated instead of standing to hug him. Instead, she motioned to the space next to her on the wall, determined to have this conversation without pushing him away entirely.

"What's going on?" he asked, sitting so close that their thighs touched and throwing an arm around her shoulder in a brief side hug.

"This is what's going on," she said, cutting the nonexistent space between their legs with the blade of her hand. "You know I'm with Christopher, so this kind of friendship is off-limits. I need you to respect my relationship if you want our friendship to continue."

Her directness caught him off guard, and the smile on his face dissolved into an offended expression. "It's not easy being so close to you knowing that if Christopher weren't in the picture, I'd have a real chance. Era, we could make beautiful music together in a lot of ways—"

"See, this is what I'm talking about. Please, I'm begging you to have some self-control. I want you as a friend in my life, and I want to work together without worrying that our friendship will jeopardize my relationship." Her eyes pleaded with him. "I don't want to give you up. Don't make me."

"Ugh," he groaned. "You're killing me, you know that don't

you? I'll do whatever you ask—but I'm not saying I'm going to like it."

"Thank you. But there's one more thing I need to explain."

She nearly forgot the second part of the hard truth she needed to lay on him.

"Oh no. What's that?"

"And I mean this in the friendliest don't-get-your-hopes-up way possible—but if you ever kiss Alex again, our friendship is officially over."

"Damn, Era, you are cold-blooded. Breaking my heart and blocking your friend—okay."

With business adjourned, she let out a quiet breath of relief. "How are things going for the 4Cs anyway?"

Chase coughed out a laugh that nearly choked him, brightening as he shifted from the awkwardness to discuss gossip. "Not gonna lie, there have been some tense exchanges in there. Your ex came at Christopher with some rude comments about taking better care of you, and I thought my man was going to lose his shit. Trust me, you don't want to see him fight. I've never seen him lose on the ice."

Era was mortified, paralyzed by the fear that Cole might have outed her lie. Anxiety tightened her chest as she thought of Christopher confronting him with the half-truth she told. It could be disastrous in either case.

"Oh no," was all she could manage, afraid that any probing would give her away.

"Yeah, Christopher called him a predator for trying to get you naked the other night. That part pissed me off too. He's definitely not getting invited to hang out with us anymore, that's for sure."

"Tell me about it. I saw him kissing Ami last night, and he ran after me when he realized I caught them," Era replied, working hard to keep her voice steady while in full panic mode.

"Nooooo... You do know this means I'm now sharing a room with my sworn enemy, right? Screw that guy."

A wave of sickening dread engulfed Era as she realized her mistake. She had foolishly mentioned the kiss to Chase, forgetting that she had refused to tell Christopher about it, even when he suspected there was more to her sudden exit than she had admitted. Panic flooded through her, but she pushed the feeling aside, placing a hand on Chase's shoulder. Using her Gift, she Pulled him in closer until their eyes locked, feeling his pulse race beneath her touch.

"Can I trust you to do me one last favor?" Her voice grew gentle, her stare holding an intense power that drew him in deeper, like a moth to a flame. He didn't need to answer; she could feel him reaching back for her with his heart, rekindling the connection they forged the night they sang together.

"Don't tell anyone about Cole kissing my roommate. It hurt more than I'd like to admit, and I didn't tell Christopher. I just want to forget," she let the hurt fill her voice, leaning into his desire to protect her. "Can I trust you?" Of course, he wanted nothing more than a secret to bring them closer.

He reached for her, grabbing her hand. The exchange nearly undid all the progress she had made by establishing new boundaries with him, but it couldn't be helped. "Yes, you can."

She leaned in and hugged him, thanking him for being so understanding before hightailing it out of there. *Two steps forward, three steps back, I guess,* she thought as she scampered away from him. In any case, she hoped that her earlier efforts would prove effective, and that her flex of the Gift would protect her secret.

Like that, Monday passed, and the next two months on campus sped by in a repetitive rhythm punctuated by flashes of the extraordinary that had become her new normal. Era attended class, shared dinners with Christopher most days, partied with Alex and Christopher's fraternity, and awaited the results of the expulsion case from her Economics professor.

Era's talk with Chase had proven somewhat effective, even if he sulked about it. No more hands hung out below her waist, and the crushing, spin-me-around hugs devolved into platonic back pats. Alex and Era officially iced Ami and Graciela (by association) out of their circle after the clear demonstration of lack of loyalty to the girl code. Cole remained morose about losing breakfast privileges but didn't make a fuss; he knew exactly what he had done and was too cowardly to bring it up.

He stopped coming to the girls' room, but Era knew he continued to hang out with Ami in the coffee house tucked away at the far end of campus. Confronting either of them would likely ignite a powder keg, so she steered clear of the topic.

Ami was an easy read; it was clear that whatever relationship she had with Cole wasn't physical, and she was pissed about it. Thank goodness Era didn't have to broach the subject with either of them to know the truth.

On the musical front, Alex released the remix of Era's song, which hit number two on the Billboard charts, right under her number one single. At this point, Era was making over $50,000 a day in revenue from a combination of royalties and monetization.

There was so much to manage that Alex brought on Arabella and Hudson from her Poly Sci class as full-time employees. The new additions made excellent replacements for their questionable suitemates. Era enjoyed watching Alex step into her new leadership role, gently guiding Arabella, her obvious mentee. And thankfully, Hudson appeared to prefer Arabella, not Era—a welcome change.

The media was positively abuzz with questions about the mysterious girl popping up, unsigned out of nowhere, stealing the spotlight, and then ditching music for a podcast. The disbelief translated into driving the viewership on Era's podcast sky high as curious people sought to solve the puzzling question for themselves.

However, despite her clear transition to furthering the mission laid out in her podcast, interest in her music remained. When the pressure for answers became too much, Era and Chase booked an appearance on a late-night show to discuss the song. Chase dogged her relentlessly to perform the song live until Era's patience wore thin, but she didn't give in.

"No live performances," she told him again and again until he almost stopped talking to her altogether. Chase began resenting being so far from the driver's seat in his own burgeoning music career and so turned his attention to Alex who he spent a good amount of time with, eating lunch together and working on the marketing plans.

Era kept a sharp eye on Alex in this regard and was pacified that they were not more than flirty friends for the time being. Chase didn't make any more moves and Alex wasn't the type to pursue. The arrangement worked out well for Era as it kept Chase from bugging her about their song.

Era's podcasts were now being broadcast live across social media instead of merely recorded and uploaded. Before each episode, she typically received her usual strange email full of attachments. It wasn't difficult to speak authoritatively on any subject after reading the equivalent of ten years' worth of preparation.

In her podcasts, she discussed a range of topics, including "An End to Hook-Up Culture and Dating for a New Generation," "What Will Become of Cities?" "Family-Centric Living," "Found Family in Your New Neighbors," and "Navigating the Transfer of Assets." As her subject matter shifted toward practical aspects of her proposition and the movement began to take off with millions tuning in to watch her live, Christopher grew increasingly jumpy about the endeavor. Several concepts began to step on the toes of his family's enterprise, and should people take her advice, entire sectors of their business could be endangered.

It became clear from phone calls with both Laura and Caspar that the Ridgewell family and their business association with Era were becoming strained. Her followers were raining down criticism on companies that held large rent interests, trapping individuals in leases and unnecessary on-site jobs that prevented people from their dreams of leaving the city.

The backlash started to mount. Era tried not to worry about the growing number of vocal opponents, including influential figures in government who had become aware of her and were speaking out against her beliefs. Articles criticized her theories and attacked her character. She even found herself mentioned on national news channels by people she never thought would care about her work.

She had been labeled as "dangerously un-American," a "cult leader on the rise," a "backwards fundamentalist," and a "delusional little girl." Yet, none of the criticisms stopped her channel or following from growing.

Era might have managed through the rollercoaster of freshman year if it hadn't been for the nightmares that plagued her night after night. Once nearly addicted to sleep, she now dreaded going to bed, assaulted by images that plagued her long into her waking hours. If her mind drifted for even a moment during a walk or a lecture, the nightmares would replay in her head. The effort to remain vigilant against the onslaught proved exhausting. Unable to cope, Era began to self-medicate at frat parties with Christopher. It seemed the only way she either didn't dream or didn't remember her dreams was when she went to bed heavily intoxicated.

Era told herself that her behavior resembled that of a typical college freshman coping with an exceptional amount of pressure. However, the drinking led to difficulties controlling herself around Christopher, resulting in growing friction between them. While she pushed boundaries without actually crossing any lines, he grew to resent her only pursuing their physical relationship when she drank. She didn't blame him even if she couldn't seem to stop the cycle from repeating.

Despite the wisdom of the Gift, she was too blind to make the connection between her destructive tendencies. Now, she drank rather than slept to escape to the truth—that she'd never get to keep him. She cursed herself for not listening to the first five warnings, knew she'd backed herself into an inescapable corner.

All of this behavior came to a head on decision day, the day Era learned, thanks to the Ridgewell family's legal team, that she had beaten the expulsion case.

The University offered her a strange deal: they would cancel her debt from the first semester and grant her an honorary Economics degree, on one condition, she must voluntarily leave school. If she stayed, she would not be allowed to major in Economics or take any more classes in the department. Ouch.

The offer tempted her even if it did leave a bad taste in her mouth. So they were against her enough to want her out, but willing to give her what she wanted, and save both their reputations. In addition, the dean handed down a deadline to decide.

Part of her wanted to celebrate, but it also left her torn about leaving Alex and Christopher behind. Rather than stew over it, Era decided to celebrate that night and leave the decision-making for tomorrow.

The heavy oak doors of the administration building creaked shut behind her, their echo swallowed by the roaring gusts that funneled through the quad. The campus gleamed under the crisp fall sunlight, red-brick facades glinting like polished stone, while palms swayed violently, their fronds rattling in protest against the Santa Ana winds.

She paused at the top of the stairs, the smoky air from a fire somewhere off in the canyons sucked the last drop of moisture from her cracked lips. A swirl of leaves chased one another across the wide paths below, scattering like the thoughts in her head. The deal loomed over her—a silent specter of choice. Leave this place and its poison behind? Or stay, digging her heels into hostile soil, knowing she'd never make it four years anyways.

Her sneakers scuffed against the concrete as she descended, her steps brisk, but not light. The wind tore at her hair, tossing strands into her face as if mocking her indecision. Halfway down the path, a flicker of movement caught her eye—a weathered flyer stapled haphazardly to a bulletin board, its edges curled and tattered. Her own face stared back at her, distorted by the sun and time, framed by bold, black letters branding her a pariah: "**STOP HATE SPEECH.**"

She paused, her pulse quickening as the wind tugged mercilessly at the flyer, leaving it clinging to the board by a single, rusted staple. Her fingers tightened into a fist at her side before she reached out, yanking it free. The brittle paper crumpled in her hand. She didn't look at it again, didn't let herself dwell. Her stride quickened, and she dropped the wad into the next trash can, the action sharp, final.

The wind howled as she walked away, its relentless force matching the quiet storm churning inside her.

"So, are you going to ditch me and sneak off with Christopher again tonight, or will we actually get the chance to dance?" Alex asked as she brushed powder across her face.

"Hmmm, hard to say, but I definitely want to dance. You should have seen Dr. Travata's face when they read the decision. I thought he was going to burst into flames," she said, laughing as she adjusted the straps of her dress and took a sip of the cocktail she had mixed for their pre-game.

"I can imagine. He should have figured out that the school wouldn't risk publicly denouncing you and should have

THE GIFT OF RUIN

dropped the case months ago. I'm glad it's over," Alex said, raising her glass. "Cheers!"

Once they were ready, the girls walked over to the boys' suite, took a shot to celebrate Era's exoneration, and then headed out. It was a typical night—large party, lots of booze, and Era in the center of it all. Seven drinks in, a sense of ecstasy swept over her as she danced. The strobe lights overhead disoriented her, and she felt off-balance and uncoordinated. Soon, she was pawing at Christopher, begging him to take her home, knowing she wouldn't be able to hold it together much longer.

Ever the gentleman, he obliged, holding her hand firmly as he led them into the cool night where a black SUV awaited to take them wherever they wanted to go.

"Home. Take me home," she begged as they climbed inside. With that, the driver sped off, merging onto the freeway toward Emerald Beach. Unwisely, Era took a hard seltzer from the cooler and continued drinking, despite her already compromised state.

In the car, she knew her behavior embarrassed Christopher but continued demanding he make out with her and pouting when he pushed her off. When they finally arrived back at his house in Emerald Bay, it stood empty. Era insisted they head to the kitchen to make another drink, but Christopher persuaded her to change first, with no intention of letting her come back down or drink anything other than water.

Era trudged up the steps, vaguely registering Christopher's arm wrapped around her waist. Once upstairs, he helped her undress. She had already unstrapped her heels in the car, but she fumbled with the mini zipper hidden into a seam at her side. Era recalled the satisfying zip sound and the weight of her dress disappearing as it fell to the floor, along with a pungent smell of sulfur.

"Eww, what is that smell?" she heard herself say aloud. Then, inside Era's head, the lights went out.

When she awoke the next morning, she was raggedly hungover and completely naked, the faint smell of recently lit matches wafting in the air. A quick peek under the covers revealed that Christopher was likewise unclothed. Desperate to grasp at any recollection, she searched her memory but found no mental images of what had happened. Then she looked at the sheets, and saw the proof of what her mind could not fathom: they had definitely had sex, and Era remembered none of it. Their first time together, and she had been blackout drunk.

Panic seized her as she dashed for a shirt and sweatpants in Christopher's closet. After quickly dressing, she took out her phone to order a ride, doing her best not to stumble down the stairs on her shaky legs. Mercifully, a car circled near the neighborhood, within two minutes of her location, and she was inside and on her way back to the dorms before Christopher even had a chance to realize she no longer lay in his bed.

She held down the phone's power button and watched the light blink out. Era began to tremble in fear and shame at how she had betrayed both Christopher and herself. The sickness of intoxication and regret tore her apart. She replayed every inch of her memory but, maddeningly, found no trace of what she knew they had done. Unable to hold back the torrent of emotions, Era sobbed for most of the ride back, alarming her driver, who occasionally murmured encouraging words to comfort her as they snaked through the morning traffic.

She knew it was all her fault and didn't blame him in the slightest. However, she couldn't shake the feeling of violation. Wasn't sleeping with someone unable to give their consent the definition of rape? She had been dancing on the precipice for some time, and it was no wonder she had fallen over it. Did she think she could drink as she had been without consequences?

There were always consequences. Christopher would now be suffering those consequences, agonizing over her abrupt departure after what might have been a special night for him.

Her stomach clenched, her mouth bursting with saliva as she fought back the vomit rising in her throat.

When the car eventually came to a stop alongside her dorm, Era raced up the stairs and locked herself in the bathroom. She sat on the shower floor for a long time, letting the water drench her, feeling broken, until someone knocked on the door. Wrapping herself in a towel, she slunk to her bed, not bothering to put on clothes, letting her dripping hair soak the pillow as she tucked herself under the covers.

Alex's phone began to ring from across the room. When she picked up, sleep still heavy in her voice, she mumbled, "Huhlo?" Peeking over at Era, she added, "She's here," before tossing the phone onto Era's bed and rolling back over. Era could hear the faint sound of Christopher's voice calling for her, and her stomach clenched.

Picking up Alex's phone, she responded, her voice wavering, "Hey."

Christopher's injured tone echoed back to her, "What's going on? Why did you leave like that?" Instead of answering, she burst into tears and hung up, burying her face into her pillow.

"What happened?" Alex asked huskily from across the room. "You guys get into a fight?"

"I think a lot happened," she replied weakly, "but I don't remember any of it."

"Oh no!" Alex said, stirring to face her. "I'm so sorry. You want to talk about it?"

"Actually, I really don't. And I don't want to see him right now, so if he calls back, just tell him I'm out or something," she said, her voice breaking as she turned away to cry against the wall. She'd suffered enough humiliation, crying in front of a strange Uber driver.

When Alex left for breakfast, Era knew she had to go too. Living on the same floor as her boyfriend meant one thing, unless she wanted to confront him, she had to get out—he would be coming to demand an explanation. She pulled on a random shirt and a pair of shorts, grabbed her keys and wallet, but left her phone and watch behind. With her mind racing, she started walking to her Jeep, desperate for an escape from the ragged torment of her mind.

Her mind, too preoccupied to care where she went, allowed her body to put itself in self-drive mode. She cruised down the freeway, and noticed the same exits she'd passed that morning. Autopilot steered her towards the same place she had come from: Emerald Beach. Her brain grappled with possible moves.

Book a last minute ticket to London? Stay with Raquel for a week or two. No, too many loose ends here. Something could go wrong with school.

Go see Mom? Era pictured her head in her mother's lap, her mother stroking her hair. *Yeah right,* she thought, tasting acid. Wishful thinking. Her mom was likely to change the subject to talk about someone she met at the grocery store.

Screw this. I should just text Jesse. That thought, bubbling up from a darker part inside her, beckoned like a cool breeze blowing through a cemetery. Ten seconds, that's how long it would take for him to arrange a table for her in the back room. It would be so easy to escape the nightmare her reality had become.

A black shimmer caught her eye on the floor of her Jeep and revulsion rippled through her. She rejected the destructive temptation and kept driving.

At long last, Era arrived at Sage Beach, her beach—the one she had visited every morning to avoid Christopher's runs. Such a fitting place to brood. Spreading her blanket under the shade of an alcove in the cliffside, she curled into a ball of misery. The sky hung heavy with fog uncharacteristic for fall, with a thick cloud resting at sea level, virtually guaranteeing her solitude.

Her tear ducts spent, she looked at the sandy wall's crevices, and a long-forgotten moment came to mind. Michael had said something to her: "The Master doesn't force anyone to serve him, but it's unwise to resist his plan." She recognized the ring of truth there.

At that moment, the path of decisions became clear. She would take the school's offer of an honorary degree and leave. She would break up with Christopher. Had there ever been any other way?

Just as the intention set like concrete in her mind, she heard a familiar voice call her name.

"Era! You're here. Please talk to me." She flipped over and saw Christopher striding toward her, anguish and determination written across his face.

When she merely sat in silence, he continued, "How could you leave like that? I didn't even know you were gone or where you went?" Pausing, he gave her a chance to respond, but when she didn't, he raised his voice in frustration. "Aren't you going to say anything?"

Era stood to address him, needing to keep some distance. "Christopher... did we—?" she began, unable to finish her question.

His face rearranged, and he choked out, "Are you saying you don't remember?"

She didn't need him to say another word. The Gift flooded her with his memory of the night—a singularly horrid experience, like watching an intimate act recorded without her consent. It felt ghastly, and she turned her head, recoiling from the images she couldn't stop seeing. "So we did then?" she asked, wanting to confirm the dreadful truth.

"Yes, we did," he replied, searching her face for answers that wouldn't come.

Now, Era saw the vision of her soul, once again united with Cole's on one side and tied to Christopher on the other, both pressing in on her from either side. She hadn't replaced one with the other after all; she had only added to her bondage.

Swallowing the hard lump in her throat, she forced out the next question, "Is there a chance I could be pregnant?"

Christopher froze, shock evident in his expression. Panic and distress clouded his eyes as he covered half his face with his hand. "I guess it's possible. We didn't use anything."

Relieved to have that part of the conversation behind them, she replied calmly, "Okay, thanks for being truthful with me." Her eyes watered as an image of a beautiful child danced in her mind—one she might have to raise alone if it came to pass.

"Babe, I'm so sorry. I had no idea you were blacked out. You sounded like yourself. You were begging me—" he tried to explain.

"I know. It's not your fault I hide my liquor so well. I don't slur and I rarely stumble when I drink too much. And I have been extremely tempted to sleep with you—pretty much every time we're together, so I'm not surprised I tried to when I was drunk. 'In vino veritas,' right?" She said this to let him off the hook, watching his hands twitch.

He stepped closer, hoping to console her, but she held up her hand to stop him. "Even though I've been tempted to sleep with you, there's a reason why I kept stopping it from happening. Something is pushing me in a new direction—and this direction, it's perpendicular rather than parallel to your path." Speaking the words felt like holding her hand in ice water until it burned.

"I've decided to accept the deal the school offered me. I'm gonna take the degree and leave."

Thinking that was all she was going to say, Christopher felt a wave of relief wash over him as he replied, "It's going to be okay. You're going to be successful no matter what. We can make it work even if you're not a student."

"You don't understand. It's over. We're over. We have to be. My future can't have you in it," she said.

"What do you mean it's over?" he asked, his anger flaring. "I love you, and we're perfect together! I know you need me now more than ever. Please..." His voice cracked as he pleaded, "Don't push me away. There's no one else for me. It's only you and it's always going to be you."

"No, Christopher, I know for certain that we can't and shouldn't be together."

"How could you know?" he demanded, desperation fully apparent in his voice.

"I know a lot of things I shouldn't," she replied flatly. "I'm sorry, but I need to go. I still love you, okay? I will always love you. I will always hate that it has to be this way, and I wish there were another choice, but there isn't. Please let me go." With that, she pressed one last kiss onto his lips and fled up the steep steps away from the beach, leaving Christopher collapsed onto the blanket she left behind.

At the sight of him prone on the sand, her heart spasmed, her breath left her body. The image seared into her, one she would never forget. *All my fault. Selfish. Selfish. Selfish.*

As she put her car in drive, Era realized two things. Firstly, he had a tracker somewhere on her car, not that it mattered now. He wouldn't follow. Two, she had screwed up the breakup. A narcissistic part of her needed to tell him she loved him and longed for a different outcome, even though it would only cause him greater pain and confusion. She sped away from the beach, knowing exactly where she needed to go for once: home.

Her fingertips brushed her lips, wishing she could bottle up the last moment she would feel his kiss. She had finally given her body to him, yet she would never experience the joy and relief of letting her walls crash down, nor bask in the incredible, unstoppable love she knew he had for her. All of it was a consequence of her own selfish actions, and she accepted the bitter medicine that coated her mouth with a pungent tang.

Walking up the drive to her empty house, she reflected on her choices. She wished she hadn't said what she did in those last moments, that she had been stronger. He was going to pine for her, to be broken. Perhaps it would have been better to cheat on him with Chase or go back to Cole. At least then, he would hate her, able to stamp out their memory and move on. But due to her own selfish words, he would not be able to.

She had seen his heart, so undividedly determined to have her forever. He would marry her without hesitation, and he hadn't exaggerated when he said he would never love anyone as much as he loved her. That truth didn't change anything, though. Furthermore, she had opened the door to her own temptation to backpedal. With Christopher knowing that she still loved him and regretted everything, he would continue to pursue her.

Era slunk upstairs to her room, uncertain of what to do in her empty house. She wondered if the nightmares would continue to haunt her and whether she should relocate to figure things out. It wasn't too late to pack up and catch a redeye across the pond; money certainly wasn't an issue these days.

She sat against the headboard of her bed and looked over at the digital clock on her side table. 3 p.m., too early to sleep and too early to eat. There was nothing to do but wait and let the day pass as it wished. Regardless of what happened, Era felt at peace. She knew she had done exactly what she needed to do. Despite the pain she knew she caused them both now, she trusted that something bigger and better awaited her on the other side of this decision. That faith held the only consolation she had, knowing she submitted to a wisdom greater than her own—one that stood outside time and could see exactly where she needed to be.

Closing her eyes, she took a deep breath, feeling her heart

thump quickly in her chest as the pungent smell of sulfur filled the room, scalding her sinuses. She opened her eyes to see a black shimmer arcing across the back wall, and a figure spark into existence in the corner.

A voice like silk and crushed glass, addressed her, sending goosebumps racing down her arms. Era stifled a scream.

"Hello, Era," the demon spoke as if addressing an old friend. "Yes, you're right where I want you to be. With ME."

To Be Continued...

ALSO BY DANIELLE FERRARO

Look for the next book in The Gift of Hearts series

The Gift of Temptation

and

Follow

@ferrarofiction on YouTube

@ferrarofiction on X / Twitter

@ferrarofiction on Instagram

@ferrarofiction on Threads

@ferrarofiction on TikTok

ACKNOWLEDGMENTS

This book wouldn't have come about without the support of my husband, who provided encouragement and admiration every time I sat down to write after putting the kids to bed, starting my second job. Thank you for every sacrifice this book cost you in time, talent, and treasure.

To my early readers who made it through the entire typo-ridden manuscript and handed over their precious feedback and criticism—thank you, especially Elyse Riff, Ashley Hitchcock, and Tess Socci.

To my Mom and Dad, for every dollar they spent knowingly or unknowingly buying me books. And since before anyone can write a book, they have to believe in themselves, I wouldn't believe in myself without the self-confidence instilled in me by them.

To some really good teachers I had along the way like Mr. McClure who loved books more than anything, Mr. Roland who graded structure into my essays without mercy, and Mr. Kroger who wrote that letter of recommendation on his lunch break that changed my life.

And whether you love it or hate it, to anyone who reads this book to the end, thank you.

ABOUT THE AUTHOR

Born and raised in California, Danielle Ferraro now calls
Newport Beach home, where she balances her life as a writer
and mother of three. Her creative journey is deeply influenced
by her academic background in Philosophy from Franciscan
University of Steubenville and her rich heritage as a Native
American writer.

As a proud registered member of the Mohawks of Akwe-
sasne, Danielle draws upon her cultural roots to infuse authen-
ticity and depth into her storytelling.

Danielle's love for books began at an early age, devouring
stories and entire series with boundless enthusiasm. At 19, she
made the transformative decision to set aside secular fiction,
dedicating the next decade to philosophy, theology, and spiritual reading.

This series represents her unique fusion of these two
passions, combining her philosophical and spiritual insights
with the power of storytelling to create a rich and meaningful
narrative experience.

Made in the USA
Las Vegas, NV
12 February 2025

17407204R00236